Praise for T

D1648112

"*The Stand-In* is a sparkly, cinematic adventure that combines emotional drama with hilarious and relatable moments. Lily Chu handles swoon-worthy scenes and down-to-earth concerns with equal skill."
— **Talia Hibbert**, USA Today bestselling author of
Get a Life, Chloe Brown

"Lily Chu's debut is wry, moving, and utterly romantic. I was charmed by *The Stand-In*'s vividly drawn multicultural cast...wit and poignancy."
— **Ruby Lang**, author of *The Uptown Collection*

"*The Stand-In* is a charming, engaging rom-com that drips in glamour and sparkles with banter. Chu's exploration of multiracial identity was resonant and nuanced. *The Stand-In* is truly a standout romance."
— **Andie J. Christopher**, USA Today bestselling author of
Not the Girl You Marry

"A sparkling debut rom-com from author Lily Chu. When Gracie is thrown into the world of movie stars, the result is a highly entertaining story full of heart—and a happily ever after."
— **Jackie Lau**, author of *Donut Fall in Love*

"Lily Chu's deft prose...had a way of taking unexpected turns, startling me into laughing out loud—or punching me right in the feelings."
— **Rose Lerner**, author of *The Wife in the Attic*

"With quick wit, beautifully developed characters, and a charming love story, this rom-com debut is a winner!"
— **Farah Heron**, author of *Accidentally Engaged*

ALSO BY LILY CHU

The Takedown

LILY CHU

sourcebooks
casablanca

Published by Sourcebooks Casablanca, an imprint of Sourcebooks
P.O. Box 4410, Naperville, Illinois 60567–4410
(630) 961-3900
sourcebooks.com

Cataloging-in-Publication Data is on file with the Library of Congress.

Printed and bound in Canada.
MBP 10 9 8 7 6 5 4 3 2 1

To everyone who tries to change the world for the better.

And Cammy—a 10/10 chameleon.

ONE

*A*ccording to the many-worlds theory—and possibly an old Gwyneth Paltrow movie—we split our universe with each decision we make. That means I've made a thousand right choices to get to this point, each littering time and space with sadder cast-off versions of me, say with dyed red hair instead of my natural dark brown or living in Tokyo instead of Toronto. Realistically, not even thousands but billions or trillions or whatever illions is beyond that.

I doubt any of those Dee Kwans are as happy as me. Thanks to meticulous vision boarding, wholehearted manifesting, and enough positive thinking to fill the Milky Way with stars, I'm exactly where I'm meant to be, doing exactly what I'm meant to do.

Waking before my alarm, I stretch in bed, warm and content under the thick duvet. The weak December sun streaming through the window lights the soft yellow walls with a golden glow that I admire before grabbing my phone to open my new meditation app. Six deep breaths and two nasal panting cycles later, I get antsy and turn it off. I haven't found the app that best suits me, but honestly, I don't need it. According to Mom, I take after her—happy by nature.

I make my way to the kitchen, where I tie back the retro dotted swiss curtains I installed in place of the old vinyl blinds with their permanently tangled cords, and put in some toast, idly counting the blooming flowers of the de Gournay–style wallpaper above the backsplash until it pops. I'm not lonely but it would be nice to share breakfast with someone. I can see him now, wearing a pair of flannel pajama bottoms as he stands at the white-and-gold marble counter, smiling fondly at me over his shoulder.

"Let me find someone," I say to the old Niagara Falls–themed thermometer I'd left in the window. "A man is not a necessity, but it would be a bonus. Preferably one who can cook. I'll do the dishes."

There, I've sent my aspiration out and trust that the universe, which I assume has nothing urgent that it needs to deal with, will manifest this man for me. I can sit back and wait for him to appear when the time is right.

I dig my toes into the Wedgwood-blue rug that covers the warm wood of the parquet floor and glance at the paper I'd stuck on my bulletin board near the fridge last January. Although "get man" hadn't made the list, it was chock-full of life goals. I read them over as I layer Havarti on my breakfast sandwich.

NO NEGATIVE VIBES!

I'd written this with little stars to emphasize the positive vibe-ness.

MEDITATE ~~DAILY~~ REGULARLY.
EXERCISE ~~DAILY~~ REGULARLY.
PRACTICE ~~WEEKLY~~ REGULAR SELF-CARE FOR WELLNESS.
BE THE BEST CHARIOTEER I CAN BE AT WORK.
REMAIN THE QUESTIE QUEEN.

My eyes linger on the last point. Oh, Questie. I'd discovered the online game last year when I needed a break from painting walls and ripping up carpet, and now spend a few blissful hours each week solving puzzles that lead to clues hidden around the city. Which reminds me, it's time for my daily Questie leaderboard check to confirm that SunnyDay remains numero uno and in the top dog slot.

I grab my phone with one hand and open the app as I bite into my sandwich, tomato spilling onto the thrifted Royal Albert forget-me-not patterned plate. I've been first for the last six months, my position unassailable, although under frequent and unwelcome attack by Teddy9. A faint sense of satisfaction suffuses me as I see that, yes, I am in the lead, a feeling deepened by noting that Teddy9 has dropped to fourth. I click over to the Questie chat and message him privately. We've been sharing good-natured taunts for the last couple months, and this seems like an excellent opportunity to rub in my continued dominance.

> **Me**: May the Fourth be with you. Get it? Because you're in fourth place?
>
> **Teddy9**: It's December and that joke is so bad I'm not going to dignify it with an answer.
>
> **Me**: Yet here we are.
>
> **Teddy9**: It doesn't matter. I have a plan.
>
> **Me**: Is your devious plan to solve clues faster and with some accuracy, unlike last week's puzzle?
>
> **Teddy9**: I stand by the fact that clue six was impossible for a normal person.
>
> **Me**: Sounds like loser talk.
>
> **Teddy9**: Winning is a state of mind, SunnyDay.
>
> **Me**: You know, I'm magnanimous in victory. My name's Dee. You can use it.
>
> **Teddy9**: I'm Teddy.
>
> **Me**: I suspected.
>
> **Teddy**: My name could have been 9, you know.

He logs off and I check if any of my friends have contacted me. I don't have many, and lately I've barely seen the ones I do. I'm usually the one to suggest meeting but I've been too busy. I'll reach out today.

I follow my usual getting-ready routine, which means after sunscreen comes my daily affirmation. Over the years, I've chanted everything from "You're good enough" to "The bangs will grow out." If I don't have anything specific, I default to "I delete negativity to live my best life." The important part is that I put my mind on a path to attract good energy and manifest my yes. My older sister, Jade, thinks this is all bull but she can go screw. Thanks to my mindset, life has turned out as I want, and there's no point messing with a good thing.

Since I've been working late all week, I'm going in a bit past my usual time, which has allowed me this unusually leisurely weekday morning. I decide to take the long route through the park near my house. It's quiet this time of day, and a sheet of neon orange with little cuts along the bottom flutters on a lamppost, like someone's advertising for their lost cat. Curious, I move closer.

TAKE WHAT YOU NEED, it says. Instead of phone numbers, the tabs read:

BREAK FROM ROUTINE
VIRTUAL HUG
MOMENT TO YOURSELF
KINDNESS

Two are missing, and I wonder what other passersby were missing from their lives. Then I shrug and turn away, leaving the tabs for someone else. I have everything I need.

Thirty minutes later, I'm walking up the stairs to Chariot Consulting. The office takes up the third floor of a small heritage building on Spadina Avenue, in easy walking distance of Queen Street's shopping and bars and Chinatown's food glories. When I walk in, it feels like home, which I suppose is natural given the amount of time I spend here.

After I wave to Nadia, the receptionist, I head to my office and stop with a little heart flutter of appreciation that hasn't dissipated since my recent promotion. The card on the door reads DAIYU KWAN because I'm always Daiyu at work. Dee, with its blond-ponytail surfer vibe, is for my personal life.

Then comes the best part of the name plate: CONSULTANT. After doing Chariot's communications for five years, they made me a full-fledged diversity consultant two months ago. It took an entire section of my vision board and endless night classes, but I'm finally in a position to make a difference by helping organizations become places where everyone can thrive. I want a world where people like my loathsome—and estranged—aunt Rebecca don't have the power to stop anyone from achieving their dreams.

I blow the card a kiss as I go in and flip on the light. More cynical people might find it pathetic, and I'm sorry for them, but Chariot gives my life meaning. It's worth every hour I spend at night and on weekends completing extra projects to prove my value. I put down my bag and straighten the copy of my CEO's book, *Diverse Paths, One Goal*, which sits on the shelf behind my desk. I'd ghostwritten it last year, and seeing my name in the alphabetical list of acknowledgments at the back continues to thrill me.

I haven't had time to decorate the space with my favorite motivational posters and soft-light lamps, but I can fix that when I come in on the weekend. The learning curve has been harder than I expected, especially since Chariot hasn't hired for my previous role so I'm currently doing both jobs. They've assured me it won't be much longer.

I look around with a sigh of total contentment and take a of sip of the green tea I brought from home. Everything—*everything*—is going according to plan.

Perfect.

TWO

I'm deep into client survey data when Nadia pokes her head around my door. "Staff meeting," she announces.

I check the time, and to my surprise, it's almost noon. "Sorry?"

"Emergency all-hands meeting," she elaborates. "Right now."

Nadia disappears down the hall before I can ask for details. Concentration broken, I drink my cold tea and stretch, unworried. It's probably a new client announcement. Our CEO, George, likes to summon us to celebrate those together, like a family.

The boardroom is crowded when I arrive, and I hide my disappointment when there's not even a box of Timbits on offer. At least the office Keurig supply was replenished, so I snatch a matcha latte, dropping a toonie into the box.

"I'm taking bets on whether he's retiring or it's a mass layoff," says Nadia as I stand next to her. Her mug says *Don't got time for maybes* in pink cursive and smells like caramel. She looks remarkably unbothered.

Before I can answer, I catch sight of my manager. He's frowning at his feet and muttering something to the IT director, who rubs his beard. In fact, the entire leadership team sports expressions from somber to grave.

"It doesn't look good," I say, heart sinking. Then I rally. "I could be wrong."

"I doubt it." She checks out the crowd over the top of her mug. "I'd say we're screwed."

George strolls in, waving cheerfully, with his tousled gray hair curling over the edge of his collar. He looks tan, as he usually does after one of his Palm Beach breaks. "Good morning, Charioteers!" he booms as he bounds up the makeshift riser at the front. He never needs a mic.

He doesn't wait for the calls of "Hi, George" to finish echoing around the room.

"I have incredible news." George gives us his trademark boyish smile. "I founded Chariot almost thirty years ago when I saw the need for diversity guidance among..."

Having heard our corporate history dozens of times, I tune out George's heartfelt exposition and Nadia's snarky commentary to check the Questie leaderboard, where Teddy9 has moved up a place. He must be completing older puzzles to pull up his score. I message him.

> **Me:** Sneaky.
> **Teddy:** Told you I had a plan.

I don't like this, but Nadia nudges me as George says, "Diversity and inclusion are changing, and so too must Chariot."

Nadia leans over. "Looks like he might be retiring after all."

"After the fuss he made about wanting to be carried out dead in his chair?" I whisper back.

"I'll be taking on a new role"—George pauses for dramatic effect—"as CEO of my cottage in Muskoka."

He chuckles, but instead of the laughter he clearly expects, the room fills with whispers. Someone calls out, "What?"

"Thank you," says George. "In the immortal words of The Byrds, there is a season."

Nadia snorts. "The Byrds or Ecclesiastes. This is what happens when you don't do his speaking notes."

"Nadia!"

"C'mon, I know you do all his writing." She tilts her mug toward a cluster of blond women standing to the side with neutral expressions. "Like the angels do the rest of his work."

George spends another few minutes extolling the virtues of Chariot and our achievements before saying, "My season, *our* season, here is done. I know you'll keep the Charioteer spirit alive wherever you go."

Understanding filters through the room, and the whispers grow to mutters. The same voice calls, "Wait, are you shutting Chariot down? We're getting laid off?"

"Bingo," crows Nadia in somewhat misplaced triumph. "I knew it."

"Chariot began with me, and I'm saddened and honored it will end with me." George dips his head down as if overcome with emotion and clasps his hands over his chest. Then he looks up. "Your manager will be in touch with details."

I don't pay attention to whatever he says next as I stand there, nauseous from the hammering of my heart. I'd worked so hard to get this job and now it's gone? I didn't even have a chance to show what I could do. I flex my hands to try to physically force my usual positivity back and breathe deep. It's a shock, but this doesn't have to be bad. In fact, it's a good chance to expand my horizons.

We join the escaping crowd after George dismisses us. "You'll need luck," Nadia says.

I steer around two women from finance who have stopped in the middle of the corridor, texting frantically as they shake their heads. "What do you mean?"

She sighs. "You sweet summer child. You've only been a consultant for two months. You think it'll be easy to get a new job? It's back to pension update emails for you."

"I can find a job." I trip on the edge of the carpet. "I have lots to offer."

"You *could* have a chance given what they pay junior consultants." Nadia looks thoughtful. "The others will be asking for much more."

She leaves me at my office, dragging my confidence behind her like tissue on a shoe as I wonder if she's right. Chariot is as comfortable as a pair of worn sneakers, and I don't want to break in new ones. Not when I was settling in for a marathon here. My throat tightens and I'm grateful the hallway remains empty so I don't need to talk.

Forcing myself to step into the office that remains mine for the moment, I sit at my desk and slide my hand up and down the seam of my notepad while staring at an old nail hole in the wall. I should make a list. What about my résumé? It's up-to-date, but can I add more? Finances. My bank account ends each month perilously close to zero.

When the phone rings, I put it on speaker, relieved for a distraction to stop me ruminating about this setback. No, this *opportunity*, because I need to start thinking about this in the correct way.

"Hi, Mom."

"Hi, sunshine. Are you taking advantage of the nice weather?" Mom is a big proponent of taking advantage of whatever the day brings.

"I'm at work." I'll tell her about George's bombshell later, when I've processed it enough to be in the proper headspace for her pep talk. I check Questie and see Teddy remains in third place.

"You should go out and get some vitamin D," she says. "It's so good for improving your mood."

It takes everything in me to not make an immature and hugely inappropriate joke. "I'll go for a walk later."

"Make sure you do, sunshine. Well, I have some interesting news."

A chill settles on my skin. I've had a long time to learn my mother's code words, and *interesting* is as close to *bad* as she gets. "Is it Dad?" I demand.

"Why would you say that? He's out for a walk," she answers breezily. "Did I tell you I'm making yogurt from scratch? It's wonderful for your gut ecosystem. Healthy body, healthy mind."

I relax a bit. The yogurt doesn't surprise me. Since her retirement,

Mom has thrown herself into trying all the things she couldn't do while working, like playing tennis, making jam, and finishing a petit point pillow featuring orange tulips that sits on my pretty teal love seat. She'd been working on it sporadically since I was twelve.

"What's going on, Mom?"

There's a brief silence before she clears her throat. "It's nothing to worry about. You know Grandma had a little problem with her hip."

It was a severe fracture that resulted in hospitalization and daily physiotherapy. "Is she okay?"

"The most important part of healing is that she keep her spirits up."

Cheerfulness is not something I associate with my grandmother, who has not smiled in years, at least not at me. I sit straighter. "Mom."

"Your dad and I have been talking, sunshine."

I try to hold on to my pleasant outlook, but dread edges out my self-control. "Tell me what's going on."

"Grandma's not able to live on her own anymore, but you know how she feels about moving into a home."

"Yeah," I say. "I know." She told Mom she'd rather be put out on an iceberg where she could die with some dignity. Exact words.

"I can't do that to her," Mom says. "She can't come live with us up north because it's too far from her medical appointments."

"Okay?"

"You can say no, of course. We won't be angry."

"Say no to what?" I exclaim. "Spit it out."

There's a pause as Mom debates whether to scold me for being rude, but she says, "I'd like to move her to your house."

I say the first thing that pops into my head. "I can't take care of her. I have to work."

"We would do that. Your father and I."

"How are you going to find a place to live?" The housing market in Toronto is so brutal it's one step away from drawing pistols at dawn for a two-bedroom.

"We'd move in with her," Mom says softly. "Back into our house."

Back into their house. Their house, which is supposed to be my house, the home I spent a year and my entire savings getting perfect. When my parents retired and moved up north, they'd generously gifted me the deed with the permission of my sister, Jade, who had no desire to take on what she refers to as the sad urban shoebox. She can take her McMansion Lite north of the city, with its consistent HVAC and enough room for an outdoor pizza oven, because I love my tiny house. Love it with a love that extends past pragma and into agape. Perhaps Eros. It's my castle, where I can pull up the drawbridge and simply be.

On the screen, Teddy moves to second place, but as of four seconds ago, I have bigger issues to contend with than my game rank.

Although it is annoying.

Mom keeps talking. "This is a lovely opportunity for our family to connect."

I don't know why that's necessary, but I'm careful not to voice this particular thought. It took my grandmother until Jade was born to accept that Mom had married a Chinese guy and to start speaking to him directly instead of filtering comments through Mom, at first claiming his accent was too heavy for her to understand. More than thirty years later, the best that can be said for their relationship is that it's not uncivil. We've been getting along fine barely talking for years.

"What about Jade's house?" Halfway through, I shift my whine to a more upbeat tone so the question ends in a squeak.

"She has more room but you know how your sister feels."

I sure do, because if my relationship with Heather Henderson is best described as distant, Jade's is nonexistent. When Jade came out as bi, Grandma refused to believe it. Flat out told Jade she was only confused and would eventually settle down with a nice boy. Things improved slightly after Jade's kids came along, but unlike Dad and despite Mom's incessant pleas, my sister is much less willing to smooth things over for the sake of harmony. She's waiting for an apology that won't ever come, because people like Grandma think they're entitled to behave however they want without consequence.

"Is this the best idea, Mom?"

"That doesn't sound like my Dee," she says in a warning tone.

"No, it's that I wonder if—"

"It will work out fine, sunshine," she interrupts. "You only need a bit of faith and an open mind."

I bang my head against the desk lightly enough so Mom can't hear it over the phone. As if I can say no. It would be monstrous. Unfathomable. Worse, not very nice of me. "Of course," I say in defeat. "It's your house. You're always welcome."

Which is true, but I pictured it more like a weekend visit, not an annexation.

"Dee, it's *your* house. We know this is a change, and we're grateful you're such a good girl."

You don't have to be good, says the mean and unhelpful inner voice I've fought to keep buried my whole life. *They gave you the house. It's yours and you don't owe Grandma anything.* I stuff that down guiltily, knowing how disappointed Mom would be with my negative perspective.

She continues to think aloud. "We'll need a place for chili, too."

"Why not the kitchen?"

"I don't like that. Too messy."

I don't have the energy to ask what she could possibly mean by that so I let it slide. "When are you coming?"

"In two weeks. We're putting Grandma's town house up for sale, and she doesn't want to be there for the showings. Does that work?"

"Sure." I'm not sure what my voice sounds like, but it feels like I'm underwater.

"It'll be fine," says Mom cheerfully. "It always is."

We get off the phone, and I drum my fingers on the table. What's done is done, and I'll make the best of it like always. Then my phone beeps and drops down a Questie notification. It's a message.

Teddy: There we go.

I scramble to check. Teddy9 is number one on the leaderboard. *Thanks a lot, universe.*

THREE

On Saturday, I wake up determined to get one aspect of my life back in line. I might not be able to resuscitate Chariot or ban my injured grandmother from the comfort of my home, but I can at least fight Teddy for the number one Questie spot. *My number one spot.* I check my messages.

> **Teddy:** The view certainly is nice from the top.
> **Me:** Better take some photos, because you won't be there long.

Teddy has triggered a strong competitive streak that's been latent since high school gym. This guy thinks he's good at Questie? Let's see what he can do. I review my plan with the focus of a paratrooper about to drop out of a C-130.

First, check that the new weekly puzzle has uploaded. Leaderboard status is determined by how long it takes to complete each clue and finish the game by figuring out the final answer, which is an anagram of the clue letters. Bonus points go to the first ten players to finish.

The green icon flashes to indicate the puzzle will open soon. The overview, listed in point-form Helvetica on the first puzzle screen, says it's limited geography, which means the clues are all within walking distance of each other. It also provides a general starting area.

Closing my eyes, I visualize SunnyDay leading the pack, then for good measure, I erase Teddy9 completely. Too bad when I crack an eyelid open, it's to see their name glowing in big letters right above mine. Seems the universe has some work to do.

I take the subway to St. George Station and begin the game, eager to get winning. The first clue appears: *The professor asks Diabolical questions. Diabolical* is capitalized, which probably means it's connected to an actual place name. *Professor. Professor, university. Diabolical?*

Of course. I give the phone such a victorious smile, it causes the woman coming through the door to shoot me a strange look and skitter away. Thanks to a Halloween city tour, I know where the clue is.

Go, me. Take that, Teddy.

Out on the street, I pass students stooped under bulging backpacks leaving small patches of dark concrete as they scuff their way through the snow. It's almost exam season, and none of them look happy. Thrilled I never have to write another essay in my life—something to add to the gratitude journal—I come into the open space of the front campus and eye my target.

Questie clues are usually images, rebuses, trivia, or wordplay. This one is a mix of the last two. It's based on a ghost story about a stonemason, Reznikoff, who attacked another mason, Diabolos, with an axe. Diabolos had planned to run away with the woman Reznikoff was in love with as well as his money.

The professor (the university) *asks* (sounds like *axe*) *Diabolical* (from the name) *questions* clearly refers to the axe mark that remains on the door in front of me. Before I take my first step to success, a man gusts past, heading straight toward the clue with deliberate purpose. I watch as he bends down, toque bobbing as if he's nodding to himself.

Questie is more niche than popular, and this is my first time seeing another player in the wild. The guy pops back up to his feet and comes my direction, stride long and shoulders straight like he's working a runway. He glances over as he walks by and falters when our gazes meet, face lifting out of the black scarf wrapped around his neck.

And what a face it is. When I was a kid, I had a battered book of fairy tales. One prince had black hair, and even ten-year-old me had known he was something special. Compared to the beaming blond and blue-eyed Prince Charmings on the previous pages, whoever had drawn my prince had gone straight for smolder and slow-burning dark energy.

Now the living, breathing 3D equivalent of that fairy tale prince stands in front of me, everything I'd imprinted on as desirable in a man minus the spangled epaulets and bejeweled sword.

I blatantly check him out. A wide forehead leads to broad cheekbones that slant down to a firm chin. The shadow of his slight stubble accentuates the strong lines of his face. His lips look full, but he's biting the lower one with white teeth as he looks at me with hazel eyes. His lashes are long enough that he could bat them in a mascara ad, and the entire look is completed by a pair of black-framed glasses, the accessories icing on his hotness cake.

He moves past me with a polite nod of acknowledgment while I take a shuddery breath, because for two seconds, I was the sole focus of an extremely attractive man. Even if he had been significantly less striking, lingering eye contact apropos of nothing always makes my heart race. It's such an intimate thing to share with a stranger.

I turn in admiration. I firmly believe it's not the shoes that make the man but the walk, and a man with a good walk is incredibly appealing to me. In my head and based on no formal data whatsoever, a sexy and confident walk is the hallmark of a well-rounded, competent, and preternaturally hot man, the kind of guy who can drive stick and give solid advice—only when asked—about good places to eat in Hanoi, how to make a campfire, and if the earrings are too much with the necklace. A prince for the modern age, if you will.

I remind the universe I am open to both adventure and a relationship with someone smart and kind and who preferably looks like Lee Dong-Wook, although that's probably pushing my luck. Then again, specificity matters when manifesting, so it's best to aim for exactly what you want. *Fine, universe, make him look like Dong-Wook. If you must.*

The man crosses the street, and I reluctantly tear my eyes away to check the axe-marked door. Then I look back. Hold on.

My head oscillates between the clue and the man, the man and the clue. Is it...? It might be? There's only one other person in the city who's as good at Questie as I am. I glance at my phone to double-check Teddy9's profile. I've never seen him in person, but his avatar is a round circle with a mop of dark hair, which could be one of a million men, including this guy. I squint at it, looking for details, when a message comes up.

Teddy: One down.

My head shoots up. Confirmed. Prince Smolder is Teddy, and oh my goodness. I wasn't picturing Questie Teddy as that attractive, and while it shouldn't matter—books judged by cover and all that—I can't help but feel it's a tiny bit unfair that Teddy be a solid ghost pepper on the Scoville heat scale, even hotter than my love Dong-Wook, and also have *my* spot on the leaderboard.

Not to mention Teddy's dazzling face and fabulous walk distracted me from the game as the clock kept ticking. I lift my chin. He might have won the battle for the first clue, but I'm going to win the war. I run up to the door and find the letter C written in marker on the stone of this historically significant building. Once I put in the letter—you get deductions for each wrong guess to prevent players from simply working through the alphabet—the next clue pops up. It's an image of a plate of spaghetti with parmesan and basil. A restaurant or... Isn't the Italian Consulate General close by on Beverley Street? I google it, note that the insignia is the same as the one on the fork in the clue, and head off at a trot, determined to beat my competition.

My phone buzzes and I check it quickly to see if Teddy has reached the second location yet. No, but the message isn't much better. It's Jade, and all it says is **WTF**.

There's no point ignoring her since my sister will escalate to a phone call within minutes if I don't reply. I keep my pace and write back.

> **Me:** Mom told you?
> **Jade:** That she unilaterally decided to move everyone in with you? Why did you agree?
> **Me:** I tried. You know Mom.
> **Jade:** You need to be firm with her. Plus, Grandma doesn't deserve it, not after how she treated us.

Grandma was never actively mean—low bar—but we aren't her preferred grandchildren. Those are Aunt Rebecca's set of matched blonds who have financially remunerative careers in banking (Ryder) and being the wife of a man in banking (Rachel). I've never met them because Aunt Rebecca moved to Calgary and cut Mom off after she married Dad, thus "contaminating the bloodline," as she put it.

> **Me:** You want me to tell Mom I won't help them out.
> **Jade:** No, I want you to apply the Cameron test.

The Cameron test is our code for asking *Does this benefit me, us, or only you?* It's from the classic movie *Ferris Bueller's Day Off*, where Cameron's the poor tagalong schmuck who gets talked into doing whatever Ferris wants, no matter what his own feelings.

Me: No one's taking advantage of me.

Jade: Please tell me you're not thinking of this in some kar-
mic points way.

Me (lying): Of course not. Anyway doesn't she deserve a
second chance?

Jade: She's not on her second chance. There have been tons
of chances over the years where she could have treated us
like the family she expects you to be now.

Me: It doesn't matter. I've agreed and it is what it is.

Jade: That's a bullshit saying created by people who want
you to believe there are no alternatives. There always are.

Me: I can handle it. Got to go!

Jade: Dee.

Me: What?

Jade: Nothing. Opal and the kids say hi. Love you!

I send back a heart, glad the conversation is over. Although I love
my sister, we are profoundly different people. Life never hands you
more than you can handle, but Jade is always more willing to deploy a
no before considering a yes.

Besides, I'm approaching my objective, a pale-yellow building
with Italian flags, where the man who I'm 99.9 percent sure is Teddy is
bending down to check the low brick wall. My dismay that he's here is
accompanied by a contradictory blast of pleasure that he's here.

My feet crunch on the snow, and when he looks up at me from under
his eyelashes, my breath stops puffing in the cold air. The glasses look good
on him, but I get the sense he's one of those men who rock everything from
tuxedos to tracksuits. Handsome men kind of go with anything.

My face flushes as he slowly rises to his feet.

"I wondered if you were playing Questie," he says. His eye contact
is a bit intense, but I won't back down from this power move. Luckily I
manage to get my breath back.

"Teddy?" Too bad my voice shakes even with that one word. *C'mon, Dee, get it together. You've met pretty, charismatic men before.* Have I though? The guy has knocked the existence of any other man clear out of my head.

His eyes widen but I'm looking at his mouth. His top lip is a bit longer and fuller than his bottom, giving it an upside-down appearance. I want to press my thumb in the middle of that lopsided upper lip to mark it like a jam cookie. "SunnyDay? Dee?"

I nod.

"We finally meet," he says. "Oh, that sounded way more like a super-villain than I planned."

When he laughs with me, it all feels better. Beautiful though he may be, this is *Teddy*, the guy I've been chatting with online for months, and no one to be intimidated by. In all our back-and-forth teasing, Teddy was good-natured and never rude or mean.

I steady my voice. "You took my place on the leaderboard."

"I did indeed." He checks his phone. "Yep. Look at that. There it is."

Confidence flows back at the sight of his smug grin. "That's my spot."

He gives me a long, slow look that gets my heart racing. "Then you'd better get moving if you want it back."

Teddy turns away before I can reply and starts down the street, giving me an irritatingly jaunty wave as he goes.

That…hot or not, who does he think he…ugh. There's no time to waste so I push aside my frustration and grab the clue, an *H.* Then it's time to check the third clue. It takes me over fifteen minutes to figure out the answer, and when I do, I jog over to the clue location, convinced I'll be there before Teddy.

To my dismay, I'm not. By the time I arrive, panting and sweating under my winter coat, the only thing I see of Teddy is his footprints. Damn. Teddy is good at Questie. Very good.

But I'm better, although it takes me a half hour to decipher the fourth clue. Teddy shows up as I leave, and I give him a big grin that he doesn't return. I'm on a roll and beat him to the fifth clue as well.

The sixth has us jostling silently when we reach it simultaneously, but I manage to get it first.

"Only one clue left," Teddy says.

"So there is. May the best player—me—win."

He snorts and heads north in what I assume is an attempt to misdirect me. I duck into a doorway to protect myself from the wind as I puzzle out the last location.

I stare at the clue, a metal snake. A cobra, to be specific. Blowing on my cold fingers, I try reverse searching the image without success before bringing up a map of the area to pore over it, taking frequent breaks to see if Teddy has moved up the leaderboard because he's made it to the last clue before me. I zoom around the map to consider my options. It won't be a liquor store or Grossman's Tavern. I come across the United Steelworkers union hall and pause.

Metal. Steel. Cobra. My friend's dad used to be a steelworker and gave her a shirt with a snake that read, "If provoked, we will strike." It has to be there.

I check the time. It's taken me over twenty minutes to figure out the clue so I walk as quickly as the icy ground allows, hoping I've figured it out before Teddy. I whoop when I turn the corner and see the unmarked snow around my destination. I won! I can already see SunnyDay back on top of the leaderboard.

Then, Teddy's gorgeous face appears at the other corner.

FOUR

I stare at him, dumbfounded, and Teddy stops to face me like a gunslinger in an old Western. We're about the same distance from the clue, and I'll be damned if I'm not there first.

He must come to the same conclusion, because he dashes toward the building like he's been training for this his whole life. I've almost beat him when he flails his arms and tries to catch his footing. "Watch for the—oww!" Teddy goes sprawling at the exact moment my feet hit what he was trying to warn me about, a long patch of black ice under the snow made more dangerous by a sloping driveway.

"Oomph." I land on my ass, thankfully well padded from my jacket, cheeseburgers, and genetics, and lie there. This could be the most humiliating moment of my life, worse than the time I gave a work presentation wearing a thin blouse only to have my manager quietly come up to give me a sweater while staring meaningfully at my chest.

For a moment, there's no sound except the two of us panting on the ground. Finally he asks, "Are you okay?"

I wiggle my arms and legs and sit up. "Yeah. Are you?"

He sits up as well and takes off his gloves to fix his glasses so they're straight on his nose. "I think so."

Next to me lies a small notepad, open to pencil sketches of what look like dresses made of palm fronds. I pluck it out of the snow, doing my best to restrain myself from flipping through because the drawings are intriguing, and hold it out. "Yours?"

"Oh God." He snatches it back and turns his face away. "Thanks."

Teddy stuffs the pad into his pocket, then jumps to his feet and extends a hand to help me up, pulling me close enough to see the snow melting on his eyelashes. I take a quick look, then another, and step back to try to restore my equilibrium as I rub the snow off my mittens.

"We're good?" he confirms. "Nothing broken or sprained? Only pride hurt?" I nod, and his eyes crinkle. "Then I can skip to the most important thing. I would have gotten there first, so I win."

I stop in the middle of adjusting my hat. "First, no way. Second." I check for the clue and see an S, which I tap into my phone. "A friendly reminder that you don't win until you unscramble the word—"

"Which is *changes*. I knew that by clue four."

I hold out my phone, where the screen displays cheerful fireworks. "And get it validated by Questie."

"Goddammit." He yanks out his phone but it's too late. SunnyDay is back in the number one spot. He looks from the phone to me, his mouth twitching. "Congratulations. Looks like you won fair and square. However, I reached *this* clue first."

"Does it matter?" I ask. "Since I won the game? The most important part?"

He gives me a look that makes it clear it matters greatly. "My slip marks start here." He walks over and taps his boot down. "Yours start a good meter farther away."

Is this the caliber of person Questie attracts? Breathtaking men willing to argue about slipping distance? I might be okay with that. Then

Teddy takes off his hat and musses up his hair. I instantly decide I am extremely good with it, because although my initial impression was positive, it's compounded when he shoves his hat back on crooked, pushing down his ears like a cat when you pet the top of its head. Two silver hoops sit in the upper part of his ear.

I suspect he's mixed like me but I'm not completely sure. Jade could tell me. She insists she has bi-dar, claiming it's good for both sexual and ethno-racial identification. To her credit, she hasn't been wrong in all the times I've seen her apply it.

Then I shake off the facial analysis because there's a more important issue, namely a trifling point to be settled against a man I've already trounced. Teddy paces my prints in the snow, placing his feet heel to toe and counting as he goes. "You were behind nine steps compared to my six. I'm the clear winner."

"I'm not going to compare skid marks with you." I clap my hand over my mouth. "Oh my God, forget I said that. Please."

Teddy is already bent over, laughing so hard I have to join in. We only calm down when a wicked wind sweeps down the street, twisting the snow into paisley curls and making us shiver.

He glances at me, a small smile lingering on his face. "Do you want to continue this over lunch to warm up? There's a pho place close by."

This is fraternizing with the enemy, but he looks hopeful. Questie's only a game, after all, and it's one I'm winning. Plus I want to. I have to, in fact. This could be the universe answering my call. If that's so, it's gone above and beyond to deliver, because Teddy is smart, funny, and breathtaking. Thank goodness Questie has shown me he also seems like an interesting and relatable guy. "Sure."

As we head toward Spadina Avenue, there's a short silence, which is akin to death to me, so I fill it right away. "Do you know ski ballet used to be in the Olympics?" My dual superpower and toxic trait are a vast knowledge of weird facts that is helpful for Questie but sometimes annoying in real life.

"I didn't." Teddy looks like I've made his day by sharing that tidbit. My shoulders relax slightly.

"It was a demonstration event, though," I say. "The medals didn't count."

"No wonder you're so good at Questie," he says. "You must kill trivia nights."

He doesn't say it as a diss but in a tone of actual respect. My bizarre general knowledge is usually a joke to people. In fact, being a joke is the best-case scenario. I had an ex-boyfriend who took it as a personal challenge to try to prove me wrong, and Jade called him Citation because of all the times he demanded references at dinner the first and only time they met.

We cross Spadina to the restaurant, and Teddy pauses at the pole topped by the statue of a cat on a chair. "We could go one day," he says to the pole. "To trivia night. If you want."

I try not to goggle at him. Is this a date request? A flush comes up to warm my wind-chilled face. Teddy stares up at the cat statue as if it's the most fascinating thing in the world.

"That would be nice," I say faintly.

"Really?" He breaks out into a huge smile, again directed at that cat, before he looks over and turns it on me. His eyes stay on mine, and I'm so flustered I miss the handle of the restaurant door and paw the glass.

"Yeah." I'm grateful I can force out any words.

"Then it's a date."

"Okay," I squeak.

Teddy pulls open the door and waves me through. The server shows us to a table near the front, then leaves a battered silver teapot and two menus. I sneak more peeks at Teddy between taking little sips of tea like I'm a newly presented debutante in a room of grande dames.

Teddy is smoother than I am, thank God, and starts the conversation. "That was fun," he says.

"Questie always puts me in a good mood," I agree. "That's the first time I had to compete in real time for the clues, though."

Teddy's glasses steam up when he drinks and he takes them off to wave around. Without the heavy frames, his eyes look sharper and tilt down at the corners to give him an almost brooding look, like a melancholy outlaw. After he puts the glasses back on, pushing them up with a single finger in a gesture so cute I wish he'd do it again so I could capture it on film to watch when I'm sad, he leans over to pour me more tea.

"Finishing the puzzle almost at the same time," he says. "I knew we were meant to be friends."

"It takes approximately fifty hours for someone to become a casual friend and another one hundred to be a nonqualified friend," I say. "Apparently."

Teddy's eyebrows raise. "Does messaging on a game platform count as any of those friendship service hours, or do we have to start from scratch?"

The server comes by and we order as I consider this. "I'd say we've banked about three hours."

"If we add in the hours we spend playing Questie, it has to be closer to fifty."

I laugh. "I'm fairly certain you have to spend the hours together."

Teddy taps his cup. "That seems antithetical to modern life. Haven't they heard of asynchronous time? I vote for at least twenty hours."

"I'll compromise at ten friendship hours banked."

He makes a face. "Compromises are the orange Popsicles of existence."

"The *what*?"

"Like, you have a Popsicle, which is great, but it's orange."

"I like orange Popsicles."

"Sure, but are they your favorite? Or would you rather have pink? Or even lime?"

I struggle with that. He's right and the smile he gives me says he knows. "Twelve hours," I offer.

"I'll take it." There's a pause. "So what do you do when not playing Questie?"

"Good question." I clasp my hands under the table. "I'm looking for a new job. My company is closing."

"Oh, that's tough," he says sincerely. "I'm sorry to hear it."

"I'm nervous," I admit, then instantly regret it. Forcing your bad mood on others is the height of rudeness, especially when we're here to have a good time. I smooth out all the places negativity might have lingered on me—the wrinkles in my forehead, the curved shoulders, and the downturned mouth—and buff myself back up to my usual shine. "It's a great chance to grow my career, though!"

Teddy doesn't look convinced that this is the good-news story I'm trying to sell it as. "Do you want to talk about it?"

I'm a bit taken aback he didn't say it would be fine or to look on the bright side. Do I want to talk about it?

"No," I say slowly. "Is that bad?"

"Not at all. I, for one, would welcome the chance to leave work unmentioned." Teddy's eyes drop.

"You would?"

"Absolutely. Let's make this"—he waves between us—"a work-free space."

"Deal." I spend so much time thinking about work that an enforced break is welcome.

"There's a world of other things to talk about, like where your love for trivia came from," he says.

His expression is curious, not insulting, so I answer honestly. "I've always liked information. My family makes fun of it. They call me a hummingbird because my mind bounces from thing to thing."

"Because you're curious."

"That's a nicer way to put it."

"It's cool," he says, smiling at the server as she puts steaming bowls down in front of us.

"Kind of useless."

"That depends on your perspective." He drops in some basil. "All knowledge is useless until you need it. Who needs to know about mitochondria in their everyday life?"

"That's important, though. Mitochondria are the—"

We chorus the rest together: "—powerhouse of the cell."

"Fair enough," he says. "Is that what attracted you to Questie?"

"Mitochondria? I'm more of a nucleus girl, to be honest."

"Hilarious."

"At first it was something to do." I look at Teddy's hands as he squeezes in the lime. They're big and capable looking, with three thin silver bracelets wrapped around his wrist. "Then I started winning and got into it."

"Does anyone play it with you?"

I shake my head, delighted at how easy conversation is with him. We could be at twenty friendship hours after all. "It's only a game but I enjoy it. I don't want to deal with people laughing at it or saying it's a waste of time."

"I get that." Teddy dips some beef into his sriracha. "Sometimes things are too meaningful to tell the people closest to us."

"It should be the other way around."

"It should," he agrees. "I find the people you love are the people who you most and least trust in the world. They have real power to hurt you."

We sit in silence for a moment, Teddy dims as if what he said came from personal experience. Then he gives me a sideways smile.

"That got heavy. Let's move to a slightly lighter topic, like if it really bothered you when I made first on the leaderboard."

"It did, kind of." I wrinkle my nose. "It's embarrassing to admit."

He stops eating, expression thoughtful. "Would you be upset if I kept playing?"

"No, why?"

"Because I'll keep winning." He says it seriously enough that I put down the tofu I was about to bite into.

"You can *try* to keep winning," I say. "I'd like to point out I won today."

He grins. "Sounds like a competition."

I raise my eyebrows. "Yeah, that's the entire point of a game. To compete. In order to win. Which I did."

"How about this?" Teddy wipes his fingers on a thin napkin. "Whoever has the fewest days at number one by the time we go to trivia pays for dinner that night."

"Deal." I pile rice noodles into my spoon, hands shaking slightly from the butterflies in my chest. "Get your credit card ready."

The rest of the meal flies by, but soon a tsunami of texts arrive from Mom, all containing instructions on what I need to do to get ready for their move. Each message ticks my blood pressure a bit higher as I see my job-hunting time disappear under moving boxes and furniture storage.

"I'd better head home," I say after the server clears the table, regretting the words as I say them. I'd love to spend more time with Teddy despite ricocheting between being utterly at ease and then freaking out when he looks at me. We tussle briefly for the bill but Teddy claims that it's his job to treat the Questie winner.

"You can get the next one when I win," he adds, and I warm at the thought of a next time. We wave goodbye, and he goes off with that admirable walk, me doing my best not to watch after him in case he turns around and sees me rubbernecking.

I'm almost home when a text comes in, but this time it's not Mom. It's Teddy, who had asked for my number, claiming it's easier than messaging through Questie. He's sent a screenshot of the leaderboard and underneath, he's written, Let the games begin.

I smile so hard that my face aches as I open my front door. It was a good day, and I remind myself to add a note in my gratitude journal. Life is coming back together.

FIVE

DECEMBER 13

I 'm in my room trying to work on my résumé, even though Jade
pointed out December is one of the slowest times to look for
a new job. I don't have a choice, though, because Nadia was right.
Competition will be fierce with every consultant at Chariot searching.

"Dee, come do the curtains with me," calls Mom up the stairs.

Mom, who has been over daily to prepare the house for their
move back, always seems to need assistance at the exact moment I
start making progress on an application. I go downstairs to where
my lovely living room has been transformed into a showroom for
Starkman's medical supply depot. Pride of place goes to the surgical
bed my mother has covered with a butterfly blanket crocheted in an
electric blue.

"What's this?" I ask. She's holding an armful of thick black fabric.

"It's too sunny in here," says Mom. "We need blackout shades so
your grandmother can rest."

"Oh." My gauzy lace curtains lie in a tumbled pile on the floor, and
Mom kicks them away before telling me to get a stool.

Once we're done, she twitches them into place. "Perfect."

The day had already been gloomy, with a low shelf of unbroken clouds stretching across the sky, and the addition of the blackout shades plunges the room into what I anticipate will be a permanent twilight.

"It makes the space a little dull," I say as diplomatically as possible.

"We can fix that." She reaches into one of the many bags littering the floor and pulls out white cotton panels printed with yellow smiley faces.

I eye the hideous curtains. "The smiley face was created to enhance employee morale at an insurance firm, and the designer only made forty-five dollars."

"What a ridiculous thing to know." Mom hands me a curtain to start hanging. "Anyway, I'm sure the joy they got out of creating something that makes people happy was payment enough."

When the curtains are done, I escape back to my room, guilt lying on my shoulders like a sated cheetah on a branch. A good daughter would be excited about helping her family. She'd be down there organizing closets instead of lying on the floor, desperately trying to manifest a better life. I briefly wonder if it's acceptable to put out an opposite affirmation, like *Keep Grandma out of my house* before deciding it goes against the spirit of the thing. After all, they're not called *negations*.

"Dee, we need to move the sofa!"

I sigh and head back down. Time enough for job hunting later.

———

DECEMBER 22

DAILY AFFIRMATION: I AM DEPENDABLE.

Teddy: Did you check the leaderboard?

The text comes as I take a break from ferrying Grandma's thankfully limited belongings into the house. It doesn't improve my mood because I know what I'll see: Teddy9 at the top and SunnyDay second.

Me: Congratulations.

Teddy: Thank you, but I detect some insincerity.

Mom comes into the room, hands on her hips and light brown hair falling out of its short ponytail. She smells faintly skunky because she's moving what seems like far more than the legally permitted number of weed plants into the grow-op Dad set up in the basement. "Dee, no lollygagging. I need you to unpack the kitchen since Jade went home early."

Jade had offered to help until noon, and Mom wasn't over the fact that she was out the door at precisely 12:01.

"I'll be right there," I say.

Mom catches sight of the blankets piled up to make a makeshift bed on the floor. "We'll get you a nice cot. Won't that be comfortable?"

Not as good as the king bed I had to put in storage because it didn't fit in the small room. "Great," I say.

I return to my conversation with Teddy when she leaves.

Teddy: I thought I'd see you today.

Me: Too busy to play.

Teddy: That makes me feel like I cheated.

Me: Don't worry. I'll come out ahead.

Teddy: I can do the puzzle with you? I won't get in your way.

It was a good circuit.

I stare at the phone, wondering what this means, and my hands get a little trembly at the idea of seeing him again.

"Dee! The kitchen!"

Me: That would be fun.

Teddy's offer almost makes up for losing my place in the game.

———

DECEMBER 26

DAILY AFFIRMATION: POSITIVITY IS INFECTIOUS! IN A GOOD, NONVIRAL WAY.

I wake up exhausted after a night of heartburn, thanks to my mother cooking enough Christmas dinner for eight although she knew Jade and her family would be in Cuba. The incessant squeak coming from the living room for hours hadn't helped. *Chili*, it turns out, is not a condiment. It's Chilly, my grandmother's pet chinchilla, who adores his running wheel at all times and particularly between three and five in the morning.

There's a message from Jade: How's it going?

  Me: It's going.

Seconds later, a video call comes through to show my sister pulling her long ash-brown balayaged hair over her shoulder.

I sit on the floor, happy to see her face. We look as different as sisters can, although we share a funny upper lip carved with an extra sharp cupid's bow. I take after Dad, with long narrow eyes, straight dark hair, and a squarish jaw. Where my face is all angles, Jade is curves, with Mom's soft rounded cheeks and wavy hair. Her brown eyes are darker and rounder than mine, and her nose has an actual bridge, which makes me eternally jealous when I have to buy sunglasses.

"You okay?" she asks. "How was yesterday?"

"Mom only asked four times why you were in Cuba instead of eating dry turkey with us."

Jade snorts, causing the video to jerk back and forth, then shows me the beach outside her window. "After years of pasting a smile on my face for the entire day, this is heaven."

"Do you remember the year we went to Italy for the holidays? I was fourteen."

"What a mess. Mom hated Rome because it was too loud, and Dad hated Venice because there were too many tourists."

"Neither of them would admit it, though."

"They kept snapping at each other through us and pretending everything was fine. Good times." There's a comfortable silence, then Jade says, "Now that the obligatory reminiscing is out of the way, will you tell me what's upset you?"

"I'm not upset."

"Liar." Jade's pale lips bend into a frown that brackets her mouth. "I told Mom this was a bad idea. She should have rented a place."

I hate having to defend Mom against her. "Grandma's sick and old."

"Grandma froze Dad out when she was younger and spry and resents being dependent on him now. She was never nice to us. Remember what happened when Mom used to tell her about an award we won or something we were doing?"

"Yeah." Grandma wouldn't say a word about us but would start talking about Rebecca's children and their soccer games or swimming lessons.

"We were only kids, and we were forced to visit her once a month so she could find us lacking to our faces." Jade shakes her head. "I don't want her near Poppy or Nick. It was bad enough Opal had to deal with her at our wedding."

"Bad vibes."

"It's not vibes," she says. "It's action. Deliberate and hurtful action. Enough of her. I don't want her to take up my brain space."

"I'll be fine," I say. "It's a change, that's it, and I've already adjusted."

"I'm going to believe you."

"Thanks." At least she won't push me for a bit, and soon it will all be back to normal. This is a blip on my life radar and nothing to arm the warheads for.

Jade needs to get to the beach, so we blow kisses and disconnect. Then I flip my laptop open. Looking for a new job will keep my mind occupied.

———

DECEMBER 28

DAILY AFFIRMATION: I RISE THROUGH DISAPPOINTMENT LIKE A PHOENIX.

It's that hollow time between Christmas and New Year. I've been look-ing forward to playing Questie with Teddy like it's a lifeline except he messages to say he can't meet me on Wednesday.

I do my best to obey my meditation app and let the disappointment pass unjudged. No go. It lingers in my chest like a summer cold.

Teddy: I can't go because I'm here.

He sends a photo. It's night and he's reflected in a hotel room window. Outside is an iconic skyline lit up with lights.

Me: You're in Shanghai?
Teddy: Last-minute business trip to sort out a supplier prob-lem. I'll be here two weeks unfortunately.
Me: Lucky. I've always wanted to see the Bund. Should we put our competition on hold until you come back?
Teddy: Hell no. I'm doing the remote version. I can maintain my Questie dominance from anywhere.
Me: We'll see.
Teddy: I'm sorry, Dee. I was looking forward to it. Promise we'll go when I get back?

He could be saying that to be polite but I want to believe he means it.

Me: Promise.

DAILY AFFIRMATION: TRYING IS AS GOOD AS SUCCEEDING. SURE IT IS.

I go downstairs to where my mother is making oatmeal. Grandma sits at the table in a beige tracksuit, which is similar to the sand, buff, and taupe outfits I've seen her sporting over the last few days. On the wall behind her, Mom has reinstated the wood-burned plaque of the Optimist Creed, its intimidating Gothic script reminding us to wear a cheerful countenance at all times. She's also hung three progressively larger carved wooden chickens with *Thankful, Grateful, Joyful* written on their bodies in flowing white script. The rust-red chickens are tied with brown string for a rustic look that destroys my pastel British tearoom aesthetic.

Grandma nods when she sees me. No smile, but that's not unusual. "Hello, Dee."

"Hi, Grandma." There hasn't been much change on the relationship front since she's been here. Although Grandma's consistent about courtesies like acknowledging Dad and me, she hasn't progressed to proactively showing interest or maintaining regular eye contact. Meals are the worst and would almost certainly be silent if it weren't for Mom and me laying down a controlled burn of busy chatter.

I wish you weren't here, says that terrible inner voice. *Jade doesn't have to deal with you.* I look remorsefully around the table as if my family can hear my thoughts. That was below me. I shouldn't think like this. I need to do better.

My phone dings as I take my first bland bite, and my stomach drops when I check the message. **Thank you for your interest in Transformity Consulting. We regret to inform you that our applicant pool was extremely experienced, and we will not be moving forward with your application at this time.**

I should be used to this by now, but each rejection eats at me.

"Where's my smile, sunshine?" Mom puts down a bowl of out-of-season blueberries that will be as hard and tasteless as pebbles.

"I'm never going to find a job," I mutter.

"Not with that attitude," Mom says. "You need to get out there and keep trying."

It was a mistake to say anything. "Right, Mom."

"A positive mindset makes all the difference," she says. "You'll see."

———

JANUARY 14

DAILY AFFIRMATION: C'MON, I'M SERIOUSLY DOING MY BEST. RIGHT, OKAY. I MAKE A DIFFERENCE TO THE WORLD BY EXISTING.

My primary hobby has become checking my phone for something, anything, to move my life ahead. I had a few condolence messages when I asked my friends about job openings, but any plans to get together keep getting cancelled. Today I find another rejection, a university friend I hadn't seen in a while and had asked out for coffee. This is normal; everyone is busy, so I type back a quick reply. Omg of course. Tell me when you're free!

Being on the second or third ring of the friendship circle never bothered me, but right now I wish I had somebody to talk to. I always made it a habit to be the friend other people could come to for support. I touch my phone with cold fingers, uncomfortably aware, thanks to my empty social calendar, that they don't seem to like it the other way around.

———

JANUARY 16

DAILY AFFIRMATION: I DESERVE GOOD THINGS.

> **Teddy**: I'm home. Ready to Questie?

I brighten. Texting with Teddy has become the highlight of my day, unsurprising since the rest of my life revolves around getting rejected from jobs, avoiding my grandmother in my own house, and watching what is left of my meager savings deplete. At least with my parents here, the last isn't going as fast as it could, so it's not all bad.

> **Me**: Welcome back. Did you check the leaderboard?

In Teddy's absence, I've regained my top spot.

> **Teddy**: I did but will triumph again. Are you free Saturday after next? We can start the new game at the same time.
> **Me**: Sure, then I can wait for you at the last clue.
> **Teddy**: It'll be the opposite way around, but you're on.

––––––

JANUARY 17

DAILY AFFIRMATION: I AM POTENTIAL INCARNATE.

"I got an interview." I whisper the news into the phone to Jade.

"Why are you whispering?"

"I don't want Mom to hear."

"Understood. The less she knows the better." She lowers her voice in solidarity. "This is great, Dee."

"I guess." I don't want to get my hopes up but then remember that negative energy attracts more negativity. "I mean, it is! I can do this!"

"What on earth are you on about?" she asks.

"Manifesting my desired result."

"Uh-huh." She doesn't bother to hide her skepticism behind a veneer of politeness.

I adjust my vision board. "Manifesting what you want makes it easier to achieve your desires."

"No, it doesn't," she says. "The big bang did not occur twenty billion years ago for the sole purpose of making sure you get what you want."

"Thirteen point eight billion years ago," I correct.

"My actual point remains. The thirteen-point-whatever-year-old universe does not give two shits about providing a better parking space because you asked a cloud to make it so."

"That's not how it works," I say. "Manifesting draws positive energy and encourages you to take steps to reach your goals."

"I accept the second. As for the first, again, I assure you preparing for the interview is a much better path to success."

"It doesn't hurt, though."

"Dee, you've worked hard." Her voice softens. "You can do this."

"Thanks."

"Go kick some ass, kid sister."

————

JANUARY 23

DAILY AFFIRMATION: I BEAT DOWN CHALLENGES LIKE BREAD DOUGH TO ACHIEVE MY OBJECTIVES.

I got the job. *I got the job.* I am a junior consultant at Gear Robins.

I lightly tap my vision board with my palm in a one-sided high five. This is the start of a great new era. All I needed to do was believe.

SIX

DAILY AFFIRMATION: EVERYTHING
I DO IS A SUCCESS. NO.
I AM A MAGNET FOR GOOD THINGS. NO.
LET IT ALL BE OKAY. PLEASE. YEAH, THAT WORKS.

It's my first day at Gear Robins and my second chance at my dream career. I wake up with my stomach churning from a combination of nerves and the smell in my room. Instead of pleasant diffusers with conceptual names from locally owned boutiques, the house reeks of cannabis, which Mom's making into oil to soothe Grandma's joints.

The mustiness competes with the sharp menthol of Tiger Balm, also used to soothe Grandma's joints. Combined with Chilly's hay, I must smell like a 1970s farm commune, which is less than ideal for the professional image I want to project.

I glance at my vision board and ignore the people at a Paris café to zero in on the woman smiling at a laptop with an uneaten iceberg lettuce salad beside her. Career success is the goal for today. Nothing will stop me. I pull back my shoulders and head downstairs.

"You're not wearing that coat," says Grandma when she sees me pulling out my parka.

"It's my only one." I dropped my good wool coat in paint when renovating and haven't gotten around to replacing it.

"It's not appropriate for your first day at work. You know that."

"It's what I have." I try to keep my voice bright, but her judgment is unwelcome when I'm already struggling to maintain my calm.

"Jessica!" calls my grandmother. "Where's my tie coat?"

"In the closet." My mother bustles over and wrinkles her nose. "Oh my, Dee, how much perfume are you wearing?"

A lot, since I'm desperate to cover the weed smell. "I've got to get going," I say.

"The *coat*, Jessica."

Mom pulls out a vintage black cashmere coat with a wide collar and a tie around the waist and hands it over. Not going to lie, it's the coat I'd been wanting ever since I saw a fashion blog post of Wei Fangli wearing one out in New York and looking like a goddess. I'm surprised this nonchalant elegance was Grandma's style at any point in her life.

"That's yours now," Grandma says.

"I can't take this," I protest.

She snorts. "When am I going to wear it?" She limps toward the kitchen as I stare after her. This is the only thing she's given me outside obligatory holiday gifts, which were usually book box sets meant for people much younger or older than I was. Is this Grandma's payment for letting her live here? I decide to be grateful and leave it at that, partly because there's no time for anything else and my attention needs to be on the day ahead.

Dad pops out to give me a hug. "Knock 'em dead, tiger!"

Mom runs her hand down my back. "The best accessory is a smile, sunshine."

Once outside, I immediately regret not wearing my parka, fashion be damned, because the February temperature has dropped low enough for the city to issue an extreme cold alert. After getting off the subway, I trudge through the valleys of icy streets toward my new office, fingers stiff in my gloves and exposed skin hurting.

Gear Robins is in a tall 1960s brutalist concrete block near Union Station. Despite the freezing wind cramping my calves in their thin nylons, I linger on the corner and watch my new coworkers disappear through the rotating doors, pale faces bleached further from the cold.

"You can do it," I whisper through chattering teeth, forcing myself to cross the street. I took two years of night school to prepare for this. I did well at Chariot. I will do well here. Damn, that's what I should have said to the mirror. I whisper this bonus affirmation as I shove through the door. *I am doing well at Gear Robins.* To work, affirmations should be said as if you've already achieved your goal, fixing it in place like a scientist observing a quantum particle.

I walk into my department on the fifth floor, walls emblazoned with inspiring quotes by Martin Luther King Jr., the Dalai Lama, and my new CEO Thomas Robins, and run into my manager, Will.

"Ah, Daiyu." Will looks like he was born to be in sales, an impression heightened by the loud voice, BBC accent, and impeccable suit tailoring. His nose is traced with red veins, prominent against his sallow skin. "Did you remember to book your desk? Come see me when you're settled."

"Okay," I say, or rather call to his navy-blazered back, because he's already halfway down the hall.

Unsure of what counts as settled, I opt for the fastest option and go to see Will as soon as I put my bag down and hang my coat on my chair. He points me to a seat without looking up from his phone. His office is as bland as a show kitchen and devoid of any personality.

"It may be difficult for you to get used to the new environment," he says as his eyes skim the sports scores. "Nevertheless you'll be expected to get up to speed quickly."

"It's an excellent opportunity to learn," I say as brightly as I can. George wanted his Charioteers to be almost incandescent with confidence and pep, and I figure it's a safe attitude to bring with me. Studies have shown that positive people are more liked and do better in the workplace anyway.

Will shoots his cuff to check his watch, which might be a Rolex, as a woman comes in and closes the door with a decisive click. "Almost on time for once," he says. "Vivian, meet Daiyu Kwan. She's new to Gear Robins. Daiyu, Vivian Shaw, one of our many senior consultants."

Vivian smiles at me. She's Black and older than I am, around fifty, with dark brown skin and long copper braids tied into a thick low ponytail. Her earrings are small gold hoops that match the thin metallic threading of her tweed blazer.

"Now that you're both finally here, I can tell you the news," says Will. "We've brought on an exciting client. Celeste."

"The luxury fashion firm?" Vivian asks, pulling out a reporter's pad and taking notes.

"Yes. My wife collects their purses." He adopts an exaggerated *ladies and their bags, amirite* expression.

My laugh is weak since even I, a fashion amateur, know one of those purses can cost well over a month's pay.

"Apparently they had a leak about their diversity numbers," continues Will.

"Not good, I assume?" Vivian jots a note on her pad.

"What do you think, since they called us?" Despite his laugh, this seems oddly combative, but Vivian keeps her eyes on her notepad, writing away. "Vivian, I'm assigning Celeste and Daiyu to you. A fashion company should be something you can handle."

Her face tightens almost imperceptibly. Is it me? Is she upset about getting a newbie? I wonder if she's into fashion and that's why Will is passing it over to her.

Will notices as well because he says, "I expect this won't be a problem?"

"I don't have time to train a new hire in addition to my current workload," says Vivian. "Particularly given the discussion we had last week regarding my capacity."

I look at Vivian, who wears a smile that shows absolutely no contraction of her orbicularis oculi muscles, and Will, who is also smiling broadly but with no contraction of his orbicularis oculi muscles. It's like sitting between two sharks.

"We can discuss your opinion further if you think it necessary, but I'm certain my decision will stand," Will says. "Daiyu is eager to learn."

I'm so uncomfortable I want to dissolve, but I want to make a good impression. "I'm determined to do well despite being new to Gear Robins," I say.

Vivian gazes at me curiously while Will nods like a proud father at what I belatedly understand was the suckiest of suck-up comments. "An excellent attitude, Daiyu, and one I encourage everyone to share," he says.

A loud knock sounds before a man opens the door and thrusts his head in. "How about that game, Will?" They take a couple of minutes to complain about the terrible ref while we wait. When Will finally waves us away, Vivian tells me to meet her in the conference room in an hour and disappears. As I boot up my laptop, my phone buzzes.

> **Teddy**: Did you know Victorians had mummy unwrapping parties?

I feel a bit of the tension leave my neck.

> **Me**: Did you know Victorian artists had a shade of paint called Mummy Brown that was made of ground-up mummies?
> **Teddy**: I did not although that would have been a logical sidebar to the unwrapping information.
> **Me**: How do you know this anyway?
> **Teddy**: I googled weird facts to try to impress you. Did it work?
> **Me**: It did.

He wants to impress me? I can feel the huge grin on my face.

> **Teddy:** Then my Monday is made. We're not supposed to talk about work but I wanted to know how you were doing. How's your new office?
> **Me:** It's different.
> **Teddy:** We can talk about it tonight if you want.
> **Me:** I like our no-work rule.
> **Teddy:** No arguments here, but you can change your mind at any time.

He leaves for a meeting, and cheered, I find the conference room and get on the network to do some quick research for the leaked documents. It looks like there's a lot to do at Celeste, which I deliberately decide thrills instead of intimidates me. I refuse to go into a project already defeated.

"Let's get started," says Vivian as she comes in. To my relief, her tone is friendly. Whatever her issue with Will, she's fair enough to give me a chance. "It's your first day, so you'll need an overview of how we work. What experience do you have?"

"I was in communications for almost a decade, including five years with Chariot before they promoted me to diversity consultant. I did that for five months before coming here."

"Five months." She seems unimpressed.

"Almost five," I clarify. More like four and there's no need to tell her my last two months were a little chaotic after George's closure announcement. "I have my diversity and inclusion certificate, too! I worked hard on it, at night."

Vivian manages a smile. "I'm sure you did. I'm familiar with Chariot's methods, so this will be a significant shift for you."

I turn to my laptop to take notes, an action she seems to view with approval. For the next hour, Vivian runs me through how it's going to go, which is basically I'll do the project and she'll oversee it. She makes it clear I'm expected to work independently as she has multiple other accounts, and it dawns on me that Gear Robins is more of an everyone-for-themselves rather than a there-are-no-bad-questions environment.

"You'll be on the ground at Celeste while the project is active," she says. "I'll set up something so we can meet their team. Sound good?"

I nod.

"Questions?"

I don't want to look ignorant, so I shake my head. I can figure it out as I go.

"Let's see what we have to work with."

We look at a screenshot of a leaked internal report that was posted to Fashion Eye, an industry gossip site, then picked up by other media. My eyes go to the bar charts of staff members and how they self-identify. For most of the charts, one bar is high. Every other bar barely clears the x-axis, if it's there at all.

"It could be worse," murmurs Vivian, eyes on her screen.

"How?"

"They could have ignored it instead of hiring us," she says.

I brighten. "That's right. There's room to grow."

She doesn't answer and shuts her laptop, ready to leave.

"Have you been here long?" I ask, eager to learn about my new colleague.

"Almost ten years."

"What do you like most about it?"

"It's always interesting." She glances at the door. "Don't forget to use the latest template, not the one from October."

Vivian's phone is on the table, the lock screen showing a teenage girl waving at the camera mid-giggle. "Is that your daughter? What's her name?"

"Maya. Did you hear what I said about the template?"

I bow down to Vivian's signals, trying not to feel hurt. Well, it's only my first day and she's busy. There's plenty of time to get to know each other when her workload lightens.

She gives me a few brisk instructions and then leaves, already on another call.

I spend a good hour searching the intranet and am happy to find old versions of analyses for other clients as well as reports I can use to figure out what I told Vivian I already knew. I hope this is a sign of a great start at Gear Robins.

SEVEN

*H*ope only gets me so far, and by the end of the day, I'm seriously worried. The reports I thought I could reverse engineer turned out to be based on an earlier methodology, not the revised Gear Robins People First Platform Vivian insists I use.

Gear Robins is nothing like Chariot, and lunch was a solitary salad taken at my desk when no one asked me to join them. The office itself is inhumanly quiet apart from Will bellowing an occasional joke or question at someone across the room. It doesn't help that I spend my commute home wishing the house was empty so I could go straight to bed without having to talk about my day to another living being. At least the cold has gone from polar to merely frigid.

When I come up the sidewalk, Dad is clearing snow again. I think it's because he wants to get out of the house, but he insists it's the neighborly thing to do.

"Dad, there's not a flake left," I say when I reach him.

"Hi, hon." He attacks my feet with his broom to get rid of the clumps on my shoes. "How was your first day at the new job?"

With Mom, I'd have to smile and say great, but Dad's a little more sympathetic. "It was okay."

He steadies the broom to look at me. His black hair, only lightly streaked with white, is tucked under a ratty plaid hunter hat with ear flaps, and his old khaki parka has stuffing coming from one of the seams. Mom hates this outfit ("What will the neighbors think?") but I like it. He's used it for decades for winter shoveling, and when I was a kid, I used to steal it to make a cave when he came in. It had that iron smell of snow mixed with his soap and felt like safety.

"Dee-bear? Everything good, lah?" Although he's been in Canada for decades, the little Singaporean interjection has yet to be completely overtaken by *eh*.

I drag my foot back and forth on the spotless sidewalk. "I need time to get used to it."

"That's right, give it a chance," he encourages. "Not everything is perfect from day one."

I'm staring into the front window as he speaks, and the words come out before I stop them. "Like Grandma?"

We never talk about it, but Dad must dislike the deliberate way Grandma treats him, as if she's fulfilling a social obligation without affection or regard. Does he resent Mom for putting him in this situation? I don't know. I have no idea what private deal they've hammered out to cope with Grandma's attitude or to recompense Dad for having to leave his beloved cottage country.

"What do you mean?" Dad starts sweeping again, his face turned away.

"Nothing." I regret bringing it up because I'm not in the mood to interrogate this too deeply. I never do when it comes to my family because we don't talk about a lot of things. It makes it easier to keep the facade that we're all content and there's nothing here to bother any of us. *Keep on that happy face!*

As Mom is fond of saying, it's better to look ahead than behind. When Jade's around, which isn't often, she counters this by pointing out that dealing with issues as they occur is the actual way to a brighter and less problem-ridden future.

Dad moves so I can see his profile, so much like mine. "I've found it's worth giving people the benefit of the doubt. Your yeye taught me to be like water, flowing around obstacles, instead of a rock that can never move."

I've heard him say this before. "Including Grandma?"

"Water flows around everything." He tilts his head. "Your grandmother is not the worst person I've dealt with in this country."

"Oh." This makes my chest tight to hear, but it's another thing we don't talk about.

"I keep the door open for your grandmother. That's it." He leans against the broom, breath puffing in the cold. "It makes your mother happy and costs me little."

"You came back here to take care of her."

"She's your grandmother, and it was the right thing to do." He pulls his broom between the sidewalk blocks. "You should go in before you catch cold. Mom is baking."

The conversation is over. When I go inside, the house smells like a barn fire instead of warm butter and sweet sugar despite Dad's hint that cookies, or at minimum muffins, will be available. I cough. "Mom? Is something burning?"

Her voice comes from the kitchen. "We're baking, sunshine."

"What, hay bales?"

"Don't be silly. Come join us!"

I eavesdrop on their conversation as I pull off my shoes.

"You're not going to get better if you sit there," Mom scolds. "You'll be fine if you get moving."

"I don't want to fall down," says my grandmother.

"You won't fall if you believe in yourself. You need more confidence."

I come in and peer into the oven. "That doesn't smell like it involves chocolate."

Mom's been trying different foods to get Grandma to eat more, so this could be the end result of catering to someone still in thrall to the ghost of 1980s diet culture. I don't think she's eaten dessert in decades. As well as anything ethnic, the list of foods Grandma won't eat runs from egg yolks (cholesterol) to grilled meat (cancer from the charcoal) to real butter (only margarine). She barely allows white rice, and that's because my father, for the only time, simply put his foot down and refused to entertain the idea of brown rice in the house.

"It's for Chilly," Mom says. "We found a great little recipe for chinchilla treats! Isn't that cute?"

I refrain from saying it smells like death. "Sure."

"Take a seat, Dee." Mom turns back to the stove. "Keep your grandmother company."

Her voice brooks no dissent, so I steel myself for some quality family time. On the kitchen table in front of Grandma is a jigsaw puzzle of Monet's *Houses of Parliament*, the pieces in tones of gray, pink, and yellow.

"Can I join you?" I ask. The puzzle will keep me busy until I can make my escape.

Grandma waves in a "you do you" gesture, so I sit and grab some of the Thames, watching Grandma's fingers shake as she tries to place her piece. The skin on her hand is thin but shiny, as if it's been rubbed with a layer of dry wax. A topographical map of thick blue veins bulges against the surface.

I don't know if there's ever going to be a way through the desert that's my relationship with Grandma. Or if there's a point. Her indifferent coldness to who Jade and I are and what we do is almost more cutting than if she showed an actual aversion like Aunt Rebecca does.

The phone rings and Mom picks up. "Hi, honey. When are you coming for a visit?"

I eavesdrop as I look for a piece.

"Your birth certificate? I thought I gave it to you," Mom says. "I'll look. What are the kids up to?"

A pause.

"Oh, Jade, why would you do that? Poppy's a baby. She doesn't need to know how bad the world can get."

Another pause.

"It's not interfering. It's for her own good… Well, I love you, too." She hangs up the phone. "I don't know what to do with that girl."

"Jade?" I ask.

Mom clatters some pans together. "She's so negative. That's not a good environment for the children."

Poppy and Nick are the most darling ankle biters in the world even though Jade and Opal, who have matching couple's shirts that say Precious Jewels, had come horrifyingly close to calling them Garnet and Jet. "The kids are doing great," I say.

"She should teach them to see the good in life," Mom continues. "Poppy was watching the *news*."

"Poppy watches a special channel for kids."

"Little girls should be protected."

"Poppy is lucky enough to be five and not have to experience a refugee camp or worse," I say. "It won't kill her to know other kids don't have that chance."

"Don't even say such a thing." Mom slams a cupboard shut.

Grandma shifts on the other side of the table, and I abandon the talk with my mother. "Did you have a good day, Grandma?"

"She'd have a better day if she left the house for fresh air," says Mom. "Exercise is good for you. All the doctors say so."

Grandma's fingers tighten on the piece. "It's slippery out."

"That's what winter boots are for!" Mom shakes her head in mock dismay as she rattles the tray of rank brown pellets she's pulled from the oven. "I keep telling you to get out there and do it. Like Nike says!"

Grandma doesn't reply but bends her head to her puzzle. A cup of tea, brewed so long it's inky, sits at her elbow, the surface dotted with dust. She doesn't look happy either, and for the first time, I wonder if

Mom had simply presented her with this move to my house as a fait accompli. Would she have preferred to stay in her own place, bad hip or not? Would having her independence have been worth the risk for her? I'm not used to thinking about Grandma as an individual and honestly doubt she's ever thought of me so deeply. Anyway, the more likely reason is that she's upset to have to live with Dad and me. Mom's voice cuts through my thoughts.

"Dee, can you run to the store? I'm out of onions."

I leap up, thrilled to have an excuse to get out of the house. "Sure, Mom."

It doesn't take long to grab the onions, and after driving back, I sit in the car, trying to summon the energy to face dinner. A text comes from Teddy.

> **Teddy**: How was the rest of your day?
> **Me**: Not sure yet.

Then I delete it.

> **Me**: Great!

I delete that, too, disliking how it feels to put on a falsely chipper persona in front of Teddy.

> **Me**: Okay. Sitting in the car at the end of my street.

This I send without edits.

> **Teddy**: Can I call you?
> **Me**: Sure.

"Why the street?" he asks when I pick up.

This is the first time we've talked on the phone, and I close my eyes to listen to the velvet sound of his voice. "I drove a few houses down so my family doesn't see me."

"I guess my larger question was why in the car down the street?"

"No reason," I sing out, eyes opening.

"Dee."

I drum my fingers along the steering wheel. "You'll think I'm a bad person."

"Did you kill someone without provocation? Cheat? Steal?"

"Not today."

"Then you're probably not that bad, but tell me and I'll see."

This makes me huff out a small laugh, which seems to be what he's looking for.

"I don't want to go inside because I'm feeling crabby," I say. It's easy to talk to him like this in the sheltering dark.

He makes a comforting noise instead of a dismissive one. "First days are stressful. You're allowed to be in a bad mood."

"Not at my house." I pluck the brown net bag holding the onions. "My mother doesn't believe in bad moods, and I don't feel like being called Oscar all night."

"Oscar?" He sounds confused. "Like the Academy Awards?"

"Oscar, like Oscar the Grouch."

He snorts.

"It's not funny," I say.

"I'm sorry, it's not," he apologizes. "It was the image of a grown adult calling another grown adult Oscar for having feelings."

"Mom is allergic to negativity," I say, surprising myself with my bluntness. "She's always finding the silver lining."

"Grinning and bearing it?"

"Making the best of a bad job."

"Mustn't grumble." He puts on a terrible Cockney accent.

"I wonder..." I hesitate because I see the value in her attitude. Life is smoother when you can face it with a smile. In Mom's world—my world—everything will be fine as long as you believe it. It's such a seductive idea, that I can control my life by fine-tuning my attitude to the right one, like fiddling with the radio to get a clear channel.

"Dee?"

"It's hard being positive all the time, but it's important and worth the effort."

"What do you mean?" He sounds perplexed.

I groan, frustrated at having to explain what to me is obvious. "Keeping a positive mindset is, like, necessary for having a happy life."

"Hell no, it's not," he says. "Not everything has to be a learning experience or opportunity. Things suck sometimes."

Like Jade, he doesn't understand. I tuck my head deeper into the seat as a kid in a snowsuit runs by with her arms outstretched. When she trips over a crack in the sidewalk, I instinctively jerk forward as if I can catch her, but she rights herself with a shriek. A few messy steps and then she's off as if nothing had happened. She moves along under the streetlights until she's out of sight.

"Look, you can say that, but you have to admit it's better if you avoid negativity," I say. "Thinking good thoughts brings goodness into your life. Makes you grateful for what you have."

"My mom used to say the same thing but trust me, when things are going bad, telling myself they could be worse isn't going to help."

I slump down, giving up. Sometimes I envy people like Jade and apparently Teddy, who can accept the valleys without feeling guilty they're not turning them into peaks. "Okay."

He must hear the defeat in my voice because his softens. "Hey, Dee, no. We have different perspectives, but that's fine. What's bothering you?"

"I don't know," I admit. "I don't have anything serious to complain about, but all together, it seems like a lot."

"I get that." There's a faint rustling, as if he's moving around. "You don't need to pretend to be happy around me."

"I am happy!" I say as happily as I can.

"I won't debate that, but since we created a work-free zone—which I love, by the way—I'd also like to suggest a bullshit-free zone. All the times you think you should smile but you don't want to, you don't."

I look out the window doubtfully. Jade had told me something similar, but with her, it felt like a reaction against Mom instead of for my own benefit. "We'll feed off each other's negative energy."

"Or we'll be able to be ourselves, good and bad. I don't want to be someone I'm not with you."

I don't like the thought that Teddy might hide what he really thinks if he feels pressured to match my attitude. *The same as Mom does to you,* says that voice. I ignore that; she does it out of love. "I don't want that either."

"It must get exhausting to have to monitor yourself all the time." His voice is gentle.

"It's what people expect," I say. "They're used to me being cheery."

"That may be, but I don't expect diddly," he says.

I lean back and hit my thighs against the steering wheel. Tomorrow is another day and all that, but at the moment, I'm stuck living this one. My chest lightens a bit to have someone unbiased to share with. "Okay. Let's do it."

"Good." I can tell he's smiling. "Total emotional honesty."

I grimace. "That sounds like a bad self-help book."

"*101 Ways to Find Your True Self with Total Emotional Honesty,*" he says in a resonant voice.

"*Girl, He's Just Not That into Total Emotional Honesty.*"

"*Emotional Honesty: The True Believer's Guide to a Better, More Productive You.*"

We're laughing when my phone beeps; Mom wants to know where her onions are. "I have to go," I say, trying not to resent being thirty years old and having to run when called.

"I'm looking forward to our Questie battle on Saturday," he says. "Named after the Roman god Saturn. You probably already knew that."

"I did," I say. "Should I pretend I didn't?"

"God, my ego's not that fragile. It'll make it even sweeter when I come up with a great fact. A knock-your-socks-off fact."

I grin at the onions beside me. "Can't wait."

"Granted, you might have to for a bit. Bye, Dee."

Then he's off, and I head home, suddenly not as blue.

EIGHT

DAILY AFFIRMATION: I OVERCOME OBSTACLES LIKE WATER OVERCOMES—WHAT? SANDCASTLES?

*I*t's not enough to start with the research," I insist to Vivian, who sits on the other side of the paper-strewn conference table. "We need to immediately engage with people at all levels who are committed to changing Celeste, not only leaders."

She regards me steadily over her screen. "Daiyu, please do it the way I told you. Not the way they did it at Chariot."

Vivian has taken the time to walk me through what's expected when I start at Celeste next week. To my dismay, she insists I follow the Gear Robins methodology to the letter. Chariot was much more flexible, and the difference is making me second-guess if I made the right move to come here, even if I was low on choices.

"Isn't it better if I...?"

"Stop." She holds up a hand. "We use the People First methodology because it works. Then we can recommend what will move the needle to help Celeste become fully diverse, inclusive, and a place people can be their authentic selves."

It's like she's giving me the sales pitch. "We can't ensure they'll do it, though," I say. How can I make change when it's up to someone else to take action? This stresses me out. At Chariot, George touted our mandate to be fully hands-on as the secret to our success.

She stares at me. "Our job is to tell them what to do, not do the work for them. They can pay extra for that."

"Should I go to Celeste's retail store before the meeting?" I sense Vivian is getting a bit frustrated with me and want to change the subject. "Field research."

"That's a waste of time you don't have," she says. "We're focusing on their corporate operation."

Her curtness takes me by surprise but I rally. "It could be useful." I'd already read up on the luxury fashion industry, including watching fashion shows and red carpets, but additional information can't hurt.

She exhales slowly. "You've been here less than a week, and this project has a compressed timeline. I need to trust you can prioritize. Otherwise I'll speak to Will about reassigning you and giving me someone with more experience."

"I can. I understand!" I almost stumble over the words. A trip to the Celeste store isn't worth this consequence. I'm a little shocked Vivian even went there without giving me a chance until I remember what she said to Will. Is the problem me or is it her having to take on the additional work dealing with a new hire? She's always on the move, and before today, I was only embarrassed about asking questions. Now I worry each one brings me a step closer to the guillotine.

"Good." Vivian gets a call and gestures she'll be a moment before she moves to a private room, rubbing her temple.

I take a sip of my cooling hot chocolate and wince as the scum on the top sticks to my teeth. I'm about to do a search on Celeste's senior leadership team—sales had told Vivian they were all white and all male except for one woman and I'd been asked to check—when she returns with a cup of coffee in her hand.

"Let's see what you've done for the kickoff presentation," she says.

I open the deck. Another day at Gear Robins.

———

The rest of the week was rough as we prepare for the initial Celeste meeting on Monday. Now it's Saturday, Questie day with Teddy, so I put aside the simmering low-grade anxiety I have failed to relabel as enthusiasm. I can worry about work more when I get home.

The stress fades with each step I take away from the house, and by the time I see Teddy near the Humber Bridge, I've almost recalibrated myself back to how I should be. Although Teddy is bundled up so tight I can barely make out his face, seeing him causes a shiver that's not from the wind. He's as attractive as I remember, with the additional glossy sheen of having a personality to match. It's cold enough that we don't waste time with pleasantries but nod at each other and pull out our phones.

"Ready to lose?" he asks, finger ready to start the game.

"I don't know. Are you?"

We open up the first clue. It's a riddle or riddle-like thing: *A strange sort of key opens the harbor's waves.*

"Okay." Teddy looks up. "It's going to be hard."

I wink at him. "For you." Then I leave.

"Dee!" he calls.

"See you at the last clue," I yell back. "If you make it."

There's a bike share depot nearby, so I grab one and ride off. Once I'm out of sight, I stop and sit on a bench to start googling ideas. A text comes.

Teddy: You're bluffing.
Me: Wrong. I know exactly where I'm going.
Teddy: I can literally see you from the bridge.

Damn, my mind game is foiled. I give him a dramatically dismissive salute and pause as the water crashing against the storm wall catches my cye. Harbor. Waves. There's a wave sculpture over at Queen's Quay at Harbourfront, which is a…strange sort of key. It's a play on the word *quay*.

Me: See ya, sucker.

I'm off.

————

Three hours later, I am a humanoid icicle, since my smugness at winning warms only my heart and none of my extremities. I sit at the café across from the last clue and admire the leaderboard, where SunnyDay reigns supreme.

Teddy arrives pale and puffing. "That was hard," he gasps.

I push over the hot chocolate I have waiting for him. "I was worried this was getting too cold," I say. "I've been here an hour."

"An hour?" His eyes are huge. "I was that slow?"

I relent. "Twenty minutes."

"Better." Teddy wraps his hands around the cup and bathes his face in the lingering heat rising from the drink. "This is the nicest thing a person has ever done for me."

We wait for Teddy's skin (with cute freckles on his nose) to gradually turn from gray to red as we rehash the trickier of the clues. It was a good puzzle, despite the cold.

"You hungry from all that gloating?" Teddy asks.

"If by *gloating* you mean *winning*, yes."

"Want to try the dim sum place a few doors down?"

I nod, pleased to have an excuse to spend more time with him. He holds out his hand to help me from my chair, and his touch causes a tingle to start in my palm and spread through my body. His hands are warm and it takes him a second longer than necessary to let go. Or maybe that's me holding on.

Five minutes later, we're at a table covered with layers of white plastic. When I return from washing my hands, Teddy's sketching. I expect him to hide his work as I would but he only looks up and pushes the open book to the side.

Teddy is an ad for effortless cool in a slouchy pullover with appliqué butterflies that shows off his collarbones and strikes me as almost painfully sexy. Hands and now a clavicle. Good God, why am I focusing on those marginal body parts when his chest is right there and perfectly accentuated by the sweater? Teddy brings out the Victorian in me.

I wrest my eyes away. "Can I ask what you're drawing?"

He flips through a few pages, biting his lip. "I don't usually show people."

I overstepped an invisible boundary and am a person of no worth. "I'm sorry."

Teddy's eyes shoot up. "No! You're the first person in ages I don't mind sharing it with."

He hands it over and fills the teacups as I relax from the embarrassment of asking for too much. It's strange. Manifesting works under the assumption that you deserve good things as long as you want them enough. Yet I hate appearing like I'm expecting more than I'm owed.

"Why me?" I ask as I look at the open page. My art appreciation barely extends past the usual paintings and Michelangelo's *David* (fun fact, Donatello had used the same block of marble but abandoned it because of a flaw), but I can tell these are not the sketches of a guy who doodles for fun. The assured lines of the half-done condiment tray are full of a kinetic energy that almost jumps off the page.

"Why you what?"

"Why don't you mind me looking?" I dare a quick glance up, not sure what kind of answer he'll give. The question sounds like I'm hoping for compliments, but I'm curious.

Also I'm hoping for compliments.

He only shrugs and I decide not to press him simply to fulfill my need for validation.

"This is incredible," I say instead, finger ready to flip through. He nods permission so I go to the next page, all ears with a little point at the tip, almost like mine. Then come trees and tricornered hats and a pair of battered women's shoes so detailed I can see the shape the foot had left over time. All of them are extraordinary.

"Are you an artist?" The last page is a dress that's been heavily scribbled through.

"I used to work in the arts." He takes the notebook back and tucks it away. "My mother was an amazing artist. She always had supplies in her bag and we'd stop and draw whenever we saw something interesting."

Teddy marks our choices on the order sheet, a standard selection of pork siu mai, lo mai gai, and shrimp cheung fun, with some chow mein to round it out. Thankfully, the food starts coming almost as soon as we order.

Teddy, who is an impressive fount of trivia knowledge himself, nibbles a bean sprout from the chow mein and tells me the best ones in the world are found in Malaysia.

"In Ipoh because of the limestone," I say, spooning out some rice from the rounded scoop in the bowl.

Teddy passes me a pork bun. "I'm impressed you know where Ipoh is, let alone the reason for the tasty bean sprouts."

"We went back to Singapore with Dad and stopped to eat them on our way to his family's durian farm in Malaysia."

To our Asian family's collective shock, Mom loves durian and insisted we take some back to Singapore. The car's air-conditioning had broken down, and the smell had been strong enough that Jade had nearly thrown up. To this day, she dry heaves at the slightest whiff of it, even if it's only the sweet tasty durian candies Mom gets in Chinatown (to the consternation of the shopkeepers, who double-check to make sure the white lady knows what she's buying).

"Is he Chinese?" Teddy asks.

"Yeah, and my mom's white."

He's smiling and there's something about the way his eyes fold at the downturned corners that transforms my suspicion into certainty.

"I thought so," I announce. "You too?"

"Opposite to you. White dad, Chinese mom. I thought you were but didn't want to say anything."

"You look pretty white, though." This is followed by immediate regret at my big mouth. Some people don't mind observations like that and some really do. "Sorry."

Teddy doesn't blink. "For what? I take after my dad. Almost every-one thinks I'm white."

"Is that strange? People not knowing you're mixed? Most people can tell I'm something."

"It has advantages, as I'm sure you can guess." He hesitates. "It's nicer to be acknowledged for who I am but I'd feel strange announcing it out of the blue. 'Hi, I'm Teddy, representing the half Chinese.'"

"Like it's a warning label?"

"Sometimes." He unwraps the lotus leaf from the sticky rice. "I had a guy at work get mad because I didn't tell him. Said I was tricking him, as if he couldn't be himself once he knew."

"Not that it's a contest, but I had a friend tell me about someone getting married to a Chinese guy and how bad that was because she'd have half-breed babies. To my face."

"Oh. Oh no." Teddy winces. "Sorry. What's wrong with people?"

I shrug. More than hurting, it had been a shock that had absolutely blindsided me. Had she thought that all those years we'd giggled at sleepovers? When she sat at the dinner table with my family and talked to my dad about school? I didn't ask because I cut her out of my life. I don't need that kind of energy. It's weird to know there are people in the world, like my ex-friend or Aunt Rebecca, who find my existence a distasteful consequence of poor decisions. *Weird* might not be the word. *Weird* is absolutely not the word, actually. At least people like Aunt Rebecca are open about it from the get-go so I know where I stand.

"I had hardly any exposure to my Chinese side," Teddy says. "Mom never talked Cantonese around the house, and I wasn't sent to Chinese school on Saturdays. I don't know if I missed out or not. I'm just me, but then I wonder if that me could have been different. Or should be."

"Do you talk to your mom or her family about it?"

"No. She died when I was sixteen, and all her family is in Hong Kong. I haven't seen them since, and Dad definitely wasn't going to be buying moon cakes for the Mid-Autumn Festival or anything. He barely remembers Christmas presents."

"I'm sorry."

Teddy looks wistful, and I wish I could hug him. "I always think about what I would say if I could talk to her one more time." There's silence as Teddy dips a dumpling into the chili sauce. "I should tell you I've been tracking our friendship hours," he says, changing the subject. "We're at fifty after today."

I'm doubtful. "That seems like a lot."

"I'm approximating," he concedes. "I'm sure it's close to fifty."

"Should we celebrate? It's a milestone." The teapot is empty, so I turn over the lid and push it to the edge of the table.

He puts down his chopsticks. "What do you think about a disclosure meeting?"

I raise my eyebrows. "Kinky."

"Dee."

"Sorry."

"I want last names. Jobs. Whatever personal history you're comfortable sharing. All that stuff we decided to avoid or never got around to talking about and it's kind of awkward to ask."

It's a good idea, I admit, watching the server fill the teapot with hot water. We should have done it ages ago, but after chatting on and off for so long online, it was almost as if we knew more about each other than we actually did. "We could do that right now. Nothing's stopping us."

"That's no fun," he scolds. "I want to make an event of it. As you said, it's a milestone."

"Should I bring confetti?"

"I'll get the party hats. I would also like to propose a motion that work talk continues at five minutes a day or less."

"I'll second that."

He passes me the last pork dumpling. "I'm looking forward to learning your last name."

"The idea of a last name was popularized in the West during the Roman Empire," I say. "What do you think of next Saturday?"

"Unusual but not the strangest last name I've heard."

"We'll *meet* on Saturday."

He laughs. "Even stranger, Dee We'll-Meet-On-Saturday, but it's got a certain ring to it."

"You're the worst."

"You love it."

Yeah. I do.

After lunch, he walks me to the subway station, and when we stop at the door, I have an awkward moment of wondering if he's thinking about kissing me. I hope so because I am unequivocally thinking about kissing him. Instead he waves as he steps away. I wave back, trying to look unbothered, and squeal as my arm gets stuck midair, yanking my head to the side. "Ow."

Teddy is with me in a second, moving my hand away to unhook my earring from the stitch where it's been tangled up.

"Thanks," I say, securing it back in my ear and trying to look cool about the whole thing.

Teddy gives me that tilted, upside-down smile and touches my hat to fix it in an action almost more intimate than a kiss. It's not enough. Before I can overthink and talk myself out of it, I raise my chin slightly, an invitation if he wants to take it.

Teddy leans down and I close my eyes, wanting to focus every iota of my attention on what's coming.

Nothing does. My eyes pop back open, and Teddy is close enough that his breath traces along my skin. He's smiling so hard his eyes crinkle at the edges, and he touches my cheek. "I like you, SunnyDay."

I drag up my bravery and keep my face turned to his. "Good, since I like you, Teddy9. Enough for you to kiss me."

Thank God for my heart and ego that he does. He tilts my chin up with a cool finger, and this time, I wait for his eyes to close before shutting my own. Anticipation makes me hold my breath, and every moment is like waiting an age.

Then, finally, his lips brush against mine in a teasing touch that forces a chill to rise through my whole body with such strength that I go up on my toes. The faint press is more tantalizing than satisfying, and I lift my hand ready to drag him in for the kiss I really want.

It never materializes because Teddy grabs my hand and kisses the palm, making me shudder. "I want to know your last name before we go further," he teases.

"All the more reason to tell each other now."

He keeps his eyes on mine as he smiles. "Nope. We made an agreement."

Then he's off, happy to leave me hanging. I can't help but laugh, and when he turns, I get a look that makes my legs trembly before he disappears.

I take a moment to get all my limbs back in working order before heading home, where I spend half the ride thinking about those lips and the other half thinking about what he'll have to tell me next week. Is he a mechanic? A teacher? Wouldn't it be wild if he was a consultant like me?

It's more than enough to distract me from the meeting coming up at Celeste.

NINE

DAILY AFFIRMATION: I HAVE THE
ADAPTABILITY TO HANDLE WHATEVER THE
DAY BRINGS. EVEN IF I PREFER NOT TO.

Remember, you're here to listen and learn," says Vivian. We're in the cab on our way to Celeste. She glances over. "Daiyu. Did you hear me?"

"Sorry, yes." It takes a moment for her words to filter through my daydream about Teddy's kiss. I'd spent much of the last two nights replaying and elaborating on that moment, which helped divert my thoughts from the meeting today.

She sniffs the interior of the cab. "Do you smell that? Like hay, but burned. A bit dank."

"It must be from outside," I say innocently, internally cursing Chilly and Mom's weed plants.

Vivian takes out her phone, and I review my background research about Celeste, mostly from their website and the informative Fashion Eye. The most recent posts revolve around Michael Madison, who was made creative director when Celeste branched into womens wear. The consensus seems to be that his first collections had been a mess—"stagnant as some of his leather lines" is how Fashion Eye phrases it—but he's been getting better by the season apart from a few big misses. Lately it has been looking uneven again.

I googled Michael to take a look at him and found a series of artistic shots where he was wearing driving gloves while perched on a table surrounded by fabric. He's an attractive man in his forties, with blond hair thinning at the front and blue eyes that could be legitimately described as piercing.

Damn, I was supposed to look up the rest of the leadership team. Too late now. I don't want Vivian to catch me and know I forgot.

Gathering data about diversity in the fashion industry is a depressing task despite knowing we are here to change those numbers for the better. *Change people's lives for the better,* I correct myself, smoothing out a scratch on the leather laptop bag I bought when I was promoted at Chariot. Because every percentage point represents real people who were passed by for opportunities they deserved or made to feel small because of who they are or how they look.

With the snail-like traffic on King Street, the cab takes about twenty minutes to reach Celeste's office, which is in a midsize brick building surrounded by small marketing firms and arts collectives. The wind whips Vivian's palazzo wool pants around her legs as we climb out.

"No ramp," she mutters to herself, standing on the wrought-iron stairs and checking around the corner. "Oh, there it is. In the back with the service entrance."

Celeste's head office is as minimalist and chic as I imagined. The back wall of the reception area is so blinding, it could be the opposite of Vantablack. It projects the optical illusion of a haze around the head of the angular young woman sitting at the desk, hair slicked back into a bun like a ballet dancer and headset as perfectly placed as a headband.

She glances at Vivian and turns to me. "May I help you?"

"Vivian Shaw and Daiyu Kwan here to see Gary Layman," answers Vivian.

"Do you have an appointment?" the receptionist asks me.

"The appointment is for one o'clock," Vivian says.

"Please take a seat and I'll ring you up."

Vivian walks to the leather love seat while I explore the space. Vitrines line the room, each with a single iconic Celeste bag displayed as if it's in a museum. At the center is one of the first Celestials, the bag that made Celeste's reputation. I read about them online, and the consensus was that they were groundbreaking because they combined two bags in one. Arranged on a Lucite platform and lit like one of the crown jewels is a black leather tote with thin straps and a detachable caramel mini bag on the front like a pocket. I personally don't see how this was particularly inventive, although it's nice enough. Is it six thousand dollars of nice? To my knowledge, it's not hand-stitched with golden thread by a virgin prince, which is the only reason I can see for the price.

While I'm internally debating the economics of luxury fashion, a trim woman in a pale blue suit comes into the room. The ivory blouse matches her skin so perfectly it's difficult to see where the fabric ends and her flesh begins.

"Are you from Gear Robins?" She's probably in her late twenties, and I wonder how she manages to balance on her stilettos. "Welcome to Celeste. I'm Jenna, executive assistant for Gary Layman, head of HR."

We introduce ourselves, and Jenna beckons for us to follow.

"I'll show you the office we've put aside for you," she says. "I'm glad we'll be working together. We're all equal under the skin, you know?"

"Sure do," says Vivian.

Jenna waves her hand at a bunch of identical corridors as we pass. "Merchandising is to the left. Finance is to the right. Data science and IT are on the floor below. Michael's design studio—sorry, his atelier—is upstairs. He's away today."

The space they've put aside for us is a small meeting room, plain and functional, with a whiteboard, a table and three chairs, and no windows. "This will be fine," approves Vivian. "HR is on the other side of the hall?"

Jenna nods. "We're a fun team if you want to join us. We do lots of cocktail nights and potlucks." She pats her stomach. "There goes your diet! Gary always tells us a moment on the lips, a lifetime on the hips, and I guess sometimes it's worth an extra few hours in the gym."

Vivian doesn't look at me, and I don't look at her. We hang our jackets on a coatrack before Jenna leads us back out. Each step ratchets up my tension, and I try to model my attitude on Vivian, who looks calm and professional. Even the way she holds her bag projects assurance, like she's confident she can handle whatever comes up.

The windowless conference room is a dull gray and white with more chrome accents, but what gets my attention is the line of high-concept black-and-white photos of young and beautiful women in contorted poses and extremely negligible clothing, holding handbags. It's like an upgraded art version of a pinup calendar.

Two men and a woman wait for us at the table. The first man comes over and introduces himself as Gary. He might be in his forties or fifties, it's hard to tell, and his balding head is shaved although patched with a pink flush. His emerald pocket square matches the sliver of sock showing above his camel oxfords.

"This is Edward Marsh, our CEO." Gary indicates the man at the head of the table. He's about sixty, sandy-haired, tanned, and tall with a perfectly knotted navy tie. He seems aggressively corporate and holds his shoulders as if he's never made way for anyone. His brown eyes drift over Vivian before landing on me.

"Gary was insistent we bring you on board," he says, holding out his hand. "Let's see what you think you can do."

"I'm looking forward to starting." I shake his hand, hoping the sweat beading on my forehead remains hidden under my hair. "Vivian is the senior consultant."

"Ah." He turns to her. "I can see you'll bring a lot of experience to the project."

My smile freezes. Did he mean with her expertise, or was he

referring to her…race? Hopefully the first, and I'm not sure if I should say something and risk making it uncomfortable. Vivian only nods, so I sit back, relieved to take my cue from her.

"I'm Liz Anton, chief financial officer," announces the woman.

Liz, who might be in her fifties, is dressed in tan leather pants and a white shirt with a bolo tie that shows off her perfectly applied bronzer. Her dark hair, streaked with white, falls straight to her shoulders, and a sweep of bangs emphasizes her blue eyes. She's striking and as lean and sinewy as a greyhound.

She gives me a generous smile. "I'm glad to be of help," she says. "As leaders, it's important for us to be seen to walk the talk."

"Very true," I say.

"Allyship is important on the personal level as well." Liz leans forward as if to speak confidentially. "That's why I put my sons in Pratt instead of Beaton Collegiate. Are you familiar with the school?"

"No."

Liz nods her head, clusters of diamonds dropping like hemorrhoids from her ears. "Pratt is known for STEM studies, so of course there are a lot of Asians. I encourage Reid and Caleb to engage with those kinds of boys as much as possible. It's so enriching for them."

"No wonder their sports teams are terrible." Gary looks at his watch. "Our vice president of merchandising is coming but we can begin without him."

Vivian checks her laptop while leading an easy conversation about the traffic and the weather as I try to recover from Celeste's version of small talk. Well, this is why we're here. Edward listens in silently, and I feel judged although he hasn't said a word. When he bends down, his profile tugs at my memory. Have we met before?

"I imagine some people can be resistant to your work," observes Liz to the room at large. "Of course there's a way to do it without alienating people, and I hope you understand that."

"We work with a variety of people, and their comfort and safety are always centered," Vivian assures Liz. She flips to the first deck slide. "You're busy, so I'm happy to jump right into our plan for Celeste."

Vivian walks them through our corporate philosophy and proprietary diversity maturity model, along with what we expect to see at each of the five stages. Although I spent the week studying the model like I was going to be tested on it, this is my first time seeing the deck presented to clients. I split my attention between Vivian and watching the others. Gary and Edward are on their phones, while Liz rotates between nodding, frowning, and checking her colleagues' reactions.

"Now, for Celeste," Vivian says as the door opens.

The CEO glances up from his phone. "Ted, nice of you to join us." The pointed tone makes me wonder if this Ted guy is on thin ice.

Gary waves. "This is Ted Marsh, who runs merchandising."

In this moment, I understand I have made a grievous error by not doing more research into Celeste's executives after getting sidetracked the other day. The man at the door has dark hair pushed off his face. He wears a plain gray suit with a white shirt matched with a blue tie so lacking in personal style it's the corporate equivalent of camouflage. He glances across the room and freezes when he sees me.

It looks like the Gear Robins sales team was wrong. The entire leadership team at Celeste isn't white—it only looks like it. In fact, despite the stunned expression, Ted Marsh is an exceedingly good-looking man I wouldn't necessarily have pegged as half Chinese.

Except I know he is, because that's Teddy.

TEN

When Teddy turns to me, hand outstretched and smile uncertain, I widen my eyes, hoping he gets the message that I want him to pretend we've never met. If Vivian was willing to remove me from the Celeste account simply for asking questions, I don't dare let her know I'm friends and hopefully on the way to something more with my brand-new client. She'll never believe I didn't know he worked here and didn't think to give her a heads-up. This early in my job, I can't take the risk that she'll consider it poor judgment, and I especially can't let her find out in front of the client at the first meeting.

In case my ambiguous facial expression isn't enough, I hope the formal way I greet him clues Teddy in.

"I'm Daiyu Kwan," I say. "Nice to meet you." There. No mention of surprises or coincidences. We're two professionals meeting for the first time. I make sure not to look at his mouth.

Teddy's face settles into a neutral expression that would be envied by any Vegas card shark although we flinch slightly when our hands touch. Well, the point of right now is to get through the meeting. The point of after the meeting will be how to get through the project.

He sits on the opposite side of the table with the rest of the Celeste team and apologizes for being late. "No need to catch me up," he says, glancing at the CEO. "Please continue."

I stare at his profile. Like Jade, Teddy's nose has a high bridge—damn him—and unlike my little snub of a thing, his is an actual feature on his face. I'm not sure I should be thinking so much about a nose, no matter how great, and particularly at this moment, so I pull my eyes away. My gaze lands on Edward as the two men turn their heads the same direction. Edward Marsh. Ted Marsh. That matching profile.

Father and son?

Vivian flips to a timeline. "We've compressed our usual six months into four because we were told, confidentially, that Celeste is looking at a sale to the luxury consortium Opaline."

"Correct. We're looking at summer," says Gary.

"Is four months enough for a project of this scope?" asks Liz, tapping her finger on the table.

"A good question," says Edward from his place at the head of the table.

"Four months will be fine." Vivian patiently lays out the methodology and timeline again. "I've worked with others in similar situations and can assure you Gear Robins is used to optimizing our clients' time."

As the meeting goes on, I keep darting little glances at Teddy. While the others ask corporate questions about strategy and resources, Teddy contributes nothing to the discussion. In fact, he barely looks up from the table in front of him. The Teddy I know would be full of curiosity and suggestions. The man in front of me is so detached it's like he's astral projected his personality to a different cosmos.

It throws me off until a sharp glance from Vivian pulls me back to the discussion, where Liz is talking about how open-minded the management team is. "We even have a suggestion box," she says.

"Is it anonymous?" Vivian asks.

Liz looks offended. "Of course not. We expect our staff to have the courage of their convictions."

I can't help but glance over at Teddy to check his reaction, but he's gazing distantly at the front of the room. At the beginning of the meeting, I'd been certain Teddy and I would figure out how to handle this revelation together. After all, no one was at fault. There were no lies about who we were or what we did, and it was clear he was as shocked as I was.

Now I don't even know who this guy is. He's being so strange.

"Ted, don't you agree?" asks Liz.

Teddy, who is Ted here, shifts in his chair, mouth lifting in an automatic smile. "Great idea, Liz."

Was he even listening? His gaze returns to the front of the room.

"You need to add some interviews with key employees," says Gary, tapping the table with his middle finger.

"I like it," says Liz. "Vivian, you'll put that in?"

Have I dropped into the twilight zone? Vivian said that already. Twice, in fact.

"Your junior colleague will be on-site for the entire project?" asks Edward, looking at me.

"Yes. Daiyu will need access to your staff and staff information as well as your policies. She'll do a survey to ensure we've accurately captured the data."

"Is that necessary?" Edward addresses the question to Gary.

Vivian answers. "Gary mentioned your priority concern is your staff demographics, which are well below the rest of the industry and don't reflect the pool of people available for you to hire here in the city. This will give us an accurate starting point."

"What Vivian is trying to say is we need a current snapshot of our workforce as a baseline," says Liz.

"Simply because the people are there to hire, it doesn't mean they have the skill sets we need," Edward says. "Or fit with Celeste."

"That's one of the data points we're eager to explore," says Vivian smoothly.

Edward puts down his phone. "Perhaps you don't understand. We were targeted by an unknown but dissatisfied staff member who leaked confidential information. The entire thing has been blown out of proportion."

I look over expectantly at Teddy. He'll say something to refute this, won't he? Those numbers told a bigger story no matter who leaked them. Instead he nods like a marionette, eyes trained on the table.

"We talked about the public perception and the need to do this," Gary says to Edward, who rolls his eyes.

"Celeste has good people." Liz plants her arms on the table. "We had a few isolated incidents, but there's no malicious intent at any level."

"I appreciate your—"

Liz talks over Vivian. "As a woman, I've had to fight against my fair share of injustice, so I completely understand how other marginalized people feel. You would know as well."

No reaction from Teddy.

There's a gentle knock on the door before anyone can reply, and Jenna pokes her head in. "Edward and Gary, your two o'clock is waiting."

We get the hint and stand.

"That was an impressive presentation." Liz turns to congratulate us. "Very articulate. I look forward to seeing what you can do."

"Thank you." Vivian's smile doesn't waver.

I escape the room before Teddy can catch my eye, looking resolutely ahead as I follow Vivian out, not sure what to think about anything.

————

I start a dozen messages to Teddy in my head as we walk to our new office near HR. By the time Vivian closes the door, I've almost decided on the simple if avoidant solution of ghosting him completely. I don't know what any of the messages could say besides, *Are you a zombie? What the hell? Who are you and what have you done with the real Teddy?* I should simply ask, in a nonjudgmental way, what was going on with him, but I'm not sure I have the courage to face the idea that the corporate robot man I saw in the meeting was the real Teddy and he's playing some long-con catfish. Part of me doesn't even want to know.

"That Ted is going to be a treat," I say for the pleasure of shit talking him. This is not showing a positive attitude, but surely I'm allowed a brief moment of open scorn.

Then I stop. Vivian is rubbing her temples as if fighting off a brutal headache.

"Are you okay?" I ask.

Vivian shuts her eyes. "Fine."

She's unquestionably not fine, but I also can't tell what the problem is. Did I do something wrong? I get the feeling Vivian would tell me if I did, but all she does is type harder than usual. I run over the meeting in my mind. It was frustrating but similar to the few I'd been involved with at Chariot. There's often some resistance to this kind of project when people are uncomfortable looking at how they might be contributing to the issue.

Finally, too tense to stay sitting, I get up and go to the washroom. I'm washing my hands and mentally bouncing between Vivian and what the hell to do about Teddy when I hear the door bang open and a gasping sniff. It's the same noise I make when I'm trying not to cry.

I freeze with my hands under the tap as the woman stops and stares at me. She's dressed in fitted jeans and a black T-shirt tucked in at the waist. Rows of beads hang from her neck with a white measuring tape. Her curly brown hair is up in a deliberately messy bun with bleached blond streaks that flatter her tan skin. A detailed tattoo of a chameleon peeks out from under her sleeve, and I feel dowdier than usual in my black Gear Robins suit.

"Are you okay?" I ask as I turn off the tap.

"I'm fine, thanks," she says shortly. She wipes at her eyes with a paper towel. We cringe at the scraping noise it makes on her skin.

"At least you're not bleeding," I say, inspecting her face. "That's good news!"

She gives me an incredulous look. "What?"

"It could be worse," I say with as much lightness as I can muster. "Your eyes aren't too red and you're not bleeding."

"Is not bleeding your standard for determining levels of good and bad? A broken leg is a positive as long as the bone doesn't come through the skin?"

"Since an open fracture is clearly the worse option, bacterially speaking, I would say yes, that's something to be grateful for." The suspicion I've come off like a fussy twit makes my voice prim.

Her lips twitch. "Holy shit, you're something else. Do you go around spouting that toxic positivity to everyone you meet?" She begins to laugh. "Yeah. I'm not bleeding. Hashtag blessed, right?"

This should make me uncomfortable, but her belly laugh is such a deep release that it echoes in the bathroom. To my surprise, I end up laughing along with her, letting out all my feelings about Vivian and Teddy.

Finally I gasp out, "I'm sorry. That was a ridiculous thing to say."

She wipes her eyes with her shirt this time. "It was. It absolutely was."

"A broken leg is bad whether you're bleeding or not."

"Good to hear."

"Let me try this whole thing again." I clear my throat. "I'm sorry you're having a bad day."

"That was better," she congratulates me.

"Do you want to talk about it?"

She looks over. "To a stranger? In the bathroom?"

I shrug. "Happens all the time in bars."

"I wish I was at a bar." She leans back and folds her arms over her chest. "To answer your question, no, I don't want to talk. You wouldn't understand. You'd see it as a little pinprick and be all, what's the big deal? For me, it already is a big deal, and enough holes eventually rip the fabric. Also, again, I don't know you."

The door opens, and we shut up as the woman ducks into a stall, no doubt to avoid her coworker, a sleek, frowning blond who looks at me curiously. I head back to the office, wondering if this is indicative of what it's like to work at Celeste. If so, it's going to be a long four months, and no looking on the bright side will make it go faster.

The woman had an interesting way of putting things, though. One more pinprick. Wait. That meeting. I review it again, removing the Teddy situation. There were a few times Liz spoke for or over Vivian. Gary repeated what Vivian had said. I frown, kicking myself. That meeting had been filled with microaggressions, those stinging little words or actions that aren't quite insulting enough to call out, and the ones directed at Vivian had almost all gone unnoticed by me, even though I'd taken workshops in how to identify them.

How had I failed? Being distracted by Teddy isn't good enough an excuse. I lean against the wall of the corridor because, incredibly, it dawns on me that at Chariot, I never sat in a client meeting led by a Black woman. It never happened because there wasn't a single Black woman consultant on staff.

Impossible. It was a *diversity* consultancy. As I run through my old colleagues, it comes to me that there were few racialized people in management overall. How had I not noticed? What did that say about me? About Chariot, which I thought was perfect? Had I been told we were doing the good work for so long I stopped looking at the company critically because I simply believed it? Wanted to believe it?

This belated realization makes me jittery, and I need to calm down before going back to Vivian. Ducking under a handy stairwell, I pull out my new meditation app. After I find the session I want—*So you've had an epiphany and it sucks*, listed right after *Seriously, get out of your own way*—I hold it up to my ear and listen to the sound of the waves as a man tells me to breathe in air because "It's only air. You know that, right? You know how to breathe, for crying out loud." Then he goes into the meditation.

"It came out of nowhere and slapped you right across the face," he says soothingly. "Now you're stuck having to do something about it or admitting you're a coward. Bwak, chicken. Oh, don't like that? Not a chicken? Focus on how your body feels as fear of taking action fills your being. Then release it, get off your ass, and do what you have to."

One more breath, and I reluctantly tuck my phone away and return to the office, grateful to not see Teddy, because I can't deal with both issues at the same time. Vivian doesn't look up when I come in.

"Vivian," I say over the lump in my throat. This is uncomfortable, and the gutless part of me wonders if it's too late to pretend I hadn't noticed a thing. She raises her head, and I decide I'm no chicken.

"I want to apologize for my behavior in the meeting," I say. "I didn't realize how people were acting when you were speaking and how upsetting that was. I should have, and I also should have said something."

Vivian's eyebrows have lifted so high, they hover midforehead. "You think I'm upset?"

I start to backpedal, worried I've made things worse. I should have kept quiet. I'm her junior, after all. Is it my place to say anything? "Or not? I didn't mean to assume."

She laughs shortly. "Calm down, Daiyu. That's nothing compared to how bad it can get. I once had a client only talk to my colleague although I was running the meeting. He had to relay all the questions to me and the answers back to the client. Absolutely ridiculous."

"I'm still sorry," I say doggedly. Then I sigh. "All my training disappeared in the moment."

"It happens." Vivian stretches her wrist. "It's not always worth my time to respond. This is demanding work, and I need to conserve my energy. It can be easier to ignore incidents like that."

"Shouldn't we try to make change whenever we can?" I say, confused. "As diversity consultants?"

"We aren't required to react in the moment to every issue that comes our way," she says. "People need to choose their battles. I decide how I want to respond and what I want from a response. You can do the same."

"I'll do better," I promise.

"Good. I'm glad you're thinking about it." She points at my seat. "Now sit yourself down, because you've got a lot of work coming."

I do, and soon she's walking me through next steps. The air between us seems lighter, which makes me happy. At least this is resolved, so I can focus on what on earth I'm going to do about Teddy.

First, though, work. Breathe in air. Breathe out more air.

ELEVEN

That night, I'm in the kitchen trying to forget the previous seven hours happened. A thin, meandering line of unanswered texts has grown over the day.

Teddy: I can't believe that was you.

Teddy: You seemed upset after the meeting, is everything ok?

Teddy: We should talk about how you want to handle this.

These sound like the Teddy I know, which confuses me further. I ignore his call.

I'm not approaching the whole Teddy thing with grace, dignity, or fairness. I should give him a chance to explain, but how he acted in the meeting has thrown me for a loop. Normally I'd be able to deal with it, but I'm too depleted to even try.

Who is he really? According to Google, Teddy, a.k.a. Ted, because apparently Teddy and Eddie and Ted and *Ned* of all things are diminutives for Edward, is the only child and heir apparent of Celeste's CEO, Edward Marsh Jr. That makes Teddy Edward Marsh III, a man with numerals. Kitty Chan Marsh, his Hongkonger mother, was the daughter of a large import-export clan and established Celeste when she moved to Canada. After her death, Edward Junior (not Teddy the Third) took the company over. Teddy was a designer for his own brand, Mars, before he started at Celeste. That was the art-adjacent job he mentioned at dim sum. Fashion designer.

If only I'd done that search on their leadership, I wouldn't be in this situation. I cover my eyes with my hands, cursing my easy distractibility and decision to focus on the industry instead of individuals.

Curiosity gets the better of me so I look up Teddy's Mars work, then put my phone down after viewing a collab he'd done with the iconic brand Harhawk. It's intimidating to see top celebrities like Choi Jihoon in the front row and congratulating Teddy with warm hugs after. It's another Teddy who has been hidden from me.

Grandma comes in to work on her new puzzle, a view of Barcelona. I want to be alone, but it's rude to just walk out of the kitchen, so I fill the kettle for something to do. "Want a cup of tea?" I ask.

"If you're making it." The words are flat but the tone is sharp. I look over, ready to flare up, but her face is tense with pain, the lines etched deep on her leathery face. She came from the generation where sun care involved half a bottle of baby oil.

I bustle around the kitchen with more energy than required to pull out two cups as a way to perform busyness and avoid talking. Eventually the kettle's whistle breaks the heavy quiet.

"What kind of tea?" I ask, hand hovering over my father's neatly cat-alogued collection. Dad has every kind because although he's never had coffee in his life, he can live on tea and Coca-Cola. No other pop because his brand loyalty is fierce. Don't get him started on New Coke, though.

"Jasmine."

Surprised, I pull out the dragon pearls. I would have put good money on her choosing English breakfast or Earl Grey, which is what Mom always gives her.

"With milk," she adds. "No sugar."

Ugh. I've seen jasmine milk teas advertised on hand-scripted café signboards, but I've never been able to get over my sense that it wrecks the delicate, pure taste of the jasmine. My taste buds revolt as I pour the milk in her cup and watch the leaves unfurl to bob up like little eels before handing it over.

Mom comes into the kitchen humming "You Are My Sunshine." She insists on calling it my song and says I loved it as a kid. That may be, but I hate it as an adult. Has she ever listened to the lyrics? Lost love is hardly joyous.

"Are you going to join us?" asks Mom as she points at the puzzle. I hadn't planned on it, but conversation about Grandma's hip and Mom's cannabis plants might keep my mind off Teddy and give my subconscious enough space to come to a solution independent of my conscious mind. Also, it's clear from Mom's expression that the question wasn't rhetorical. I pour her a cup of peppermint tea and take a seat near the wall.

"How was your day, sunshine?" Mom searches through the pieces for the blue sky.

"Great, thanks." I give the proper answer, and we work for a few moments until I say, "Did you know that most one-thousand-piece puzzles actually have one thousand and twenty-six pieces?"

Grandma catches my eye. "Why not one thousand?"

"The usual layout is thirty-eight pieces across and twenty-seven down."

She looks down at the puzzle. "Interesting. I wonder if that holds true for five-hundred-piece puzzles. Or five-thousand."

"Where in the world do you find these useless bits of information, Dee?" asks Mom.

I press my lips together and start searching for the edge pieces. My mother prefers to work on random sections of the puzzle, and it's soon obvious I am not the only one who finds this aggravating.

"First edges, then you can do what you want," Grandma snaps at her. Mom takes a noisy sip of tea. "Mother, it's a puzzle. For fun."

"It's the proper way to do it," Grandma says. I catch her eye and we nod at each other. She's right, of course. There are only three rules in jigsaw puzzles—turn over all the pieces before you start, do the edges first, and don't work on another person's section. My mother ignores all of them.

Every time we forge a tiny connection, Grandma unbends a little more. In a decade, we might tolerate or even enjoy each other's company, but does it matter? I've gone without having her as a loving presence in my life for thirty years. I'm used to it, plus it's easier to hold a grudge, which can last unexamined for an eternity. Forgiveness means I need to think more deeply about topics that generally I've left untouched.

"Is something wrong, Dee?" Mom leans over to grab my chin in her hand, but I shake her off. "I don't like that look on your face. You'll get frown lines like Jade. I sent her a new wrinkle cream, but I told her only fixing her attitude will erase them completely."

"I'm fine, Mom. Tired from work." Work and worrying about what to do about Teddy because it only occurs to me in this moment that we'll be at the same office for the next four months. Fantastic.

"Get some fresh air." She sits back. "It's the same as I say to your grandmother. Moping around the house is no solution."

"Oops." I accidentally on purpose knock some pieces to the ground in an attempt to change the conversation. It doesn't work.

"Are you eating well?" asks Mom. "A banana in the morning helps keep your energy up."

A huge wave of irrational anger sweeps over me but I choke it down. "I'll try that."

"Whatever it is will pass."

"You're probably right." I take two gulps of tea so massive I finish the cup. "All done," I announce. "I've got a few things to do before bed."

Grandma doesn't look up from the puzzle, while Mom wishes me sweet dreams. Once upstairs, I sigh and sink down the door until my butt hits the floor.

What's wrong with me? All this is stuff I usually brush off, but it's as if I've been roughened up with coarse sandpaper that's taken away my smooth slide and is making me catch on everything. *Because you're thirty and don't need to be nagged about snacks*, snipes that voice. I sit up, and a seam rips on my pencil skirt.

Tears spring up in my eyes but I dash them away. I am not going to cry because a skirt I don't even like ripped. A skirt is nothing to cry about, and I am someone who manifests the change she wants to see in the world. I will buy full skirts. I will crack open a vanilla-cardamom fragrance diffuser to get rid of the persistent smell of chinchilla chow. I will put on my cheerful face and do something about Teddy and impress Vivian and find one, just one, friend to go out with me, and speak kindly to my old and sick grandmother and think pleasant thoughts until life goes back to how it should be, and I will do it all while putting out good energy because I only need to believe harder that it will all work out, and I *will not cry*.

Too late. I curl up on my side and stare at the wall as the tears trickle over my nose, skirt hiked in a tube around my waist so I don't make the tear worse. My desk has been shoved into the corner to make room for the cot I bought from Canadian Tire's depleted off-season camping section. Every extra blanket in the house is piled on the thin egg-crate foam mattress to try to cover the support bar of unforgiving steel that digs into the middle of my back when I try to sleep.

I reach for my gratitude journal to improve my mood and manage to swing my hand down on the cover. I don't bother to open it.

What am I grateful for? There's so much I should list because I have everything I need to thrive. I'm healthy. Loved and fed. I'm privileged to have a whole house for myself, so how can I be so selfish to not share it with the family I'm lucky to have in the first place? I have a job. I was raised to count my blessings because there are so many people worse off in the world, and I'm an awful person for letting any negative thoughts surface when I have so much. That's asking for trouble.

I don't text Jade, not wanting to wreck her evening, but our sister bond somehow activates, the same way I knew when she went into labor with Poppy. She calls, and it doesn't take sisterly intuition to know I'm not in my best place.

"Jesus, you look like shit," she observes through the screen. "What the hell happened?"

"I had a bad day."

She regards me through squinted eyes. "A bad day for you is like a Category Five hurricane for anyone else."

"The World Meteorological Organization chooses storm names years in advance, and you can find them online," I mumble, rubbing my face. "What do you want?"

"First, to be regaled with your extensive knowledge of storm nomenclature." Jade's tone is light but her eyes are concerned.

"Second?"

She shrugs. "I was making cookies and thought of you."

"How domestic."

"Wookie cookies with extra milk chocolate chips because semisweet are trash, so there's no need to swipe at my baking skills."

"I like cookies," I say conciliatorily.

Jade tells me about her day amid the chaos of the kids playing tag with Opal in the background, giving me space for my thoughts. Her life is ideal. How can it be so perfect when mine is a dump? She was always the one who was depressed and angsty as a teenager, so how did she get so content when I'm the one who was born with a smile? When I was the one who worked so hard on keeping happy when that natural smile faded? Who refused to let misery be an option? Why does she deserve joy and I don't?

Jade sees the tears filling my eyes before I smear them away with my sleeve.

"Dee?" she asks. "Do you want to talk about what happened?"

"No. Nothing happened." My voice is squeaky.

"That's it." She mumbles to Opal and moves upstairs to the bedroom where I can hear the click of the door. "You're going to talk to me."

"There's nothing to talk about." There's a huge and unacknowledged obstruction sitting in my chest, and I need it dislodged before I erupt or choke. I don't know how to do it. I've never had to. I was never allowed to.

Jade sits on the bed. "You never say what you're thinking, and I'm worried about you."

"I'm fine," I say automatically.

"I've told you before, you can tell me the truth. You don't need to be a sprightly ray of sunshine every minute of the day."

I rear back as if she's hit me. "And I've told you I am naturally a positive person."

"Then you wouldn't have to work so hard at it," she says softly. "You're struggling to fit into a narrative you've written for yourself. Or that someone wrote for you."

I frown. "I don't want to talk about this. You're not making me feel better."

"Sometimes you need to face facts." Her voice rises.

So does mine. "Jade, this is not what I need right now."

"Sorry." She winces. "Sorry, Dee. I love you and I get worried. I want to support you."

I sigh, not wanting to fight or think about what she's said. I'm not in the mood. "I get it. I love you, too."

We hang up with the unresolved tension between us making me feel worse. Sometimes she's just like Mom, trying to make me be more like her instead of accepting the way I am.

The phone dings again with a text, and I grab it to see if it's Jade. It's not.

Teddy: Can we talk about this.

I've been weakened by my emotional breakdown, and this time I give in.

Me: Ok.
Teddy: Can I call you? Are you worried?

I don't know how I want to answer this, so I sidestep the second question and address the first.

Me: Now's not the best time.
Teddy: Can we talk tomorrow after work?
Me: Somewhere no one will see us.
Teddy: Got it. I'll be off-site but I'll text you where we can meet.

I turn off my phone without answering. I have a day to figure out what to say, and the countdown's on. I close my eyes, tears leaking out, as Mom's bittersweet song drifts up the stairs.

TWELVE

DAILY AFFIRMATION: I LET GO OF WHAT
DOES NOT SERVE ME. THAT'S RIGHT, WORLD.
I LET GO OF WHAT DOES NOT SERVE ME.

*I*t's my first official day at Celeste, and Jenna meets me at reception. "I wanted to make sure you have everything you need," she says.

"Thanks." I yank my bag onto my shoulder since it keeps slipping out of my hand from sweat and do my best to avoid thinking about Teddy. The possibility of seeing him—*What if his off-site is canceled? What if he comes back early?*—has worked me into such a state of strain that not even my meditation session, *It probably won't kill you but how can you know?*, was able to help.

Jenna is talking about the Wi-Fi, and I tune back in. I'm here to do a job after all, and I need to do it well. "IT has given you access to the network," she says. "I recommend—"

"Well, well, who's this?" A voice comes from an office as we pass. "Looking good, Jenna. Where's my smile?"

"Oh, Travis. Daiyu, meet Travis. He's on our sales team." Jenna makes the perfunctory introduction.

I give him a big smile because work will go much easier after I establish trust with the Celeste staff. Travis is an average-sized man with watery blue eyes, and as I shake his hand, he invites me to eat his nuts.

"I beg your pardon?" I ask, suddenly less pleased to be meeting people at Celeste.

"My nuts." He grins with no teeth showing. "They're salty. I love when the ladies in the office come by for a taste."

I extract my hand and glance down at the bowl of almonds he points to on his table. "I'll pass. They look a little small and shriveled."

Travis smacks his lips and winks at me. "Good girl. You'll do well here."

Jenna tugs me away, face tight with exasperation. "Oh my God, Travis. She's our diversity consultant."

"Hey, hey." Travis steps back with his hands high, that shit-eating grin wide. "It's just a joke."

Before I can reply, Jenna steers me down the hall. "Travis is something else. The CEO loves him." She looks at me. "They play racquetball together."

"Great," I mutter. I get the hint. Travis is untouchable.

That run-in with Travis turns out to be one of the least aggravating parts of the day. Apparently Gary wants to approve any data that gets sent to me, but Gary is in meetings. Celeste has limited my network access, so it's almost impossible to find any useful information on my own. Even getting a full staff list might take a few days, Jenna tells me apologetically, since Gary wants to look through it first. Her expression tells me she finds this as perplexing as I do.

By the time I get to the bar where Teddy is waiting, I'm wound tight as a coil and not in the best mood to maintain an open mind.

I thought Ted the vice president would choose some bougie haven where the wine costs twenty-five dollars and comes as a thin layer coating the bottom of a glass as big as your head. Instead we're in a shabby pub above an Indian restaurant. Guinness signs share space with Spice Girls posters on the dull burgundy walls, and the savory smell of curry drifts up the narrow stairs.

Teddy sits alone reading a book, hair falling over his forehead. His gray blazer lies crumpled on the banquette beside him like a discarded skin, and his shirtsleeves are rolled up to reveal those silver bracelets. He glances up and my treacherous heart skips a beat.

I slide into my seat as the server puts a beer down for Teddy, then winks at me with illegally good cheer. "Something for you?"

"A Dark and Stormy, please."

"You betcha."

We wait until she leaves and then Teddy says, "I get the feeling you're angry with me."

Even his voice is different from the one he used in the meeting yesterday, warmer and more lively.

"I'm not angry."

"Please, give me some credit." He gives me a look. "You haven't even taken your coat and gloves off."

"I wasn't sure what to say." This has the advantage of being true.

"About what?" Teddy looks confused. "I don't know why it's an issue. You report to Gary, and I can recuse myself completely if you want. It's not like I'm going to make a difference anyway."

What does that mean? I ignore it for now.

"It's not that." I already want this conversation over and we haven't resolved a thing. How do you tell someone you don't like who they are, or at least part of who they are?

"Help me out here, Dee. I don't get it." He tilts his head. "That talk we were planning is well-timed. Why didn't you tell me you were working with Celeste?"

Me? He's blaming this mess on me. "I don't know. Because we made a pact to not talk about work? Why didn't you tell me you were Ted Marsh? Sorry, Edward Marsh III?"

He frowns when I say his full name. "Same reason."

"Is it true that your father owns Celeste? He's the CEO?"

"Yes." Teddy says it reluctantly. "I'm not my father. We're different."

"Yeah? You seemed on the same page yesterday."

"Let's treat this as our disclosure meeting," he suggests, frown turning to a scowl as his fingers pick at the fraying seam of the red cloth napkin. "Full disclosure. Total honesty, emotional and factual."

The server drops off my drink, and I take a sip to buy some time. If I don't hear him out, I'll always wonder what his deal was. I pull off my jacket and stuff the gloves down the sleeve. "You start."

"All right." Teddy looks at the wall, then the table, then me as if unsure where to begin.

I do him a favor and break the silence. "You were a fashion designer." I shrug when he looks at me. "I saw it online."

His smile is crooked. "Mars did sustainable, fair labor, luxury street-wear, but fashion is a tough industry. I had to close the label."

"I'm sorry." We may be fighting, or at least I am, but the loss is obvious in Teddy's tone. It's the voice of a man who lost more than a company. He lost a dream.

"It happened and I've been at Celeste for three years since."

"It was your mother's company."

He looks out the grimy window to the snow falling. "She considered it her legacy. Dad became the CEO after she died and we made a deal. He'd let me use my inheritance to fund Mars, and if it didn't work out, I'd come back to Celeste. If I proved myself there, he'd retire and I'd take over."

"Okay." He gets a company as a present, fantastic. I get socks at Christmas.

He looks at me. "I can tell you I worked my way up the ranks, and that's true, but it was also like having rockets attached to my ankles. I'm good at what I do, but I had a huge head start."

"Then that's why you were acting like that in the meeting. You play at being all artsy but you're a typical corporate puppet sucking up to the CEO." The words are harsh because I'm mad at myself for being taken in, and it's mixed with a dull sense of defeat because, as usual these days, another part of my life is not turning out.

That seems to hit him like a slap because he jerks back in his seat. "Is that what you think of me?"

"The guy in that meeting wasn't the Teddy I met playing Questie."

There's a long silence as he stares at the table, poking the varnished wood with his finger. Then he throws his head back and speaks to the ceiling. "You're right. I know I'm different at work."

This quick admission takes me by surprise. "What?"

After a few seconds gnawing his lip and staring intently at the lights, Teddy looks back down. "You know, Dad hated me studying design instead of business. He sees fashion as a product. It is, obviously, but my mother taught me it can be more as well."

I might be a bit with Edward Junior here. Teddy must see it in my face, because he gives me a wry smile.

"Think back to when you put on an outfit that made you feel good. No, that made you feel like the outer you matched the inner you."

"That must have been one of my grade school picture days. I wore a big pink princess dress."

"Did you like it?"

"Loved it," I say truthfully.

"I wanted to make people feel like that every day. That's why I opened Mars. When I came back to Celeste, it was in merchandising and not design, but I thought I could impact people other ways."

"How?"

"Mom designed the first Celestial bag and started the company, but she was more interested in fashion as art," Teddy says, looking again like the old animated him. "I want Celeste to be that and more. I want to make a real difference in the world."

"Make a difference through *fashion*?"

He laughs mirthlessly. "Luxury fashion is a three-hundred-billion-dollar-a-year industry. Not a single person on earth can avoid fashion, because we all wear clothes. It's also a huge environmental disaster. Do you know how much it contributes to global greenhouse gas emissions?"

"No." That hadn't been my focus in my research, and it hadn't occurred to me to consider it in my normal life. I may know a lot of trivia, but Teddy is shaming me with information.

"Between two and ten percent. Economies of scale mean it's cheaper to overproduce, so millions of items are sent to landfills each year, never worn or sold. Then there's working conditions and agricultural impact."

"You think a luxury firm from Canada can change this?" I ask.

His smile is small and sour. "I did." Then he gives a fierce nod. "No, I still do. When I started at Celeste, I insisted we needed to be a different kind of business, one that looked at more than traditional financial success metrics. We should consider our entire impact, including what happens to the environment and people, the way I did at Mars. How can an extra percentage profit for someone already rich be worth locking people in a room without breaks or ventilation to make your products? No purse is worth more than a person."

"That's not what your father thinks?"

"He doesn't care because growth is his only goal for Celeste," Teddy says. "He rejected every change I suggested until I...I don't know. I stopped. There was no point and it seemed easier to wait until Dad retires."

"Is that why you weren't supporting us yesterday? You gave up?" Even as I speak, I know I'm being a bit hard.

"You don't know the full story." He runs his hand over his face. "You've known the company's problems for what, a week? You think I don't understand the issues we're facing? Do you know how many plans I've submitted that could improve our environmental impact? How we pay and credit designers and ensure fair labor? Help young designers? Improve our hiring and people's experiences at work? Even the ones that were approved died from under-resourcing and were used as an example to prove that my other ideas were unfeasible."

"I might not know everything about Celeste but I do know change only happens if you keep trying," I say stubbornly.

"I didn't stop trying. I'm biding my time and waiting for a better opportunity." His hands lay flat on the table. "That it's longer-term than you want doesn't make it bad."

"It's not about Celeste!" I lean forward. "It's about you."

"Me? What are you talking about?"

"Be honest. I saw what you were like in that meeting. Did you decide to back off as a deliberate decision or so you can avoid it in the short-term?" I think of Travis Eat My Nuts and having to work with a guy like that day in and day out. "Things need to improve *now*."

"It's not that easy. When I tried, all that happened is that Dad got upset at me for not focusing on my actual job. If he fires me from Celeste, I'll lose any chance I might have." His voice has gotten more intense as he speaks and we glare at each other across the table.

"Ah..." The server has come up and looks between us. "Sorry, wrong time to ask if you want another round?"

That breaks the strain and we sit back in unison. Teddy raises his eyebrows at me and I nod. Then he nods.

"Okay, another round and how about food?" she asks. "Since I'm here."

"The onion rings are really good," Teddy says with the detached tone of an observer. "We could share them."

"That sounds good."

"Good."

"Good," echoes the server. "All righty then."

She escapes the tent of tension we've erected over the table and we take deep breaths. Something from the meeting occurs to me. "What about that company that wants to buy you. Opaline? How does that factor into your long-term strategy?"

"I don't like it but what can I do? Dad wants us to be bigger, more global. That money will help us expand."

"Why don't you like Opaline?" I ask, trying to keep my tone casual and our emotions down.

Teddy frowns. "They're the worst. Opaline won't sign any

environmental charters, and they only care about maximizing quarterly profits."

"If they buy Celeste, won't they replace you?"

"Opaline prefers to keep the current leadership to maintain consistency, so there shouldn't be a problem with me taking over. Dad is planning the sale for June while he's still here and for me to take over in the next quarter after the transition," he says. "I've tried to talk him out of it, but Dad doesn't like being challenged. There's nothing I can do until I'm CEO, and then I can try to mitigate the Opaline influence."

The server goes up to the jukebox and delivers a swift kick to the corner. The Cure starts playing in the background.

I sit back and regard him, utterly baffled. "I don't get it, Teddy. You want this company, but you don't fight for it. You want to make change, but you're willing to knuckle under to your father. You say Opaline is bad and you're ready to sit and watch them take over."

Teddy hunches his shoulders and the silence grows until he speaks in a low voice. "It's just Dad and me since Mom's gone. I don't want business to get in the way of our relationship. It's better to let it go for now even if that means pulling back a bit on the changes I want."

"There's a difference between being careful and being completely disengaged," I say gently, although I understand his desire to maintain family peace.

A deep line appears between his eyebrows. "I hear what you're saying."

That might be the only win I get at the moment. "Did you leak those diversity numbers?"

"That wasn't me, although it forced Dad to do some damage control." He shakes his head. "I want to know who it was."

"To turn them in?"

He looks me in the eye, wounded. "Of course not. They had guts. I wish I had the same courage."

That's all I need to give it one more shot. "You do. I can tell you're tired, Teddy, but think about the impact you could have on people at Celeste. They might be struggling but, unlike you, don't have the means to change what's going on."

"It's hard." He blows out his breath in frustration. "I tried. I *tried*."

We sit quietly. Teddy's expression is almost like stone but his eyes flicker between the window and the wall behind me, back and forth.

When he speaks, it's to that window. "I hadn't had time to process losing Mars before starting at Celeste." The words are slow, almost if occurring to him in the moment. "To have all my ideas shot down right away hit me where it hurt. I felt I couldn't make a single good decision."

"Then you started to doubt yourself."

"I did. I'd always had confidence in my work but losing Mars and then all that happening was paralyzing." He nods, expression clearing as he considers this. "I think I shut down a bit."

My anger and confusion have settled into sympathy for his situation. He looks beaten, and the difference between the Teddy I know and the man he's created to keep the approval of his CEO father is nothing short of heartbreaking. It can be hard to keep your hopes up that things will change, especially when the person you want to impress continually tells you nothing will. Luckily, my naturally positive disposition helps bring me through those dark times. *Or you varnish them over*, says that voice. I shut it up.

We sit quietly as the fresh drinks come. Teddy doesn't even taste his. "Maybe I gave up too soon," he says to the table. "After all, Dad agreed to hire Gear Robins. That means he might be open to other changes."

I nod as he continues his train of thought. "It would be good to set a foundation for people, so they know I'm not going to be like my father when Celeste is mine."

"You seem to have different values for the business." I smile politely at the server as she returns to deliver the onion rings.

Teddy looks drained and we take a break to eat. "I'm tired of being tired," he finally says, straightening his shoulders and wincing. "I don't want to be a ghost anymore."

"What are you going to do?"

He looks at me. "I'll need time to figure that out completely, but for now I can support you better at Celeste."

"I wish we'd been more open about who we were from the beginning."

He offers me a small smile. "We're here and can do that now. Almost like we planned. No party hats, though."

"There's a leftover banner and some deflated balloons on the wall from someone's birthday."

That makes him laugh. "Now it's your turn to fill in the blanks."

It only takes me a minute to provide a summary, because unlike Teddy, I'm not the heir to a luxury fashion firm. I tell him about my time at Chariot and the new job at Gear Robins, and answer a few questions about Vivian and my diversity night classes. Then, because I realize how one-dimensional it seems to only describe my life in terms of work and work-adjacencies, I tell him about my family moving in with me.

"Do you like it?" he asks.

"It's crowded," I say. "But we're coping."

To my relief, he takes that at face value. "We're all up to speed." He looks pleased.

"Which is great but, Teddy." I play with my coaster as I get my thoughts in order. Over the course of the conversation, something has become clear to me, and I hate having to say it. "We can't hang out like this anymore."

He nearly drops his glass. "Why not?"

"What do you mean? It's a conflict of interest."

"I don't understand."

"We kissed," I point out, going red. "You *kissed* me."

"And I am more than willing to do it again." He looks at my expression. "After you're done at Celeste. Only if you want. Also, I'd consider that more of a peck than a kiss."

"You can't work with someone who you've kissed *or* pecked. Not to mention I'd have to tell my boss, who I'm fairly sure would not be pleased I didn't tell her before I started."

"You didn't know," he points out.

"I don't think she'd believe me," I say ruefully. "I'll look like I was hiding it from her or that I have relationships where I can't be bothered to find out someone's full name. I'll look flaky at best."

"I can see your point," he says slowly. "It would be better for me to keep my work and personal life separate as well. My father thinks workplace relationships are toxic."

We sit for a moment.

"Are you open to a proposal?" he asks.

"Tentative yes."

"Good enough. What if we hang out as friends?" he says. "Platonic friends. We can both use an ally at Celeste, and we have Questie in common."

Friends seems like a monumentally bad idea given the amount of time I spend looking at his mouth and those hands. There are so many problems. The aforementioned conflict of interest. Trying to keep my attention on work, knowing he's right there. Not straddling him in a chair.

Too bad I'm lonely and I want something—anything—with him, because the idea of no Teddy is too upsetting to contemplate. He's become a huge part of my life, from our fights about Questie to his texts. Not to mention the kissing.

There is no issue that I can't rationalize away, and to my disgust, I've already done it. There won't be a conflict of interest as we'll only be friends and I report to Gary anyway. Keeping my attention on work would be difficult no matter what.

The chair straddling, well, I'll depend on willpower. What can go wrong?

"It needs to be completely professional while we're working together," I say. "That's important to me."

"Of course." He nods vigorously.

Well then, problem solved. "Okay."

Teddy pauses for a moment. "I should tell you something."

I cover my face with my hands. "I'm not sure I can handle much more."

"I am committed to maintaining a nonromantic relationship while you're at Celeste, I promise." He looks at me until I move my hands and meet his gaze. "However, I plan to ask you out the day you hand in that final report."

My heart goes fluttery. "You will?"

"In four months," he says firmly. "The second that report is sent."

"Not after the payment is received?"

"We have net ninety, and Liz pushes that as far as possible to get supplier discounts."

"Wow."

"Yeah, and I don't want to wait that long, so it's going to be when the report is in." He grins at me. "Until then, Best Questies?"

I can't fight my smile. "That's a terrible name."

"C'mon, you know it's awesome."

"It's okay at best."

He holds up his glass. "I'll take it."

We cheers to it, and Teddy scans my face carefully.

"Are we good?" he asks. "I'll think about what you said about work."

"We're good." I won't push him more at the moment, not until he has some time. Changing a mindset can be as hard as maneuvering an ocean tanker but at least he's already started to turn the wheel.

He goes to see if the jukebox plays anything besides the Cure, and I do a surreptitious check on my phone for the exact day the Celeste report is due. When I glance up, Teddy is pressing buttons and doing a tiny dance to the end of "Boys Don't Cry," work slacks not leaving a lot to the imagination.

I swallow hard. It's going to be a long four months.

THIRTEEN

DAILY AFFIRMATION: I CELEBRATE MY DECISIONS
AND MOVE CONTINUOUSLY FROM THE PRESENT.

*A*s part of the listening and learning element of the Gear Robins People First Platform, I've set up a series of interviews with people across the company. It took me over a week, and today is the creative director, Michael Madison. By now, I've heard enough gossip—Jenna is a godsend—to know one word from him can tank a career.

Although Teddy and I have relaxed our no-work conversation rule, he refused to talk about Michael when I asked. "The man wrecks my day by existing," he'd told me, which I suppose conveys a lot of what I need to know.

After our disclosure meeting, we haven't been able to meet in person, not even for a Saturday Questie day, as Teddy was at a work conference. I'd sent him a photo of SunnyDay topping the leaderboard (again) and he texted back a sketch of me laughing over a Questie clue. The Dee in the sketch was engrossed in what she was doing, fully in the moment and loving it. She was also beautiful—confident and lively. The image left me speechless. Is that what I look like to him?

Me: I don't know what to say. I love this, Teddy. Thank you.

Teddy: I did it the day we met. I'm glad you like it.

I saved that sketch to my phone for whenever I needed a mood enhancer, which means I've looked at it about twenty times this morning to psych myself up to meet Michael. By 10:57, I decide some positive self-talk is in order and spend the next two minutes whispering boosts that would make Dale Carnegie proud. *You can do this. You are capable and talented. Smile and the world smiles with you.*

Shit, it's 10:59. I hurry up the stairs to arrive at the design studio slightly out of breath and juggling my laptop as it threatens to slip out of my hands, the exact opposite of the smoothly professional and in control Daiyu I wanted to present. Dale Carnegie's displeasure radiates out from his grave.

I compose myself and walk in the room, where a wall of windows pours natural light into the big open space. A wide aisle separates rows of tables piled with pattern pieces and fabric. Women in rolling chairs and perched on stools bend over half-stitched garments while others adjust clothing on dress forms.

"Can I help you?" It's the woman I saw crying in the bathroom. We recognize each other at the same time, and she shoots me a warning look that puts me on the defensive. Does she think I'm going to rat her out?

"I'm Daiyu Kwan, the diversity consultant from Gear Robins," I say. "I have a meeting with Michael."

Before she can answer, there's a clatter at the door as Michael comes in. "Slacking off again, Allie?"

Her lips thin as she sits at a desk overflowing with paper and swatches. Michael looks at me curiously and I remember we've never met, so I introduce myself and reach out to shake his hand.

Michael keeps it clasped in his and looks me in the eye. I instantly see why some people here speak about him with awed tones—he exudes self-confidence, an intimidating level of self-confidence that demands attention. "Let's go to my office," he suggests, "where we can be alone."

As opposed to the organized chaos of the main studio, Michael's office is almost spartan, with only a few photos of Celestial bags and rows of awards lining the cabinets. He tosses his bag in the corner and leans in to look at me closely as I sit down, like I'm a butterfly on an entomologist's tray.

"You have quite the face," he says. "What's your mix?"

I curse inwardly at the phrasing but want to get this over with. "I'm half-Chinese."

"I thought so," he says, satisfied he's put the proper label under my pinned wings. "It's the eyes."

I ignore this and point at his cabinet. "That's a lot of awards."

It's enough to get his attention away from me, and he gives me a TV-ready smile.

"As you probably know, I was named Best Accessories Designer for multiple years," he says. "My Celestial bag made the Celeste brand."

"That's so interesting," I say, wondering if I misheard. I thought Teddy's mother designed it.

Michael starts talking. Every time I try to interject to get us on track for the questions I need to ask, he talks over me. As he's listing the famous people who clamor over his bags, the woman from earlier knocks on the door. He looks up, irritation evident. "What now?"

"We've had a fabric shipment but the linen is too heavy for the drape I want," she says. "Did you change it?"

"The drape you want?" Michael sounds mild.

She freezes. "Sorry. The drape you wanted."

"I did change it. That fabric needs to have more—" Here he makes an incomprehensible gesture with his hands. "I wish you could understand what needs to be done without bothering me with details."

"Also, merchandising wants to know what happened to the patterned shorts they had on the road map," she says, ignoring his comment. "Martine says you cancelled them."

"I did. Ted is a numbers man because merchandising is a numbers game. He knows nothing of the art of good design."

The dig seems both petty and incorrect given what I saw of Teddy's work online, but Allie ignores this too. "It's on trend."

"Trends are for people without imagination," Michael says. "Go back to the mood board I had you lay out. It's all there if you bother to look. I can't do all your thinking." She leaves and Michael gives me a generous smile. "Allie has some skill but needs a lot of supervision," he says. "Now, you had some questions for me. Fire away."

I pull out my list with relief. It takes an extra forty-five minutes to go through them—no surprise, he feels completely at ease at work and knows for a fact his team feels the same—and by the end, I'm exhausted.

I can't imagine what it's like to work with that guy. Poor Allie.

———

There's no time to recover as I need to hurry for my meeting with Liz. As I come around a corner, I stop dead when I see Teddy and his father arguing in the hallway. I duck back behind the wall and try to figure out an alternate path that doesn't bring me in the middle of a dynastic struggle.

"It's worth working with the supplier to improve their infrastructure," Teddy says. "We can keep building a mutually beneficial long-term relationship."

"Too expensive," says Edward dismissively. "Break the contract and find someone cheaper."

"Fine." Then Teddy pauses. "No, hold on, Dad. That's not right. We've worked with them for years."

His voice sounds stronger, like the Teddy I know. He must have taken our conversation to heart. I do a silent clap from my hiding spot.

"We've had this discussion, Ted, and I thought you understood. Your job as CEO is to grow the business. Our business, not theirs. This is what Opaline will be looking for."

"I told you I don't think Opaline is good for Celeste."

"That's because your vision is small. I think global. Get your head in the game, son."

There's a long silence. "I understand," says Teddy tightly.

"You'll see I'm right."

Teddy doesn't answer, and my heart hurts for him. It must be soul-destroying to have to give in like that. If this is what's he's been dealing with, no wonder he was so discouraged.

The two of them leave, and I wait a minute before making my way to Liz's office. I'm bursting with apologies that she waves away as she arranges the huge light over her desk.

"My heliotherapy lamp." She pulls a green juice out of her mini fridge, then counts out some almonds from a small glass container. "Self-care is so important, don't you think? How have you been settling in at Celeste?"

"Very well, thanks."

"It was a pleasure meeting Vivian the other day." She puts an almond back. "She has such a distinctive look, don't you agree?"

"What?" I'm not sure what she means.

"Well, that hair certainly stands out." She looks thoughtful. "I suppose her job gives her more leeway in her appearance."

I need to speak up when I can. "I'm not sure what Vivian's hair has to do with her ability," I say stiffly, wondering if I should be firmer. Or something.

"I never said it did. It's only an observation," she says.

"It is," I reply. "I'm not sure for what purpose."

She looks at me. "Making conversation. Before we start, I want to say I've always felt change best comes from within, and I'm pleased to facilitate it at Celeste."

It's my job to listen right now, so I put aside what she said about Vivian to wait for her to continue.

"During my finance career, I've been in many rooms where I'm the only woman," she says. "It was hard, but it also makes me the perfect person to talk about women's experiences here at Celeste."

"I'll keep that in mind," I say.

"I have good friends well-placed in media outlets eager to interview me to get our message across. They often say I'm an inspiration. I'll send you their names so you can work with Kylie, our head of communications, to set them up."

"I'd love to have some more time to understand the Celeste story before I take action," I say with as big a smile as I can muster.

"Oh, you're a thinker. We tend to be doers here." She leans over the desk. "A word of advice. It's important to silence our inner critics and show up, because only vulnerable bravery results in change. I suggest you sit with that."

I'm at a loss for an appropriate answer, so I scramble to get this meeting back on point. "You've been with Celeste a few years, I understand? How do you find it here?"

"Incredible organization." She gives a little laugh. "Of course, despite the perception of fashion being a women's industry, we see a drop in numbers the higher we go in the organization, which we can attribute to society rather than a failing of management. Nonetheless, that needs to change, so I do my best to promote and amplify those on my team."

I glance out the window of her office to her team, who are indeed women but, as I recall, none are women of color. Calling that out directly isn't on my Gear Robins approved list of questions, and I know I need to use gentle and supportive language so clients don't think they're bad people.

"You need buy-in, because once they get defensive, it's game over," a Chariot consultant had told me. "It's all about self-image at that point, and it's hard to see past that. All you'll get is stonewalling and protests and excuses and, from a certain kind of person, big old tears."

Ah, fuck it, says that inner voice, and for once, I don't ignore it. Being with Michael sucked out a lot of my willpower to keep quiet, and lately

I've been struggling with setting my default outlook to positive. I'm tired of people like Liz acting as if they can only be part of the solution and never part of the problem.

"That's so wonderful," I say. "Tell me, what are you doing for others?"

Her complacent smile freezes. "I beg your pardon? The other what?"

"Your primary focus is on women as if we're a generic whole. What about those who might have different experiences in addition to their gender? Women of color or queer women? Women with disabilities?" I check my notes, knowing I'm being reckless and feeling my pulse bunch up in my throat. "When you eventually hire them."

"I prefer to look at unity and not division. Being women is where we all intersect with the same experiences, so that's where I target my efforts instead of head counting," she says.

Before I can continue, she raises her voice to control the conversation.

"I see people as individuals. Not everything comes down to race." She says the word like it's a little dirty and she's trying to be polite in good company. "Or those other things. The women on my team have worked hard for what they've achieved, and I do not appreciate your insinuation that they don't deserve their success. Now, don't you have real questions to ask?"

Choose your battles, I hear Vivian say. I swallow down the words that were ready in my mouth and open my laptop.

———

I come out of Liz's office feeling flayed, and after sitting and staring at my screen for five minutes, decide I need to get out. There's a fancy café down the street, which is empty except for a familiar face. I grab my tea and walk over to say hello to Allie.

She looks up, eyes unfocused as if I've taken her out of a daydream. "Hi?" She shakes her head. "Oh, hi."

"Do you mind if I join you?" I ask.

She gestures at the empty chair. In front of her is a tablet filled with whimsical drawings on a croquis, the quick sketch of a figure used to set the proportions of a design.

"You're Allie?" I ask.

"Alejandra Diaz," she says. "Michael thinks my real name is too long."

"You work in the design studio with him?" I don't add, *Is it as much of a nightmare as it seems?*

"His second." She laughs wryly. "Lucky me."

It's not professional, but I can't help making a commiserative face.

Alejandra stares at me like she's taking my measure. "I heard you met with Liz today," she says.

That was fast. "How do you know?"

"Her assistant heard you talking."

That's not good, and I get a little sweaty at what Vivian would say if she found out Celeste staff were gossiping about my meeting.

Alejandra tilts her head to the side. "She said you had a disagreement."

Even worse. I try to keep my expression calm as I weigh my options. I can stop this right now. I can excuse myself and be the company stooge. Or I can play this out and let Alejandra know how I really felt about that meeting, an option that might lead me to a deeper understanding of what's going on at Celeste so I can make the right recommendations and succeed at my damn job. The People First Platform isn't infallible, and despite what Vivian says, it might require a few side journeys to get what I need. The result is what matters.

I make my choice and take a sip of tea to combat my suddenly very dry throat.

"We had a discussion where we didn't see eye to eye," I say in a mild tone that belies the adrenaline tingling my skin. I take the plunge. "Liz seems like quite a person."

There. I put myself out there first to give Alejandra an opening. I hope she'll take it.

"That she is." Alejandra's reply is cautious.

Although encouraged, I try to play it cool as I venture a little further. "She values her opinion."

Now Alejandra puts down her stylus to look at me straight. "I've found the same thing," she says. "Occasionally."

"A few times, she didn't seem to understand where I was coming from." I wave my hand. "Which is fine! Everyone's here to learn."

"Liz likes to say she's listening and learning," Alejandra says, her lips twitching.

I'm definitely not misreading this. I click my tongue. "Sounds like she's trying."

"Oh, she's trying all right." Alejandra says this without cracking a smile, but I grin at her.

"I bet she is." I clear my throat. "Then there's Michael."

"What about him?"

"Remarkable man. Eager to share information about himself. Unasked."

"I've noticed that myself many times," she says.

We regard each other across the table.

"You hate them, right?" Alejandra asks. "To be clear."

This is the moment of truth, the declaration of a budding alliance. There's no going back, and if Vivian finds out, the best-case scenario is a strong lecture for deviating from the Gear Robins path. It's worth it because if I can do well here, I can prove to Vivian that my way of approaching work has value. "*Hate's* a strong word, but they're not my favorite people to deal with."

Alejandra blows her breath out. "You know we're in a mutual destruction pact," she points out. "If you tell, I'll take you down with me."

I gesture to the table, tension and relief pulling me between sagging in my seat and leaning forward in excitement. "While we sit here, we're in the cone of silence."

"Nothing leaves the cone?"

"Not a word." I open the lid to my tea to let it cool faster and for something to do. Should I jump right in with questions? I don't want to scare her off.

Luckily, Alejandra takes the lead. "I don't know why you're bothering." She moves her tablet to the side. "Nothing's going to happen. I've been trying to change who we bring into the studio for years."

"I thought Michael did the hiring."

She curls her lip. "Michael rolls in and coasts on his reputation for a few hours while I do the work. A couple times a year, he gives us his vision, which almost never has to do with what merchandising needs or is workable in any way, and I formulate it into something feasible and rush around making it happen."

"That's a lot of work."

"I prefer it to when he's involved, because then I have to fix everything while making him think his mistakes are my fault and my corrections are his ideas."

I shudder at the intense ego management. "Has it always been like that?"

She snorts. "Hell, no. It's far worse since he's started—" The door jangles open, and she casts a worried glance over her shoulder, then relaxes when she sees it's a dad with a stroller. "I should go," she says. "Cone of silence?"

After I nod, she leaves. Vivian might have concerns about this unconventional method, and although I want to impress her, I'm certain I'm doing the right thing. After all, the Gear Robins People First Platform focuses the attention on manager level and above. That's an issue if we miss information from people like Alejandra, and I'm going to do my best to change it.

I wish she'd told me more. I sit over my tea and ponder next steps to figure out the best way to get what I need until it's time to go back to the office.

FOURTEEN

DAILY AFFIRMATION: I AM ACTION ORIENTED AND THE UNIVERSE ENSURES MY DECISIONS WORK OUT FOR THE BEST.

*V*ivian checks in with me every couple of days, which would be nice if I didn't dimly suspect it was more to make sure I wasn't screwing up than out of care for my well-being. On Wednesday, we meet in person at Gear Robins.

I unpack my bag at my desk behind a pillar and check my phone. As usual, there's a text from Teddy, who has taken to sending me good-morning facts (yesterday's was that the word *ferret* comes from the Latin for *thief* and that a group of ferrets is a business). He seems down, so I go into a phone room to give him a call. He goes right into what's bothering him.

"I've been thinking about what you said, but it's like playing Whac-A-Mole," he says. "Every time I see an opportunity to make a suggestion, it disappears."

Thanks to Mom's unbeatable optimism, I have a lifetime of experience to call on to help him out of this funk, and I happily prepare to share some of it. "You need to tell yourself to—"

Remember you wanted to throw something when you felt like this and Mom said to stop complaining and look for the good in the situation, the voice reminds me. *You weren't ready to hear that yet, and he might not be either.*

I try a new approach. "It sounds hard."

"Thank you, and it's infuriating." He sounds relieved I understand.

"I appreciate that you're trying." I pause. "I accidentally overheard you and your dad fighting in the hall the other day. About some suppliers."

"You heard that?" The sound of traffic rises in the background, like he's at an intersection.

"I was behind a corner. It gave me an idea of what you're up against," I say.

"Then you see it's pointless."

He's having some sort of a crisis, and I don't know if I should prod or not but decide to speak my mind. "I'm not sure of that. There are other things you can do. What if you start smaller?"

"Smaller like how?"

"Well, is everything as good as you can make it in your department?"

"I do my best with my team," he says stiffly.

"I'm sure you do, but when was the last time you checked in with them? You said you've been disengaged lately." I try to keep my tone as nonjudgmental as possible.

A car honks and Teddy swears. "I hate that you could be right. Shit, what if I let them down? They're a great team."

"Talk to them, then."

"We have a meeting today about the resort wear collection." He sounds like he's thinking it through. "I can do it then."

"They might have ideas that you don't need your father to approve."

"I'm sure they will." He sounds rueful. "Why did I get so caught up in thinking I had to run everything by him? I'm a vice president, for God's sake." With each word, he sounds more confident. "Thanks, Dee," he adds. "Sometimes you need someone to give you a wake-up call."

"That's me, a living alarm clock." I see Vivian through the window. "I'd better go. Meeting time."

"One thing first. Are you busy tonight? We can do an archived Questie puzzle for fun."

Two friends playing a game isn't a date, so we set a time and I hang up as Vivian walks in. Despite her careful makeup, there are heavy bags under her eyes, as if she's crammed a week's worth of lost sleep there. I know better than to ask about her personal life, so I say nothing.

"How's Celeste coming along?" she asks. "It's been almost two weeks, and according to our timeline, you should be completing the in-person interviews."

I put thoughts of Teddy aside and scramble for my notes. They're more like a script because Vivian makes me nervous, and I overprepared. "There are a few issues at Celeste," I say.

"Like what?"

I go through what I've learned. Their company demographics confirmed the damning leak to Fashion Eye, and someone finally spoke to me candidly, a South Asian woman who was looking for a new job since she'd had enough of being excluded and made to feel like she couldn't do her job. "My manager tells me how impressive my English is," she said. "I was born in *Brampton*."

"That's fairly typical," Vivian says. "Anything else?"

I hesitate. "There are issues around some of the senior people, but I don't know what." Alejandra cancelled the meeting request I'd sent her, so this is coming more from the gut feeling of having met Liz and Co. combined with Alejandra's cryptic final comment. Maybe it would be better to talk to her away from work.

"It's probably nothing significant," Vivian says. "Keep to the Gear Robins plan."

"Vivian," I start slowly. Since the conversation with Alejandra, I've been thinking more about Celeste and what Teddy told me. "Is sticking to the plan the right thing to do? The best choice for real change?"

She glances at the screen. "The methodology will get the buy-in we need."

"That may be, but is this *right*?" Teddy's comments at the bar weigh on me. "Most of their products are made in poorly regulated factories. They don't do anything sustainable. Their business directly contributes to inequity."

"As do most of the companies we deal with." She raises her eyebrows. "When the problems happen in some other, poorer country, it's easier to ignore."

"It's all so useless," I burst out. "How can we say they've reached maturity when we don't address any of those problems? Our methodology needs to change."

"Those problems being global issues that every person in this country contributes to by dint of being alive?" She sounds almost amused, like I'm naive. "Including you."

"Yes," I say stubbornly.

Vivian looks at me, and her face is weary. I never realized how much effort she must make every day to cover her exhaustion. I should have, given how many of her emails come time-stamped with obscenely late or early hours. "You want the truth?"

I nod.

"Here's the truth." She points at my screen. "Forget the global perspective. This is a company located in a city with about fifty percent visible minorities and over fifty percent women. Celeste is over ninety percent white, most of their senior leaders are male, and no one at the company disclosed a disability on the survey, which could be because they don't have one or, as I've often seen, don't feel safe saying so, even anonymously. Sexual and gender diversity are where we would expect but almost disappears in leadership positions. This is so bad I can't believe it's not deliberate, but so common I could plot it in my sleep."

"Then why are they bothering—"

"The leak caused questions, and Celeste wants to be an attractive investment for Opaline. Shareholders and investors like to see companies take action if there's a possibility of scandal."

"People are watching to make sure they change, though."

"Not really," she says. "Hiring us will be enough that most of their critics will consider it a respectable effort, leaving them to feel good about shopping there again. They won't be monitoring for real long-term change."

"That's cynical," I say.

"That's the truth." Vivian sees my face collapse. "Don't worry. We'll go in and give some recommendations that they'll shelve immediately or after discussing them at an all-hands meeting. Nothing will happen, but you can tell yourself you made a difference."

"This isn't what I thought the job was," I mutter.

"No job ever is." She clasps her hands. "I know what you mean. I used to be the same as you. Idealistic, let's say."

This boggles me. "Then why are you going along with it?"

"Because there's always the chance that you'll still change minds this way. A small change is a change."

I examine her face. "Do you think so?"

"Yes." Her expression shifts to become sardonic. "Also I need this job, so I make it work."

"Oh."

"You have a choice." She taps the table with her finger. "You can make Celeste feel like they're good people who can't be blamed for any of this because it's enough that they're trying."

"Hold on," I protest.

She keeps going. "Or you can tell them they've created and maintained an environment hostile to people unlike them and designed to protect people like them. In one scenario, you keep this job, and in the other, you don't. I can assure you the second option will cause no more change than the first."

I sit straighter. "What we do isn't working. Maybe the key isn't to keep people comfortable. Maybe they need to be shocked."

Vivian rolls her neck like a prizefighter about to enter the ring. "How long have you been doing this?"

"A few months." I try not to sound defensive. "That has nothing to do with what I'm saying."

"On the contrary, it has everything to do with it." Vivian sighs. "I understand where you're coming from, but I need you to commit to our method."

It's on the tip of my tongue to say, *What if I don't?* but I need this job, too.

"Fine," I say finally. She's right, after all. I was hired by Gear Robins and they can expect me to do the work the way they decide no matter my own feelings.

"Good. After Will's meeting, I'll walk you through how to structure the report."

This last is given like a concession, and I'm glad she's willing to move on. That will have to do for now.

I'm early to meet Teddy, so I text Jade. She's always a good sounding board, and I want a third-party opinion. Despite my decision to be a good little Gear Robinser (Robinsite? Robinsian?), not being able to go beyond the vaunted People First Platform feels wrong, even though I'm doing my best to visualize a positive outcome.

> **Me:** Let's say that you've started a new job. Hypothetically.
> **Jade:** Why bother with hypotheticals. I know it's you.
> **Me:** HYPOTHETICALLY there's something bothering you at this new job. What do you do?

The dots come and go for a minute as I check to see if Teddy's coming. Finally her answer arrives.

Jade: There are a few things to consider in this unbelievably vague scenario. How bad is it? Is it a moral or values thing or a process thing or a personal preference thing? What are the consequences? Is it possible to do what they want now, and when you get more information, to act on it then?

Me: All good questions.

Jade: Can you give me more details?

Me: My new boss wants me to stick to the way they do things at work and I don't think it's right.

Jade: How many times have I told you the first rule of corporate life?

Me: Never come late to a meeting holding a coffee?

Jade: That's the second rule. The first is that if you bust your ass and suck up the first six months, you can set your reputation and be golden for the next decade.

Me: Then you think I should do it the way they want.

Jade: It's safest, and they have far more experience than you.

Me: You're probably right.

But Vivian said she used to feel the same way. That means something, doesn't it?

Jade: I have to go. Nick got something stuck in his nose again.

Jade's comment that I can change my mind hadn't occurred to me. I can do what Vivian wants and keep on investigating what's plaguing Celeste in my own way. Information gathering is part of the Gear Robins methodology, so I'm not even crossing the company. The more I mull this over, the better the idea gets. For added assistance, I send out a strongly worded plea to the universe to let the situation unfold to my benefit.

When Teddy arrives, he seems like his old self, or at least the self I met first. It's unseasonably warm for early March, and his open coat shows a white varsity-style cardigan over a black T-shirt that makes him look mouthwatering. My gaze keeps drifting up to his shoulders and then down again whenever I walk behind him.

If I thought Questie was entertaining on my own, Teddy elevates the entire experience. His enthusiasm makes me warm and happy. Real happy, too, the kind that glows like a banked fire and I haven't felt in a while. That's odd. If this is happy, what have I been the rest of the time?

That we're evenly matched makes it even better. He'd gotten the first clue, *This café is the bomb*, which had led us over to the Grenadier Café in High Park, where I'd found the letter *S* on a railing. The puzzle is by TigerCloud, who we agree is the best. A twinge of envy goes through me at how well they construct their clues. Sometimes I wish I could do that. I even have a list of clues on my phone that I jot down when I get an idea.

"How did your team meeting go?" I ask as we walk down Bloor Street.

"Amazing." He almost glows. "It was awkward at first, so I was honest and told them I'd been frustrated and burned out, and apologized."

I wish I could hug him. "It's brave for you to admit that."

"I let them down, even though I told myself it was a strategic retreat." He rubs his hands together. "This is only the beginning. I need to rebuild their trust, but I already had someone take me aside to give me a list of ideas they've been working on. Good ones, too, that we can implement quickly."

He's wearing that lovely upside-down smile, and I swallow over the thump of my heart. "Good for you."

"You gave me the hand I needed," he says. "Like pulling me out of quicksand."

"I always thought quicksand was going to be much more of a threat in my adult life than it is," I say.

"Me too! Cartoons are so misleading."

Our mood is light as we keep going. Teddy slows his stride to check a store display with a headless mannequin wearing a pleated skirt and pokes his tongue in his cheek. "Are you trying to see what's good for Celeste?" I ask.

"In part, although we depend more on data from SKUs and what our sales teams report. It's often too late for a trend by the time we see it in the wild. Also this is a vintage store."

I ignore that. "Skews?"

"S-K-U," he spells. "Stock keeping unit. Codes that track each item. They tell us what's selling where, so we know if pants are doing better than skirts and black pants rather than red." He turns his attention to a dusty-rose blazer. "Fashion is a highly monitored industry."

"I didn't know."

"Most people like to see the art rather than the science," he says. "I work on three collections at a time, analyzing the past, responding to the present, and forecasting the future."

"That's cool."

"It's an interesting part of the job." He sounds enthusiastic, and this is the Teddy I know.

"I wish Questie could be a job," I say as we keep walking. "I love this."

"What in particular?" He grins. "The game? The winning? Spending time with me?"

I refuse to look at him. "The game, of course. It's not like I would die if I had to stop, but life would be duller, you know? Drearier."

He frowns as a chorus of yells drift out from a bar showing the hockey game. "Yeah."

"Is there something wrong?" I ask.

Teddy shakes his head and gives me a small smile. "Sorry. I was thinking."

"About what?" His face did not reflect good thoughts.

"Sunday evenings," he says obscurely.

"What does *that* mean?"

"I'm tired of hating them." He turns back to the puzzle. "It's this *break a leg* part that's confusing me," he says, referring to the clue. We've been arguing about the meaning of *Even when you primly assume, there's a good chance you can break a leg,* and tossing ideas back and forth.

I look at the clue. "Assume. I assume. You assume."

Teddy tucks his hands in his pockets. "I had a collaborator who always said when you assume, you make an ass out of you and me."

"An ass." A memory sparks. I turn to him, then check the clue again. "Broken leg? Primly?"

We stare at each other before yanking out our phones. I'm the first one to find it but my cry of discovery is closely followed by Teddy saying, "I *knew* it was familiar."

We high-five and get on the subway to Bay Street. Teddy glances at a woman at the end of the car with a Celestial bag slung casually over her shoulder.

"Suede and patent leather from 2000," he murmurs.

My eyes drift back to the woman. "You can recognize when a purse was made?"

"Not always," he says. "It was a limited colorway for that year."

That reminds me of my conversation with Michael. "Hey, I thought you said your mom designed the first Celestial bag."

"She did, in 1990, right before she opened Celeste."

"When I met with Michael, he gave me the impression it was his work."

"He's a liar." Teddy's eyes darken. "Mom brought him on board to expand the accessories line, but he had nothing to do with the Celestial bags besides reissuing them with different materials."

"He's taking credit for your mom's work?"

"Unfortunately, and I've tried to set the record straight many times. I talked to Dad about it but he doesn't consider it an issue since it's all Celeste." His jaw sets. "Can we talk about something else?"

"Sure." I rack my brain. This is like being forced to tell a joke on the spot. "Uh."

This at least makes him laugh. "Sorry, Dee."

The train slows, and I get a reprieve on generating conversation topics. "We're at Bay Station."

We go south to where a statue of Primrose the donkey stands with two casts on its legs. There's an N on the pedestal, and Teddy smiles at me after he puts it in the game. "Teamwork wins again."

I nod, trying not to look at his shoulders silhouetted in the street-light. Or hands. Or the silver rings in his ear. His entire being is a giant booby trap of attraction.

Oblivious, he bows his head and checks for the next clue. Still Best Questies, at least for the time being. It's better than nothing.

FIFTEEN

*DAILY AFFIRMATION: EACH DAY OFFERS
A CHANCE TO GROW AND IMPROVE.*

Work settles into a predictable routine. I come into Celeste every day and hunch over my computer, hunting and gathering information to fill in the blanks of the Gear Robins standard template. Policies. Complaints. Interview data. Occasionally I consume a hot or cold drink or hot or cold food. Jenna comes by to check that I'm alive. Gary does not. I avoid Travis because he's gross. I try to avoid Teddy because of chair-straddling concerns, but I notice his visits to HR seem to have increased.

"Is it me or I am seeing you at work more often?" I ask one mid-March evening. Teddy wanted to try a new coffee shop, and we're sitting at the front window counter eating gigantic Japanese soufflé pancakes and watching people pass by on the slushy street.

"It's you." He sips his mango latte.

"Really?" I glance over. "Because in the last two days, you've walked through HR at least seven times."

Teddy looks affronted as I slice into my pancake. "I'll have you know I am a very important executive conducting essential HR business."

"You were using the photocopier."

"That was once." He goes red. "It's nice to see you sometimes during the day, but I feel strange about going and talking to you. I can stop."

I stare into my strawberry lavender tea. "I might have walked by your office a couple times to see if you were there."

Teddy laughs so hard he snorts some of his drink, which makes him cough. "We're not doing anything wrong," he says finally. "We can talk to each other if we want."

"It *feels* wrong," I say.

"Oh?" he asks. "I think it feels right."

Then he grins at me and puts his strawberry on my plate. "Want another pancake?" he asks.

"Sure."

When he takes out his phone to scan the menu, it opens to the calendar app, which shows the first week of June. On the Wednesday in all capitals is an appointment that says, "DEE DATE DAY." There are exclamation marks before and after.

Teddy doesn't notice that I've seen it, and he flips to his web browser before I can check that I didn't misread. "Matcha white chocolate?" he asks. "Or Nutella banana? That sounds good."

I nod, unable to speak. He meant it about asking me out. Even though I trusted him and we've been flirting, seeing that he's looking forward to the next step pushes away any doubt. He's as into me as I'm into him.

"Dee?" He looks at me with those big eyes.

"Nutella," I manage to say.

There are too many days left until June.

———

On Friday, I'm on my way to ask IT if there's something wrong with my network access, which has again blocked me from the HR area, when a raised voice comes from behind a closed door.

"Who the hell do you think you are?" Michael says. "I'm the creative director here. I set the vision, not you. You have one job, and you can't even do that right."

The other voice is lower and muffled by the door, but it sounds like Alejandra. There's a cracking sound, like something being slammed down, and I jump before I take a step forward, my body deciding to intervene before my mind can make a choice. Not even Vivian could disapprove of me poking my nose in a situation like this.

The door slams open, and Michael strides out, calling, "I don't want a fucking excuse, Allie. Stay late to fix the mess, and stop wasting time on your useless designs."

I catch sight of Alejandra's face, furious and defeated, before she reaches out to close the door.

Mind buzzing from the shock of witnessing such a scene, I hesitate before moving on. Although I've seen Alejandra cry, I don't think she'd thank me for barging in on her like this. I'll check in on her later, when I can find a way to do it privately.

Forget my intranet access problems. I make my way back to my office and slump in the chair to think through what happened. Should I report this to Gary? Tell Vivian? What's the right thing to do? I pick up my phone to text Teddy but put it down. He's an executive at Celeste, and I don't know if Alejandra would appreciate him knowing, or anyone for that matter. I'm on my own.

The most important thing is to make sure Alejandra is okay. I doubt this is the first time he's blown up like this, and since he remains at Celeste, it's probably accepted as his star temperament and how he is. Michael had told her to work late, so I can go up and talk to her when she's alone to provide some moral support.

The day drags by, and Jenna pokes her head in my door a little after five. "Not going home?" she asks, tucking her hair behind her ears.

I pretend to be engrossed in my file, not wanting to say I'm waiting to talk to Alejandra, which might cause undesirable questions. "I want to finish before I lose my train of thought."

"I get it. Don't stay too late. This place empties out fast on Friday and it's spooky." She shudders.

Twenty minutes later, the office is silent as I head up the stairs. The door to the studio is ajar, and I give myself a final check with my hand on the knob. Do I want to do this? Yes, I do. If she thinks I crossed a boundary by coming up to talk to her, I can apologize and leave.

I push open the door, but to my dismay, it's empty and dark. Alejandra isn't here, and although I'm glad she's not staying late because of Michael's tantrum, this messes up my plan to check in. I should go, but instead I linger because the studio is a fascinating place. I step inside and turn on the light before moving over to the big board with its colorful sketches of outfits, fabric swatches, and trimming. The breezy, glamorous looks resemble the design I saw on Alejandra's tablet, and I suddenly come to my senses. What on earth am I thinking, hanging around the design studio alone on a Friday without permission? I don't know if industrial espionage is a thing in fashion, but I don't want to find out. This was not a good idea. Vivian was right, at least for this. I should talk to Alejandra the proper and accountable way, through an official on-the-books interview.

Then the door clicks, and in a panic, I duck under the table.

The moment I crouch down between the chairs, I regret it because there's no reasonable way to explain this. I do my best to slow my breathing and hope, toddler-style, that because I can't see them, they can't see me.

"Who left the lights on?" a woman murmurs as she walks around the table. Too bad she's a neat freak and I left a chair slightly out of place. She pauses right where I'm hiding. "Messy," she says.

Then she shoves the chair into my side.

The first thing that alerts her to the fact that all is not right with the situation is that the chair won't go in. The second is my wail of pain, which sets up a feedback loop of her shrieking in fear, which causes me to sympathy scream.

"What the fuck!" she yells, stepping back into the design board and causing it to fall over on top of her.

I recognize the voice. "It's only me," I bleat from under the table. "Daiyu?"

I poke my head out to look at Alejandra's astonished face. "Hi?"

She stares, one hand holding up the mood board and the other raised in a fist. "What the hell are you doing here?"

I crawl out. "I wanted to talk to you."

She looks unimpressed. "You thought you'd find me under a table?"

"No, you scared me, and I hid."

"Good Lord. I can't believe you think that's close to being an acceptable explanation." She shoves the board in place. "Why do you want to talk to me anyway?"

I see the open door behind her and lower my voice. "I heard you and Michael earlier. I wanted to see if you were okay."

Alejandra looks taken aback. "You what?"

"He was out of line. I'm sorry I didn't come in to see you when he left, but I thought you might want privacy."

Her expression morphs into astonishment. "No one has ever asked how I feel after one of his explosions."

I grimace. "Does it happen a lot?"

"It..." Alejandra suddenly looks around as if also remembering that open door. "You know what? After that near-death experience, I need a drink. How about you?"

I'm not sure Vivian would believe this counts as information gathering, but I do, even though it's unconventional. Plus I'd like to get to know Alejandra better. It's been a while since I went out for drinks with a cool woman. "Sure."

We get out of Celeste without anyone seeing us and debate fancy cocktails versus cheap beer before splitting the difference and going to a pizza place with a good wine list. "I deserve all the cheese after the day I've had," Alejandra says.

"Does he do that to everyone?"

"Mostly me. I try to shield the rest of the team as much as I can." She takes her hair out from the bun and massages behind her ears.

"I'm sorry."

"First, priorities. Let's order." The restaurant is having happy hour with mini pizzas, so we get a few to share.

"Should we get a bottle?" asks Alejandra, looking at the wine list.

I have to meet Teddy early tomorrow for Questie, but they're on sale for half price, and I have poor impulse control, as was amply demonstrated this evening. "Yes. Did you know there's a place in Spain that has a free wine fountain?"

"Yet here we are, paying for it like losers." Alejandra bundles her hair back up in the bun. "Why were you sneaking around the design studio? Was it really to talk to me?"

"Why else would it be?"

She laughs. "I have no idea. That's why I'm asking."

I debate my answer. This is the next step of what we started in the café. It's entirely possible she'll go back and report this to Celeste. I might get fired for being inappropriate. Or I could make a difference, the way I always wanted to.

Across the table, Alejandra's expression turns from curious to concerned as the seconds tick by and I work up my nerve to answer.

"I want to know what you were going to say the other day." I look her in the eye and try to ignore my pounding heart. "Tell me what's going on, for real."

"Why should I?" she asks reasonably.

"So I can help change it. I want people to be happy at work, or at least not unhappy, because everyone deserves that."

Alejandra raises her eyebrow. "Noble."

Here I go. "I'm also tired of people getting away with their bullshit because they know they can. Please. I'm nosy but I want to help."

I don't know what internal calculus decides it for her, but after a minute, she mutters what sounds like *Fuck it*. "I'm only telling you because I need to get this off my chest," she says. "Same cone of silence rules apply."

"Absolutely." I can barely restrain my satisfaction that I'm finally getting somewhere.

She plays with her water glass. "You know," she says finally, "a creative director doesn't have to be the most artistic in the company or the best at technical drawing."

"I thought that would be table stakes."

"It's not. What they need to succeed is a vision and to inspire people to work together to achieve it. Michael was an excellent accessories guy, but he thinks he's superb at everything. He's not. We all pretend he is because we're expected to."

"His clothing designs have been praised, though."

"That's me." Her voice is low and serious. "My work, because Michael doesn't have what it takes, although he's certain he does."

"Incredible." I look up. "He's not embarrassed to take your credit?"

She tugs on a curl. "You've never worked with someone that shameless?"

Like George, my old boss at Chariot, who would tell the jokes I wrote into his speeches and bask in the applause without even thanking me in private. I push the disloyal thought away and remember what Teddy said about Michael rewriting the history of his mother's Celestial bag. "What about the rest of the company?"

"For Edward and the others, it's in their best interest to maintain the illusion that their creative director is creative, although he patently is not."

"Then why hasn't he been fired?"

There's a long silence. Alejandra releases the curl, which springs up by her eye. "Michael kept growing Celeste's reputation in accessories after Kitty Marsh died, and Edward eventually made him creative director. No matter what you say, no matter what you recommend, the CEO is loyal to Michael and will never get rid of him."

There's something in her voice. "Is there more?"

The server comes, and we break off our conversation for Alejandra to approve the wine—it's a screw top, so I'm not sure why this ritual is necessary—and then tap our glasses in a dismal cheers.

"Michael," she says after taking a sip that empties about half the glass.

I wait for her to get to the point. Vivian warned me about this before I started doing interviews at Celeste. *People will talk about subjects that are deeply uncomfortable, and you need to be patient,* she'd said. *Listen to what they're not telling you. Wait for them to stop talking around what's on their mind until they can bring themselves to say what they need to.*

I do this now, sipping my wine and watching Alejandra tap her fingers on the table, then her thigh. She looks weary and discouraged.

Finally, she blows out her breath and looks me in the eye. "Super mega cone of silence?"

"I promise. This won't go in my report at all."

"Mutual destruction," she warns me.

"It won't come to that."

It takes another minute, and then she speaks.

"After his first womens wear collections got panned, I took over most of the designing behind the scenes. We did a fall/winter collection of all my looks, and not to brag, it was fucking *amazing*. The best we've done. Got into *Vogue*, pieces on the red carpet, the whole bit. Outside Celeste, Michael was the golden child, but everyone in the design studio knew the score. They started coming to me instead of him."

"He didn't react well?"

"He started treating me different. Cut me out of meetings. Changed my designs and told vendors to go to him instead of me. Suddenly he was all over me, mocking my work. Nothing was good enough, but his own ideas were worse, and we all knew it except for him."

"Why couldn't he keep things the way they were?"

"Ego and delusion, I assume," she says. "He's a big deal in Canadian fashion, so he's used to people kissing his ass, and they have for years."

I drink my wine and wait for her to go on.

Alejandra sighs. "I had some success and he wanted it. He told me to step back and brought in his own ideas again. It was strange because his work had changed. He'd always drawn on classic styles, but these were almost edgy."

"That's unusual?"

"For him, and there was no unity in his ideas." She bites her lip. "You know, when he takes my designs, it's irritating but understandable. He's the creative director, and it's on his head if the collection is a failure. My work is under his vision, or what we tell everyone is his vision."

"There's more, then?"

She gulps down the wine and puts the glass down so hard it's a shock it doesn't shatter. "Michael is stealing designs. I don't mean he's inspired by other designers. He's taking their work and using it for his own."

"Oh," I say weakly. "Do you have proof?"

"Nothing for sure. I saw a couple of portfolios in his office from other designers, and lo and behold, almost identical versions appeared in Michael's initial sketches. He also never used to do those, too. He'd leave that work for me."

"He left the portfolios out for anyone to see?"

She looks me in the eye. "They were hidden in a back cabinet in his office."

"You snooped?"

Alejandra laughs. "I was looking for something unrelated. I was shocked he kept them so close, but I suppose he thinks he's untouchable. I haven't risked looking again."

"That seems smart. Those designers never said anything?"

She refills our glasses. "They're young. They don't have the clout to go up against someone like Michael, and he knows it and they know it."

"How about you? You can't tell anyone?" I keep my voice curious because I don't want her to feel judged for not acting.

"He'd deny it, and if those designers won't come forward, how can I? If I tell, I'm done in the industry, same as them."

I don't know what to say. "Alejandra, I'm sorry."

A long platter of mini pizzas, each cut in quarters, appears in front of us, and we decide on an eating break. There's one of each type: pesto and sun-dried tomato, Alfredo, and Halloumi, pear, and pecan. All conversation ceases until we sample and rate each pizza.

"Halloumi," I say.

"Pesto first," says Alejandra. "Then Alfredo because I don't like the honey drizzle on the Halloumi. That's not a pizza topping. I am not a bee."

"More for me." I say. "Back to Michael. What are you going to do?"

She pours us more wine. "I'll wait and see what happens. What can I do?"

"You could find proof and confront him."

"Sure." She pulls the collar from her throat as if it's choking her. "That'll be fantastic for my career, since there is zero chance of anything improving."

"I think you should."

Alejandra's eyebrows shoot up. "Easy enough to say when you're not the one risking anything."

"Okay," I say after a short silence, since that was a direct hit and also the truth. "Well, I suppose it could be worse."

"Probably not." Alejandra pushes the last Halloumi slice to me and takes the pesto.

I open my mouth and shut it. She's right. We finish up the wine and go back out into the cold wind. I wish I could talk to Teddy or Vivian. Too bad for the cone of silence. Sorry, the *super mega* cone.

SIXTEEN

*W*hen I wake up on Saturday, my mood is already a bit low thanks to a minor hangover, and it tumbles further when I recall what Alejandra told me. I shake it off and put on my StarLune playlist to stretch the kinks out of my back. She's given me a challenge to figure out, that's it. It's not a nuclear-grade problem but a *challenge*.

"You like challenges," I say out loud. "You love challenges. You're grateful to them. They provide stretch goals."

"What's that, sunshine?" asks Mom through my door.

"Nothing."

"What do we say, then?"

"Good morning!" I try not to shout it.

"Saying good morning makes the morning good." She goes humming down the hall.

I grit my teeth. Mom's insistence on wishing each other a good morning so aggravates Jade she refuses to say it at all, even on those perfect summer mornings that are objectively fantastic.

A text comes from Teddy, confirming we're on for Questie.

Teddy: Can we get saganaki at lunch?

Me: Never had it but I'm in.

Teddy: It's cheese they set on fire.

Me: You had me at cheese but clinched it at fire.

I sneak out so I'm not delayed by my mother trapping me in a conversation about my day and plans. Despite a chill in the air, it's sunny and I'm glad, because I want to be in a good mood for Teddy. I rephrase. I want to be in a good mood not for him but because I want to enjoy my day.

It's a subtle but important shift.

———

I arrive a few minutes early at Broadview Station, but that's no big deal since I'm used to being the one waiting for people. To my surprise, Teddy is in the station when I walk up the escalator.

"Dee!" He comes forward with two paper bags. "We need energy for today. I got us a chocolate chunk cookie and a baklava blondie."

He's dressed as Generic Man: Toronto Winter edition, with black boots, black jeans, and a black parka unzipped to reveal a gray cable-knit sweater. His glasses—lenses unsmudged from errant greasy fingers—and the starkness of the outfit highlight his features.

"A baklava blondie?" I ask.

He peers into the bag. "I thought it sounded interesting. We can split them even Stephen." He gives me a sideways glance. "Even Stephen?"

"Apparently that phrase comes from a Jonathan Swift book."

He whistles. "God, you are so brilliant. I can't stand it." Then he looks as if suddenly concerned. "You know I'm not testing you, right? I love that you know all this, but I'm not trying to put you on the spot or anything."

"I know," I assure him. "I like it. Usually people get bored of me being a *factory*." I wait to see if he gets it.

"Nice." Teddy shakes his head. "I can hold my own, though. I can talk your ear off for hours about what makes Lana Breton runway shows memorable."

The name rings a bell. "The one with the robots?"

He lights up. "Autumn/winter 2017. It was a commentary on the industrialization of fashion and loss of creativity. Thirty looks, all made completely by robots."

"Not hand-sewn?"

"No, that was the point. Only the robot looks were shown, but when attendees left the show, every look was displayed next to a version that had been done totally by hand. Iconic."

"That's fascinating. Have you met her?"

He nods. "She invited me to the show. Now for food."

The baklava blondie is a chewy vanilla brownie with layers of honey-saturated baklava on the top and the bottom and sprinkled with bright green pistachios. Teddy licks around the honey, and my eyes follow his tongue before I snap out of it. We're on a friendly outing, and ogling Teddy is not appropriate.

Even if he's well worth an indirect and respectful ogle. This isn't only my opinion. People have been glancing in our direction as they pass through the doors, and there have been more than a few double takes.

Teddy gives me a half smile. "Why are you looking at me so intently?"

"You don't dress like a fashion designer," I say to avoid the somewhat spicier truth.

"Technically, I should dress like a merchandising executive. What does a fashion designer dress like?"

"More...trendy?"

"Most of the designers I know don't bother much with their wardrobes since the focus is on dressing others." Teddy passes me a napkin. "You want to be comfortable, and there's a lot of moving around."

After the last bite of cookie, which was good and had a crunchy sprinkle of salt, he takes my paper bag to throw away with his. Outside we stand blinking in the sun as I start the game and read out the first clue. "Broadly speaking, when a prince pelts rocks at lions, they duck out of the way," I say. "*Broadly* must be Broadview Station, so we're off to a good start."

We head out to the Danforth, falling in step as easily as if we were meant to walk all paths together.

"Pelts rocks at lions as they duck out of the way." Teddy is cute when he thinks, teeth nibbling on his short lower lip as his eyes dart around his surroundings. "Duck. Duck."

"Goose," I interrupt.

He shoots me a look as he fights a smile at my admittedly juvenile joke. "Duck out of the way."

I happen to be looking toward the bridge as he says this, and suddenly it clicks. "It's like a homonym. *Duct* with a *t*."

His eyes lift to the sky as he thinks through the next connection. "Duct. Via. That's *way* in Latin. *Duck* out of the *way*. The Bloor Viaduct."

We head west toward the bridge, where we stop at a pillar. "There aren't any carvings of lions," I say as I circle it.

Teddy looks at the bridge, then starts googling. "Try literary."

I peer down to the Don Valley, where cars drive beside the sluggish brown river. "Do any authors live around here?"

"Think Canadian literature."

"Bloor Viaduct," I say, rubbing my nose and glaring at the bridge with its tilted crosses lining the edges. A glimmer of Ms. Sweed's English class breaks through. "Lion. Oh my God. Michael Ondaatje's *In the Skin of a Lion* features the Bloor Viaduct."

He high-fives me. "Brilliant."

I find the clue, an R near the word Prince (its official name is the *Prince Edward Viaduct*), and we input the answer at the same time for fairness.

"Good job," I congratulate Teddy. "You got that fast."

"I have a strong motivation that other players might lack."

"You do?" I frown. "What?"

"They're not trying to impress the person first on the leaderboard."

I try to get rid of the smile creeping over my face as Teddy holds my gaze. He's serious.

Then I panic over the proper thing to say and ruin the moment by choosing the saddest and most pathetic response: a thumbs-up. "Ah, ready for the second clue?"

Teddy is unbothered by my awkwardness. "You bet."

———

We find the next two clues with relative ease and make our way along the Danforth. Teddy's eyes linger on a pair of open-backed clogs as we pass a shoe store. "Those would look cool as sneakers, wouldn't they?"

I have no idea if they would or not. "Is this how you get ideas? Looking at other designs?" I listen closely because of the conversation with Alejandra and because it's a pleasure to hear his thoughts.

"It depends. Sometimes it seems to come out of the blue, but if you try, you can usually trace an idea back to the exact moment of inspiration." Teddy touches some early pussy willows tied with twine in a green bucket.

"The exact moment?" I dodge a woman pushing a stroller with a dog leash tied to her waist.

"Well, I did these sukajan jackets once."

"I saw one online. I loved it." The embroidered jackets were in denim instead of satin and currently $8,000 at a resale shop.

His entire face creases into a huge smile. "You like them?"

"I do." We wait at the corner for the light to turn. "Continue with your jacket story."

"It's embarrassingly straightforward. I saw a woman wearing a black-and-gold satin jacket with an embroidered tiger and thought, *Wow, that would be great in denim.*"

"That was it?"

"For the idea. The research and design took longer. I did a collaboration with a retired artisan in Okayama."

"The home of Japanese denim."

His hand grazes mine and I want to grab it. "I'm not surprised you know that."

We take a break to argue about the next clue before finding it tucked near the WELCOME TO GREEKTOWN sign that spans the street.

"You sound like you miss designing." His voice had been regretful.

"It's not an option for me at the moment. I promised my father I would focus on Celeste as part of our deal, and I can't interfere with Michael. He can be...well." Teddy kicks some old ice down the sidewalk.

"I bet," I mutter. It's my turn to kick the ice, and it flies into the street to get crushed by a passing car. Teddy knocks over another bit. No shortage of ice in Toronto, even in March.

Teddy looks at me curiously. "What do you mean?"

His hazel eyes are keen, and I realize how much I want to talk to him about what Alejandra told me. The cone of silence means I need to control my tongue. "Nothing," I say. "Only that you make a good point. I can see there'd be tension."

"There is," he says.

I kick the ice again and wonder what about this exchange seems a little different. Then it comes to me.

"You don't seem as stressed talking about work," I say.

Teddy raises his eyebrows. "Was I that bad?"

"There's been a significant change." I think back. "It really started when you talked to your team."

Teddy's brow furrows as we check around a small park for the next clue. "My perspective might be changing?"

"Is that a question or a statement?"

"I don't even know. The relationship with my team is improving. I started a new project, and that's interesting, but you're right. Six months ago, I don't think I would have bothered to *be* interested. It would have been another thing I had to do."

"What shifted your attitude?"

Teddy pauses near a bust of a serious-looking man and tilts his head to the side as he rubs his finger along the plaque at the bottom. "I'm not sure, really. It might be you."

"Me?" I turn around to see if he's serious. "How so?"

"You're passionate about what you're doing." Teddy watches me with a small smile. "I wanted that back in my life. I'm not going to give up on Mom's company. It's mine now."

"I'm glad," I say, glowing. Knowing you made a difference is the best gift.

"Me too."

There's a softer feeling between us as we finish the game, typing REALITY into our phones and confirming our top two spaces on the leaderboard. We head for lunch, and at the table, I relax into the warmth, rich with the smell of garlic and roasted meat. Teddy pulls off his hat and does all his usual little adjustments to maintain order—glasses up and hand run through hair. I don't know why these actions are so appealing to me.

"Do I have hat head?" he asks, seeing me watching him.

"Not at all." Teddy looks fantastic even with his nose red from the cold. He would look incredible in anything. Or nothing.

He smiles at me, and my whole body tightens because I've come to crave this expression. It lights up his whole face, crinkling the edges of his eyes and making that upper lip more delectable.

The server drops off the menus and we order tea to warm up. Teddy insists on the saganaki, and I want the Greek fries.

We look at the dips. "What's tirokafteri?" he asks, going to search it on his phone. "Damn, my battery died."

"It's made with feta."

"Thanks." He tucks his dead phone into his pocket. "Who needs Google when I have you?"

I'm toasty but can't tell if it's from being with Teddy or the satisfaction of being inside after hours in the cold. Teddy looks around, bringing that stellar profile into view. Oh, it's absolutely because of him. It's going to be torture to make it to June without touching him.

We talk about Questie until a waiter swoops down on us, holding a metal plate with what looks like a golden slab. He sprinkles some clear liquid from a bottle—ouzo from the licorice smell—and lights it on fire as he and Teddy yell, "Opa!" The flame leaps up blue and yellow before quickly extinguishing, and he sets the platter on the table with a flourish.

Teddy squeezes some lemon over the saganaki. "Try it with the bread."

I take a taste and, wow, I'm in love with a cheese. I would marry this cheese. The ouzo burned off to leave the outside golden and crispy and the inside a luscious, melty goodness. "This is delicious."

Teddy looks tickled I'm enjoying the dish he chose and passes me some more. After we eat, he takes my phone to check an online Questie thread when he jolts to attention.

"What's up?" I ask, cold premonition prickling at me.

Teddy's face is grave when he looks up. "Alejandra texted you. Alejandra Diaz from work."

I remember we'd exchanged numbers last night and straighten in the chair. "Were you looking through my messages?" I demand.

"The notification dropped down, and I tapped it by accident."

I glare at him. "By accident. I bet."

"Believe me or don't, but it's true and I have questions." Teddy looks down and reads. "'Changed my mind about M's designs because fuck that guy. Let's talk.'"

He passes over the phone, and I confirm, yes, that's the message. My legs go numb and I shift to let the blood flow through, making a bit of a fuss to buy myself some time and wishing I could manifest myself out of this mess. This is Alejandra's story. I can't squeal it to Teddy.

"M. Is that Michael Madison?" he asks.

I look at the email, wanting to talk about it but knowing I shouldn't.

"Dee, what's going on?" he demands.

"It's something to do with work. With Celeste."

"Thanks, I figured that out. What is it?" His eyes are fierce, and he's frowning so hard his mouth is bracketed with white.

I make my decision. "I can't tell you," I say. The trust I have with Alejandra is new, and tattling to the CEO's son isn't the way to build it. "I'm sorry."

He takes a deep breath. "Doing good by my team is only the start. If there's something wrong, I want to help."

I feel like a heel. "Alejandra trusted me. I can't until I ask her."

Teddy bites his lip. "You're right. I know you're right."

"You don't need to make up for lost time," I say softly, holding his gaze until he nods. "Give me a day."

He sighs but then he touches my hand, looking more determined than I've seen him apart from finding a Questie clue. "I can wait."

We finish up, but the rest of the afternoon is more somber. I blame Michael. The big jerk.

SEVENTEEN

DAILY AFFIRMATION: I LIVE MY TRUTH. WHAT
DOES THIS EVEN MEAN? I NEED TO CHECK
A BETTER WEBSITE FOR THESE THINGS.

On Monday, Grandma is in the kitchen when I come down for work, her hands already curled around a mug and Chilly on her lap. That's strange. Mom is upstairs getting ready, and Grandma hasn't made her own tea since she arrived. It's become a bit of a routine between the two of us, and like many routines, it's forced at least the perception of a connection.

"Your father made it," she says. "It's not as good as yours."

I glance down and see it's not quite opaque. "Needs more milk," I say as I pour it in.

She sips with satisfaction. "That's better."

"It was nice of him to make it," I remind her.

Grandma nods, and again, it's such a small thing for her to acknowledge him but so huge at the same time. Chilly's whiskers tremble, and I reach out to give him a pet.

"Do you want to hold him?" She lifts him into my hands. His light grey fur is so soft it gives the strangest sensation of not touching anything but warmth.

"I've never felt anything like this," I say.

"He's a good chin," she says. "Comforting. You can hold him when you need to. Most chinchillas don't like it, but he's always been social."

He starts to wiggle, and Grandma takes him back to put in his cage. Why does she need comfort, and why does she think I do? I think about what it would be like to ask her that and what I'd do with the answer. I'm not sure but I might want to try. One day.

Teddy's usual text comes as I'm eating a banana left out by my mother and listening to Grandma fill Chilly's food bowl. Instead of a trivia fact, it's a single question.

> **Teddy:** You'll talk to Alejandra today?
> **Me:** It has to be tomorrow. That was the soonest we could meet.

I hadn't wanted to put anything potentially incriminating in writing, so when I'd texted Alejandra back I'd only set a date and time.

> **Teddy:** Thank you. Also do you know Japan has almost seven thousand islands?

I leave the house with a wave to Grandma, who is sitting alone on her bed in the cluttered living room, hands folded in her lap.

The morning at Celeste goes by without me seeing anyone but Jenna and a sea of spreadsheets. In the afternoon, I head over to Gear Robins for my one-on-one with Vivian, where we're going to go over my initial findings deck. The meeting with Celeste isn't for a while, but she insisted I get it in early for her to review since it's my first time doing one. I'm confident it's what's needed, and I'm eager for Vivian's praise and the confirmation that I have a handle on this job.

Vivian greets me and then points to the conference room. "Let's talk in here, where it's private."

There's nothing to be nervous about. I poured my heart and soul into that deck, staying up until three in the morning typing to the accompaniment of Chilly's wheel and Grandma's robust snoring. I visualized the hell out of it and manifested success. This deck is faultless.

"This deck is subpar," Vivian says as soon as she shuts the door. "I'm disappointed."

I blink, unable for a moment to reply. When I do, I try to at least sound as if I'm open to feedback. "It's what you asked for. I looked at all the qualitative and quantitative data before I pulled it into the model."

"The numbers are not the problem," Vivian says. "The language is."

"The language?" I echo.

"Look at this wording. *Celeste is behind the industry on every measure.*"

"Well, they are."

"They don't want to hear that. We talk about opportunities for growth."

I was in communications, so I get this, but still. "Don't we need to be honest about the findings to know where to direct the effort?"

Vivian taps the deck printout. "The numbers are honest. How we frame the numbers is art. A list of allegations is not going to facilitate moving the client along the model."

"They're facts, not allegations."

"That's not my point, Daiyu."

I flip through the deck with shaking hands. Much of the document is covered with red marks from Vivian's pen, and her edits make Celeste sound like it's one step away from beatification. The anodyne pull quotes are all about the beauty of belonging and the benefits of diversity. People technically said them, but not in this context. At all.

"This isn't right," I say stubbornly.

"We talked about this. I don't know how else to get through to you." Her irritation is clear as she plants her hands on her armrests. "I've been doing this work for decades."

"I know and—"

"You will not interrupt me. I need the work *done*. I don't have the space to deal with you banging your moral drum. Celeste is expecting this project to be completed to the standards that Gear Robins, the company that hired you, has laid out. I'm going to ask you one more time. Can you do your job?"

"This is my job! It was in the job description! I'm supposed to design and deliver best-in-class diversity and inclusion recommendations to improve the working lives of stakeholders!" Or something like that, but I'm too upset to remember the original wording.

"Which you do by following our proprietary model, not your gut."

She doesn't *get* it. There's more at stake than a silly model, which can't possibly address the needs of every company and definitely not Celeste.

"The creative director is stealing work from young designers and passing them off as his own," I burst out. "He's useless at his job and bitter about the woman who's actually running the studio. He's ruining people's lives. I need to do something about it."

She twists her head to look at me, astonished. "You? That has nothing to do with you. Your job is to look at where the company is on the People First model and make recommendations based on that, not play vigilante."

"But, Vivian—"

"But what, Daiyu? Do you have proof?"

I shake my head. "Not yet."

"You have no proof, so you have an unsubstantiated claim that you should recommend the person report through the proper channels so Celeste can deal with it. It's not your job."

Not my job. I shift around the papers on the table.

"That's wrong," I say, heart pounding, and move my hands down so she can't see them shaking. "I'm going to do my best to make a real change at Celeste. That's why I got into this work, and you want me to stop?"

"Your motivations are not my concern, Daiyu. Talk to Will about nurturing your career here. My problem is the job you were hired to do, which is what the sales team has negotiated with Celeste. For money, because they are paying for a report and recommendations based on our assessment, which is in turn based on our methodology."

"I have to do what I think is best." I'm not going to lie. Surely she has to see I'm doing the right thing.

Vivian's expression doesn't change. "That's your choice."

I look up, glad she understands.

"However, it's not the answer I need to hear." She stands up. "I'll discuss this with Will. Work out the rest of the day here until we decide a plan of action. I'm sorry it came to this, but I've given you plenty of opportunities to listen. I have deadlines to meet and you insist on thinking you know better than me or the company."

I stare at her as she leaves. I'd seen enough movies that I'd expected Vivian to agree with me. She was supposed to be struck with my eloquence and passion and promise to support me or something. At least hug me as music rose in a crescendo behind us.

She wasn't supposed to leave.

I tuck my hands between my knees and rock back and forth. I should have kept my mouth shut, but I thought once she knew, Vivian would be on my side. How could she not? Will that be me in a few years, telling the newbie to suck it up and do the job she's paid to do, not the work that matters? I guess not, since Vivian might have fired me. Can she even do that?

The silence of the conference room amplifies the little voice in my head whispering, *Wow, you really blew it.* It's too late to visualize a better outcome, and the voice scoffs anyway. I could have said what she wanted to hear, done what Jade suggested, and kept my head down until I had better information. But I have proof now, or at least proof that's good enough for me because I trust Alejandra. I try to focus on the sounds of the office around me to get my mind off my own thoughts. Two women are debating where to go for coffee. A man laughs about some sports ball game. Vivian is talking to someone about another client right outside the door. Then Will calls her name, loudly interrupting her.

"Excuse me," she says to whoever she's talking to. "Will, can I help you?"

"I asked you for that budget report. I expected it on my desk this morning." That man does not know how to modulate his voice.

"You told me about it yesterday afternoon, and it takes two days to get the information," says Vivian evenly. "I told you this already, but you'd also know if you did your own budgets."

There's a silence, and then Will speaks again. "One more day, and then this will be another issue to discuss on your performance assessment."

Does everyone in this office immediately go to the most extreme option? I stare at the door, wondering if I'm allowed to leave or if that will upset Vivian more, then jump in my seat when it bangs open. Vivian stands there, and for the first time, it seems like I'm seeing the human being, not the professional who flows between corporate cheerleading and irritation.

"You have no idea, Daiyu. No clue at all."

"Hey," I protest faintly.

She closes the door and regards me. "You know, every time someone thanked me for my bravery in a training session, I thought I was a role model. I liked my job. I loved my job, in fact. I was extremely good at it. Still am."

I blink at her. "What happened?"

"At first, it was the little things, but they got bigger," she says. "I was the most senior in the department, but they brought in a man, gave him my promotion, and told me they couldn't lose my expertise but he was a better fit for the role. They gave me half his responsibilities and a tiny raise when it turned out he couldn't handle it." She laughs. "I thanked them because I thought it meant they valued what I did. That they valued *me*."

I shift on the chair and keep quiet. She must be at her breaking point to be opening up like this.

"Then people started leaving because of the workload, so I took on more. How could I not? Things were happening, and people were finally open to change. Gear Robins saw it in terms of the bottom line, but I saw it as changing the world, and I was dedicated."

"You sound burned out," I say.

"Isn't everyone these days?" She looks at me, head tilted to the side. "What I've realized is this is a job, Daiyu. We're disposable. You can gussy it up with as much meaning as you want, but Gear Robins is a business, and businesses need to make money."

"I don't want to be like that," I say. "I started this job so I can make a difference. That's what I want to do. You wanted that, too. You said you were like me."

Vivian looks at me with a distant expression, and I force myself to not look away. Will's loud laughter comes from the hall as he jokes around with one of his usual buddies, and she purses her lips as her gaze shifts to the door.

"You know what? All right, Daiyu. Okay."

"Okay?" I repeat.

"You want to make a difference? I'll tell you how to make a difference. You will keep your nose down and do your job. You will also take notes."

"Notes?" My head is spinning at her about-face. It's like she's snapped, and I wonder if she'll regret this in the morning.

"You and your informant will gather evidence, as much as you can get. Dates, names. Who is he stealing from? They won't fire him because he treats people badly, but they might if Celeste's creative reputation is on the line. Keep it absolutely quiet. Who else knows?"

"No one but the person who told me."

"Never use your corporate email or the Wi-Fi for messages, either of you. Find out if your friend's phone is issued by Celeste, and if it is, make sure they don't use it to gather information. Don't search anything online at work or when hooked into the VPN. Make sure you're never seen together."

"For how long?"

Vivian picks up her neoprene lunch bag and her work tote. "How long what?"

"Do we take notes and not action?"

She tugs the top of the bag closed, then curses when it pops back open. "Until your contact gets fired and turns it over to an employment lawyer, or you find something so egregious it can't be ignored." Her mouth twists. "Mistreating staff is unfortunately not enough."

"Have you seen this before?" I ask.

"Oh yes. Come to me when you have the information, but in person. Never message me details, got it?"

"Why are you helping me?" I ask, confused.

Will's loud voice comes again, and she looks back at the door.

"Let's say I remember how you feel." She nods at the deck. "We've wasted enough time. That's the deck we're going to present, not your version. Am I clear?"

"Yes."

"Can you do that?"

"I can." Knowing I'm working behind the scenes to make change means the deck edits are much more palatable. She's given me the orange Popsicle of compromise, but it tastes like pink.

"Good. I'll talk to you later."

She leaves. Vivian is not what I expected, and I am uncomfortably aware that I had thought about her more as a representative of Gear Robins than as Vivian herself. I should have tried harder to talk to her, to get to know her. I could have shared about my life first, taken the first step. Perhaps I will next time we meet.

For now, I have work to do. Invigorated, I turn back to my deck.

EIGHTEEN

DAILY AFFIRMATION: I TRUST MY INTUITION
TO LEAD ME ON THE CORRECT PATH AND NOT
INTO A BUNCH OF, LIKE, BRAMBLES.

The next day at work finds me thinking about Teddy's hands. I've wasted an inordinate amount of time doing this when I should be contemplating Alejandra's problem and Celeste's woes. I guess I'm into hands now. Well, there are worst things to be into. Knees maybe. Elbows. Teddy's hands look sure and talented. I think about how they'd feel on me and instantly shut that down. Right now, as we potentially hover on the edge of conspiracy, the safest and smartest thing to be is friends and friends only.

However, it's work time, not Teddy-hand-fantasy time. Actually, it's lunchtime. I meet Alejandra at a little Cuban place on a side street that she guarantees offers total privacy from Celeste people.

"This is real Cuban," she says as she pours out water. "Not fancy Cuban fusion. You come here to eat with your mouth, not your eyes."

She banters with the server in Spanish for a minute and orders the paella while I go for the chicken. The restaurant has salsa music on low enough to not interfere with conversation but loud enough to provide atmosphere. Cuban flags hang from the walls with bunches of fake flowers, and the waxed tablecloth is worn. Two women passing a baby over the table sit in the front window, and nearby a man eats alone, chatting to the phone held up in front of his face as he forks up rice and beans.

"I need to tell you something," I say after the server leaves.

"I don't like the sound of this," she says.

"I'm sorry in advance."

"I definitely don't like the sound of this."

Over the course of the morning, I've tried to figure out a few ways to tell Alejandra about Vivian but all my eloquence disappears when she waves her hand to hurry me up. I come out with it all at once. "I had to tell my boss at Gear Robins about Michael. I didn't tell her your name, though."

"What? You did *what*? Without asking me?"

"She was about to fire me for not doing things according to the Gear Robins plan."

"Jesus, I wasn't expecting that as a reason." She looks around the restaurant. "It makes it harder to be mad you're a blabbermouth who did not respect the cone of silence, but not impossible."

"I'm sorry."

"You're sure you didn't use my name?"

"Absolutely."

"I should thank you for that at least." She puts her face in her hands and talks to the table. "What did you tell her?"

I recount the conversation, Alejandra with her head down but listening. Then she looks up, tossing her curls out of her eyes.

"Not that we have a choice, but you're sure we can trust her?"

"We can. She's implicated because she gave me advice on next steps."

"Next steps?"

I go through Vivian's instructions, Alejandra getting increasingly spooked by the level of corporate surveillance they suggest, and when I finish, she agrees they make sense.

She studies her phone as if a team of spies is listening. "I don't like that you told her, but you getting fired wouldn't help either of us, so I'll let this slide."

Thank God I kept my mouth shut with Teddy. I feel a wave of relief that I made the right decision.

The great thing about Alejandra is that, apart from with Michael, she doesn't seem to hold grudges. The server puts down the food, and Alejandra starts eating, her mood improving with every bite and her irritation at my big mouth fading. "This is so good," she says. "Want to try?"

I take it as complete forgiveness when she puts a few spoonfuls of paella on my plate and helps herself to my chicken when I push the food in her direction. The spicy chicken has been served with a fresh and tangy coleslaw that sets off the savory rice and beans. I try Alejandra's paella, which has about six grains of rice packed around chunks of sausage, shrimp, and peppers.

"There's something else I want to talk to you about," I say. The more I think about it, the more I like the idea of combining forces with Teddy, who will have access to information we don't. The problem is that Teddy is in management, and it might take some convincing for Alejandra to trust him.

"Given the first part of this conversation, I'm feeling a bit nervous."

"That's reasonable. You know who Ted is, right? At Celeste?"

She rolls her eyes. "Yes, I know who the owner's son is."

"What do you think about him?"

Alejandra pulls a mussel out of the shell and pops it in her mouth. "Why do you—"

"Dee?"

We stop eating and Alejandra looks at me, surprised. I turn around to see Teddy standing beside the table holding a white plastic takeout bag.

"Teddy?"

Alejandra goggles at him. "Dee? *Teddy*?" She looks between us with narrowed eyes. "You know each other?"

"Yes," I admit. "We're friends."

"Friends," Teddy confirms.

"We know each other from a hobby group," I add. That's true, although it sounds like we play Dungeons and Dragons each weekend before hitting the Ren Faire.

Teddy shifts his bag from one hand to the other. "Good to see you, Alejandra. Are you two talking about"—he belatedly remembers he's not supposed to know anything about Michael and ends with a weak—"stuff?"

Too bad Alejandra is smart and on the alert. "Oh my God. What does he know?"

"Nothing!" I hasten to assure her.

"I trusted you!" She gives me an injured look. "First you tell your boss, and now you tell him? A vice president? The owner's son, of all people? What's the matter with you?"

"You told your boss and not me?" asks Teddy.

I shoot him a look that says *later*. "Alejandra, I didn't say anything. This is what I wanted to ask you about."

"Ask *what*? How does he know about Michael if you didn't tell him?"

Teddy waves his hands, bag swinging close enough to my head that I need to duck. "It's not Dee's fault," he says. "I saw the message from you on her phone and asked her about it because I suspected it was about Michael. She wouldn't tell me anything until she spoke to you."

"Oh." She sounds mollified but then gives him a suspicious look. "So you can tell Michael what I'm saying about him?"

"Whatever it is, no."

She snorts. "Yeah, right."

"Can I sit?" he asks.

Alejandra looks conflicted, then waves him down. "Only because I'm not done eating," she grumbles. "I'm not letting you ruin a good paella. This shit's expensive."

Teddy sits down and opens his bag to offer his yuca fries. I take control of the conversation to formally ask her permission. "Alejandra, I want to tell Teddy what you told me. I won't if you say no."

"This seems like an idea with more downsides than up," she says. "Not to mention you've put me in a bit of an awkward spot with him right here."

"I can move away," offers Teddy.

"Too late now." She turns to me. "Convince me why this is a good idea."

"We can work together to make change at Celeste," I say. "You want to get proof about Michael. I want to help Celeste become a company where this kind of thing doesn't happen."

"What about you?" Alejandra directs this at Teddy.

"I want my company to be a place I'm proud of. If something is happening with Michael, I want to fix it," he says firmly. There's no trace of the old disengaged Work Ted in him.

She sighs. "Look, I'm going to declare another cone of silence here. No offense, Ted, but it's not like you've been a voice for revolution at the office lately. Why should I believe you?"

"I've been doing a lot of thinking about the way I've been approaching work and making adjustments, starting with myself and my team," he says. "I want to do more."

Alejandra chews thoughtfully, her eyes flitting between us. She looks unconvinced.

"Alejandra, you know what I did with Mars. You were there when I started at Celeste and saw what I tried to do in the beginning," he says quietly. "I'm trying again."

That seems to convince her. "You can tell him."

I turn to Teddy and look him in the eyes to emphasize the importance of what I'm going to say. "We suspect Michael is stealing designs from young designers and passing them off as his own. He's also trying to sabotage Alejandra, who has been doing his design work."

"Oh." Teddy pulls off his glasses and rubs his eyes. "Fuck." He puts his glasses back on and looks at Alejandra. "I'd always wondered how he managed to be so good after those shitty first attempts. Of course it's because of you, not because he did some soul-searching and managed to dig up some inspiration." He pauses, deep in thought. "Damn, you're good, Alejandra. You should be in Michael's role."

She looks at him but he's unflinching. "You mean that?"

"Absolutely," he says. "This proves he's incompetent and out of his league, even if my father refuses to see it and he credits Michael with Celeste's success." His expression darkens. "Which was originally based on my mother's work, so you can see that it's not the first time he's pulling this."

There's silence around the table as we look at each other. Finally I say, "That's it. We're in this together."

"What are we in exactly?" asks Teddy carefully. "What's going on? Were you plotting?"

"We were about to," I say. Teddy's foot brushes mine under the table, and we pull back quickly enough that my chair squeaks. A soft blush comes up to paint his cheeks.

"We don't have anything if people don't come forward," says Alejandra. "There are some suspicious shifts in how Michael approaches design, but that can be explained by wanting a new start or different influences."

"He's built up his relationships in the industry, too." Teddy eats some more fries with those exceptional fingers. "Some don't like him, but enough will give him the benefit of the doubt."

I take a fry. "Can you talk to your father about it?"

Teddy laughs out loud. "Not going to happen."

"Why not?"

He squints at a fork. "He won't believe me. He'll suspect I'm angling for Michael's job, and the idea of me designing makes him irrationally angry."

"Thinks it shows a lack of commitment to your current role?" asks Alejandra.

He nods.

"Then for now, the best thing we can do is pay attention." I try to ignore Teddy's foot near mine again. We aren't even touching, but I'm so aware of him that I might as well be sitting in his lap.

"That makes sense," agrees Alejandra. "I wish I knew the names of the designers, but the drawings were unsigned and the contact information pages were missing."

I frown. "We need to start looking for proof. Let's be stealthy and keep each other in the loop."

Alejandra pokes me in the arm. "Only us. No one else."

"No one else," I promise.

"Fine."

"Then I declare this cone of silence to be lifted. You may go about your business," I say in a lofty voice, like someone invoking Robert's Rules of Order.

Alejandra rolls her eyes and Teddy snickers. We're off to a good start and I lean back, happy we're working together. I can already taste success ahead of us, and it's sweeter than the tres leches cake Alejandra insists that we split.

NINETEEN

A few days later, Teddy invites me for an inspiration walk. "What's that?" I ask.

"It's when you walk around and look at things for inspiration."

"A walk, then?"

"Yes, but an *inspiring* one," he says. "I'm feeling flat and want to exercise whatever side of the brain boosts creativity."

"The right."

"See? I might have known that if I was being inspired."

High Park turns out to be too desolate, the skeletons of trees barely clothed in green even though it's almost officially spring, so we go over to Roncesvalles, where we grab coffee and sit in a parkette. Teddy perches on a tree stump with his sketchbook, turning the fractals of a bush into a fabric pattern, while I huddle across from him and eat overpriced gourmet cookies. I pick up my phone out of habit and then blink.

"Hey, Questie is looking for volunteers," I say.

Teddy glances up, eyes dipping down when he smiles even as his hand continues to move across his sketchbook. "For what?"

"That's pretty," I say idly, looking at the design. It has an art nouveau feel, like William Morris set in a Jetsons future. Teddy's right brain is working overtime, and it occurs to me that this is the first time I've seen him working on a fashion-related piece. I keep that to myself, not wanting to put him on the spot, but pleased for him.

"Thanks. Questie?"

I check the email. "They're expanding so they're looking for puzzle creators in cities around the world."

He puts down his pencil. "You'll be fantastic at that."

"What do you mean, me?" I eat another cookie—chocolate pretzel chunk—and offer him the last one.

He plucks it out of my hand, breaks it in half, and hands part back to me. "You're going to apply, aren't you?"

"No way. That's too hard. I'm a solver, not a creator."

"You could be." He looks at me intently. "Why do you think it's too hard?"

"It's not my thing," I say uncomfortably. That private list of clues on my phone is only for fun, a brain exercise not meant for public consumption. "I like doing the puzzles, not making them."

"I get it," he says in a gentle voice. "Although I'd do any puzzle you created." He sits up. "Whoa."

"What?"

"Shh," he whispers, bending so his ball cap covers his face. "Michael walked by."

"He did?" I crane my head around, and he grabs my arm.

"That was the most obvious thing I've ever witnessed," he grumbles, pushing up his glasses and leaning over to watch Michael go down the street. "You look like a meerkat on guard. What's he doing here?"

"What do you mean?"

"Michael doesn't live around here. He lives near Yorkville."

"The guy's allowed to go to a different neighborhood," I point out. "He's probably meeting someone for dinner."

"Unlikely. Michael eats at one of two spots, neither of which are close, and he goes to be seen."

"Then he's shopping."

"He wears thousand-dollar Prada T-shirts. Trust me, he's not shopping here." Teddy frowns down at his sketchbook. "He's up to something."

We look at each other, thinking the same thing. "We're going to follow him," I announce.

He snaps his sketchbook shut and stuffs it in his pocket. "Let's go."

This starts a brief debate on the best way to follow Michael without being seen. Teddy, having seen James Bond and *Mission: Impossible* movies, favors a more aggressive approach. I, who have seen those movies but additionally read an SAS book on effective surveillance, suggest we pretend to be shopping. "It gives us plausible deniability if he sees us."

"We'll have to explain why we're together."

"Because we're out shopping," I stress. "As friends do."

Teddy looks up as if mentally calculating, then gives me a smile that makes me draw in my breath. "For another seventy-nine days."

Oh, heart, stop jumping. "We're losing him."

We speed walk for about half a block to get Michael back in sight before we start window-shopping. "He's walking," reports Teddy.

I pick up a waxy apple from the greengrocer and pretend to check it over. "Okay."

Four steps later. "Walking."

"Good. I see him, too."

Another three stores down. "He's—"

"Walking?"

Teddy pouts. "No, checking his phone in front of a seedy bar."

We turn to gaze in the window of an antiques shop, trying to appear fascinated by the dusty sconces on display as we sneak peeks around the corner.

"He's looking around," whispers Teddy. "Pretend to shop."

He leans in as we turn back to the window, not touching me but close enough. Teddy feels safe, I realize. We're supposed to be friends right now, but I give in to the temptation to step closer. Teddy slides his arm around my waist and pulls me in. He's cider in front of fireplaces and a warm hand in the darkness. Belonging and comfort and honey in tea and butter in rum and soft fluffy pillows. It doesn't take long for my mind to stray from those PG thoughts. Now he's like hot hands on a summer night, the sheets a tangled mess. Slick skin under my mouth.

"Dee?" He looks down, so close, oh so close. "Are you cold? You're shivering."

I have a brief unfriendlike fantasy of shoving him against the store window and shocking the sensibilities of the woman on the other side looking at a mid-century modern lamp when I come to my senses and step back, mind sluggishly recalling why we're here at all. Michael. I glance down the street.

"He's going inside," I say. "Let's go take a look."

It takes Teddy a moment to move his arm. When he tugs me out onto the sidewalk, I fold all my feelings up into an emotions taco and eat it down. Seventy-nine days is a lot of days, and I'm already on thin ice with Vivian without adding Teddy into the mix. We decide to stroll by the bar casually so I can glance in. There's a better chance of Michael not recognizing me than Teddy.

"A quick look," Teddy coaches as he puts his ball cap on my head. It's too big and dips down over my eyes until he takes it back and tightens it. "Not for long."

"I've got this," I tell him. "I've been looking at stuff for years."

"Okay, okay."

When we pass, I see only one table is taken and it's near the door. Michael, unluckily, is facing me, talking to someone in a hat and black coat.

"He'll see us," I say, ducking my face away slowly so the sudden movement doesn't catch his attention.

"Damn."

We loiter in the alcove of the head shop two doors to the east until the door to the bar opens. The reflection in the window shows Michael striding by, face buried in a scarf and a wide black case in his hand.

Once we're sure Michael's gone, we return to the bar to see who he was meeting. There's no one there. Nor is anyone around.

"We missed our chance," I mourn.

"Michael was carrying what looked like a portfolio," says Teddy. "That helps."

"How?" I ask. "Also, why a portfolio instead of digital files?"

"Less of a paper trail?"

"That's something at least," I say. "We can get Alejandra to check the studio for the portfolio and find the designer."

"He's behind on the resort collection, and I've heard there are issues with the looks he wants to present. He'll be in a rush. He needs this."

The wind cuts down the street, swirling up dust. We look up.

"I don't like that sky," observes Teddy.

Over the last hour, the clouds have become gradually darker and lower. It starts to hail as Teddy speaks, marble-sized ice pellets falling one by one until suddenly the skies open.

"Under there," Teddy says, pointing to the alcove in a deserted storefront where we can shelter.

"Ow," I say in answer, because hail knocked into my eye when I looked up. We hustle over, and Teddy takes off his glasses and rubs them fruitlessly on his scarf before tucking them into his coat pocket.

Then he looks over. "You're shaking."

The chill combined with the delayed stress of trailing Michael has been enough to set me off. "A bit." My teeth chatter as I answer.

Teddy positions himself to block the worst of the wind, which is driving the hail toward us, then undoes his jacket and opens his arms in invitation. I walk forward like a sleepwalker, and he wraps his arms around me, tucking me inside the warmth of his parka and against his chest.

"I swear this wasn't on the forecast this morning," he murmurs into my hair.

"March," I mumble, eyes closed to absorb every sensation. "The only thing to expect is the unexpected."

"This is nice," he says. "Not the hail. That sucks. Being with you."

I nod against his sweater. His cologne is so light it's barely there, a warm, clean laundry scent that makes me want to curl up under a huge fluffy duvet with him.

We stand in silence for a few moments before I open my eyes to watch people on the street run by with bags over their heads as the ice pellets bounce on the ground. The hail turns to rain and the rain keeps coming. Teddy glances down at me. "I have a suggestion. I live close by. We can escape the weather and get warm before I drive you home."

I'm nodding before he finishes. The cold has frozen me right through, and the idea of taking the TTC or sitting in a café with wet clothes waiting for the storm to pass is unappealing. Seeing Teddy's place, on the other hand, is an attractive alternative.

"Yes," I say. "Lead the way."

When the weather shifts from downpour to drizzle, we make a run for it. Teddy's place is only a few blocks away, but we're soaked by the time we reach the door. My reflection confirms my suspicion that I look like a drowned rat, hair straggling down, but at least my mascara has held strong.

I hop from foot to wet squelching foot to keep warm as Teddy screws up the code, swears, and eventually gets us in. The lobby is small and empty, with exposed brick and a single black leather couch. A big painting of a fern sits above a real fern, and I don't know if it's a joke or a meta commentary on art reflecting life.

"I'm on the third story," says Teddy, directing me to the elevator. He presses the button, and I watch my jacket drip water on the shiny marble floor.

"The third floor of three? The penthouse?"

He pauses. "Yeah."

Then we're in front of a wide black door, and I get my first peek at Teddy's place.

TWENTY

I instantly love it. Teddy has a one-floor loft, and the wide rain-streaked windows reveal a terrace lined with big pots ready for spring planting. He starts fussing as I stand near the door taking stock.

"Let me get you a towel and some clothes," he says as he leaves a trail of wet footprints down the hall.

Not wanting to make more of a mess on the floor than I have to, I stay in the hall and peer around. The living room is bright and cheerful, with furniture that looks like it was chosen because it appealed to Teddy rather than to fulfill an aesthetic. There's an Eames chair with a low table piled messily with battered books, a big daybed with lots of pillows, folded blankets on a stool, and a deep couch in a pleasant pine color. The walls are exposed brick with a gallery wall of what looks like mini portraits that I can check when I won't wreck the silky Persian carpet with my rain-soaked self.

Teddy returns with an armful of towels and clothes. "There's a shower if you want to get warm," he says, handing the bundle over and slicking his wet hair back. "I can use the one in my room."

For a naughty moment, I wonder what he would do if I suggested we have one together. Then he shivers and runs his hands over his arms. Pressing our clammy skin together as we shower to fight off hypothermia is less sexy than I'd like our first naked encounter to be. I only wish it could happen now, or least when we warm up, and not after I'm done at Celeste.

This bites. I hate work. I detest impulse control. *Friends* is not a good enough silver lining to get me through this temptation.

"Thanks," I say.

I'm so cold that my skin prickles when I get under the hot water, but I'm soon dressed in a cozy sweatshirt and sweatpants so long I need to roll them up to keep them from dragging on the floor. Thank God my underwear is dry enough that I don't have to go commando in Teddy's borrowed clothes. That stretches the bounds of good guest behavior.

The whistle of the kettle sounds, and after I do an obsessive wipe - down of the bathroom floor, sink, and counter and check for stray hairs left in the shower, I pad out with my bundle of wet clothes and towels. Teddy is in the kitchen taking down some mugs, and when he turns around and blinks, I feel almost painfully cute and dainty. His voice sounds a bit choked when he asks if I'm warm enough.

I nod, doing my best to be cool about the way he's looking at me. Teddy's hair is damp and falling over his face. He's in jeans and barefoot, with the sleeves of his gray hoodie shoved up in a classic boyfriend look.

I hope something happens to make him less attractive, like he has talons for toenails, but no go. They're regular old toes. Actually, they're kind of pretty for toes. I groan inwardly. I'm not made of steel. I've already spent the last ten minutes picturing him under the shower, eyes closed and arms up to rinse his hair like he's starring in soft-light porn created solely for the woman's gaze, or at least one woman's. It's unfair how difficult he's making this for me.

"I'll make ginger tea," he says, tearing his eyes away from the wide neckline of my—his—sweatshirt. "Do you want me to put those clothes in the dryer?"

"Yes, please." I hand them over.

"Make yourself at home." He disappears through a door, and I go to check out the portraits. They're a random selection of objects, from hammers to lamps to jellyfish.

Then I catch sight of another room.

The sound of the dryer starts up, and Teddy brings over my tea. "You lied to me," I accuse as I take it.

He freezes. "No. Did I? I'm sorry. About what?"

I point to the room or, more accurately, studio. "You didn't stop designing."

Teddy deflates. "I didn't lie," he says. "Not exactly."

"Then what am I looking at?"

"This is recent." He pulls the door open all the way. "It was shut for years but you inspired me to try again."

"Why didn't you tell me?"

"I was embarrassed." He leans against the wall and stares into the room, which is a smaller and messier version of the Celeste studio. A long worktable fills most of the space, its surface mountainous with fabric and pieces of paper and flanked by a sewing machine. On each side is a dress form, one with a half-made blouse that shines under the lights and the other with a high-waisted A-line skirt. Bolts of fabric lie along the back wall next to neatly labelled boxes.

"Why?" I ask, bewildered.

"I'd failed at something I loved. Something I wanted so bad it hurt." He gives me a shy look. "You know I cried when I decided to fold Mars? I fought to the very last moment, hoping, praying to the goddamn universe that something would save it. Dad wouldn't extend me a loan, and I'd tapped out all my other resources. I'd worked so hard, and I had to let it go."

My instinct is to say something along the lines of how it all works out, but I crush that like a frat boy with an empty beer can. I don't want him to feel like this doesn't matter. "I can tell how much it hurts."

"I thought I'd made my peace with it," Teddy says, walking into his studio.

I follow him in and reach my hand out to the fabric, which slips across my palm, warm and soft with a drape that belies its thickness.

"Then you started designing?"

He looks around the room. "You know I love Questie, right? It's like all the fun I used to have was funneled into that single bright spot. Then we were playing one day and you said something about life being duller without it."

"I remember."

"That was it." He shrugs. "Apart from Questie, I'd been living in grayness everywhere, not only work. I couldn't do it anymore. You inspired me to want to be all of me again, at work and with this."

"Oh," I say faintly. Such a big change to come from such a small comment. "I'm glad."

He picks up a zipper and slides it through his fingers. "Me too."

He looks at me and I feel my face heat up. I put down the fabric and point to the dress forms. "Tell me what I'm looking at. What are you making?"

Teddy transforms into a human happiness beacon. "It's an evolution of Mars," he says. "Multiuse designs in sustainable fabrics I've spent years sourcing. I tried to get Celeste to use them."

"Did they?"

"Of course not. Michael's idea of an exciting fabric is printed linen."

"That is a deeply niche insult."

He laughs. "True, though."

"The clothes are multiuse? What's that mean?" I trail after him to a hanging rack where he pulls out what looks like a toga.

"This is a shirt, a skirt, a sarong, a cape, and a dress to help reduce overall consumption," he says, shaking it out. "Made of a new fabric created from renewable kelp in a clean process."

I touch it. It's a knit but I can tell it's not the kind of fabric to cling to lines and lumps, if that's something you worry about.

"Want to try it on?" he asks.

I look at it doubtfully. It's voluminous but there are fastenings along the seams. "I won't fit into a size two sample."

"Few do, so I design for an average-sized North American woman." He waves his hands at the dress forms, which, now that I look at them, are closer to my size than I'm used to seeing.

"How does it work?" I ask, lifting up a fold of material.

Teddy wraps it around his waist and deftly belts the sash before taking it off and turning it into a dress that ties at the neck. It looks comfortable but also elegant and sophisticated.

I take the garment—there's no other word that accurately describes it—and Teddy slips out of the room so I can strip off my sweats and put it on along with the bodysuit he left.

It's easy to get the hang of the design, and the first look I try is a long flowing skirt with a glam 1970s feel that reminds me of Studio 54. Then I pull up some hidden ties along the seams, hike up the top, and it becomes a minidress, cute but easily wearable.

"How is it?" calls Teddy a few minutes later.

"You can come in." I'm busy checking myself out in the mirror. I've turned it into a strapless dress, which admittedly would look better without the top of the bodysuit sticking out.

Teddy pushes the door open and stares at me until I feel self-conscious.

"Did I do it wrong?" I ask, pulling at one of the ties.

He shakes his head emphatically. "You look gorgeous." He comes closer, eyes not moving off me and swearing when he walks into the table. "It's...this is the first time I've seen it on a person."

I do a spin. "Feel free to test it out."

His eyes widen. "Can I?"

"Sure. How often do I get to be a fitting model?"

"More like a muse," he says. "Let me get some pins. Tell me if you get bored, though. Or want to stop. This is a huge favor you're doing me."

Teddy grabs a plastic bracelet with a pincushion attached and drops to his knees in front of me. Then he looks up, mouth quirking to the side and instantly supplanting my earlier shower fantasy with some extra premium material.

"My mom used to have one of those pincushions that had the people with little queues holding hands." I stare at the wall so I'm not thinking about Teddy's position. "Dad bought me my own in Chinatown when I was a kid, and I kept it on the shelf like a figurine."

"My mother had those, too, and ones that looked like tomatoes from my nonna." He hesitates. "I'll need to touch you. Is that okay?"

I nod, not willing to trust my voice. He looks up at me as he trails his hand across my hip and tugs the dress slightly. I try not to gasp, but it escapes me and Teddy's eyes widen as he bites his lip, teeth indenting that gorgeous mouth.

Then he looks down, takes a pin, and twists the fabric in place.

TWENTY-ONE

I try to cover how quick my breathing has become. It's quiet as Teddy works, muttering to himself about ease and gathers as I turn to the left or lift my arms according to his gentle guidance. He takes off his glasses to peer at a section of the dress, leaning so close his breath warms my skin through the fabric.

The rain beats steadily against the window. It's a struggle to avoid looking at his hands—my weak spot on the best of days—as they flicker across my body, and I end up training my gaze on a pair of scissors on the desk. It offers a much less interesting view, and I eventually calm down.

After a few minutes, Teddy sits back on his heels, and I look in the mirror at what he's done. I'm not sure how, but with a few pins, he's transformed the dress into a brand-new look. The material is nipped at the waist and lies on my hips in a way that accentuates my curves.

"I can add some internal ties to make another dress option," he says, groping across the table for his glasses. I hand them over, and he puts them back on.

"Anything else you want me to try?" I ask. The offer feels almost selfish since it's such a thrill to see him work.

Teddy rises to his feet and picks through the rack before handing me a dress. "How about this?"

I pull it on when he leaves to give me privacy. This time, the material is so sheer it's almost invisible, and he's somehow layered it so it covers the goods but maintains a fairylike lightness.

Teddy comes in to find me examining the sleeve. "This is a new technology that spins recycled plastic like cotton candy," he says.

"It's amazing," I say, holding my arms out to see how it falls.

"Mmm." Teddy is already looking at the darts. "I knew those should be farther back." Off go the glasses and on goes the pincushion wristlet.

By the time we work through another dress, a pair of wide-legged pants that were the exact flattering design I've been searching for my whole life to fit my short and curvy legs and can be buttoned up to make culottes, and some skirts paired with a tank made of the same recycled material as the floaty dress, the rain has stopped and night has fully fallen.

Teddy sits on a rolling chair in front of me, hands hidden in the folds of my shirt and occasionally brushing the bare skin of my stomach as he pins the hem. Each touch leaves an electric tremor in its wake. Teddy takes my hand to bring me over to the long mirror hung on the far wall, pulling the curtains shut on his way.

There's no huge transformation. I haven't put on lipstick or high heels to suddenly become the most beautiful woman in the room. No crowd of onlookers falls silent as I descend a staircase. I have a crooked part in my hair, which has dried stringy. My face, except for that incredible mascara, is bare and shiny.

But the blouse Teddy gave me to wear is a lovely sherbet orange that doesn't wash me out as I would have expected. My skin glows, cheeks a soft pink that I've never been able to achieve with rouge. Same with the eyes. Normally a basic brown, in the mirror, they look sparkly.

"What kind of light do you use in here?" I ask, looking at the ceiling. "Those soft white bulbs are magic. The outfit, too."

"It's not the clothes or the lights. It's you." Teddy stands behind me looking at us in the mirror, and I forget about telling him that bulb brightness is measured in lumens while energy consumption is watts. He makes a motion as if to brush my disheveled hair behind my ear, then flushes and drops his hand to his side.

"Teddy." My need for his touch is almost a physical ache.

"You know," he says in a contemplative tone. "I've never thought so much about time in my life. Never thought about how long four months can be. One hundred and twenty days. Two thousand eight hundred and eighty hours."

"You calculated the hours?"

"Of course I did. The day we decided to limit this to friends. It would almost be easier if we'd decided to not see each other until June, but I get glimpses of you at work. We play Questie and go for coffee, and each time I wish I could have more."

We watch each other's reflection, and Teddy is the one to break.

"We made an agreement about being friends while you're working at Celeste," he says. "I'd never pressure you, but I want you to know that if you want more, like immediately, I'm willing. Very willing. If you don't, I understand and won't say another word. I value your friendship on its own and can handle another one thousand eight hundred and ninety-six hours."

Then he stops talking so I can decide. Wanting Teddy is a given, but I should wait until I'm done at Celeste to pursue anything. That's the smart thing to do. Absolutely the wisest course of action and of course the one I'll choose. It only makes sense.

I meet his eyes in the mirror. "I don't want to wait."

That was not what I was supposed to say, but when his lips part, I have no regrets.

"Good."

My knees weaken at his husky tone but I don't move yet. There's more to say. "If work finds out that we're..." I don't even know how to end the sentence. Dating? Together? Potential bang partners? I let it go and move on. "It would be a problem."

He moves forward so he's almost touching me. "We're in a conspiracy to get rid of the creative director," he says. "I'd say we've already crossed the line of what they'd consider questionable workplace behavior."

"That's true." What's one more risk on top of the others? "It's not like we'd be making out in the boardrooms."

"Unless that's something you're into." He grins and my chest almost hurts with how many beats my heart skips. "I wouldn't judge. Or complain."

"Whatever happens would be totally private until I'm done with Celeste," I say. "Gear Robins would not be pleased with me, even if you're not actively involved in the project."

"Agreed, because my father would be even unhappier." He frowns. "He'd see it as a total lapse of judgment as well as a hit against him personally, thanks to his views on workplace relationships. Did I tell you he fired two people who were dating even though they were in different departments?"

"No." I raise my eyebrows. "Are you sure you want to do this?"

"Are you?"

A heavy silence falls over us. Am I sure? Parts of me are extremely sure. My internal struggle is over before it even begins because I want this. I want him and the universe has put him right in my path. I would be inviting cosmic wrath if I didn't do this. I nod. "I am."

"Me too." His answer is nothing but a breath, and those hands, big and a little rough from not using a thimble, come up to grip my arms. In the mirror, I can see my pulse beating under my skin when I tilt my head to the left. It's enough for him to trace his lips along the side of my throat, my skin almost lifting to his gentle touch. He pauses when he reaches the base of my neck and tugs aside the collar of the blouse to kiss my shoulder, pulling out the stitches of the basted seam with a popping noise.

"I've wanted to do this for a long time," he says. "That kiss at the subway was torture."

I watch this all in the mirror, his body dipped down behind me as he kisses along my shoulder, his one hand holding the collar free for his mouth. His other hand has dropped to spread over my stomach as he brings me closer. Then he pulls back and our eyes meet again, his lips red and mine pale, both of us breathing hard.

He shifts his weight to purr in my ear. "By the way, did you know the first recorded kiss is in the Vedas from around thirty-five hundred years ago?"

Obscure trivia as seduction tactic. "Come here," I say, turning around.

He laughs as I wrap my arms around his neck. Those lusciously full lips of his are almost insultingly soft. I have no shame as I step into him.

When we resurface, Teddy's lips are swollen, and this time, I give in and press down on his mouth with my finger to see it dent. He kisses my hand before tracing his thumb along my jawline as he dips back in to kiss near my ear, then lets his head rest on my shoulder.

The phone rings, a strident, shrill sound that breaks the silence of his studio.

"Forget it," Teddy whispers, but I glance over. Why does he have it set to ring instead of ignoring calls on silent like normal people?

"It's your father."

He steps away from me and glares at the phone. "Shit."

"You'd better take it." My voice cracks and I clear my throat. "I'll get changed."

Teddy drops a kiss on my head and grabs his phone, answering it as I leave to get my clothes from the dryer. "What's up, Dad?"

In the laundry room, I bury my face in my clothes, which smell a bit like Teddy and far better than the Chilly snacks/weed combo I'm used to from my own house. I'm almost sad to take off Teddy's work, which makes me feel striking in a way my jeans don't. The clothes in his studio are phenomenal. It's a different level from what Alejandra does for Celeste, no shade to her since she's constrained by a corporate brand identity. Teddy's looks are unique and meant for someone who wants to be different, rather than a typical Celeste customer, who wants to look the same as their friends.

Through the wall, Teddy talks about budgets and something called allocation. I run my fingers through my hair to try to restore order but soon give up. Jade's hair always falls perfectly in place, but I inherited Dad's cowlick at the back of my head, making clean, straight parts an eternal struggle.

"Dee?" Teddy calls from the living room.

I come out, carefully holding the skirt and blouse, and hand them over. Teddy is frowning and bunches them up before tossing them on the couch without looking, a far cry from the delicate pride of earlier.

Except when he ripped the collar to kiss me.

"Everything okay?" I ask.

"I need to go into the office," he says. "Dad wants some forecasting done, and I need my files from work."

"At this time of night? On Sunday?"

"Not unusual. I'm sorry about this. Do you want a drive home?" He touches my sleeve and rubs it in his fingers. "Oh good. All dry."

At least the clothes are one thing that's dry. I nod. "I'd like a ride, thanks."

Before I get out of the car, he gives me a last kiss, this one a sweet press of his lips on my cheek as his hand smooths my messy hair, and I float into the house.

TWENTY-TWO

DAILY AFFIRMATION: WHEN FACED WITH A CHOICE,
I AM A WOMAN WHO DOESN'T ALWAYS MAKE
THE SMARTEST ONE. I VALIDATE THAT TO MYSELF!
THE UNIVERSE WILL BLESS MY INTUITION.

*T*he word *clasp* is from a combination of *clutch* and *grasp*. *Ginormous* is *gigantic* and *enormous*. *Nervouscited*, according to *My Little Pony*'s Pinkie Pie, is a mix of *nervous* and *excited*. I need a new portmanteau to match how I feel.

How about *guilpy*?

First, we have *guilt*. *Guilt* because kissing Teddy was a possibly unprofessional action that I would not like to have to defend in front of Vivian. Combine that with *happy,* for the complete satisfaction of being able to replay the moment he pressed against me.

Or there's *regliss*. That encapsulates regret that I've made a sticky work situation worse and mixes it with the bliss of knowing Teddy wants me the way I want him.

Fuck it. I stand by my choice, which is confirmed when Teddy sends me an affectionate good-morning text that has me grinning at nervous strangers for the rest of my commute. The morning passes relatively quickly even though my head pops up every time someone walks by my door in the hopes of seeing Teddy. It never is.

Around eleven, it's snack time, and I wander out to the vending machines in the back hallway to see Teddy in a fitted navy suit and no tie. He looks good. Very good. Good enough to stop me dead.

"Oh, hi." He checks to see if anyone is around.

"Hi." I try to look serious, a coworker greeting a coworker. I stand beside him, then step back, then forward. What's too close for work? A step away? Better make it two. "This is weird."

"I feel like we're sneaking around and we're literally beside a watercooler, corporate shorthand for the place you're supposed to hang around and talk." He asks what I want and hands over the chocolate after it bumps down through the machine, letting his fingers linger on mine. "You're good for tonight?"

Alejandra had summoned us, saying she had news.

"Yes, I'll meet you there." We all decided to go separately to avoid speculation from other Celeste staff.

He makes a face. "I get it but look forward to the day when a streetcar ride together doesn't feel dangerous."

Voices come from around the corner, so we head out in opposite directions. The rest of the day has me thinking about Teddy to the point of accidentally writing his name in my document, forcing me to do a search to make sure I haven't missed any others. He texts before I leave.

Teddy: Should we tell Alejandra about us?

Us. I like the sound of that.

Me: Not yet. There's enough going on.

That's an excuse, though. This thing we have is so new I want to hug it to my chest like a secret, at least for a while.

I arrive at the bar after Teddy and Alejandra, who sit on either side of a back booth. Teddy is pouring out red wine from an opaque blue-and-white pottery jar with a narrow neck. They greet me and shift down to give me space. Dilemma. If I sit with Alejandra, I can look at Teddy but won't be able to touch him. If I sit with Teddy, it's the opposite. Is that too obvious? I debate my options until Alejandra points beside her.

"Jesus, sit down already."

I bundle my coat up and give it to Teddy—as the person with more space, he's obliged to keep the coats on his side—and do as I'm told. Alejandra pushes over a glass, and we begin an introductory round of work/weather/transportation complaints.

When we're done, Alejandra refills the glasses with an air of cere-mony. "I've got something," she says in a low voice.

Teddy and I lean in.

"About *him*?" I ask. I don't want to say Michael's name in public, although we look so shady it would be clear to people working on the International Space Station that we're up to something.

"Yes. I was at a party and someone asked if I wanted to know a wild story." She lifts the bottle and shakes it to gauge how much is left.

"Of course you said yes," Teddy says.

"Damn straight. The story wasn't that wild, but we were talking about work and he asked me if it was true designers stole from each other."

She pauses to ask the server for another bottle and something called a beige platter. Then she drinks her wine, looking into the distance.

"Stealing," I prompt.

"Right. I gave him my biggest and most innocent eyes"—she turns on a soft, doe-eyed gaze that wouldn't be out of place in a cheesy per-fume ad—"and asked him what he meant."

"Is he a designer?" I ask. Teddy's foot presses against mine, and I momentarily lose focus.

"No, but he was at some *other* party, and this *other* guy was there and that guy was, like, hammered. Apparently there was some pissing contest about who's been screwed over the worst, and the drunk guy told a story about how a big-name fashion designer stole his work."

"There are a lot of guys in this story," Teddy notes.

"Blame patriarchy. Anyway, I did some digging and found him online." She casts another look around the restaurant to confirm no one is paying attention and hands her phone over. "Meet Jean-Pierre."

Teddy and I scroll through his work.

"I see it," says Teddy. He turns to a web page of Celeste's past collections and points to the same oversize tunic as in Jean-Pierre's designs, then an identical skirt cut to give an airy swing.

The server puts down the wine and the beige platter—a combination of mozzarella sticks, fries, spring rolls, and jalapeño poppers, making the etymology of the name abundantly clear. It smells like a grease trap and my mouth waters.

"How did anyone not notice?" I ask as I grab a popper.

"Who in Michael's circle is looking at what some Black kid barely out of school does?" Alejandra asks. "Even if they knew, they'd say it's the business, that ideas circulate."

The two of them embark on a discussion about technical sketches and design stuff that goes right over my head. It doesn't matter, because I'm not thinking about the designs. I'm focused on what it means. This could be it, our big breakthrough.

When they pause, I say, "It sounds like we need to find Jean-Pierre."

Alejandra dips a fry in the pinkish mayo. "That's the problem. He's in Paris."

"We can call him," I say.

"Already put out some feelers. He won't do calls or video calls. He regrets what he said and he's worried about getting recorded. His future career is on the line."

I frown. "That's a problem."

"No, it's not." Teddy looks eager. "We go to him. We'll see him in Paris."

"We can't go to Paris," I say.

"Why not?"

"What do you mean, why not? We can't afford it," I say. "Or take time off work. We need to find a more feasible way to talk to him."

Alejandra pokes me under the table, and out of the corner of my eye, I see her mouth the words, *Rich boy*.

Teddy confirms this when he says, "I can pay and we'll go on a weekend."

"To Paris," stresses Alejandra. "France."

"Are you serious?" I ask. God, people with money see the world in a different way. It's like nothing's impossible. It only has a cost.

"I can't anyway." Alejandra pours us all more wine. "I help my sister with her kids on the weekend. It's the only time she gets a break."

"How bad do we need to talk to Jean-Pierre?" Teddy asks.

"I haven't been able to find any other proof," she admits. "If he'll talk to us, then we can try to convince him to come forward."

"Hold on." Teddy pulls out his phone. "I forgot, I'm going to Paris for business next week. I can talk to Jean-Pierre while I'm there."

"You forgot about going to Paris." Alejandra is not impressed.

"It's a short trip," says Teddy apologetically.

"You're in management, so he might see you as being on Michael's side." Then she cocks her head. "Then again, you're Teddy Marsh of Mars. It's hard to say."

"If Dee comes, she can make contact instead, just in case." Teddy turns to me. "Will you?"

Teddy wants to buy me a weekend trip to Paris. There's no way I can accept it, but Alejandra looks at me with the same pleading wide eyes she demonstrated for us earlier. I'll have to take one for the team. "I suppose so?"

"Thanks, Dee," Alejandra says. "It's a lot to ask." Then she wiggles her eyebrows at me and I pray my face isn't red.

Paris with Teddy. What have I done?

———

"He replied." Alejandra catches me in a stairwell two days later. This time, the *he* isn't Michael—she's been working on making a connection with Jean-Pierre since we embarked on this scheme. Yesterday, her go-between managed to pass on our request to meet. Jean-Pierre's level of paranoia garners my full respect.

"And?"

"We should talk about this outside."

Ten minutes later, we're standing in an alley sharing a little beam of sunlight to take advantage of its weak heat. "What's going on?" I ask.

"Jean-Pierre is a little freaked out by the idea of you coming overseas to talk to him." She doesn't sound happy, and her forehead carries three horizontal lines. "It's sounding like a big deal, and that's making him nervous. I told you he was already regretting it."

"Damn." I run through options. We could lie to him and say I was in Paris anyway, but I don't want to start this on a foundation of mistrust. "What did you tell him?"

"That I heard about his story and wanted to talk to him about it."

"Any details? Did you tell him we suspect Michael? Tell him what we're trying to do? That we're from Celeste?"

She shakes her head. "I didn't want to commit us to a stranger."

"We might have to. He might be more open to us if we're the first to show ourselves to be vulnerable."

Alejandra makes a face. "That's my least favorite word."

"Worse than moi—"

She holds up her hand. "Don't even."

"Fine. It's a sensitive situation, but let's look at it from his point of view. He's drunk at a party talking shit, and then some stranger calls his friend to try to get in touch with him about his accusations."

"I'd be scared," she admits. "I can't believe he answered at all."

"He'll want to know how much we know." I think this through. "We could change our plan and have Teddy try to talk to him? I know we were worried about how Jean-Pierre might react but

Teddy's on the spot so it's not like Jean-Pierre is the target of a special trip."

"No, now I'm even more sure that would backfire." She turns her face to get some sun on it. "Mars was a big deal in fashion. Meeting Teddy is kind of like meeting a legend."

"It is?" I knew he was good but this famous?

She looks a little shy. "I nearly passed out when I heard he was coming to Celeste before I understood it was basically so Daddy could have him under his thumb."

"Harsh."

"True. Ted was a fashion darling for trying to make it his own way, because the industry loves a rebel." She shakes her head. "That he failed almost makes it more appealing for a lot of people, like a romantic figure."

"So absolutely no Teddy," I say. "That leaves our original plan of me going to Paris, which means we need to take the first step. If it makes you nervous, you can say you don't know the details and send him over to me. I'll do it."

"I'm in this, too." She takes a deep breath. "Let me do it before I lose my nerve."

Alejandra takes out her phone and types out the message—that we work with Michael, suspect he wasn't the only person Michael had done this to, and are contacting him without the company knowing. No identifying names besides Michael's but enough to show we're serious. Then we stand there.

"How long until he gets back to us, do you think?" I ask. "I'm getting a bit cold."

"It's about eight in the evening in Paris. Let's head back to the office and give him a chance. Also this alley smells."

We grab some drinks to give us an excuse for being out, and as we leave the café, Alejandra's phone dings. It's Jean-Pierre.

"That was fast," she says.

I look over her shoulder at her phone. "It worked!" He's given us a date, time, and location to meet, which is Saturday morning at a café in Belleville, in the northeast part of the city.

"Congratulations." She nudges me with her elbow because she's got a crinkly paper bag of pastry in one hand and a coffee in the other. "I guess that Brené Brown vulnerability stuff works after all."

I have a brief sense of satisfaction that's almost immediately followed by panic. "I can't believe I'm going to Paris," I say.

"Yeah, don't fuck it up." Alejandra looks worried. "What if this gets back to Michael?"

"First, it's too late for us to be concerned about that. Second, how? Jean-Pierre has as much to lose as we do. He won't tell on us." He'd better not, because I don't want to explain this to Vivian, at least not until I get the proof I need about Michael.

"I hope so. How's your French?" she asks.

"Vraiment terrible."

Alejandra flinches at my accent. "Noted. Thank goodness Jean-Pierre speaks English. Are you comfortable meeting him for breakfast?"

"What's he going to do, throw a croissant at me?"

She gives me a look. "Do you know what you're going to tell him?"

"Pretty much. I'm going to be honest," I say. "I'll tell him what we know, what we think, and ask for his help in trying to remove Michael."

"He's young," Alejandra reminds me. "With a lot to lose."

"He could have a lot to gain." I rub my temple with my free hand. "In the end, it's not about gain or loss. It's about whether he's the kind of person who wants to do this regardless of risk."

She sighs. "Yeah. Do you want to role-play different scenarios?"

"Absolutely I do not." I smile at her over my tea. "Don't worry. I've got this."

Alejandra juggles her pastry to switch her coffee to her other hand. "I hope this was the right decision."

"It was," I assure her. "Trust the universe."

"I'm trusting *you*."

"It's going to be fine. I promise."

Alejandra looks at me for a long moment. "Okay."

She goes in first so we're not seen together, the way Vivian said.

Looks like I'm going to Paris.

———

"Come on. You know this one." Teddy's face disappears and a building takes his place on the phone screen.

I'm taking a break from packing to chat with Teddy, who is walking through nighttime Paris on his way home from drinks with old friends. He took such joy in telling me the latest gossip—apparently Jasper and Mila are striking out for themselves, Frankie has a new girlfriend everyone loves, and Henry's millinery venture is a huge success—that I didn't even care I had no idea who any of these people are.

"Is it Chanel?" I hazard a guess.

"Yes! Thirty-one rue Cambon." He tilts the phone to show me the stark black-and-white sign on the wall. "Coco had an apartment upstairs but slept at the Ritz every night. Mom wasn't a fan of Chanel."

"Why?"

"She thought the bags were uninspired, but more than that, she was disgusted people were so willing to gloss over Coco Chanel's support for the Nazis." He shrugs. "That people would ignore such a moral failing, even years later, because the clothes are nice was something she found sickening."

"Your mother sounds like she was an incredible woman."

Teddy stops and leans against a stone wall. "She was. She loved Paris. She took me here one summer when I was twelve and Dad had to work. It was August, so half the city was shut down for the holidays, and the cobblestones smelled like history." He starts walking again, passing in and out of pools of lamplight. "That's when she took me to

Thirty-one rue Cambon and told me fashion is art and art has influence that should be used for good. I think about it often."

"That's what you want to do."

"That's what I'm going to do," he corrects. I love this new Teddy, the one who's worked his way back to reaching for what he wants. He's inspiring. Then he yawns and I want to pinch his cheeks, then kiss them.

"Are you near your hotel?" I ask.

"God, no. Not even close. Did I tell you I tried the Parisian Questie?" As he walks, I can see small backdrops of the city pop into view. A double door here, a tiny car there.

"How was it?"

"It would have been more fun with you," he says.

I preen. "Isn't everything?"

He takes me seriously. "Yes. It is." He pauses his walking and shows me a dark cave that I don't immediately recognize as a flight of steps. "I'm at the Metro. I have that meeting on Saturday so I can't meet you."

"I'll see you after."

"I wish I could go with you, but you've got it under control." He blows me a kiss. "Bonne nuit."

I disconnect the call and open up a map of Paris, looking at Place Vendôme, then panning over to the sixteenth arrondissement and the café where I'll soon see Jean-Pierre. The street view helps detail the visualization in my head. I see the crumbs on the zinc table with the empty cups, Jean-Pierre agreeing with our plan, his face determined.

Satisfied I've done everything I can do to ensure success, I go to bed.

As I told Alejandra, I've totally got this.

TWENTY-THREE

I arrive at Charles de Gaulle at seven in the morning.

The red-eye had been as comfortable as a transatlantic flight can be and greatly alleviated by the amenities of business class. I even have replenished skin because they provided little zippered bags that included sheet masks as well as shoe socks. I'd texted Teddy and he'd pointed out that unlike first class, business didn't provide pajamas. I made fun of him for being spoiled and he didn't deny it.

It's easy enough to get through the airport and find a cab. I do my best to stay awake and manage to keep my eyes open until we hit a gray expanse of industrial and warehouse buildings. I wake in a narrow street facing an unremarkable building with walls of dark chiseled stone in need of a power clean.

"Qu'est-ce c'est l'hôtel?" I know that's not right even before the driver gives me a confused look. I try again. "Est-ce que c'est l'hôtel?"

The driver nods. "Oui, c'est ça."

I pay and grab my bag, wrestling it over the curb and trundling it through the gateway into a gorgeous courtyard lined with cherry blossoms. Through the back is what looks like a cloister leading to a small verdant garden. Spring is much further along in Paris, and I breathe in the soft morning air as I walk over the black-and-white tiles to the reception desk. To my shock, Teddy stands up from one of the ivory velvet chairs.

"Good flight?" he asks, pulling me into a hug.

I relax into him and soak in his sunny clean scent. I hadn't realized how tense I was about meeting Jean-Pierre, and Teddy's touch is a reminder that things will work out.

My hand lingers on his chest to feel his heartbeat. "I thought I wasn't seeing you until later."

"I was finally able to move that meeting back so I could meet you." He hands me a huge metal key suitable for a dungeon. "No key cards. It's an old-fashioned place."

The vintage charm continues to our rooms (two, I note with mingled chagrin and relief), which are utterly divine. Mine is small but has a sitting room with a writing desk that looks like it was used by the comtesse du Fontaine to handwrite invitations to the ball. Long muslin curtains open to reveal a small patio in what might be a third garden, which is filled with spring flowers and fresh green shrubs. Teddy puts my bag on the little stand before coming over to give me a lingering kiss that makes my knees wobbly.

"I could spend all day here," I say. The *with you* is implied.

He checks the time. "Too bad you have a meeting with an up-and-coming designer in ninety minutes."

"Right. Shower time."

I unpack and shake out the outfit I brought. Jeans, a white T-shirt, and a blazer, to be worn with ballerina flats. Simple and hopefully elegant enough to suit Paris. The shower is hot, and I let the water beat down on my head to wash away my doubts along with the bergamot-scented lather from the fancy shower gel. I can do this. I can convince Jean-Pierre. It will be fine.

"It will be fine," I say to the shower curtain. "I trust in myself and it will be fine."

I dry my hair quickly, get dressed, and open the patio doors to wait for Teddy. Jean-Pierre might be on his way already. I hope he shows.

If he doesn't, at least I tried, and that's all anyone can ask for. Whatever happens is what's meant to be.

———

We walk to the café, which is located on a corner under a cream-and-red awning that hadn't been in the online street view. Round tables and woven seats line the sidewalk in front, and it looks so stereotypically French, I half expect a mime to pop out. A man with a stiff white apron wrapped around his chest and waist snaps a cloth away from the only customer.

"That's not Jean-Pierre," I say, looking at the middle-aged white guy in a cheap blue suit reading *Le Figaro*. "He's not here. Where is he?"

Teddy takes my hand and runs his hand over my wrist. "I can feel your heartbeat." He smooths the skin. "Take some deep breaths."

I do as he suggests. "This is a bit scary."

"I know." Teddy gives my wrist a gentle squeeze, then pulls me close to kiss my upper lip, then the lower. "I wish I could wait with you. You can do this, and I'll see you right after my meeting."

"Right." My nerves go into overdrive as I watch Teddy disappear around the corner. If this gets back to Celeste...no, I won't court negative consequences by thinking them into existence. It *will* work out.

I take a seat facing into the street, appreciating the bald Parisian admittance that people watching is fun. The server comes by and I order, excited to use my pathetic French. "Un, ah, une? No, un chocolat chaud, s'il vous plaît." I never managed to get the articles right in school and tend to default to the masculine.

The server asks me something and, at a loss, I nod.

There's nothing to do but wait. I check my phone every thirty seconds for a message as eleven approaches. The hot chocolate comes, along with sugar cubes and a bowl of whipped cream that I'm not sure if I should eat now, eat later, or stir into the drink. A voice comes from my left.

"You are Daiyu?"

I jump to my feet, almost knocking the table over. "Jean-Pierre?"

He leans over before I can stretch out my hand. Oh my God, he's going to kiss me. I have never been cool about this and stay ramrod straight as he air-kisses to my right, then left, and back to my right. I make a smacking sound and hope it's passable on the etiquette front.

We sit and look at each other. Jean-Pierre has dark reddish-brown skin, his hair shaved at the sides and bleached locs coming down from a high ponytail on the top of his head. His short beard is trimmed to a small point under his chin. He's dressed in pale jeans and a black V-neck shirt with a tastefully distressed burgundy cardigan styled to reveal a sleeve of tattoos on his right arm that resemble plate armor. Like Alejandra, he's cool. Like, head-turningly stylish and so, so young.

The server comes, and Jean-Pierre orders a café au lait before looking at my mound of whipped cream. "You like Chantilly cream?"

"Yeah, but I'm not sure what to do with it."

"Stir it in your drink."

"All that?" There's a good cup of it.

Jean-Pierre clucks at me. "No, no. A spoonful only."

"Aztec warriors had drinking chocolate as part of their rations," I say as the cream dissolves into the chocolate. "It was made into wafers that they mixed with water."

"They also used cacao beans as currency," he says, raising his cup. This exchange of culinary trivia breaks the ice enough for Jean-Pierre to relax for a moment. Then he says, "Let's not waste time. You came all the way to Paris to hear my story."

"I did."

"Why?" He crosses his arms and looks out at the street as the shopkeeper across rattles up his storefront grate.

"Because I heard what happened to you and I want to know more."

He raises his eyebrow, making the silver ring through it glint as he waits for me to continue.

I take a fortifying sip of hot chocolate, which the cream has made into an elixir of the gods, and send a brief hope out. This is it. Go time. "As we told you, we suspect Michael Madison is stealing designs and claiming them as his own. The problem is we have no proof."

"What would you do with proof if you had it?" he asks.

"I'm not sure yet," I say. "It would help us understand what he's doing, but I'll be honest. Even with proof, we might not be believed."

"I see," he says. "If this thing happened to me, why should I help you?"

He's playing it careful with his language. I turn to face him. "I could tell you that it's the right thing to do and you could stop the same thing from happening to other people. You already know that, and part of you agrees because you're here with me in the first place."

"If that's not what you're telling me, what is the reason?" His accent makes the sentence almost mocking. I wonder what my own accent sounds like. Probably much less classy.

I debate a few things that could win him over and decide to go with the most visceral and true. "To fuck over Michael because he deserves it."

There's a moment of startled silence before Jean-Pierre laughs and slaps his hands on his thighs. "Bien. Tell me more."

"Michael is in over his head at Celeste," I say. "He takes from others to make himself shine."

"Some would say it's a skill to recognize talent."

"It is, and he has that in abundance. It's a greater person who can do that and support those with talent instead of claiming it for their own because of their ego."

"You want to take him down?"

"Or at a minimum, make him face justice."

"Do you work for Celeste?"

"My friend who contacted you does. I'm a diversity consultant doing some work for them."

Jean-Pierre looks at the street. "Then you aren't directly involved in this. What does it matter to you what he did?"

"It's wrong," I say. "You can't treat people like that. You can't go around doing whatever you want because you think life owes you more than it does others or because you can't admit you can't cut it."

"You're all right." He looks at his coffee and finally gives an insouciant shrug. "What the hell? You already know that it happened."

For the next thirty minutes, I sit and listen as Jean-Pierre speaks. When he finishes, I pause to consider his story. It's as we heard from Alejandra, but what gets me angrier is Jean-Pierre's assumption that Michael will get away with it.

Because he always has.

"Will you come forward if we report this?" I ask finally. That's the million-dollar question after all. We don't have anything until we have proof, and Jean-Pierre has a very persuasive story. If we get him on our side, we might be able to find others with similar experiences.

Jean-Pierre squints at a space in the awning where the spring sun filters through. I don't want to pressure him and do my best to simply sit and visualize my outcome. I see Jean-Pierre agreeing to help and focus on that image.

"Someone needs to stand up to him," he says, looking at me. "I'll come forward."

I nearly jump up from my seat to hug him, I'm so thrilled. Proof manifesting works because this is what I wanted. "Thank you."

"When do you leave for Canada?"

"Tomorrow."

He fixes the rings on his hand. "Then you'll tell my story?"

"I need to talk to my friend first," I say. "We need a plan to make sure we maximize the impact. I can keep you updated."

"A plan." Jean-Pierre nods with a slight frown. "Good luck. I hope this helps."

I wonder if I should urge him to stay and chat longer, but he stands to indicate our meeting is over. I'm a bit taken aback, but he probably has other plans for his day. I manage the farewell without accidentally kissing him on the lips or smearing lipstick on him.

When he's gone, I sit back down and savor the moment before picking up my phone and texting Teddy and Alejandra a single word.

Me: Success.

TWENTY-FOUR

*A*s agreed, I meet Teddy in Montmartre. He's still winded from the steps at Abbesses Métro station when he grabs me in a hug, panting in a way that puts my mind right in the gutter.

"He agreed!" I don't temper my elation.

"I knew you could make it happen." He tucks my hair behind my ear. "What happened?"

"Give me a second to get my thoughts in order." I'm flying so high with this outcome—although it was to be expected as I'd done my best to visualize it perfectly—that I can't even talk about it yet.

"You got it."

"What should we do since we're in Paris?" With the stress of the meeting over, I'm suddenly greedy for experiences.

Teddy kisses my cheek. We're well beyond friends, this much is clear, and we should talk about how far into the next category we are, but I've maxed out on heavy talks this morning. "Anything you want," he says.

"Let's wander, then."

We head toward the street where people go about their day. A woman walks a small dog while smoking a cigarette, and a man carrying an armful of narrow baguettes passes under a pharmacy with its little green cross.

"Those thin baguettes are called ficelle," Teddy says. "It means string."

"I didn't know that."

"You didn't? All that trivia research is paying off." There's an expression of pure delight on his face. "I'm glad I can finally pull my weight with you."

"You bring lots to the table," I say.

He gives a bow and then says, "Unfortunately, patience is not one of those things. I'm dying to know what happened with Jean-Pierre."

"It's all true but he told me more." We pass an alley, the sidewalk stained dark, and I wrinkle my nose. "After Jean-Pierre saw the Celeste collection with his designs, Michael tried to pretend they never met. When Jean-Pierre pulled out the text messages, Michael changed his tune."

Teddy waits for a white delivery van to rumble by on the street. "He got mean."

"But subtle. He made it sound like Jean-Pierre was threatening him, and he needed to protect himself. Jean-Pierre decided it wasn't worth the aggravation and moved to Paris. He's got family here."

"That piece of garbage." Teddy says it like a pronouncement. "That utter asshole."

"Yeah."

"I wanted Michael out before this. This makes it a mission." His mouth is a line.

"Good, because that's what we're doing."

"That's right. We are." Teddy shakes his shoulders as if physically throwing off his mood. "Enough of Michael for now. We've done what we can, so let's forget all this until we get back and talk to Alejandra. I won't let him mess up Paris for us."

"Screw him."

"Screw him," Teddy agrees. "We're in Montmartre. Do you want to walk or take the funicular?"

"Always take the most fun option, and *funicular* has it in the name. Fun-icular. Get it?"

He groans. "I get it."

The little funicular takes us up the steep hill, more like a ride than a transportation method. At the top rises Sacré-Coeur, and we walk over to sit on the steps that overlook the entire city. Teddy passes me some hand sanitizer, then a rustling paper bag.

"Macarons!" I say, looking inside.

"I got them from a patisserie on my way to meet you."

There are six and we split each of them, teeth sinking through the crisp shell into the gooey center. Teddy is boring and decides the delicate burnt almond is the best, while I waver between salted caramel and ube.

Teddy dusts the crumbs off his knees. "Now what?"

"Sit and enjoy the view for a moment?" I contemplate the city before us, an endless cream and gray vista punctured by the Eiffel Tower and the business district of La Défense in the distance. It takes a moment to notice Teddy is looking at me instead.

"What are you doing?" I ask.

"Admiring the view."

"Oh my God, you didn't say that."

He smiles. Then he kisses me. There on the stairs, tasting like the sweetest of French cookies, he kisses me, and the polyglot conversation surrounding us fades away. Teddy's kiss starts so soft that it's not much more than a brush of our lips. He doesn't pull away but waits for me to move in, my hand sliding up to the back of his neck, and then he makes a small sound as I glide my mouth across his.

How can I describe kissing Teddy? It's not fireworks, with their frantic explosive high and disappointingly quick fizzle. He's the opposite, so deliberate that he builds a wall around us with every movement until it blocks everything but his hands in my hair and his lips on mine.

It doesn't take long to get to a point that will soon be inappropriate given the public setting. I pull back a bit and Teddy follows me so we're tucked up beside each other. His arm wraps around my waist and I press into him, a silent demand for more kisses. Teddy gives me one on the tip of my ear, then on my temple. A man comes by, shaking a handful of key chains at us, and Teddy stops him to buy one.

"Here." He hands it over. It's one of the tackiest things I've ever seen, with an anthropomorphic baguette wearing a mustache dancing in front of a montage of the Arc de Triomphe, the Eiffel Tower, and a carousel. I adore it.

"Thank you." I tuck the unlikely love token in my pocket for safe-keeping. A year ago, I added the Paris scene to my bedroom vision board, and I have a moment of wonder at how well it worked. Then again, surely the universe could have found a more direct way to get me to Paris than messing around with Jean-Pierre. Well, I should enjoy it and be grateful instead of nitpicking.

We decide to start walking and weave our way through the dozens of people crowding the stairs. Once we arrive at the top, Teddy takes my hand as we head down a winding street filled with souvenir shops. There are more postcards here than a person could send in a lifetime, and Teddy points to a store with salt and pepper shakers of cancan dancers.

I pick up the pepper brunette. "The reason the cancan was scandalous was because of the high kicks."

"I guess it was risqué back then."

"Also women's undergarments were split down the middle at the time."

"Oh," says Teddy. Then he puts it together. "*Ohhh.*"

"Yup."

We hum "dum-dum-dadadada-dum-*dum,*" Offenbach's classic sadly better known to both of us through an ad for a muffler repair company, as Teddy steers me through more winding streets until we end up at what looks like a vineyard in the middle of the city.

It's peaceful here compared to the chaos of the streets closer to

Sacré-Coeur. Teddy leans against the wall, smiling at the sky, and I stand in front of him. His eyes fly down to me and then to where my hands press against his chest.

If the kiss on the steps was heated, this one is blazing. Because we're standing, I can crush my whole body against him and feel his every reaction. He flips us around so I'm against the wall and cages me in with his arms on each side of my head.

"We're going to be a public spectacle," he says in my ear, edging his leg between mine and making me gasp. Then he pulls away, laughing as I swipe at him. He smooths out my clothes with quick and careful hands, then runs his finger over my mouth. "Pretty," he says, looking at my lips, before kissing me one last time. "Come on. Exploration time."

"I was exploring," I grumble.

His ears go bright red. "Explore Paris."

A few more couples have come to appreciate the quiet, and Teddy stands closer to me. I give him a side-eye. "What's this about?"

"I like to be near you," he says shamelessly. "I want them all to know that this beautiful, brainy woman chose me."

I pop up on my toes to give him a kiss on the cheek. "You know what I like?" I glance down his body in as suggestive a manner as I can. Teddy's breath hitches and his glasses slip down.

"What?" he whispers.

"Ice cream. You want to get some?"

He bursts out laughing and catches me in his arms. "Come on. I know the perfect place."

———

The ice cream is actually gelato shaped into little flowers in the cup, labneh and fig for me and honey pistachio for Teddy. After, we take the Métro to the Latin Quarter and wander around the narrow medieval streets before stopping at Shakespeare and Company, where Teddy buys a book about perfume bottle design.

Then we're off to his favorite shop, Deyrolle. It's a taxidermist, of all things, and we gaze at the posed animals like a zoo of the dead.

"Are you hungry?" asks Teddy as we flip through botanical posters.

"Yes." I look at the stag staring at me with shining eyes. "Something vegetarian."

We bid the animals farewell and head toward the Marais on a walk so romantic it's almost a cliché. The clouds cover the sky in pillows of soft ash gray, and we pause on Pont Royal to look over the Seine as the bateaux mouches slip under us with their rows of tourists. Today is better than the time I got a haircut that looked as flattering on me as it did on the woman in the photo. More exhilarating than getting to the top of the Questie leaderboard. More joyful than starting my new career as a diversity consultant at Chariot.

"Paris is like walking through memories I have but didn't make," I say.

Teddy nods as he takes a photo. He's been documenting the strangest things, like tiny details of stonework or metalwork or the petal of a flower. Looking at lines, he says, and how they flow.

We step onto the Rue de Rivoli where we're nearly trampled by a woman holding a closed red umbrella over her head and the small band of visored and fanny-packed women who follow in her wake. Soon we're in another small neighborhood filled with people and the smell of cooking onion.

"The Marais," says Teddy. "With the best falafel in Paris over there."

He's clearly not the only one who thinks so, because there's a line about twelve deep at the green-painted stall. The Marais is like its own little town, and after we eat the truly delicious falafel, I poke my head into a gate to find a tiny garden with herbs and grapevines curling over a trellis. We walk around stores looking at tea and gloves and adorable house decor until Teddy glances at the sky. "It's getting late. Want to go back to the hotel before we eat?"

I nod, yawning. It's been a long day, not including the stress of meeting Jean-Pierre. This time, the Métro is crammed with tired Parisians swaying with the rhythm of the train. An influx of passengers crowds in at République, pressing us close.

"Are you okay?" Teddy asks, one arm coming around to hold me.

I do my best to keep a polite distance, but a woman shoves her shopping bags into my legs and forces me into Teddy. He doesn't say anything but his heart beats against mine.

You'd think a jam-packed train would be the antithesis of sexy thoughts, what with the baby screaming and the smell of worn-out people and someone's roast chicken filling the small space. After all, not even Paris can make commuting appealing or romantic.

Yet Teddy can. He's been touching me all day, and I wonder if he's deliberately trying to rile me up to see what I'll do. I mean, the answer is anything at this point, and if this train had been empty, I couldn't be held responsible for my actions.

"What are you thinking about?" he asks.

I don't want to say, since my mind is absorbed with a tiny freckle on his ear that I want to kiss, and that would be strange to declare on public transit. Teddy's hand slides a little further from my waist, low enough to grasp my hip. As revenge, I give the smallest of grinds. Teddy twitches and moves back.

I grin. "That the Métro font is called Parisine."

"I love when you talk trivia to me."

Belleville comes too soon and not soon enough, and we behave on the way back to the hotel, probably in part because the city grime has settled into every fatigued pore. We separate with a promise to meet on the patio after we shower.

Alone in my room, I see my socks have left an imprint of the fabric's weave on my skin and a thin line of dirt on my ankles. With a sigh of relief, I grab a washcloth for an intense scrubbing session that leaves me clean, moisturized, and perfumed in strategic areas, because my goal is to get Teddy between those white hotel sheets. There's no manifesting here or asking the universe for a boon. I'm the one who will make it happen. Me.

I slick on some raspberry lip balm, pull on the terry robe that's been folded in a tidy square on the bed, and walk out to the patio. Teddy lounges in a chair looking at his new perfume book with two glasses of white wine sitting beside him on the table. "The reservation isn't until nine, so we can relax for a couple hours," he says, smiling at me.

I try to sit down gracefully but simply collapse. "We did so much today."

A pleasant silence falls over us as we drink the wine and look out into the garden. Part of me is happy to enjoy the moment because the air is warm, the wine is cold, and the garden smells like lilac and freshness after the stone and concrete of the city. Then I notice Teddy glancing at my legs. The robe has fallen open to show my knee, and I decide on my plan of action. Reaching for my glass, I adjust the robe so it reveals my thigh. It's not so wild that if someone walked by it would be a problem, but it's a definite invitation.

Teddy tosses back the rest of his wine before reaching out with a finger to trace a cool line up my leg. "Are you doing this on purpose?" His voice is rough.

"Yes."

"Good to know." He stands abruptly and pulls me to my feet. "My room or yours?"

A pulse surges through me. "Mine."

He pauses. "I don't want to be presumptuous, but I should go to the store. I don't have anything."

I look over my shoulder. "I have no problem being presumptuous, so I came prepared for any contingency."

"You were planning to seduce me?" Teddy's eyelids flutter. "Holy shit, that's hot."

He ushers me in through the patio, then carefully closes the curtains. The early evening sun filters through to fill the room with a dreamy glow as I stand in the middle and wait for him to come to me, heart racing. Teddy takes off his glasses and puts them on the table before pushing the robe off my shoulder. Then he bends his head to lay his mouth on mine, pulling on the tie of the robe so slowly I reach down to do it myself.

He captures my hands in his. "Patience," he scolds.

I wait, and he makes it worth my while.

TWENTY-FIVE

We linger in bed until the room starts to dim, and Teddy insists we leave to go eat. "I want to show you the view from the restaurant," he says. "I promise you won't regret it."

I take the robe he hands me. "Let me have a quick shower."

When I get back in the room, Teddy is sitting in bed, fidgeting with his bracelets.

I give him a look. "What?"

"What do you mean, what?" He stops. "Nothing."

"Teddy. You want to say something."

He waffles a moment more before saying, "Wait here." He gets up, and I switch on the light to get a better view as he pulls on his clothes. "Dee, what are you up to?" He's smiling a bit and I laugh as he flexes to put on his shirt.

"Admiring."

"That's fine, then."

He stops to kiss me, hand teasing under my towel, and leaves only to return a moment later with a hanger in his hand. He shoves it toward me, face bright red and chewing on his lower lip.

"What's this?" I ask, intrigued.

"I made it for you," he says. "You don't have to wear it. I swear it's totally cool if you don't want to. I'm not trying to change how you dress, because you always look great."

"You made me something?" I take the hanger to find the pants I tried on at his place, black with a high waist and pleats all around that cause the soft fabric to fall like water. He's added a black shirt I haven't seen, with a high neck and cap sleeves. A chain belt completes the look.

"You seemed to like them," he says.

"Like isn't close to describing it." I can't help running my fingers over them. He takes a little step forward, and I look up. "Teddy?"

Teddy looks at me steadily although he's rubbing his fingers together as if he needs to get energy out in some way. "They're a thank-you."

"For coming to Paris?" Which he paid for.

He shakes his head. "For making me want to create like this again. For giving that back to me."

I put the clothes on the bed so I can walk over and wrap him in my arms. "Thank you," I whisper into his neck. "They're gorgeous. I love them."

The tension seeps out of his body and he leans against me. "That's the first set I've done in years." His laugh is shaky. "I changed my mind about giving them to you about twenty times and almost didn't pack them. I was more nervous than when I put on my first runway show."

I give him a kiss on his ear freckle and go back to my new clothes. He watches as I pull them on, telling me about how he constructed the pants ("I wanted a more elegant, flowing look so I added pleats to the back instead of fitting them with darts") and showing me the extra button to increase or reduce the waist if needed ("Clothes should change with you to add to their longevity"). My short hair shows off the collar of my shirt, which has intricate shirring on the top, and Teddy informs me he hand-embroidered the little leaves along the edge. There are optional long sleeves that can be attached, but he left those at home.

He looks me over after I belt the pants. "You look beautiful." When I catch his eye, he's not looking at the clothes and admiring his work but at me.

"It's my first time in designer," I say as I consider myself in the mirror. He's right; I do look incredible. Moreover, I feel fantastic. This is what he meant by how fashion can change your entire self-perception. I could take on the world dressed like this.

"I can make you a whole wardrobe if you like," he says, watching intently as I put on lipstick.

"Please. I'd love that."

He shakes out a diaphanous short black hooded cape fit for a movie star. "This also turns into a dress, a skirt, and a top," he says as I run my hands over the fabric, which is the same warm cotton candy weave I saw before. "I can carry it until you need it later."

When we leave, I strut through the magnificent hotel lobby with as much panache as I can summon, catching more than a few flattering glances. This is new and I'm not complaining, because Teddy's clothes have made me the chicest woman in a city famous for them. I wish I could feel like this all the time.

We walk up a cobblestone street, holding hands and laughing about my embarrassing French pronunciation between stolen kisses, when I gasp. "Teddy, look."

We've reached the top of the Parc de Belleville, and the sun sets over the city in an explosion of orange and red. Streaks of violet paint the sky behind the distant silhouette of the Eiffel Tower, and the entire scene is so beautiful that I can't believe I'm seeing it.

Teddy stands quietly beside me amid the crowd until the sun falls behind the horizon like a puppeteer has dropped her strings. Then he points to a café. "This is us."

We get a seat on the patio, and the tables and chairs are brightly colored and a little unsteady on the uneven stones. The French buzz makes me feel richly traveled, and we order some wine, or Teddy does since

I usually only differentiate by red, white, or rosé. Trivia I love, but my oenophilic knowledge level is so low I thought orange wine was made with real oranges, much to Jade's disgust and my own disappointment. We decide on a selection of small plates and nibble at the warm bread the server drops on the table with some sage butter.

"I've been thinking about work," Teddy says. I raise my eyebrows, and he frowns. "This situation with Jean-Pierre has made it clear that I've failed more than I thought at Celeste."

"You can't keep beating yourself up about it."

"I'm not." He catches my eye and gives me a faint smile. "Maybe a bit, but it's like my eyes are open now. Things were getting bad, but I didn't realize how deep the rot was."

"What do you plan to do about it?" I break off some more bread. Every culture has its own carb dishes, and there's something about the crunch of a French baguette crust that's exquisite.

He drums his fingers on the table, staring at the chalkboard with the menu on the wall. The patio has little fairy lights draped around the edge of the awning, and under the amber glow, his face is shadowed and severe and beautiful. "That's the issue. The appropriate thing is to sit down with my father, but that won't go anywhere. He wants to keep me in my place, at least until he's gone and I'm finally CEO."

I sprinkle some salt on my bread and butter. "Are you sure that's happening? What if he changes his mind?"

"He won't." He speaks with certainty. "Dad and I might not see eye to eye on the best way to run the business, but he told me Celeste will be mine. He knows how much the company means to me, even if he doesn't agree with the changes I want."

The first of the plates come, a burrata with fresh tomatoes and basil drizzled with pale green olive oil. Teddy cuts into the cheese to reveal the liquid interior.

"Your father hasn't changed, though. He's still not going to see it your way."

"I know." He looks at me with a serious expression. "The negotiations are moving quickly on the sale to Opaline this summer. I don't have time to waste if I want to stop it. Dad won't listen to me, so I'll have to work around him."

"That's big." This is such an about-face from where he was a couple months ago that I feel I've watched a butterfly emerge from its chrysalis.

"It's necessary. I tried to fool myself into thinking otherwise, but once they own Celeste, my hands will be tied as CEO. Getting rid of Michael will cast some doubt over the stability of Celeste's creative side and help me."

We thank the server, who has brought a mushroom terrine with little golden crostini. The terrine is savory and flavored with tarragon. When Teddy sees me shiver, he comes over to drape the cape over my shoulders. It's like being cocooned, and a woman shoots me an envious smile, then raises her glass in approval when she catches sight of my companion.

My phone beeps. It's Mom, asking when I'm back from my work trip so I can pick up Grandma's prescription at the drugstore. I have no idea why she's internally assigned this task to me, but it's easier to do than argue.

"Something wrong?" Teddy watches me with concern across the table.

"A message from my mother that makes me very glad to be here with you." A small salad of pea shoots decorated with petals arrives.

"I'm flattered." He eats a pink petal. "You want to talk about it? You said your family moved back into your house. For how long?"

"Indefinitely." I take the tuna carpaccio he passes me. "You know how your dad's family didn't really care about your mom being Chinese? They respected it?"

He nods.

"My grandmother didn't approve of Dad when Mom married him. They're polite but it's tense to be under the same roof. My gross aunt doesn't talk to us at all. No loss."

"I'm sorry." He puts a chicken medallion on his plate and drizzles the sauce over. "I hate to say that I was lucky with how my dad's family treated us, because that should be standard. I know it's not."

I eat some artichoke dressed with lemon that squeaks in my teeth. "Don't take this the wrong way, but your mom didn't get any negative comments?"

"Her side was more upset about having a gweilo in the family, to be honest. On my dad's side, it was clear they thought Mom was different but they liked it. Nonna once told me she was grateful to my mother for opening her eyes to new experiences. Like, soy sauce was new to her."

"Grandma thinks garlic is exotic."

"Nonna worked up from fried rice, but before she died, she was in love with spicy curries." He takes a fig with some goat cheese. "My mother created a fusion dish that involved noodles, cheese, and chopped squid arancini served with a curry laksa sauce. Nonna loved it once she got up the nerve to give it a try."

That doesn't sound appetizing but I don't say so. "I'll take your word on it."

"I'll make it for you. We call it curry squid cheese, and Nonna asked Mom to make it every time she came over."

"That's sweet." I'm a little jealous of his family's affection.

"What I'm hearing is this wouldn't happen with your family."

"God, no. Although—" I hesitate. "Sometimes it seems like she might be trying."

"She might be embarrassed or unsure about how to fix the situation," Teddy says.

What if Grandma got caught in a mindset that she wants to change? Do I owe it to family harmony to be kind? Do I owe it to her, even if Jade disagrees?

Do I owe it to me?

We eat quietly for a bit, and when the plates are cleared, Teddy says, "Questie."

"What about it?" I finish my wine and put the glass down with a soft clink on the metal table. We've ordered more cheese for dessert as well as a fruit tart to share.

"Have you thought more about volunteering to make a game?"

"I decided no. I'm a good player but not good enough for that."

He raises his eyebrows. "You don't have a file of perfect clue ideas?"

"They aren't good clues," I say, a bit flustered he read me so well.

"I find that difficult to believe. You should try for one of the puzzler roles. You're so good at it, Dee. You could be the next TigerCloud."

"TigerCloud is apparently a Mensa-level genius who has crosswords published in the *New York Times*."

"Good for them. You've been top of the leaderboard for months. You dominate this game."

Despite the clothes and food and romantic setting, I'm getting annoyed. "I don't want to do it."

"Are you sure? Or are you scared?"

That he's probably right makes me even madder. "What if I am? What if I'm also happy with the way things are?"

Teddy looks at the table. "Sorry, I was out of line. You don't have to want more."

The fruit tart arrives with coffee and has a flaky crust that melts in my mouth. I hardly pay attention to the dessert because of what Teddy said. I was happy with my job and my house and my life before it all went to hell a few months ago. A small snake of unease curls around my heart and squeezes tight with each beat. Should I want more? Isn't that what manifesting is for? Getting more money or peace or whatever?

He offers me the last bite of tart and I calm down. I have enough for now, and it's time to enjoy it while everything, for the moment, is working out.

———

Teddy wakes me up with a slow line of kisses along my bare back. I flip over and stretch as he trails his fingers along my ribs and the curves of my stomach. He's lean and tight with muscle, whereas I'm neither of those, and the contrast between how we feel when he drags me over so I'm lying on top of him makes me wish we had another day to spend in bed.

"I set the alarm a bit early," says Teddy.

"Why's that?" I let my legs drape down on each side of his hips as he sighs against my shoulder. This is much better than straddling him on a chair, although I wouldn't mind doing that one day, too.

"Thought you might want more time to pack." His hands slide down my hips to hold me in place. "Stop that. Oh my God, you're killing me."

"I only have one bag," I say, grabbing his wrists and pinning them down over his head. "Plenty of time."

"Good." His head goes back when he tries to move his hands and I press down harder. "Oh, very good."

TWENTY-SIX

*S*hit, shit, shit." We run through Charles de Gaulle, desperately trying to make the flight before the gate closes. Airports are never as big as when you're late. "I thought you were watching the time," I call to Teddy. He's got our bags.

"I *was busy*," he protests, voice drifting back to where I'm a couple steps behind.

We make the gate as they're doing last call and collapse into our fancy business class seats.

Teddy leans back with a sigh of relief. "Made it."

Luckily, there are bottles of water waiting for us, so I guzzle down half before I put on my seat belt. "Thank goodness." I didn't relish the idea of telling Vivian I was stuck in Paris because I was too busy getting laid to get to the airport on time.

He kisses my temple. "Even if we'd missed the flight, let me be the first to say it was worth it."

Easy for him to say. I shift on the seat, belatedly realizing that after a night—and morning—of more sex than I've had in the last year, this eight-hour flight is not going to be the most comfortable I've ever had.

At least I have room to stretch my legs and don't feel like I'm actively courting deep vein thrombosis. Business class is heaven compared to economy.

I look out the window and tick over the weekend's wins. When we get home, we can figure out how to best use our Jean-Pierre information. If all goes well, Michael might be out as soon as Tuesday. Then there's Teddy, currently struggling to get his bag back under the seat, who has given me possibly the best two days of my life. I might even be building something with Alejandra, who has texted me photos of her nieces and their cats over the weekend, like a friend would.

I shiver at how well everything is coming together, like it was meant to happen.

As the flight attendants walk down the aisle to check seat belts, I wiggle my phone out of my bag and turn it over to put it on airplane mode. There's a message from Jean-Pierre, who'd taken my number before he'd left the café yesterday.

Daiyu, it reads. I've reconsidered my decision and you may not use my story. Should you do it anyway, I will deny everything.

That's it. Direct and unsoftened by apologies or regrets.

I let out a long, soft sigh, and Teddy looks over. "Dee?"

Silently, I hand him the phone. It only takes him a moment to read the message, and then he hands it back. "Shit. Do you think you can talk him into it?"

"I'm not going to try."

"Why not? He might only need a bit of convincing."

I shake my head. "He has to be in this with his whole heart. If I push him, he might say yes to get me off his case, but could we trust him to come through when we need?"

Teddy hesitates. "I don't know."

"Me neither, and that's not good enough." Jean-Pierre's choice has to be respected. I loosen my grip on the phone and send back a single message—I understand and will be here if you change your mind. No guilt trips, no accusations. Nothing to close the door if he decides to reconsider. Teddy watches me but says nothing.

If it's meant to be, it will be. Que sera sera, although apparently Doris Day didn't even like that song. I close my eyes as Teddy takes my hand.

"It was all working out." I say it to the window but Teddy hears.

"You did what you could."

Had I, though? Had I done it all, covered every contingency? Obviously not. Teddy and Alejandra had counted on me and I'd failed. I'd been so focused on picturing my success that I hadn't done the practical planning that might have prevented Jean-Pierre's second thoughts.

"No, I didn't." I close my eyes. "Alejandra wanted to know what I was going to do, and I told her I had it under control. I thought it would all turn out because I wanted it to."

"You're taking responsibility for something that's not solely your problem."

The plane starts to move down the runway. "I could have come up with a detailed plan to convince him," I insist. "I was the one meeting Jean-Pierre, and instead of doing any preparation, all I did was envision a good outcome."

"There's nothing wrong with that," Teddy says. "Visualizations can work."

"Only when you do the work as well as hoping for the best," I mutter, but my voice is lost under the roar of the engines.

"We'll think of something."

"What if we can't?" I ask morosely.

He kisses my head. "Then we can't and we deal with it. This was only our first try."

I like that attitude, but I don't know if I can get there. I feel the need to somehow mitigate his realistic assessment with some sort of encouraging statement to keep the good energies on my side. Jesus, am I positive or simply superstitious? Is this the modern equivalent of throwing salt over my left shoulder? I shake my head and Teddy leans close.

"Dee..."

"I don't want to talk about it right now. Please."

"Later then."

I fall into an uneasy doze and find Teddy's comforting hand on my thigh every time I'm jostled into semialertness. I'm grateful for his touch because self-recrimination perches on my shoulder like a gremlin.

I'm not sure how long we've been in the air when Teddy wakes up, slowly blinking himself alert before squeezing my leg. "Hi," he says.

"Hi." I was already awake, mulling over the Jean-Pierre situation and trying to get back to my usual self. I'm sure there's a benefit to what happened, even if I can't find it at the moment.

"It's later," he says softly, or as softly as he can while being heard over the brown noise of the plane.

"What are you talking about?"

He sits up straight. "You agreed to talk about Jean-Pierre later. It's later."

"It's all fine," I say.

"Dee. *Talk* to me."

"It's no big deal. Things go wrong, and you're right. I need to stop being oversensitive and move on."

His frown goes from a dip of his lips and tiny furrow between his brows to a full-fledged glower.

"That's not what I said."

"You basically did." I sip my water.

"We said we'd be honest."

"I am being honest."

"Not with yourself," he says, taking my hand. "It's normal to be disappointed. I, for one, think this is a total shit sandwich. You can, too."

No, I can't. After all, I'm a card-carrying member of the cult of positivity, joyfully indoctrinated at birth. To admit I'm upset goes against our first commandment, which is to always look on the bright side. "It's not useful, Teddy." I look down as he laces our fingers together. "What's the point of being upset? It doesn't change Jean-Pierre's mind."

"So you're happy with the situation? Not a single part of you is thinking, Well, *fuck this*?" I can tell he's getting a bit frustrated.

"Obviously I'm not."

"Then why do you insist on pretending it's not a big deal?" he asks. "It's almost like you're scared to admit this sucks."

"Because it's bad." I can't believe I have to explain something so simple. "Being upset is bad, alright? Being unhappy is bad."

He looks at me with serious eyes as he thinks this through. "Are you telling me that you think being upset about Jean-Pierre—not even with him, but with the situation—somehow makes you a bad person?" He speaks slowly, as if testing each word.

I shrug. It sounds strange when he says it like that.

"Dee." He twists to look at me. "Do you think I'm a jerk for being mad?"

"No, of course not."

"Only you, then. Why?"

I shrug again. "It's different if it's me."

Teddy looks like he's going to explode. "No it's not. It's not different at all."

"It is," I insist.

"How?"

"Because..." I peter off. "It just is."

Teddy's groan of exasperation is interrupted by the flight attendant with trays of food, including a little round of brie, which is exciting. Teddy gives me his in exchange for my fruit salad and by mutual consent, we stick to neutral conversation topics until Teddy dozes off again.

Then I stare bleary-eyed at the row of movies displayed on the headrest screen in front of me and think about what he said. Even I know *just because* is a weak answer but I'm struggling to find a better one. It's possible Teddy's right and I'm scared, but admitting that to another human being is impossible when I can barely think it to myself. After all, I know what Jade and probably Teddy would tell me. There's nothing to be scared of. They don't understand that to me it would be the tiny sound that sets off an avalanche that would bury Mom's Sunny Dee. And at the end, who would I be?

Mom's voice comes to me, a childhood memory from one day after school, telling me to brighten up because tomorrow is another day. She's right. Things will look up when I'm rested.

Despite my swirling mind, I go back to sleep. When I wake up again, jostled my seat, I'm groggy and my skin feels both dry and oily. However, I'm pleased to note that my plan worked, and I'm far more composed than I was an hour ago and able to see a way forward.

I had a setback and I won't give up, but this time, I'll depend on more than affirmations and hope. I'm going to make a plan instead of expecting it all to go the way I want. I'll start as soon as we're back home because my frustration with what happened with Jean-Pierre has morphed into an iron determination that Michael is not going to get away with this. Not on my watch.

Teddy wakes up. "How do you feel?" he asks.

"Better. A lot to think about."

"Do you want to talk about the feelings thing?"

"I get what you're saying," I say because that much is true. "I need to think about it."

He leans over and kisses me. "Okay."

Thanks to time zones, when we land in Toronto, it's about two hours after we left Paris, which is convenient if unnerving to my body clock. After we pass through the baggage claim, Teddy and I stand outside arrivals. "Can I take you home?" he asks. "We can share a cab."

We're close enough in the same direction that I don't feel needy for saying yes, and I'm not quite ready to say goodbye. Teddy holds my hand, and we sit quietly as the cab comes into the city and starts to wind its way to my house. My mind jumps from thought to thought, with my hormones on a consistent high after a romantic weekend in Paris and my emotions varying between a low thinking about Jean-Pierre and what Teddy said, then a high after my decision on the plane to make things happen. I shut my eyes and will my brain to calm down for a minute.

Teddy looks out with interest at my neighborhood, and when we pull up at my house, he says, "Your place looks cute."

"I only wish it was less crowded," I say.

He leans over for a last kiss, and I let myself be comforted by his touch.

I'm halfway up the walk when a text comes from him.

Teddy: I miss you already.

A small smile starts on my face as I open the door to Chilly's wheel squeaking away despite the regular oiling Dad's been giving it. Nothing to worry about.

Because things are going to start changing.

TWENTY-SEVEN

DAILY AFFIRMATION: I AM ENERGIZED WITH
PURPOSE AND INTENT. WAIT, ARE THOSE THE SAME?

I t's time to talk to Vivian about what's going on with Michael and
Jean-Pierre and get her thoughts on next steps. But she's been
away from work, making me progressively antsier as she declines my
coffee meeting, then cancels our lunch. I'm wondering if it's worth
sending her an email with no details but making it clear I have an
update, despite her orders not to, when I finally snag an opportunity
after our usual meeting at Gear Robins. I'd prefer to talk to her away
from the office, but I'll take what I can get.

Vivian looks as professional as ever but it seems as if she's moving
a little slower, like she's dragging herself through water. She puts
down a huge cup of coffee and lowers herself into the chair as if her
bones ache.

"You seem a bit tired?" I ask the question carefully, not sure if asking
would constitute an overstep but feeling as if not asking would be rude.

"I'm fine." She brushes off my concern with a quick flick of her wrist.
"Let's get started."

The meeting is fairly straightforward, and she only has a few suggestions about where I can make changes. She brushes her hand down

her hair, then picks up the coffee, and puts it down without drinking. "Are we done? I need to leave."

"Oh, umm, okay." I'm a bit taken aback.

"Was there something else?" Vivian seems a bit impatient. "You know what you need to do?"

"Yes, but I booked a meeting with you. For after this one."

Her phone beeps, and she shuts her eyes briefly after checking it. "Sorry. Right. What about?"

"It's the issue we talked about."

This settles her back in her chair. "Oh?"

Lowering my voice, I say, "I thought we had proof against Michael, but the designer who told us won't let us say anything."

"That happens. Quite often, actually. Retribution is a real fear." She presses her lips together. "They're young, I suppose? New to the industry?"

"Yes. He lives in Paris, and I went to see him but he—"

She holds a hand up. "Slow down. You what?"

"Saw him in Paris."

"You physically went to Paris? Paris, Ontario?"

"France. He refused to talk to us any way that could be recorded."

Vivian looks more alert. "Did he now?"

"He was worried after Michael threatened him." I give her a brief rundown of the conversation.

"When was this?"

"Last weekend."

She closes her eyes and visibly counts to ten. "You didn't tell me immediately?"

"I'm sorry," I say. "You weren't at work, and you cancelled the meetings I tried to set. That's why I wanted to talk to you today."

"Daiyu." She shakes her head. "What were you thinking, chasing this man to Paris?"

"You told me to take notes!"

"How is this taking notes?" She sounds infuriated. "This isn't notes! I also said don't do anything until you talk to me. You think I haven't dealt with this kind of thing before?"

"I didn't know."

"No, because you acted first. Instead, you go to Paris, interview this Jean-Pierre." She looks at me. "He has your name?"

"Yes."

"He can find out where you work. That's a reputational risk for Gear Robins as well. Excellent." She rubs her hands together, and the dry rasp puts my teeth on edge.

"Vivian?" I ask uncertainly.

"Daiyu." She looks drained. "Do you know how many years I've been coming into this Gear Robins office?"

"No."

"Eight years. Eight years, and you know what I do? I work. I get the job done the way it's supposed to be done, because I do not have time for this. I have a child who is in the hospital. I have an ill mother I am caring for at home. I have more clients than any other consultant. Now I also have to deal with you."

"I didn't know," I say, looking down. "I'm sorry."

"I don't need you to be sorry. I need you to stop and think about reality and consequences instead of acting like things will work out." She sighs. "You're frustrated. I am too."

"I'm sick of waiting," I say. "I want change now. What's happening is not fair or right or...anything."

"I know," she says.

"Ah, there's more." I might as well lay it all out since I can see the dribble method of information sharing is not Vivian's preferred process.

"More?" She closes her eyes.

"I went with Teddy. Ted, the VP at—"

"I know who Ted is," she breaks in. "What do you mean, *went with*? You need to clarify this."

"I didn't travel there with him, but he was in Paris at the time and, yeah…" I trail off before I saddle up and spit it out. "We're seeing each other. Dating?"

Her blinking becomes more rapid. "You are romantically involved."

"Yes!" I'm about to thank her for finding the correct wording when I realize now is not the time and it was not done as a favor to me.

"Are you planning to continue your relationship with Ted Marsh?"

"Yes."

Vivian looks at the door as if wishing I was on the other side of it. "Ted isn't our direct contact at Celeste, so our policies don't expressly forbid a relationship," she says as if mentally consulting the employee handbook. "However, I shouldn't have to tell you it's ill-advised at best."

"We know and we're keeping it private. Teddy's adamant no one at Celeste knows, too."

"You've known him how long?"

"We'd been chatting online for a couple months, but I didn't know he worked at Celeste until I started there." I rub my eyes in the hopes it will dispel the slight headache from the fluorescent overhead lights.

Her eyebrows raise high enough for her forehead to fold on itself. "That seems like a fairly common thing to have covered early on."

"It was complicated."

"Daiyu." This time, her voice softens. "For once, think about what you're doing. Wait until you're done with the project. It's not that long."

"I have thought about it." I try not to sound stubborn but I'm only sure about one thing in this mess, and it's Teddy.

"Have you truly considered the impact this could have on your career?" Vivian flattens her hands against the table. "Your career and probably not his?"

"Teddy has a lot riding on keeping his father happy, and his father would see this as a lack of judgment. Both of us have a lot to lose."

She shakes her head. "It's different for you, and you know that."

"It will be fine," I assure her. "We're going to be cautious."

"This is an extremely bad idea," she warns me. "I can't stop you, but I hope I never have to say I told you so."

"You won't," I say confidently.

Vivian blows her breath out. It takes several seconds. "All right."

"Are you telling Will?"

She hesitates. "No. As I said, this doesn't contravene our policy."

"I'm sorry to have dumped all this on you today."

"Me too," she says. "Let me make it clear that if you want to stay with this client, if you want to stay with *Gear Robins*, you will tell me in advance before you do something, especially if it's something reckless. By that I mean by normal-person standards, not whatever scale you use. Is that clear?"

"Yes."

"Is there anything else?"

Now is not the time to ask her advice on next steps. I shake my head.

"The only reason I'm giving you any slack is that you tried to tell me earlier." She puts her laptop in her bag. "Otherwise we would be having a different conversation, no matter how good the quality of your work has become here."

"I understand."

She levels me with a look. "I also want you to do some deep-down soul-searching on whether you'd be pulling this kind of thing if you had to answer to Will and not me."

This floors me, and I pull back my knee-jerk reaction to think about it seriously. I picture Will in her chair before I imagine a woman who looks more like Jenna or Liz. Or me. And I think very hard about what Vivian has asked.

"No, I wouldn't," I say eventually.

"You think it's acceptable to challenge my authority like this and not someone else?" Her voice is arctic cold.

I can feel the red coming up my face. "I know what you're saying, but if it was anyone else, I don't think I would have told them at all. I wouldn't have trusted them for advice, and I definitely wouldn't have told them about Teddy or going to Paris. You don't agree with what I did, but it doesn't mean I don't respect you. I do."

"Strange how it doesn't feel that way because you keep not listening."

"I am listening." I frown down at my hands. "I can respect you and your expertise while wanting to act differently from the Gear Robins way. If you transferred me to another consultant, I wouldn't change what I do, but I'd change what I tell them about it."

Vivian shoulders relax slightly. "A good thing there won't be any more bombshells to drop on me."

"There won't." I can't look at her when I say this. "I like working with you. I'm learning a lot."

This makes her laugh even though it's a bit dry. "Let's hope some of that is how to be patient."

Then she leaves. Of course I should have told Vivian before I left for Paris. Be real. I didn't tell her because I knew how she'd react. I didn't want her to talk me out of it or forbid me, because I knew it was something I had to do.

Like I have to keep trying, although in a less spectacular way. More behind the scenes, to keep my word to Vivian. I send a thought to the universe asking for success out of habit. It can't hurt for some extra help.

———

Alejandra is disappointed but unsurprised when we tell her the full Jean-Pierre story over drinks the next day. "It was always a long shot," she says. "This is a guy who crossed an ocean to get away from Michael."

"I also updated Vivian," I say. "She wasn't happy."

"Did she say to stop?" asks Alejandra.

Teddy says nothing, as I'd told him earlier that Vivian now knew about us. He'd taken it in stride, luckily, after I'd assured him she wouldn't be informing Will or Celeste.

"She said to be careful." This is technically true. "Which we will be because I have a plan." I fish my notebook out of my bag and open it to the first page, which has "PLAN" written at the top. The page is crowded with bubbles filled with my messy writing connected by arrows. In the middle is a big letter M with an X through it.

"Have you been sleeping?" asks Alejandra with concern. "Do you want some red string and pushpins to cement that conspiracy vibe?"

I tap the page. "This is where we begin, but before that, a check-in."

They look at me expectantly.

"Stage one is confirming that we're all in this together," I say. "This is the point of no return. If you want out, no hard feelings."

"I'm in," says Teddy.

Alejandra nods vigorously. "Me too. This has gone on long enough."

It has. I put my hand facedown in the middle of the table. Teddy puts his on mine, and even this small touch in a high-stakes conversation is enough to cause my thoughts to momentarily veer into a brief fantasy of those damn hands. Then Alejandra puts her hand on top, pressing down to seal the deal.

"Do we need a cheer?" I ask.

"U-G-L-Y, he's probably got an alibi," chants Alejandra. "He's ugly. I hate him."

"That's got spirit," approves Teddy. We bounce our hands and wave them in the air.

"Looks like Team Mutiny is a go," Alejandra says.

Teddy frowns. "Can we get a better name?"

"What is it with you and group names?" I ask.

"They're really effective for morale," he says earnestly. "How about the Mutineers?"

"How is that better than Team Mutiny?" scoffs Alejandra.

Teddy shrugs. "That's a bit basic."

"*What?*"

"We should focus on our next steps," I say, intervening.

"It's too bad Jean-Pierre is a dead end," mourns Alejandra. "He was our best bet."

"Never say never," I say. "I'm working on that and will have some options to present soon. In the interim, we need some alternatives. I open the floor to your thoughts."

Alejandra points at the notepad. "You don't have any ideas in that collection?"

"They're not great," I admit. "My jet lag was catching up on me."

Teddy looks at Alejandra. "I wouldn't have any excuse to get into his office, but how about you?"

"Locked," Alejandra says. "I'll keep trying because we know he's arrogant enough to keep the designs there. I'm also trying to track down who else he could have stolen from."

"I looked in the HR files I have access to, but there was nothing," I say. "Is there anything an executive can find?"

Teddy clicks his tongue as he thinks. "Let me try, but we put in a new HR platform last summer that tracks any activity, including logging in. I need an excuse."

"Hiring a new intern?" Alejandra suggests. "A crossover between your department and Michael's?"

Teddy snorts. "He'd love me coming into his territory. Good idea, though. It gives me a reason to at least be in the system. I can also suggest to Kylie in communications that Michael's design process would be a good story for the company newsletter. He might let something slip."

"Do you two have any industry contacts you trust?" I ask. "There might be some rumors, other people with the same story as Jean-Pierre."

They nod. "It's been a while since I've talked to my contacts," Teddy admits. "It's time I change that anyway. Meeting up with friends in Paris was a blast."

I decide there's no need to tell Vivian until we have some actionable information. None of these count as reckless actions.

He glances at his phone. "Sorry, I have to head out for a meeting." Teddy leans in as if to kiss me, then thinks twice, since we're in public and Alejandra is watching us like a hawk. "I'm honored to be part of the Mutineers."

"Team Mutiny," corrects Alejandra. "The clearly superior name."

Alejandra goes to the washroom when he leaves and I check my texts. There's already one from Teddy, and I'm smiling when Alejandra slides back into her seat.

"What happened?" she asks. That woman is observant.

"Nothing."

She follows my eyes to my phone in time to see a notification pop up to show another text from Teddy. I need to redo my phone settings.

She sighs. "Do you want some advice?"

"Probably not."

"Too bad. It's what my abuela told me when I started working. Don't chase your honey where you get your money."

I make a face into my drink. "Is that a classier way of saying, 'Don't shit where you eat'?"

"You got it."

"There's nothing between us," I lie.

She raises her eyebrows. "Paris? The city of love?"

"Honest, nothing," I lie again. I need to talk to Teddy before spilling the beans to someone at work, even if it's Alejandra.

"No one being honest says *honest*."

"Well, I do."

"He's upsettingly attractive," she says in an indifferent tone.

"If you like that kind of look." Which I do, quite a lot.

"Well-dressed. Bedroom eyes. Those hands."

"I know, right?" I enthuse. Then I catch her smirk. "I mean, stop objectifying people."

"Those are facts."

I lay my head on the table. "They are."

We sit in silence for a minute, then I lift up my head and dust the crumbs from my forehead. "What if?"

Alejandra raises her eyebrow. "Yes?"

"If one did like Teddy. I mean Ted. Is that so bad?"

"I should lie about this to save you from yourself, but no." Alejandra tucks her chin down. "I feel bad for him. He's wasted at Celeste. Daddy Marsh must have threatened to cut off his inheritance or something if he didn't come on board because he's a genius. I told you he was a fashion darling but that's also because he was an extraordinary designer."

"That good?" I knew this from my research and personal experience, but it gives me a thrill to hear about it from Alejandra, like hearing your favorite song on the radio despite having it on a playlist.

She gives a fervent nod. "A version of one of his jackets hit every runway when he launched Mars. Chanel copied it. Valentino. Celine. He had a rabid following, and his designs still get referenced in collections."

"Seriously?"

"He was cool, too. No advertising. Total commitment to sustainability. Paid fair and completely transparent. Like, Stella McCartney wanted to partner with him."

"I thought Mars didn't survive."

"No, he definitely made some business mistakes." She rubs her eyes. "It's a crime he refuses to have anything to do with the design side of Celeste. I'd love to work with him but that'll never happen. Michael would lose his mind."

I do my best to keep a big smile off my face. Hearing good things about Teddy makes me giddy.

"When he started, Ted pushed hard for inclusive sizing," she says. "It makes a lot of sense on the business side, and if Celeste wants to expand, it needs to court women of all sizes. Do you know how bullshit it is that I can't even fit into my own company's clothes?"

"What happened?"

"Michael said if women wanted to wear Celeste, they needed to look good in it."

"Why am I not surprised?"

"Typical for him. Edward agreed that we needed to focus our womens wear on a target desired audience, with the insinuation that larger ladies could stick to handbags." She shakes her head.

"Teddy fought them on this?"

"He tried. He had stacks of spreadsheets and numbers about how it would improve sales since he knew that would be the only argument that had a chance to sway them. Michael complained he was hampering the brand vision, and Edward made it clear to Ted he was overstepping publicly in a staff meeting."

"Wow." Poor Teddy.

"I'll say. In any other case, I'd tell you to go for it, but here? Now?" She makes a face. "Seems like a bad idea. Like a career ender."

"Yeah?"

"Yeah." She eyeballs me over her glass. "I suggest you keep that in mind."

TWENTY-EIGHT

The next night, I'm staring at my vision board and thinking about a fitting inspirational image to represent retribution when Mom calls me down to eat. Pancakes, as it's breakfast for dinner.

I sit down and reach for the jam. "Pineapple?"

"It's your grandmother's favorite," Mom says. "When she eats jam."

There's no accurate personality test based on jam preference that I know of, but I'm a little surprised. I'd pegged Grandma as a strawberry enthusiast, with brief forays into the dangerous world of seedless raspberry if she felt a bit edgy.

We've finished a relatively peaceful meal when a knock comes at the door. "Ignore it," says Dad. "We're not expecting anyone."

"David, we can't do that," says Mom as she gets up, holding her back with one hand. "It's not polite."

"I'll get it, Mom."

To my surprise, it's Jade, standing with some books she'd promised to lend me. "Hey, sorry for the late surprise visit," she says. "We're taking the kids home from skating but thought we'd drop..."

"Is that Jade?" Mom bustles up to the door. "Come in! Where are the kids?"

"In the car." Jade thrusts the books at me and glances back at the car where her family waits. "Sorry, Mom, we're about to..."

"I haven't seen my babies in so long; you can stay a few minutes." Mom is out the door toward the car before Jade can answer. Her voice drifts back to the house. "Who wants to see the chinchilla?"

There's an eruption of cheers, and Jade pinches the bridge of her nose as Opal, gracefully giving in to the inevitable, unbuckles the kids and lets them loose.

"What the fuck," Jade says softly to Opal as Mom takes the kids in. "I'm sorry, babe. I thought she said she'd be out."

"It's fine. Hi, Dee. How's my favorite sister-in-law?"

"I'm your only sister-in-law."

"So you are." Opal gives me a hug, her short red hair tickling my cheek. "Jade, don't worry. Seven minutes and then we're off to dinner before the kids melt down." She goes in the house after setting her phone timer.

"I don't deserve her," Jade says with admiration. "How can she be so kind and so cold?"

"She's amazing," I agree.

We follow Opal in to see the children looking wide-eyed at Grandma and holding Mom's hands as everyone tries to find some space to stand in the crammed house.

"Hi," Jade says, keeping her distance.

"You look well, Jade." Then Grandma gives a small smile to Opal. "Hello, Opal. It's nice to see you again."

This unexpected olive branch to her wife is enough for Jade to engage politely instead of grabbing her kids and packing them back in the car, chinchilla promise or not. She introduces Poppy and Nick with the standard, "You remember Great-Grandma," which they do not. No surprise. They've only met her once or twice.

"Give Great-Grandma a hug," Mom insists, tugging them forward.

Poppy pulls away before putting her hands behind her back and shaking her head.

"Poppy," Mom says in a warning tone. "Be a good girl, like your brother is being a good boy."

Nick, an inveterate hugger, went up right away. Grandma pats his shoulder awkwardly as he clings to her legs.

Jade steps in front of her daughter. "Poppy is allowed to choose who she hugs," she says evenly.

"My God, Jade, why do you have to make such a fuss over the simplest things?" asks Mom. She glances at Grandma and lowers her voice. "It's only a hug."

"If it's only a hug, then it won't be a problem." Jade stands her ground, and I glance between them. Both have mulish looks on their faces, and memories of teenage standoffs about everything from curfews to Mom promising the neighbors Jade would babysit flash before my eyes.

Dad must see the same thing, because he bends down as Opal puts a hand on Jade's arm.

"Do you like animals?" he asks Poppy and Nick.

The kids nod, Poppy peeking out from behind Jade.

Grandma releases herself from Nick. "I do, too. I have a chinchilla you can pet if you're careful. Would you like that?"

More nods, and the tension in the room fades. Grandma gives instructions on the best way to hold Chilly to keep him calm and safe as the kids listen closely.

"Grandma was never that nice to us," Jade whispers to me, her eyes trained on her kids. "Remember when you broke her candy dish and she didn't talk to us the rest of the visit?"

"What about when you showed her the painting you were so proud of and all she said was that horses weren't blue?"

The two of us share these memories in soft whispers, kind of laughing and kind of not. Then Mom comes closer to ask Opal about work and we shut up.

Disaster strikes a minute later when Poppy's grip slips and Chilly, seeing his opportunity, leaps out of her arms.

"Chilly!" Poppy's panicked cry grabs our attention away from tedious talk about gas prices. Jade and Opal move forward, but Grandma brushes her hand over Poppy's hair.

"It's okay," she says. "Can you help me find him?"

"I can help!" Poppy's tears stop as she drops to the floor to look. Jade's surprise is written on her face. This is not the grandma we grew up with. This is like a *Twilight Zone* grandma from the world of what could have been, maybe a transplant from that alternate universe where she was kindly Nana hanging out with red-haired Tokyo Dee.

Despite my hatred of his squeaky wheel, I've formed a soft spot for the little guy, so I join the kids on the floor to peer under furniture and make a clicking noise. It works for cats, so I assume it'll track for chinchillas. Eventually Poppy finds him huddled next to a wall and looking like a fretful beach ball with gigantic ears.

"Everyone, you're scaring him." It's Dad, coming into the room with some raisins. "I have an idea."

It takes some coaxing, but to everyone's relief, Chilly is soon back in his cage. Once he's safe, Poppy looks up with big wet eyes. "I didn't mean it," she says in a small voice.

"Oh, Poppy, it's nothing to cry about," says Mom. "Give me a smile. You'll upset your brother."

"Enough, Mom," says Jade, breathing deep.

"She's being a little silly bean is what she's being. Right, silly bean?" Mom waits for Poppy to nod uncertainly. "Aren't you a big little silly?"

Jade's jaw clenches, but before she can explode, Grandma leans over to Poppy. "You were a big help," she says, her voice softer than I've ever heard it.

Part of me is pleased at how gentle she's being with the kids. Part is bitter that she couldn't have done the same for Jade and me at that age. *Maybe the Chinese blood has been diluted enough for Poppy to be acceptable,* says that unpleasant voice.

"Time to go," says Jade, herding her kids toward the door. Grandma struggles to stand, but before Mom can come over, Dad holds out his hand. Grandma looks at it for a moment, then lets him help her up.

For the first time I can remember, Grandma looks at Dad in the face as she speaks. "Thank you," she says, so quietly it's almost lost in the background noise. Dad hears it, though, and his smile is genuine. Is this the success of water around an obstacle, eroding bad feelings over the long years? Or has simply being around us helped her be more comfortable, like exposure therapy but for people instead of heights or open spaces?

I walk Jade to the car, Mom behind us chatting to the kids and Opal about the skating rink.

"Would you come back and visit?" I ask in a low voice. "A real one? I miss you."

"I don't know." Jade makes a face and looks at the sky. "You should come to our place. We have more room, that's for sure, and no one will nag at my kids."

"There you go again, making a mountain out of a molehill," Mom says loudly, materializing behind us. "You should encourage your children's natural happiness instead of trying to turn them neurotic. It's not like they have any real problems."

Jade stops, forcing Mom to do a little dance back to avoid walking into her. "Mom, I have told you not to comment on our parenting. We are doing what we think is best."

"I've told you a thousand times you're too sensitive," says Mom. "You should listen to me. I raised the two of you, and look how you turned out. You were always my sunny Dee and jolly Jade."

I can tell this pushes Jade past her breaking point, in part because being called jolly when one is not dressed as Santa is utterly obnoxious.

Opal, sensing trouble, ushers the kids over to the car, calling, "Great to see you! Jessica, do you want to come say goodbye to the kids?"

"They can't go without giving their grandma a big kiss!" Mom bustles around to the other side of the car.

My sister stares after her. "How do you stand it?" she asks me in a low voice.

I check that Mom's not listening. "It's not that bad."

"No, Dee, it is."

"Mama, dinner!" Poppy calls from the back seat. Mom has already gone back in.

Jade's shoulders relax. "Call me if you need me, okay?"

I give her a hug, thinking about the way Opal smiled at her and how Jade gets to go back to her own home, filled with people she chose to be in it. Good for her. It's not like I'm jealous.

Well, I have Teddy. At least secretly.

TWENTY-NINE

*DAILY AFFIRMATION: I AM RESILIENT AND
CAN RECOVER FROM ANY DIFFICULTY
AS LONG AS IT'S NOT TOO BAD.*

This sucks," complains Alejandra. It's a month since Paris, and every attempt to get undeniable proof that Michael is taking advantage of young designers has failed. I couldn't find anything in the HR files I had access to. Teddy's request for an intern was denied by Gary, and when he tried to access the new HR system, he found he could only look at his direct reports, which naturally did not include Michael. Although Teddy had mentioned that staff at Celeste would be most interested in the behind-the-scenes secrets of Michael's process, Kylie's fawning newsletter feature had mostly focused on Michael bragging about the Celestial bag, which had Teddy grinding his teeth down to nubs. We couldn't even find out who leaked the initial diversity data, thinking they would be a good ally.

We sit morosely around the table. "I refuse to admit defeat," I say.

Alejandra takes a sip of her lavender latte. It's lunch, and we're in a tiny hole-in-the-wall that serves what Teddy claims are the best drinks in the city. I have a crème brûlée hot chocolate and Teddy chose matcha. They're excellent drinks, but as Alejandra pointed out, for eight dollars each, they should be.

"There has to be something," says Teddy. "Anything."

"The only thing could be..." Alejandra thinks. "I have access to his calendar."

"Seriously?" I ask.

She gives me a look. "To make it easier for me to book his meetings. He forgets I can see everything on it, and he sometimes he puts in personal things like dinner dates."

"Have you checked it recently?" I ask.

"Order for Teddy," calls the barista.

Alejandra eyeballs me as Teddy goes up to the counter to collect the plate of mini muffins we ordered. "How are things going with lover boy, Dee?" Like Teddy, she's started calling me Dee.

"Good." With his agreement, I'd eventually told her Teddy and I were together. Her reaction had been almost identical to Vivian's, accompanied by a chant of "I knew it! I *knew* it!"

"You're not too gross to be around," she says grudgingly. "That's a blessing."

"Seems like a challenge." I grin at her.

"Please no."

Teddy comes back with the muffins, warm from the oven and smelling like heaven. "What are you two laughing about?" he asks.

"Nothing," we chorus.

"Sure." He gives my shoulder an affectionate touch that causes Alejandra to sigh heavily. "Anything on his calendar?"

"A bunch of boring work stuff," Alejandra says as she scans it, picking up a bright pink raspberry muffin. "Some events I didn't put in."

Teddy peers over her shoulder and points at something. "What about that?"

"J at one in the afternoon today." She checks her watch. "That's now. Is he meeting someone? Going to a place that starts with a J? Smoking a big old jay?"

Teddy starts ticking through his fingers. "Jane Keen is in Vancouver.

I talked to her the other day. Stanwick Jackson from the Fashion Council?"

"Whatever it is, he needs to come back to the office because we have a meeting at two," she says.

We each take another muffin. "Why are tiny muffins tastier than regular ones?" I ask.

"Like how Timbits are better than doughnuts," agrees Teddy.

We look at the calendar. Every other event except the one with J has details—who, where. "This has to be something," I say.

Teddy nods. "Let's get back to the office and see if he looks shady when he comes in."

"He always looks shady," mutters Alejandra.

We each jam a last muffin into our mouths and head out the door, having decided that Alejandra and Teddy will keep an eye out for Michael since I have a meeting.

They take the TTC on separate routes, and I grab a cab to make my meeting, a pleasant and long-awaited sense of possible victory humming inside me. It's been a hard month, and we deserve a break. At least Vivian has warmed up to me after our Paris discussion. It helps that we've been in perfect alignment over my recent work, which has built some trust, and we've avoided talking about Celeste issues related to Michael and global inequity, although I've been doing more research privately on the latter.

Then there's Teddy. Last week, we'd gone to a movie and walked around making puns about street names. The puns had been terrible, but he'd held my hand and we'd ducked into every dark corner to kiss. That had been incredible.

I also continued as number one Questie player, which is pleasing.

After my meeting, I check my phone, eager to see if we have any news about the mysterious J. I'd had to silence it and keep it in my bag to focus on Jenna's HR policy discussion, and I scroll almost faster than I can read.

Teddy: I'm in reception but not sure if he's back.

Alejandra: Negative. He's not in the studio.

Teddy: Here he comes. He's not holding anything. No bag. No portfolios. Maybe the meeting was with his proctologist or something.

Alejandra: No, he puts the details of his medical appointments in his calendar and that was last month.

The next message from Alejandra comes forty-five minutes later, after her meeting.

Alejandra: We have him. There was something in his coat pocket, like a sketchbook. I'm going to try and find it. It must be in his office.

Teddy: Is that a good idea?

That's the end of the text thread, and I type out a message as fast as I can.

Me: Don't do it! It's not worth the risk of getting caught. It might not be anything. Meet me near the vending machines. We need to talk. Teddy, can you make it?

There's no answer—he must be busy—so I head down jingling a pocket of change, my worry about getting caught making the very normal trip to get a drink feel hazardous. Alejandra is there feeding quarters into the pop machine.

"I'm going to do it," she mutters. "We don't have a choice."

Luckily there's no one in the hall. "I'm working on a plan for Jean-Pierre. He'll come through. Trust the process."

"I'm tired of waiting."

"So am I, but we need to be careful when taking action." I jab A5 for a bag of Cheetos that will turn my fingers orange, then decide I also want a Coke.

"That hasn't worked."

"I don't think you should do this. Well-considered action is our method."

Alejandra waits until my drink tumbles down to speak. "I'll think about it."

"Thanks."

She cheers me with her can and opens it to spray brown foam over the edge. "Goddammit."

"You forgot to tap it."

"That's a myth." She shakes the pop off her hand.

I hold up my Coke, tap it three times, and open it to an even bigger spray of foam.

She smirks at me. "Considered action, my ass."

"Shut up."

"You shut up."

Laughing, we salute each other with our dripping cans and head off. Vivian would be pleased that I did the right thing here, and I'm satisfied Alejandra will agree once she considers it.

———

When I arrive at Celeste the next morning, Jenna is in the middle of a small knot of women, all of them talking excitedly.

"They had to get security to escort her out," says one, eyes wide.

"Are you kidding?" asks Jenna. "That seems extreme."

"God knows what else she was up to," says another righteously. "Snooping around in Michael's office? It's a good thing I lock my stuff up at night."

"Hey," says Jenna sharply. "That's not cool. She's not like that."

The other woman smirks. "Security begs to differ."

"I don't care," Jenna says. "There must be something else going on."

Oh shit. They're talking about Alejandra. I wait until Jenna is alone at the printer to approach her.

"Did something happen?" I put my hands in my pockets to hide the trembling.

She glances around, then leads me over to a little closet. "Don't put this in your notes, okay?"

I nod.

"Michael says someone was spying in his office early this morning, but I don't believe it," Jenna whispers. "That person does most of the work in the design studio, so if those are her designs in the first place, why would she need to steal them?"

"Wouldn't he want to keep her around then?"

"God, no. Michael? He'd see this as a good way to get rid of her, the snake." She claps a hand over her mouth. "I didn't say that."

"Why didn't you tell me this earlier?" I ask, trying not to be annoyed. How can I do my job if no one tells me the truth?

Jenna looks astonished. "Why bother, since nothing would happen? Every place I've worked at has a bunch of women doing what needs to be done but without the pay or credit they deserve."

Like how I ghostwrote the book with George's name on it. "It matters," I say, getting angry. "It's not fair."

"Oh, fair." She rolls her eyes. "Life's not fair."

"It could be."

She turns to head back to the printer. "It's not, though."

I rush back to my office and text Alejandra.

Me: Is it true?

The reply comes in a minute.

Alejandra: It's possible you were right and I made a bad call.
Me: That's not important now. Are you okay?

Alejandra: I'm only angry. It's true he caught me but I'm sure whatever he's saying is bull. I need to see what my lawyer says. I didn't find anything.
Me: I'm sorry.
Alejandra: Only one person did anything wrong, and it wasn't you or me. I'll keep you updated.
Me: Tell me if you want to talk.

There's no answer. I go back to my work, wishing I could talk to Teddy or anyone. But it's time for my first meeting, and the day goes by without me learning any more.

THIRTY

*A*lejandra throws her head back against the couch. It's the next night, and we're having an emergency Team Mutiny—I have to agree with her that it's the superior name—meeting at Teddy's place for privacy. She shrugs off our attempts at sympathy to focus on her primary grievance. "I can't believe I didn't even find anything," she says.

"Nothing at *all*?" I ask again.

"No, I told you he left his door unlocked, so I looked around his desk drawers." She tugs her hair. "That he reacted so badly means I was on the right track. A few more minutes and I could have had my smoking gun."

Teddy leans forward to drop his hands between his knees. "Right before resort wear, too. What a mess."

"Sorry I screwed up the collection by getting fired?" Alejandra grabs a crostini and tops it with a wedge of brie. Triple cream—Teddy didn't stint on snacks. "I should have planned it better."

He winces. "I apologize."

She shrugs. "It's okay. You're right. It'll be an utter shit show without me."

We eat for a minute. "We need to think of our next steps," I say.

"What if we acted first?" Teddy asks. "We could write a letter to my dad. An FYI."

"You want to be a narc," says Alejandra.

"It's more like a private anonymous feedback form outlining what we know," he says.

"A rat. A snitch. A stool pigeon."

"That term came from setting up captive pigeons on stools as decoys to hunt other passenger pigeons," I say.

"That's pretty cool," Alejandra admits.

"Look, there's how Michael treats his team and how he's never hired a single diverse intern and few diverse staff," says Teddy. "We know there are changes in his work that point to him stealing designs. That's enough to at least start Dad looking into it."

"You think a letter would be better than talking to him?" Alejandra asks.

"We've been butting heads lately," he says. "It's not a good idea to have this come from me."

I grab some mimolette, my favorite, but the cheese is a small consolation in this particular moment as I try to choose my words. "Teddy, your father knows. It's that he doesn't care enough to make the change. It's not a priority for him."

He sets his jaw. "He doesn't know how bad it is."

This conversation can only go downhill, so I let it be. "We should talk to Vivian." I don't want to bother her, but when I told her about Alejandra getting fired, Vivian told me to be careful although she agreed I'd done what I could. Checking my phone, I see she sent me an email only a few minutes ago, even though it's seven in the evening. "Should we ask her now?"

"No time like the present," says Alejandra.

She and Teddy start talking about this season's bag designs, reluctantly noting that Michael could still deliver when it came to leather goods. They move on to whether the data says it's a good idea to shift into leather neck-wear as I email Vivian to see if she's free to talk. Before I can ask them if they're seriously considering suede fringed scarves for fall, the phone rings.

"What's happened now?" asks Vivian in lieu of a more standard greeting.

"Hi, Vivian. We want to ask you about an idea. I'm putting you on speaker." I put the phone on the table next to the cheese tray.

"What idea?" Vivian sounds apprehensive. "Who's on speaker?"

"Ted and Alejandra."

"I'm listening."

"What do you think about writing a letter to the CEO to outline our concerns with Michael? An anonymous one."

"It's a bad idea," she says.

Teddy leans back against the cushions, eyes closed.

"Why?" I ask. "He might not know the extent of what's happening."

"Doubtful," she says. "I can see why you think it's a good idea, and I've even seen it work once but in a very different situation. Here, you lack proof, and the corporate culture is different."

"How so?" I ask. There's some whispering on Vivian's side. "Vivian?"

"Sorry, dealing with some things at home. Celeste has shown that they only react if something's public. A leak, for example. A letter is private, and an anonymous letter is very easy to discount. Nothing will come of it except defensiveness."

"Okay, what about...?" There's more whispering in the background.

"I'm sorry. I need to go," says Vivian. "Don't do the letter, Daiyu. For once, listen to me."

"I guess that's that," says Teddy when she disconnects. Then he laughs. "I kind of knew it wasn't a god-tier idea."

We eat some more cheese. "Vivian said we need to keep the scandals coming," I say.

"Is that what you got from the conversation?" asks Alejandra. "That is not what I got. I got big *don't poke the bear* vibes."

I nibble on a chewy cracker that's filled with nuts and cranberries. "You said resort wear will be a mess."

She nods. "Apparently he decided to redo a bunch of looks within hours of firing me."

I pull my gaze up from the cracker to look at her. "You're kidding. This close to the show?"

Teddy stares at his Stilton. "It's become obvious Alejandra was the one to lessen the impact of his more disastrous decisions."

"Can he even do that?" I ask.

"Sure but it's a dick move." Alejandra hauls herself off the deep couch to pace. "It puts stress on the team because you have to refit the new looks on the models, and you can run out of time. It's going to be a fiasco." She only sounds a little pleased.

"I need to talk to my father," says Teddy. "Michael doesn't like me, but I can't let the collection fail like that. I can help out."

Public failure. "Or," I say slowly. "Or you let him suffer the consequences."

Alejandra stops near the windows. "What do you mean?"

"Michael has been propped up for years," I say. "Now that you're gone, people will have the chance to see him for who he is."

Teddy stands up, face going pale. "Are you saying I should stand aside and let the company humiliate itself when I can help?"

"Oh, whoa." Alejandra's eyes snap between the two of us. "You know, I'm going to the washroom."

She rushes out and leaves us alone.

"Is that what you're suggesting I do?" Teddy says quietly.

"Yes." I look him in the eyes. "He's never had to deal with the fallout of his actions. Now is the time."

"You don't get it, Dee. Celeste is more than Michael. My mother started the company with a single bag and it's going to be mine. I can't do that." He faces the window, but our eyes meet in the reflection. He looks heartsick.

"I can't force you do it," I say. "All I can say is that people like Michael depend on others to cover for them. If he's good for Celeste, then the resort wear show will be a success. All he has to do is keep Alejandra's work. If not"—I shrug—"is he that good for the company? That's what your father needs to see."

"I don't like it."

"I know and I'm open to alternatives that get us a result." I look at him. "This could be what you need to impact the Opaline sale as well."

He comes to sit beside me on the couch. "It's hard," he says after a minute, resting his head on my shoulder.

I turn around to give him a fierce hug. "I know."

We haven't moved by the time Alejandra comes back. "All sorted?" she asks in a cautious tone.

"What do you think about the idea?" I ask.

She sighs. "We should do it."

"The poor team," says Teddy. "The sooner the truth about Michael comes out, the better for Celeste." There's a moment of silence, with Teddy gripping my hand. Then with a final squeeze, he releases me. "Let's do it," he says. "You're right. This is totally in his hands. I'm not responsible for his bad decisions."

"I also have an idea about Jean-Pierre," I say. "I want to contact him with a new plan to see if he'll change his mind."

"Will you tell him what happened to me?" Alejandra asks.

I nod. "Is that okay?"

"Sure, but I don't think it'll help your case any. What are you going to say?"

"I'm going to give him a solid plan. Teddy, I've kept your name out of this so far, but can I tell Jean-Pierre you're involved as a show of transparency?"

Teddy considers his response, and I don't rush him. "As long as he can keep it confidential."

"That's fair."

He stands up and gets some grapes. "I can talk to him about his designs as well."

Alejandra pours some water. "You can offer me as a sounding board with Ted if you want. I've got plenty of time."

"I want to tell him what protection we can offer if he comes forward," I say.

"Not much," Alejandra says. "It's not like we can stop Michael from doing anything."

"We can promise to keep his name private." Teddy sits back down. "Mind you, give one detail about a single look, and Michael will know he squealed."

"What if we keep it broad strokes?" I ask. "Tell the story without dates and identifying details?"

He and Alejandra look at each other. "It will weaken the accusation, but it might be enough to get some action from people," he says.

I tap out a note to Jean-Pierre and read it aloud.

"It's honest," Teddy says. "I like it."

"Send it," says Alejandra.

There's no reply by the time I go to bed, but a message comes in from Teddy.

> **Teddy:** Thanks for understanding.
> **Me:** Thanks for doing this.
> **Teddy:** All for one and one for all, right?
> **Me:** That was the Three Musketeers.
> **Teddy:** I knew I had it wrong. Also are you busy day after tomorrow? Up for an adventure to get our minds off this?

It's the day before the big presentation of my initial findings to Celeste, but I've practiced that thing out the wazoo. I deserve a break.

> **Me:** Depends on what.

Teddy: You can have it be a surprise or know the plan.

Me: Surprise.

Teddy: Meet me at College and Bathurst at 8 pm. Wear a red flower so I know who you are.

Me: You know who I am.

Teddy: You'd look cute with the flower anyway. Sweet dreams, Dee. Wish you were here.

I wish I was too. I wish I didn't have to answer to my mom about what time I come home at night. I wish a lot of things. In the past, wishing was enough. Not anymore, and it's time to look at what's in my *wish* category and move them over to the *doing* side. I'm ready to make more changes.

THIRTY-ONE

DAILY AFFIRMATION: I REVEL IN MOMENTS OF
BLISS WHEN THEY APPEAR AND INVITE THEM TO
COME WITH GREATLY INCREASED FREQUENCY.

I get off the streetcar to see Teddy leaning against a wall watching people walk by. He waves when he spots me on the other side of the street. "Wait there!" he calls.

"Rules against jaywalking are the result of a propaganda campaign by the auto industry," I tell him when he reaches the sidewalk.

"I believe it." He tilts his head, causing the quiver in my stomach to wing out over my entire body. "Taking part in small acts of rebellion makes me feel alive."

Teddy is wearing a peacoat, this time with a blue scarf woven with impressionistic storks and clouds. I glance down at my black pants. "I came from work, so I hope I'm dressed right." Knowing Teddy is a designer makes me a bit more self-conscious about my clothes even though he doesn't seem to care.

"You always look lovely, even without the red flower. We're headed over there." He points at the Tex-Mex place on the corner, covered in faded and chipped murals and with a small patio space in front that might seat two tables in warmer weather.

"We're getting nachos?" This is fantastic news.

"That we can eat as we smoke some ass at trivia night."

We cross the street. "You were serious about going out for trivia."

"I signed us up as a team, but we can play against each other if you want." He stops and looks down at me. "Or we can do something else? I thought it would be fun. It's been a rough month with all the Michael drama and what happened to Alejandra."

"Are there prizes?"

"Like free food or something."

I'm already yanking the door open. "Let's go."

Teddy's laugh chases me up the rickety staircase covered with ridged black rubber matting coated with sand and salt from the street. A woman with pink hair in a sloping beehive hands us a few sheets of paper as we come into a big room with mismatched tables and chairs. Depeche Mode plays over the speakers, and it smells like old fried food and spilled beer.

"Hope you brought your own pen." Her gravelly voice is tinted with nicotine. "We stopped giving them out when they all got stolen. Can't trust anyone these days."

Teddy pulls two pens out of his pocket with a flourish and passes one to me. "I got it covered."

We take a seat in the middle of the room and scope out the competition. The majority seem to be there for drinks and fun, but a few tables are ready to roll. Teddy looks at the menu. "You hungry?"

"Always." We order some potato skins, nachos, and beer.

"Hold on." Teddy lays his hands down. "This makes me look like I'm weaseling out of paying for dinner."

"How so?"

"We're at trivia, and if we win, the nachos are free." He points at his phone. "You've spent seventy-eight percent more time in the number one spot on Questie. Do you remember our bet?"

"I do now." That's a good percentage to be leading. I'm pleased and even happier that Teddy doesn't have an issue with me ranking higher than him. "We might lose and have to pay."

"Then tonight is on me. If we win, I'll happily take you out again."

"Deal. Let's decide on the team name. You should love this."

"You know me well," Teddy declares. "How about the Winners?"

"A little bombastic. Also, that table took it." We fake glare at them, but the Winners don't notice. I decide they're going down tonight.

A few tables are choosing the dirty route with adult-themed names, and others, like Marley's Team, are going straightforward.

"How about Answer Gods?" He reconsiders. "The Olympians?"

I make a face. "La Trivia-ata?"

"Getting there." He looks at the ceiling. "I've got it. On Wednesdays We Quiz."

"It's not Wednesday."

"That's why it's perfect." Teddy gestures to my blouse. "Plus you're wearing pink."

I nod and he writes it down with penmanship so good it makes mine looks like chicken scratches. Everything his hands do is artistic. The potato skins come, and he pushes over a container of sour cream for me.

"How was your day?" I ask.

The gossip coming from the studio isn't good, and he's been struggling with his decision to let Michael do as he will with the resort wear collection and to limit his own involvement purely to what his department needs. "Apparently the entire design team is taking shifts working all night to make his changes."

"That's a mess."

"I'm angry now." His eyes are narrow. "I keep thinking about what you said, that he only had to build on what Alejandra had put in place. It's his ego making a mess of this, and my father is letting it happen."

"Only a few months until you take over."

"It's not fast enough. At this rate, Michael will ruin our brand name before Opaline has a chance to. He has to go, now."

I double-dip my potato skin. The blessings of each having our own container. "We're trying."

"We are." He runs his hand through his hair. "Enough about that. How about you? Ready for your presentation tomorrow?"

"I can recite it in my sleep."

"Then you had a good day?"

"This is the best part of it. You are anyway." I wonder if that was too much to admit, but Teddy's expression removes all my doubts. His face is almost shy with pleasure.

"Mine too." Teddy looks at me intently as we sit in the crowded room of that seedy bar. He leans forward over the table to cup my face with his hand, eyes flickering down to my lips, which I pray do not have sour cream on them.

"Good evening, trivia nerds," booms a voice from the front. "Who's ready to show off some impractical knowledge?"

Teddy delivers a quick kiss, then sits back down, eyelids dipping as he takes a breath. Then he gives me that smile and I'm about to grab him back over the table.

"Ready?" he asks.

"Ready."

"Then let's kick the tires and light the fires. It's trivia time."

———

The winning of the nachos—technically a hundred-dollar food certificate—would have been easier had I not been so distracted. Teddy has effectively thrown a hand grenade into my concentration, and it's not getting better because he keeps touching me, small light brushes on my hand when he passes me something. Worse—or better—is that he watches me. When I whisper an answer, his gaze goes from my eyes to my lips. When I write, he focuses on my hands.

I'm doing the same to him. He's in a white T-shirt with a slight V at the neck, revealing enough to be disturbing to my well-being and focus. He leans back to stretch his arms over his head, showing off the trim lines of his body, and my mouth goes dry when I remember how he felt over me. And under.

The room gets hot during the second round. I take off my blazer and Teddy's eyes linger on my shoulders, revealed by my sleeveless blouse. His gaze is like another kind of touch, and when his knee brushes mine under the table, I almost jump.

However, despite my Teddy-lust-induced agitation, I want to win and, as a side quest, impress him. The trivia questions are a mix of easy and tricky. Teddy has a solid hold on music, and I've gotten us in the top three teams after the sports category thanks to knowing that the highest score you can get in a round of darts is 180.

"This is Degas," he says, tapping the clue sheet and diverting me with his hands again.

The art component came as sheets printed with thumbnail details of famous artworks. We've identified Dalí's *Lobster Telephone*, Emily Carr's *Church at Yuquot Village*, and now we're looking at what could be the edge of a ballerina's tutu.

The women behind me, team name the STARlings, are having the same conversation. They've been our closest competitors, and we've created a fun rivalry. One of them glances over at me. She's Asian, with black hair cut in a bob. Her friend, also Asian, has hair down to her waist in a thick shiny braid and perfect bangs that show off exquisite earrings.

"The Buds thought that was a Banksy," the one with short hair whispers to us. We've jointly bestowed this name on a group of ball-capped guys who greeted each new arrival with a hand clasp, one-arm hug complete with back tap, and "Hey, how ya doin', bud?"

"That's because you said, 'Number three is Banksy; that's so easy' loud enough for them to overhear," says her friend.

The first woman grabs her beer. "They shouldn't have been cheating off us."

"They're in first place," Teddy points out.

The woman snorts. "Only because sports and music were the first categories. They're massacring art. This is the beginning of the end for the Buds."

Her prediction is correct. The Buds (actual team name: First Rule of Quiz Club) drop back in the standings with each successive round. By the geography category, we're leading the room with only two points over the STARlings.

"For our final question of the night," announces the quizmaster, "what country was the setting for Tatooine in *Star Wars*? To clarify, this is *Star Wars IV: A New Hope*."

Muttered debates erupt around us. A *Star Wars* question is always going to be seen as a challenge for a certain subset of nerd.

"It was in the desert," comes a drunken voice. "Like, the Sahara? Or is it the Sonora? Sonoma?"

"How is this a geography question?" grumbles the STARling with long hair.

"It's Algeria, you jackass. Lucas wanted..." This is the contribution of the lead Bud.

"Algeria," says Teddy, about to write it down.

"It's Tunisia," I say.

"I'm sure it's Algeria, though." He doesn't look up before scribbling the answer.

My heart sinks that he didn't believe me.

The host calls out, "Five seconds left! Four, three, two, one! Hand your papers over for marking."

We trade ours with the STARlings, and the room cycles through claps and accusations as the host gives the answers. Finally he gets to the last one.

"The answer is...Tunisia." A chorus of cheers and squeals rise from the crowd.

I was right. We could have won.

Beside us, the STARlings start whooping. "Fifteen out of fifteen," the one with short hair hollers. "We have a winner!"

My head whips around. "What, us?"

"You!" They pass over the paper, and I look at the answers.

"You put Tunisia," I say to Teddy.

"I did."

"You thought it was Algeria."

"I did."

"Then why?"

Teddy looks confused. "Dee, if it's my gut against yours, naturally I'd go with you. You're amazing at this." He raises his eyebrows at me. "Surely by now you know I like winning."

The host comes over to check our sheets and lifts his mic. "Congratulations to our new winners, On Wednesdays We Quiz!"

The room applauds, and since we don't need all one hundred dollars for our bill, we give the rest to the STARlings, who laugh and thank us. I watch them as we get ready to go, their easy camaraderie and open affection. They look comfortable, and it occurs to me I never felt that way with my friends. My spectrum with them ran from feeling judged to excluded to like a performing monkey, always ready to bang some cymbals to chase their blues away. I don't want that anymore. I don't need that.

It's a convenient revelation, since none of my friends seem to want to hang out with me either.

Outside, the night is crisp and cold and a welcome change from the closed atmosphere of the bar. "That was amazing," I say.

"I thought you'd like it." He turns around to face me as he walks backward down College Street with his hands in his pockets. "You were my ace."

"You only asked me so you could get some free drinks?" I fake outrage.

"That was a bonus." He stops dead and I do, too, so I don't run into him. "What I wanted to do every time you got a question right was to kiss you."

My breath catches. "I got quite a few right."

"You did." He lifts my chin with his finger. "It made concentrating difficult for me."

For a moment, the sounds of the street get loud in my ears.

"Dee?" he murmurs.

"Yes?"

"I didn't ask you because I want to win at trivia."

It only takes a second before he has me back against the brick wall of some building, and maybe it's the drinks or the high of winning or Teddy, but I have no shame. Honestly, I haven't had a make-out session this hot with someone in public like this in years, and the faint sense of transgression combines with the huge thrill of simply kissing Teddy. I yank up his shirt and he yelps when my cold hands rest against his skin, making me laugh.

"Let's go, Herbie." A voice comes from startlingly close to us, and I jump to see a man tugging a small white dog on a leash. Teddy stands in front of me but the man, on his phone, doesn't seem to notice us at all. I suppose that's good for my modesty, but it's hard to deny that he and Herbie have broken the spell.

Without speaking, Teddy and I tuck in our shirts, then link hands and start walking back down the street. "I should get home," I say reluctantly. I don't want to. I want to drag Teddy into the dark parkette and sit him down and feel those lips on mine again and hear his sounds when I grind down on him. Then I want to go back to his place. However, my mother is currently texting me nonstop, asking where I am, and I have a big presentation in ten hours. Either would be aggravating, but combined, they're lethal.

"Can I get you a cab?" he asks.

"I'll take the TTC."

Teddy walks me to the stop and pauses to kiss me every few steps. Or I lean over to kiss him. Perhaps five or six kisses in, we stop at a crosswalk, laughing about nothing in particular and waiting for the light to change. It's odd the things you notice when you're happy. The small cat twitching the curtain of a second-floor apartment. A woman cycling. A cab window lowering and rising again, showing a sliver of tanned forehead. Witnesses to your joy.

We cross the street, and he tucks me in close, as if he likes having me near.

I like it, too, and I curl into him, feeling nothing can go wrong.

THIRTY-TWO

DAILY AFFIRMATION: TIREDNESS IS A STATE OF
MIND. THINK YOUR WAY TO ALERTNESS! COFFEE
MIGHT WORK BETTER. SOME EYE CREAM.
SECONDARY AFFIRMATION: STOP DOING
THESE LOOKING IN A MIRROR.
OH, AND ALSO LET ME SMASH THIS PRESENTATION.
NO, I WILL SMASH THIS PRESENTATION.

I fell asleep thinking about Teddy and woke up at three in a panic thanks to a nightmare about the Celeste meeting. The rest of the night was fitful, and I'm almost jittery with nerves by the time I hit the coffee shop on the way into work.

The woman beside me glances over. "Better than cold potato skins, huh?"

With a hat covering her hair, it takes me a moment to place her as the woman from trivia. "Hey, you're a STARling!"

"Guilty. I'm Hana," she says. She orders a black coffee, then changes her mind and gets a matcha latte and white chocolate scone. "What would you like?"

"Oh no, it's fine."

"I owe you for the nachos." Hana grins at me. "Unless you order an espresso with twelve blueberry syrup pumps or something. That's too embarrassing to have on my credit card."

"Can I please get your order?" asks the guy behind the counter. "I got a line here."

"Sorry. I'll get the same but no scone." I move aside with Hana to wait. "Thanks. I'm Dee."

We chat about the Buds and other trivia nights in town. Hana is easy to talk to and fills in the conversation gaps before I start freaking out over what to say.

"Do you need to get to work?" she asks finally.

"Yeah." That presentation won't give itself.

"What do you do?" Hana makes a face at her drink. "Should have gotten a vanilla shot with this."

"I'm a diversity consultant."

Her eyes snap up. "No way. Me too—or I was. Where do you work?"

"I was at Chariot and now I'm with Gear Robins."

"That's quite a change. You like it there?"

"I'm learning a lot." It's wise to be careful around others in the industry, even if Hana seems like good people.

She gives me a sideways look. "I bet. Well, if you want to talk, I've got lots of time. Since I quit, I live the life of doing not much except dealing with my burnout."

"Sorry."

"No, it's wonderful." She toasts me with her cup. "My friend—you met her at quiz—made some big changes in her life that inspired me. I'm only mad I didn't do it earlier."

"What kind of changes?" I ask nosily.

"Literally uprooted her entire life after meeting her soul mate. He did the same. They're sickeningly cute." Despite her words, Hana sounds fond and she's smiling.

"Wait," I say as we reach the corner. Testing the waters for a prospective new friend is more nerve-racking than flirting with a guy. "Give me your number so I can get the next coffee round."

She gives it to me. "Make sure you call, otherwise I'll charge interest. I always remember a debt."

I wave as she goes. I made a friend. Possible friend. This bodes well for my day. I walk up the street with a spring to my step that hadn't been there earlier.

––––––––––

By the time I arrive at Celeste eight minutes later, unease about the presentation has returned with a vengeance. Vivian takes a long look at me under the bright lobby lights. "There's nothing to worry about," she says. "We've gone through the deck, and you have it down."

Vivian herself looks blasé and not like me, with the butterflies in the backs of my legs. She must have done a thousand of these during her years at Gear Robins. I aspire to her level of cool, because not even touching my Paris key chain for good luck helps calm me down. I only need to believe. *Not believe*, reminds the voice. *Don't just let this happen to you. Take control.*

I can do that. Jade once told me she deals with stress by facing the feeling head-on, and what the heck. I might as well give it a shot.

I'm anxious, I tell myself. I'm worried about how this presentation is going to go. What if I don't know an answer? What if I freeze?

At first, I doubt Jade's method, because allowing yourself to feel anxious, shockingly, means feeling anxious. I don't like it at all. Then I remember Vivian is here with me. I memorized the presentation. I've done similar work for Chariot, and it was fine. I can do this. My breathing regulates and my heart rate slows. The anxiety fades into the background.

Huh. Jade's advice worked.

I enter the conference room with a little more confidence and put hard copies of the deck down on the huge oak table. Vivian makes small talk with Jenna, who is punching at the buttons on the remote to turn on the screen at the end of the room. At least Teddy won't be here distracting me.

Naturally, that's when he walks in wearing a black suit with a black shirt open at the throat and a jeweled tiger brooch on his lapel, sending me a pleading look.

Jenna looks up from where she's reading through the deck in the corner. "I thought you were sending Amber."

"She's not feeling well, so I told her to go home," he says, nodding to Vivian and then me. "Good to see you again." He's so much more self-assured than in our first meeting; it's like dealing with a new and even hotter man.

Vivian doesn't look at me as I mumble a response, but I'm saved from further interaction as Gary, Michael, and Liz come in followed by the other department heads, who I recognize from our meetings. If I thought I was on edge before, it's kicked into full dread.

Breaths: Take them.

Smile: On face.

Affirmations: Desperate times, so I resort to the most basic: *You can do it!*

Manifest: The hell with that right now.

"How was the gallery opening last night?" Liz asks Michael as they take their seats.

"Oh, tedious," he says, sending a big smile my direction. I check over my shoulder to see if anyone is behind me. There's isn't. "I only went to support Peppa's daughter but there were too many young people thinking they have something new to show when they're nothing special."

"Experience can make such a difference." Liz opens the deck in front of her.

"It's been a long time since I was in that neighborhood, but I should go more often. There's so much to see from a cab on College Street," he says, looking at me and then at Teddy, who is observing him with a slight frown from across the table. "People walking dogs. Couples kissing as they cross the road."

Liz laughs. "You don't believe in public transit but imagine what you'd see if you took the TTC."

Panic: Full blown.

I barely listen because static has filled my ears. No. Is he? Did he? I

refuse to look at Teddy and do my best to keep my expression uncon-
cerned as the sweat rolls down my ribs. Michael opens his mouth, but
Edward walks in and the room quiets.

He nods in Vivian's direction. "Let's see what you have," he says, not
bothering with pleasantries.

"Of course," she says. "Daiyu?"

I stare at the deck for a moment, mind on Michael, before Vivian
clears her throat. Thank God I read this over forty times, because
muscle memory kicks in. My voice shakes at the beginning, and I have
no idea what I'm saying as my mouth moves independently of my brain.

Out of the corner of my eye, I see Michael training his gleeful little
smirk on Teddy, who is concentrating on my presentation as if we hav-
en't been rumbled. How could Michael have seen us? Is he going to say
anything? My worries make it hard to focus, but I wipe my hands along
my thighs and try to breathe before starting in on the next section.

Most of the people in the room follow along with their hard copies.
I can tell I'm going too quick as I stumble over my words, and out of
the corner of my eye, Vivian mimics a deep breath. I try but Edward's
body language is about as welcoming as a Doberman watching a mail
carrier approach the gate. I want to fix whatever he thinks is wrong, but
I don't know what it could be, so I keep going. With Vivian's help, I'd put
the brightest spin imaginable on what I'd found at Celeste, but risking
a glance around the table, I see Teddy and a few of the others frowning
at the numbers. It's clear they see the real issues and equally clear that
those issues center around Michael and his department, although Liz
is a solid runner-up.

Then I finish and look up to see Vivian nodding. My chest unknots
slightly. If she'd shown any other reaction, I might have bolted for the
door. Teddy catches my eye and gives me an almost imperceptible
smile. Having him here wasn't as bad as I thought it would be. It was
comforting to feel his silent support, although I doubt I can expect more
than that, given what happened at the last Celeste meeting.

There's silence around the table as everyone waits for the CEO to speak, like a patriarch eating first. Edward leans back in his chair, looking at the final slide summarizing the next steps to get Celeste a few rungs up on the Gear Robins People First model. It would bring them from the basement to about the mezzanine.

"Some interesting findings," he says finally.

Liz jumps on it. "Everyone here knows how supportive I am of this project, but my read is that you've created a lot of problems where there aren't any," she says. "I must say I found that many of your questions in the interview section led to specific answers. I don't doubt that it influenced these numbers. It's disappointing."

"Those are standard questions," I say, a little surprised at how defensive Liz is. I continue after a pause to see if Vivian wants to answer, but she lets me take the wheel. "They're designed to be open-ended to allow for thoughtful responses."

Liz points at the screen. "This is obviously exaggerated because it doesn't reflect my experience at Celeste at all." She laughs. "We definitely have some drama queens on staff."

"We do." Michael smiles at Teddy. "There can be drama anywhere."

Teddy ignores him.

"It's not our fault if people are too lazy to take advantage of what we have," adds Michael. "We offer plenty. Look at my internship program."

I debate letting this go so I don't antagonize him. No, that was my presentation, so it's my job to discuss the findings. "That's an excellent point, and an expanded paid program would help immensely for those who can't afford to work without an income."

"Then they don't want it enough," he says, smiling to show more teeth than necessary. "Unlike some, who go for what they want regardless of risk. They need to show *passion*."

He's so horrible.

"I want to amplify what Michael said," says Liz. "I'm disturbed by the level of sheer entitlement here. We hire the best and we promote on merit. You're suggesting we lower our standards."

"It's curious you think opening up your hiring pool would lead to a decrease in quality," I say, throwing caution to the winds. Vivian shoots me a look across the table that's fairly easy to interpret as *Watch your tone*.

"This is a lot to consider," says Teddy, jumping in before Liz can speak. "I have to disagree with you, Liz. I had Gary post jobs in my departments more widely, and the level of applicants was much stronger."

He glances across the table at me as I try to hide my surprise. This is my Teddy, the one who wants to stand up for what he thinks is right.

"This is a shift from your previous tune," observes Michael. "What made you change your mind?"

"Vivian and Daiyu have provided solid reasoning behind their recommendations, which are beneficial to the business and support many points I've brought up before," says Teddy coolly. "Unlike some, I'm able to adapt when new information arises."

Although grateful for the support, I wish Teddy wouldn't aggravate Michael. There's a stony glint in his eyes, and Michael seems to decide he doesn't want an open confrontation at the meeting in front of his peers. He gives a casual shrug at he looks at the CEO.

"Well, you deal with numbers," Edward says dismissively. "On the design side, culture fit is key, and I trust Michael knows what he needs."

"The data here is showing us that might not be true," Teddy says, locking eyes with his father.

"Quotas are not the answer," says Edward.

"That's a straw man, because no one mentioned quotas," snaps Teddy. "At all."

"Look, I'm a visionary and an artist," says Michael, running a hand over his chest. "I understand the anger people feel. These days, no one hires white men. We're the real underclass. I have to fight for everything I get."

"First, that's not true." Teddy taps the deck in front of him.

"What would you know about it?" mutters Michael, barely audible.

Teddy plows on. "Second, judging from these numbers, you need to step up your game anyway."

"Keep to your lane, Ted," warns Edward.

Michael glances at me with a sly expression. "Perhaps I need some one-on-one training. I hear that's a possibility."

I can tell my face is doing something, because Vivian looks closely at me. Then the conversation moves on.

"Some of these comments are simply rude and hurtful," says Liz, looking at her package. "This one about lack of respect is clearly a personal grudge."

"I'm sure that's Allie," says Michael. "I always said she was a troublemaker, with that temper of hers, and we're better off without her. I wouldn't be surprised if she was the one to leak our diversity numbers in the first place."

"I believe it," Liz says. "She complained that Nicole on my team was deliberately holding back payments to some of our vendors. Of course, Nicole would never do such a thing."

"Did you investigate?" asks Teddy.

"There was no need." Liz taps the table. "I know Nicole."

I look to Vivian, telegraphing nonverbally that I need assistance on how to handle this, and she jumps in. "It's not helpful to try to identify people from the comments," she says smoothly. "Shall we move on?"

"What we're seeing here is that there's room for improvement," Teddy says, looking directly at his father, whose expression doesn't change. "A lot."

"Gary, as head of HR, do you want to weigh in?" asks Edward.

There's a pause as everyone looks at Gary. "Ah, you know, it's a situation with a lot of nuance," he says, throwing himself into Michael's camp. "We need to take a bit of a three-sixty, high-level view."

Teddy gives him an infuriated look.

"Instead of these extreme changes, we should start with wellness webinars to help people help themselves," says Liz. "In-house yoga. My heliotherapist is a yogi, and she'd be happy to come in. We could charge staff twenty dollars per session to cover her hourly fee. That's affordable."

"If we have it at lunch in one of the event rooms, convenient as well," adds Gary. "I wouldn't want people taking that time during work hours."

Edward makes a noise from the end of the table, and the others fall silent.

"All right, thank you," he says. "I agree with Liz. I'm a little concerned about the direction this is going. A lot of the problem we see is a pipeline issue."

"I've provided at least six ways Celeste can take a leadership role in helping change that," says Teddy tightly. "They were all rejected."

"It's not Celeste's responsibility to solve," says Edward. "Let someone else worry about it."

"There's also the lack of women at higher management levels," I say. "That's not a pipeline issue."

"That's right," says Teddy.

There's a silence as most of the table looks elsewhere as if we've said something embarrassing. Edward stares at me and then keeps talking as if I hadn't said a word.

"We need to focus on what we can do here to support our current staff, and more of those other applicants will come when they see what we offer. Mentorship, that's good."

"What does this even tell us in the end?" says Liz. "We look for diversity of thought. That's what's important, not some arbitrary number. After all, we're all unique in our own way."

Edward stands up. "Incorporate that feedback and show me the revised recommendations. Gary, keep them on target. Ted, my office."

He leaves and the meeting is over. That was it. Strangely anticlimactic and also unfulfilling. I do my best to not sag in my seat and to keep the bright professional expression on my face as I pretend to make notes so I have time to breathe. Michael without speaking to me, and I'm grateful for small mercies. Teddy lingers at the door, talking to Gary but trying to catch my eye. I give him a little smile, and his shoulders relax before he ghosts me the tiniest of winks. I'll text him later for the best way to deal with this and to see what his father said.

Across from me, Vivian gathers up her belongings. Now that I know her a bit better, I can see how tight her jaw is. She was right all along. We were being paid to make some people feel good, not make lives better. Apart from Teddy, the people in that meeting didn't care. They don't want to change. Despite everything, I had hoped she could be wrong, but there's no fooling myself. If we want change to happen here, then we need to keep doing it ourselves.

We will. Unless Michael opens his mouth and ruins everything for me. For us.

THIRTY-THREE

We go back to the office Celeste has put aside for me, and Vivian shuts the door behind her. Suddenly she looks a decade older, her face releasing the polite expression from the meeting to become worn and weary. But the smile she gives me is real and brightens the room for the moment she wears it.

"That went well enough," she congratulates me. "I'm pleased with the work you're doing here at Celeste. You've gone above my expectations."

I'll take this as the compliment she means it as, although my heart sinks to know she'll regret saying that once I tell her about Michael. "Thanks. It didn't feel that way."

"That's nowhere near as bad as it can get. I had one client leave halfway through and send his assistant in to tell me to pack up and go."

I sit down across from her. "Wow."

"As I said, not that bad." She checks her phone. "You need to work on keeping your replies more professional."

"It's hard." I frown, trying to organize my thoughts.

"That doesn't mean you get a pass from doing it."

"It's frustrating that they try to block the smallest change, even when it doesn't affect them at all. Liz doesn't do her job postings. Jenna does. Why wouldn't she want to open it up to more people? She keeps telling me how supportive she is."

"She probably believes she is." Vivian smooths her sleeve. "I suspect deep down they worry that if they agree with those changes, they're admitting they're wrong and the way they've been working is unfair."

"What's wrong with that?" I demand.

"Do you like being wrong?"

I think about my breakdown on the airplane. "No."

"If opening up their jobs leads to a wider pool of qualified applicants, they might have to ask themselves if they benefited from a similar narrow field. People like to think their accomplishments are based on personal merit and don't like being challenged on that." She lowers her voice. "I was impressed with the change in Ted from the first meeting. Your doing?"

"His choice," I say, taking secondhand pride in her praise.

Vivian gets ready to go, and I follow her out, wanting to talk to her about Michael.

"When you do this, it makes me feel bad news is coming," she says as we come out onto the sidewalk and head toward King Street. "I'd love to be wrong, but past history has me doubting I am."

I don't sugarcoat it. "Michael might know about Teddy and me."

She stills. "*How*?"

"From what he was saying today, he might have seen us on the street last night."

"Were you doing anything?" Her face scrunches up. "Couple things? Wait, I don't want to know. What I want to know is if there's proof."

"I don't know."

She shakes her head, and I can *feel* her disappointment. "What's your plan?"

"I need to talk to Teddy, but my instinct is to deny it."

"You need to be prepared for backlash," she says. "I warned you, but I can't help you here."

"I understand." She's done more than enough for me. Although it's hard to hear, every word she's saying is true. I made the choice, and it's my responsibility to deal with the consequences.

She shuts her eyes. "Anything else?"

"No."

"Daiyu, really?"

"Honest. We're going to let what happens happen."

She stops. "That seems unlike you."

"You've been a good influence." I pause and decide to go for it. "You probably would have preferred to work with almost anyone else. You could have dealt with me with much less patience, but instead you mentored me, even when I made decisions you didn't agree with." I shuffle my feet. "So thanks."

She stares at me, then drops her head in her hands, there in the middle of the sidewalk. This is so unlike Vivian that I step back as if seeing her at a distance will help me know what to do.

"I'm sorry!" I exclaim. "I didn't mean to make it weird."

"It's not that."

Vivian looks so worn down that this time, I take the risk. "You're pretty private at work, but I feel something happened?"

To my absolute horror, Vivian's eyes fill with tears that she dashes away. "It's fine."

My hands give a sort of weak flutter as I waver between reaching out or not. Her expression decides me, and I tuck them by my sides. "Is it? Or not. You don't need to talk about it," I hasten to add.

"I asked Will for a leave of absence," she says. "Maya needs me."

Her daughter. My heart twists at the devastation in her face. I've been forcing her to deal with my bullshit when she has a little girl who just wants her mom.

"I'm sorry." She must be at her end to be opening up like this. "What did he say?"

"He said I was too valuable a member of the team to have out of the office. Then he reminded me sick days were only to be used if I was sick myself." Her voice is bitter. "I've already used my vacation taking care of her."

"Things will look up," I encourage her automatically. "You need to look on the bright side."

"No." She looks at me in scorn. "No, they won't look up, and there is no bright side."

Her words hit me like a slap, and I regret speaking without thinking. I can't know if things will get better. "You're right." This time, I say what the little voice urges me to say, the way I do with Teddy. "You sound like you feel trapped."

"I am," she says with surprise. "I hate it."

The last is said with such vehemence that she freezes, like she needs to recover from it.

"I hate it," she repeats. "I hate this life."

"It sounds like a shitty situation."

"It is shitty." She glances at me. "I've never said that out loud."

"My sister says ignoring negative emotions makes them bigger."

"Wise woman. Does she have advice about what to do when you stop ignoring them?"

"She's more unclear on that, but I assume we're supposed to do something about it."

"Harder." She looks at me. "Not impossible. It would help if you kept out of trouble for the next month until this damn project is done."

I'm taken aback by her quick move back to work issues, but sometimes work can be an escape from real life. I nod. "I will."

"You should know I told Will this project is under control. Don't make me a liar."

She's gone before I can reply, and I stand in the shadow of the building looking after her. This time, her abruptness doesn't bother me, or not as much as it did. It's not about me although I'm grateful to have been there for a moment when she needed someone to listen. It's about the situation, which is terrible.

I hope she can get it sorted out. Vivian deserves better.

———————

I call Teddy on my way home. "Do you want to say it or me?" I ask.

"Michael saw us last night."

"Did he talk to you about it after the meeting?"

Teddy snorts. "He didn't get a chance because I was getting reamed out by my father for not supporting the management team."

"I told Vivian, and she says we're on our own to deal with this. Denial is the best policy."

"I agree." He sighs. "I hate that he has this over us. Dad's already angry."

"It might be easier to come clean."

"No way. Dad is rabid about dating at work."

I get a rush of fear. "Could he complain to Gear Robins and get me fired?"

Teddy's momentary silence says enough. "It won't get to that," he assures me. "We're in this together, and if you get terminated, I'll leave Celeste."

"You can't do that."

"I can." He says it simply. "We'll worry about it if the time comes."

We get off the phone, and when I arrive home, all the lights are on in a way that irritates me further because it bodes no peace. I stand outside looking at the front windows. Closing my eyes, I visualize each room and the people in it. Grandma, stuck in the cramped living room with no privacy. My parents, back in the city instead of their beloved cottage country. Me, on a cot in my old childhood bedroom with an unofficial curfew. None of us happy but all of us making the best of it.

What if this isn't the best of it? What if there's another option? The one I should have explored months ago but didn't have the courage to pursue?

I don't know if I have the guts now. My new goal of taking action wavers. If this was Teddy, I could tell him that we have a problem and need to talk. The same with Vivian. It wasn't fun, but I didn't have the sense of it being an unmovable obstacle the way I view my family.

Some of that role-play Alejandra suggested before I met Jean-Pierre might be useful. I clear my throat and test out the words.

"The house is..." My voice fails even though I'm alone on the sidewalk. Oh, not alone. I give the woman walking by with groceries a small wave and try again after she passes.

"This living situation is not... Hi, Mr. Silva." I wait until he's gone for a third go. "This isn't working, and you need to find a new home."

Oh God, I can't say that to my own family. I panic and call Teddy back.

"I want to tell my family to leave my house."

"Wow. Okay. Now?"

"Yes?" My voice is trembling even with the one word.

"What do you plan to say?"

"How about, *I'd like you to move out*?"

This time, he pauses. "That's certainly direct and gets your point across."

"I can't say that to my family!" I wail. "It's horrible."

"What about softer language?" he suggests. "Focus on what's in it for them."

"Like I would at work." Weird how I did communications for years and can't manage to make my point to my family. "My grandmother would be more comfortable in her own place. Dad loves being up north. He hates the city. Mom would have more time to do her other hobbies if she's not growing weed for Grandma all the time."

"Or not. It might be lucrative."

"Let me try again." I take a deep breath. "Maybe it might be an idea if we possibly look for another place for Grandma to go. It's crowded in the house, and she'd be more comfortable in her own place, and you could go back up north and enjoy your retirement."

"That's perfect, Dee," he congratulates me. "Very soft language at the beginning."

"Too soft."

"If that's what you need to be comfortable enough to say the rest, go for it."

"I'm going to do it."

"You can. I'm here if you need me."

We hang up, and I square my shoulders and look at my house again, lit up like the holidays even though everyone will be on one floor.

I can do it. I need to do it.

When I get in and hear Mom chatting with Grandma in the kitchen, my nerve fails despite my practice session with Teddy. Instead, an intense exhaustion takes over. I can do this tomorrow. For now, I'll sneak in.

"Dee?" calls Mom.

Damn it.

She looks at me when I come into the living room. "Goodness, Dee, you look like a little thundercloud. Time to turn that frown upside down."

"I didn't have a fantastic day," I say.

"I'm sure one good thing happened," Mom insists.

"Maybe, but overall it sucked."

"Come now, that's no way to think," she says. "You need to count your blessings."

She doesn't ask what's wrong, because the only thing that matters is I not show it. When we were growing up, Mom always used to say she knew she'd done a good job parenting if we were happy. *Did she ever truly care how you felt?* asks that horrible voice. *Or does she only want the assurance? The lip service that everything was hunky-dory so she can feel good about herself?*

That's cruel. A terrible thing to think about my own mother, but now that I've thought it, I can't let it go. Perhaps that voice isn't so horrible after all. Perhaps it's saying all the things that I never let myself consider but should. This time, I listen without judgment. What did Mom do whenever I had a problem? She listened, but only to tell me the problem was no big deal.

"Mom—"

"Take a seat. You'll feel better after a snack."

That's it. All the years of being told that the problem was with my mindset and not the teacher who hated me or the friends who left me out, the decades of being forced to pretend to be happy and feeling I never had a right to be upset or disappointed because everything happens for a reason, all culminate in what I can only call a whiteout. I honest to God see white. She taught me that my feelings didn't matter, but Teddy showed me they do.

"Enough, Mom. I don't want to hear it."

"Dee, you are the only one with the power to change your perspective. Why don't you go upstairs and take a bath? That works wonders."

The words pour out from where they've been trapped. "I don't need a bath. I've tried baths and yoga and journaling and gratitude, and none of them are working. You know why?"

"Dee, what are you...?"

I steamroll over her. "Because some things are not in my capacity to change! I need my work to not be horrible. I need people to not be selfish. None of that is up to me, and what I don't need to hear from you is how this is all my fault because I don't have a positive attitude or take regular exercise."

Normally, I would have agreed that although I can't change other's actions, I can control my response. Today every word I said feels true and like my response is warranted. No number of affirmations will change Celeste. My thoughts won't change Michael or Liz. Then what do you do? What if my response is rage?

I don't know. Being positive means not dwelling on the negative, whatever that is. If you can't turn a problem into a challenge, you're the issue. If life is a matter of perspective, that leaves only one person to blame if things aren't working out and you're not successful.

You. You're the problem, and no one else. Not another person. Not an unfair and unjust world.

I don't like that. Part of me always knew that wasn't true, but I hadn't been able to admit it. When you believe you shape your reality, having those thoughts is to invite failure, like a positivity catch-22.

"What's up?" asks Dad as he comes into the kitchen.

Mom ignores him. "Dee, you need to get a good night's sleep. We'll talk in the morning when you feel better."

Dad waits until she's out of the room and then sits at the table with Grandma. She shifts over, but to make room for him—not get away.

"Dee?" asks Dad carefully. "Did something happen at work?"

"Yes." I thump my elbows on the table. "It was incredibly fucking bad."

It shows the depth of Dad's concern that he says nothing of my language. "I'm sorry," he says.

I sit back in my seat. "Why can't Mom say that instead of telling me that I've got nothing to whine about?"

"It's how your mom is, Dee-bear." He rubs his chin. "That's part of what I love about her. She's always optimistic."

"Too optimistic," I mumble.

"She's never been able to handle bad news." Grandma fills in some blue sky on her puzzle, this time of St. Basil's Cathedral in Moscow. "Always smiling. She got awards for it in school, you know."

Dad and I glance at each other. "For what?" I ask.

"Congeniality, they called it back then." Grandma starts in on a colorful tower. "She was scared of what would happen if she told people what she thought."

Dad hums as if this makes sense.

"It started when her father left us," Grandma adds.

"What happened?" I knew he'd left but he'd died before I was born. Dad leans forward as if this is new to him.

"He moved in with another woman when your mother was young. The last thing he said was that he needed someone who appreciated him the way he deserved."

"Appreciated him?" My grandmother is speaking to me like a peer for the first time, and although this is the direction I want our relationship to go, it will take time to get used to it. Dad, however, watches her calmly, almost as if he'd been waiting for this kind of a moment.

Her mouth twists. "He meant laugh at his jokes and take care of everything with a smile and without complaining. Your mother internalized that. She was always cheerful from then on, as if the rest of us would leave if we saw her sad."

"That's horrible."

"It is." Grandma stares at Dad. "You've been good for her, David." The words come out haltingly.

Dad smiles. "That's my job."

There's a moment of awkward silence, broken by Chilly jumping on his blasted wheel, and then Grandma turns to me. "Do you want to talk about your day?"

"No."

"All right."

I stand to leave the room, then hesitate and turn back to her. "You know when things aren't going right but you don't know how to fix them?"

"Yes."

"I know what Dad does. What do you do?"

She puts in another puzzle piece. "You live with it with as much grace and mercy as you can manage. That's all you can do when you can't find a solution."

That sounds a lot like Dad's water. "What if you can't?"

In goes another piece. "I've found a good screaming fit into my pillow helps."

This startles Dad and me into laughter. I leave them at the table working on the puzzle and try not to think about how strange it is to see them together and possibly enjoying rather than only tolerating each other's company.

What a day.

THIRTY-FOUR

The day for the Celeste resort wear show dawns gray and cold. It's taking place at Sugar Beach, a sandy strip on a pier down by the lake that's pleasant in summer, but less so in early May when the weather can be variable. Like, it snowed last week. Knowing the wind will be worse by the water, I pull out my winter coat to wear. Or Grandma's coat that is now mine.

I receive the usual morning trivia text from Teddy, although he's busy getting ready for the event, and curl up on the bottom of the cot to hug my phone to my chest for a moment before texting him back to wish him good luck. Today will be hard for him if Michael does as badly as we suspect.

There are no other messages, although I keep hoping for a reply from Jean-Pierre. Each time I see my own block of text staring back at me, my spirits get a bit lower. I wish he'd give me an out-and-out rejection instead of silence, even though that's unfair to him. It's hard to accept that the decision is out of my, and the universe's, hands.

When I arrive at Celeste, Jenna is staring out the window.

"Today is going to be a nightmare." She sounds tense. "I heard

Alejandra had the show booked inside at some gorgeous art deco pool and Michael changed it last minute."

"Why?"

"No doubt because it was her idea and it was good. The show producer had a fit and nearly quit."

People gradually filter out over the course of the morning, chattering animatedly as they walk by my office. Finally, I shut my laptop and pack up. It's a pain to get to Sugar Beach by TTC, especially in this blustery weather, so I grab a cab. On the way, I get a message from Hana, the STARling I'd been texting since we met at the coffee shop.

> **Hana:** You up for drinks? I got a new job, which means I have discretionary income again.

We set a date (tomorrow) and place (I don't know it). After an interminable time in traffic, the cab passes the Redpath Sugar building with its whale mural and pulls up behind a line of other cars. My attention turns to the artificial sandy beach that lines the waterfront near the battered freighter floating next to the sugar refinery. Except for the golden sand, nothing about the scene screams "resort." Waves whip up against the side of the pier, their tips edged with white. To the east is a huge black tent, which I assume is for the models. It's cold enough that I wish I had my parka instead of Grandma's wool coat.

I join the line of people waiting to get in, only some of whom have thought ahead and dressed for the weather. In front of me, two women are laughing. "I thought the location was a joke," says one, clutching her light jacket. "Or that they'd heat the beach with a dome or something."

"They could be doing après-ski," says her companion, snug in a shiny fur that looks real. "That counts as resort, right?"

I get to the front, where Jenna waves me through. "You're right on time," she says, teeth chattering. "The show starts in ten minutes. Thank God."

I sit down on the collapsible chair, part of a shaky double line weaving in and out of the permanent metal umbrellas that line the beach. The sand is wet enough to cause a chill to climb up my calves, but the seats keep filling up. Despite the cold, there's a sense of anticipation. After all, resort wear is a new direction for Celeste, and the crowd is eager to see what Michael can do.

My anticipation lies in a different direction.

I'm here to see how badly he fails.

I wish I could focus on the show to get my mind off everything, but there's no show to focus on. The start time comes and goes, and I and everyone around me get more miserable, except for a man wearing what looks like a snowsuit. The women's gossip behind me turns progressively nastier, as if the energy they're expending to maintain their basal body temperature uses up the effort they would have used to be nice. I listen to them rip apart one friend's weight gain, another's weight loss, and debate if a third is having an affair.

Then they turn to fashion, and I nearly fall over backward to eavesdrop as they talk about Michael. "He's always given me a creep vibe," says one. "He looks like the kind of guy who hits on the interns. Plus he's a smile talker."

"Don't say that too loud." The friend starts laughing. "And what the hell is a smile talker?"

"You know, those people who smile when they talk. Like a robot you can't trust."

"God, I wish I was a robot so I didn't feel this cold," the other says. "This better be worth it."

A text comes from Teddy.

Teddy: You here?
Me: Yes, in the middle.
Teddy: Look past the photo pit.

There he is, bundled in a parka.

Me: Are you ready?

Teddy: Strangely, yes. This morning, I was told to mind my own business when I asked a very reasonable question about the show related to my team, and I thought, you know what? He doesn't deserve that job. He's not owed it.

Me: He's not.

Teddy: I'm ready for him to fail. Luckily he was also too busy to threaten me about us.

Me: It's only putting off the inevitable.

Teddy: One crisis at a time.

Me: You haven't seen anything at all from the show?

Teddy: No one's seen the whole thing. Michael made a bunch of last-minute changes and only let the people involved into the tent.

Me: Not even your dad?

Teddy: He trusts Michael. Michael told him he's going to push boundaries.

Me: Sounds ominous.

Music blasts out of the speakers to start the show, bringing a ragged mutter of relief from the shivering crowd. There are no spotlights, or any lights, but a screen has been erected at the end of the makeshift runway above the photo pit. A short video plays of an old-fashioned train running through mountains and along the shores of lacs (they're clearly better than boring North American lakes) to come whistling into a station. The camera lingers on the words ORIENTAL EXPRESS painted on the side, then moves to the doors of the train where turbaned servants bow.

The models hit the sand runway. The first looks have a kind of Gatsby tennis vibe, and a murmur of appreciation rises around me as people hold up their phones to record the show. However, the cool rich-girl aesthetic is weakened by the lurching gait of the models. The sand shifts treacherously under their heels, causing one woman to almost walk on the sides of her ankles. We're close enough that I can see threads trailing from the clothes after last-minute alterations. One has pins along the hem. It looks messy and unkempt and shows a lack of attention to detail.

Then I hear, "What on earth?" and someone snickers. It takes me a moment to see what the problem is because I've been looking at their feet. Michael has matched the models so the first in a given pair is blond, with a classically lovely English rose look, while the second wears a black bobbed wig with bright red lips and eyeliner winged out to give the impression of long eyes. None of them, I notice as they wobble by, are actually Asian.

Teddy: Are you seeing this?
Me: I can't look away.

The smart sporty look is reserved for the English-looking models, while the fauxsians have been made to look like they've come straight from a paddy field via a *Blade Runner* set, with stiff wide-legged pants, garishly colored and patterned sleeveless Mao jackets, and conical hats combined with geta sandals and tabi socks. They also aren't wearing anything under the jackets, and there's an abundance of outdated shoulder pads and some zipped pockets. It's as if Michael put ideas for twenty looks in a bag and fished around with his eyes closed to make some rather hideous outfits. Even I can see it lacks harmony.

I look over to see Teddy slack-jawed while Edward looks on, nodding his head. Teddy turns to his father, whispering urgently before Edward says something that makes Teddy slap his hands on his thighs.

Teddy: Dad doesn't see a problem. Unbelievable.

Me: Not one?

Teddy: Apparently not. He says Michael knows what he's doing. How was he ever married to my mother?

The models keep coming. There have been about twenty so far, so we're more than halfway through.

Teddy: LOOK DOWN

When I check what he's doing, he's not looking at the models but at the ground, and I follow suit. I didn't think this could get worse, but it has. The models' shoes have carved soles that act like stamps, leaving little images imprinted in the damp sand when the women lift their feet. Cartoon anime versions of Amaterasu and Kali and Guan Yin are mixed in with roses and castles and crowns.

"Is this a joke?" asks a nearby man. He's in a turtleneck with his ginger hair in a ponytail and moving his phone to record first the models, then the prints on the sand, shaking his head.

His companion giggles hysterically, repeating, "Oh my God, oh my God. Do you see this? What is he thinking?"

"I love those female empowerment sandals," says the woman behind me, the one who thought her friend was having an affair. "They'd be so cute for the cottage."

When the finale comes, I'm too scandalized to confer with Teddy via text. Michael sends one of the English rose models out with a Shiba Inu on a leash, followed by a woman with gigantic chopsticks piercing her hair. She's also wearing a fez with a tiny net veil tilted forward on her forehead. There's dead silence until someone starts laughing, an uncomfortable snicker that is instantly shushed. Although the two models try to keep their aloof expressions in place, they look hugely self-conscious.

Teddy: I did not think it could be this bad. What did I see?

The models return to the tent, leaving the runway clear and the crowd chattering. The music changes, and out comes the first model again, followed by the rest. At the end, his arm slung around the slender shoulders of the final model, forcing her knees to bend with his weight, comes Michael, smiling and blowing kisses. There's a smattering of applause, but the silence, made heavier by the snow that's started to fall, gives me secondhand embarrassment so bad I can only look at him with brief glances. He takes a bow as the models do a final chaotic group tromp through the sand.

There we go, my first fashion show. What a doozy.

THIRTY-FIVE

I stare at the footprints, wondering if I can offer assistance in dealing with the inevitable fallout or if I should sit back and get the popcorn. Since this seems like the kind of situation Vivian would want me to check in about, I give her a call.

After a summary of the show, which is made longer by Vivian laughing, saying, "Are you kidding me?" or making me repeat things because she couldn't believe her ears, she agrees I should assist with Celeste.

"You said your background is in communications?" she asks.

"Yes."

"That's a bonus. You're an excellent writer, and it will do them good to have a third party look over their statements."

She hangs up, and after a moment to bask in her compliment, I find a cab to take me to Gear Robins, excited to be part of what's happening. Change! This has to bring in the change we want to see.

Teddy: Need to deal with this. No words.

A text comes from Alejandra, a combination of keyboard smashes and *WTFs*.

> **Me**: Were you here?
> **Alejandra**: Had someone stream it on their phone so I could see.
> **Me**: Was that your original plan?
> **Alejandra**: Are you kidding? First, I wasn't going to freeze my ass off outside. I had it booked for an indoor rooftop pool. Second, the only designs he used of mine were the sporty ones.
> **Me**: Those were the best.
> **Alejandra**: Damn right they were. Apparently he also had some of his fabric printed with Chinese calligraphy he found off the internet.
> **Me**: Like those tattoos people get that are supposed to say freedom but say mashed potatoes?
> **Alejandra**: If he's lucky it'll say mashed potatoes. Now you know what I've been fighting against for the last few collections. It's like he saved up all his worst ideas and let em rip.
> **Me**: He's got to be out. There's no way.
> **Alejandra**: Michael will say the publicity is good for the brand, and he'll convince Edward. You'll never be disappointed when you expect the worst from people.

No hashtags are trending when I leave Sugar Beach, but that ends by the time I get to the office. The same site that published the leaked numbers has taken aim at Celeste, and the story has started to appear on other fashion blogs, big ones. It's only a matter of time before major media weigh in. I turn to Fashion Eye and start reading.

> Celeste's debut foray into resort wear was gearing up to be a big success for the Canadian luxury brand. Recent years have seen some design missteps—who could forget the outdated

pseudo prom dresses of their last spring/summer collection, ideal for the modern woman who considers high school her zenith—but overall, the brand's creative director, Michael Madison, has overcome the disappointment of his first womens wear collections to build a modern global look.

This isn't bad. I keep reading.

Until today, when we can only assume Madison is playing a rather excruciating prank that is funny only to himself, like that of your boomer uncle at Thanksgiving dinner. A freezing crowd watched in shock as Madison trotted out hypothermic models in an incohesive, misguided attempt to capture what he hyped in a quick preshow call as the confluence of "Oriental exoticism with Western familiarity."

The review goes on to rip the show apart.

...disgracefully unprepared...
...racist, but we couldn't tell if it was out of maliciousness or ignorance.
A travesty made worse by the contrast of the few standouts, dashing tennis glamour looks that call for a Pimm's Cup after the courts.

Overall, it's not looking good. The story finishes by referencing Alejandra's firing, Celeste's deplorable lack of diversity, and reports they've hired a consultant to "bring them into the modern age, for all the good that's done." Oh, Will won't like that, and Edward will jump on it.

I get out at Celeste and walk through the empty halls to the big conference room next to the CEO's office, ready to work. Liz is already there with Kylie. "The others are at Sugar Beach," Kylie says as she looks at me in confusion. "We'll conference them in."

It turns out Kylie has been prepared for this day, which tells me a lot about how Michael was viewed internally. She has everything she needs, including the apology social media post and the Q and A for their spokesperson, who is Edward.

I seat myself, happy to join and experiencing the rush of being in the middle of things. "Is he usually the spokesperson?"

Kylie doesn't bother to look up from her laptop. "Of course. He's the CEO."

"It would be an idea to have someone else give the initial statement," I say. "It gives you an escalation path."

"If we need to go out with another statement, we want someone higher on the totem pole to deliver it?" asks Liz.

"Ladder," says Kylie mildly. "Higher on the ladder."

Liz glares at her. "Language is not our priority right now."

I consider whether Edward is the kind of man to stick to a prepared script, particularly in a situation where he might be held accountable. "You might not want to offer interviews at all," I say. "It could be safer."

Liz shakes her hair over her shoulders. "I'll be the spokesperson."

"You will?" says Kylie.

"While I obviously disagree with the commentators online and think Michael put on a very innovative and frankly *remarkable* show, I'm the best person to speak on issues of diversity here at Celeste, as I told Daiyu when she began," Liz says. "I can talk about how progressive Celeste is for the women who work here, an obvious good news story."

"I'm not sure that's the primary issue," I say diplomatically. I remember I don't need to protect this woman from herself, and decide to give her one last chance to listen to me and save herself humiliation since I have a good idea how the interview would go. "You know, Liz, I understand what you're saying, but I advise against you as the spokesperson."

She doesn't even ask why. "Nonsense. Kylie can email Priya at Fashion Eye to set it up. She loves me."

Kylie looks torn, but Liz stares her down. "Is there a problem?"

"No, no, of course not." Kylie doesn't look at me as she turns to her laptop.

"Uh, Kylie?" The other woman holds up her phone. "Michael has been posting."

"Let me see." Kylie sounds resigned.

We read it over. "All fashion is appreciation," he's written. "Nothing is forbidden in the hands of an artist." It's getting ratioed to hell.

"Get Ted to steal his phone," Kylie mutters.

"On it," says the woman.

"I was kidding." Kylie pauses until Liz turns away, then lowers her voice. "Tell him to try."

"We've got media requests coming in," says the woman. "Do you want me to reply with no comment or not at all?"

"Hold off answering all requests until we talk with Edward," says Kylie.

"I've got Sugar Beach on the line, Edward and Michael," the assistant says, making it sound like NATO's calling with the heads of state. No Teddy, though.

Kylie's voice shifts to become smooth and calming. "Hi, Edward. We have my team, Liz, and, uh, Daiyu from Gear Robins here."

"What's the status?" Edward says.

"We recommend a social media post to clarify our intentions for the show," she says. "Media want statements, so that should cover it."

"This is ridiculous," Michael breaks in. "I refuse to kowtow to a few jealous assholes. All the big brands push boundaries, and none of them have hurt for sales. This is a witch hunt. I'm the victim here. Good fashion generates an emotional response. Art is under fire."

There's a brief silence after this deranged rant, then Edward says, "Let's hear it, Kylie."

Kylie clears her throat. "Today Celeste presented—"

"I don't understand why we need to do this," says Michael.

She continues: "—a unique—"

"This is fucking ridiculous, Ed. A waste of time."

"—experience to—"

"Why the hell we're bothering with these pieces of shit is—"

I've had enough. "Michael," I say loudly. "Kylie is speaking. Let her finish."

There's silence on the line, and Kylie rushes in with the rest of her statement: "—to showcase the breadth of our creativity. We are proud of our reputation for innovative fashion and our corporate values, which include respect for all."

There's a long silence now that she's gotten it out. I stare at her across the table. "I can see where you're going with this," I say as a polite formulation of *hell no*. "It might be an idea to go through the text together. You know, give it a bit of wordsmithing."

"It's fine," says Liz. "Good work, Kylie."

"Why don't we take a few minutes and brainstorm some other options?" Releasing this will be like throwing gasoline on a fire. It's like none of them have ever been on social media. "For instance, there's language, and lack of language, that some might take issue with."

"Like what?" demands Michael. "Soon I won't be allowed to speak at all. You might as well muzzle me. I'm being cancelled. We should be like the royal family. Never explain."

I ignore his raving. "It's a great start, but specificity and accountability are key. How about, 'We apologize for the inappropriate representation of Asians and Asian culture in the Celeste resort wear show. We're reviewing our processes and will make changes based on our findings'? I assume the last will happen, since an apology is nothing without action." I look at them expectantly.

"No, no," Kylie says as I finish. "We need to reference our company and values. Those are our key messages."

"Plus, the comments arc utter garbage written by illiterates," says Michael. "People have told me it was a fantastic show, a total inspiration. It was about contrast. Dichotomy, do you know what that means? Innocence and sex. Those girls looked exotic. Sultry. What girl doesn't want to be sexy?"

I do my best to keep my temper and try to channel my inner Vivian. "Kylie, I'm not sure this is the place for corporate goals, particularly given that most of the criticism is pointing out a perceived lack of respect for all."

"Daiyu." Liz raises her thin eyebrows. "Perhaps you're a little overly sensitive, given your own background?"

I want to tell her to stuff her heliotherapy lamp where the sun don't shine, but I restrain myself. "Luckily, my background gives me a perspective that's missing around this table and was also apparently missing from any of your design discussions."

"Bullshit," says Michael, loud enough the phone line crackles. "I don't have a racist bone in my body, if that's what you're accusing me of. Ask anyone. That whole show was celebrating those people and their culture."

"I disagree," I say.

"Well, who cares what you think? You're nobody." He sounds irked. "This is a storm in a teapot. Get a brand ambassador or something. Who was that Indian one who was up for an Oscar? Get her."

Be cool, I internally chant. *Cool like water. Like ice. Focus on the end goal. Also be polite so he doesn't spill about Teddy and me.* It's a fine line. "Michael, I understand seeing comments like this is upsetting. However, please don't refer to people as *that one* or *those people*. Perhaps we can consider other ways to have a discussion about art and appreciation where you can expound further on your views."

I'm lying, of course. It's an ego sop for Michael, although I'm ghoulishly intrigued by how bad a garbage fire that discussion would be. On par with an interview with Liz, I'm sure.

"Tell Fashion Eye to delete the post," says Liz. "That will stop this mess."

"I'm afraid it won't," I say. "It'll put more attention on it. The Streisand effect."

"I know what you're doing," says Michael. "You and your boyfriend Ted want to make me the bad guy. Figures you'd think the same, but two halves don't make a whole."

The room falls silent. I stare at the conference phone, and out of the corner of my eye, I see Kylie and her assistant make identical *oh shit* expressions. "What did you say?" I ask slowly.

"Boyfriend?" asks Liz, naturally focusing on that.

"What did you say about Ted?" asks Edward. "*Boyfriend?*" Then before anyone can answer, he says, "That's enough. Let's get back to the issue. I agree controversy is good for the brand, but I don't want people getting carried away."

The dating part is the only part of Michael's comment he cared about? He's not even going to stand up for Teddy? I grip my hands tight under the table during the ensuing back-and-forth, breathing through my nose and remembering I can choose my battles and this isn't one I want to have right now. Later, though, when I'm better equipped to deal with him, I definitely want it.

Finally Celeste signs off on a diluted apology, mostly, as Edward says, "To get this over with."

"You should also have a town hall," I add, forcing myself to do my job. "As soon as possible. Your employees are your best ambassadors."

"There was nothing wrong with the show besides a few snowflakes getting all offended," says Michael loudly.

"Kylie, get a town hall organized," orders Edward. "Tomorrow at noon."

They hang up, and Kylie's assistant frowns. "I didn't think he'd go for that," she says.

Kylie doesn't look up from her laptop. "He wants to tell people to keep their mouths shut in person."

I look at Kylie. "Michael is a problem for the company," I say. "Speaking honestly."

"Well, and didn't we bring you on board to stop issues like this before they start?" snaps Liz. "Michael needs some training. That's it."

I glare at her. "Did you need training to step in after what he said to me?"

How dare she say the real problem is that if no one's ever sat people like Michael down to tell them what they're doing is wrong, then their actions aren't their fault or responsibility?

As if the world wasn't education enough. As if existence wasn't education enough. I suppose if you consider your experience the standard, it isn't.

She waves her hand. "You're reading into things. Is it true about you and Ted? Edward will hate that."

"We can take it from here," says Kylie loudly. "Thank you, Daiyu."

I get the hint and leave without answering Liz's question.

Once outside, I suck in lungfuls of fresh air. It's done and I handled it despite a huge provocation from Michael. Vivian should be pleased at how I did. Mind you, she won't be thrilled about Michael accusing Teddy and me of having a relationship, but I didn't confirm it.

I can't let Teddy get caught unaware and text him.

> **Me:** You weren't at the meeting.
>
> **Teddy:** What meeting? I was with the sales team doing damage control.
>
> **Me:** Your father, Michael, Liz, and the comms team, also doing damage control.
>
> **Teddy:** No one told me.
>
> **Me:** Ah. Michael called you my boyfriend.

The call comes through immediately. "What?" Teddy's voice is hushed under the buzz of conversation behind him.

"Said me and my boyfriend—you—are trying to put all the blame on him."

"Shit. Did you confirm it?"

"No."

"Good."

Oh, that actually hurt even though we agreed to keep this a secret. Now that it's out, I'm anxious but a bit relieved that I don't have to worry about hiding anymore.

Then he says, "Dad's going to be furious." He sounds like he's at the end of his tether. "What else?"

"Michael said two halves don't make a whole."

"About the two of us?" Teddy snorts. "Because we're biracial?"

"I assume so."

"Jesus, that's the most pathetic insult I've ever heard. It's not even mathematically correct."

"I guess that's why you're the numbers guy." Making jokes about it with Teddy helps.

"Are you okay?" His voice is serious. "Did anyone stand up for you?"

"No."

"Not even my dad?"

"He told Michael that was enough, but that was it."

"Oh." He breathes out. "That's…I'm sorry you had to hear that."

"I'm fine," I assure him. "Angry but fine."

"Yeah," he says in a strange voice. "Me too."

"Teddy, about your dad—"

"You know what?" he says. "This is why we're here. His attitude is causing the problems. He can't keep doing this."

"Right."

A beep comes from his end. "That's Dad. Can I call you later?"

We hang up, and I lean against the wall and feel my legs weaken. I did as well as I could and kept my temper after Michael insulted me.

Not bad, me, and I didn't ask the universe for a thing.

THIRTY-SIX

*DAILY AFFIRMATION: I ACCEPT THAT WHICH
I CANNOT CHANGE BUT ALSO ACCEPT
THAT THIS ACCEPTANCE IS BECAUSE I AM
IGNORING WHATEVER IS HAPPENING.*

Teddy asks us over to his place to talk about our post–resort wear plan, but when Alejandra declines ("I appreciate the invite, but if I have to talk about Michael and his collection of cock-ups one more time, I'm going to set the entire city on fire"), I go alone.

Teddy gives me a warm kiss, then a few more, when I arrive. "I thought I'd do dinner," he says. "We can talk while I cook and then be done with it."

"Deal. What are you making?" I follow him into the kitchen and survey the ingredients. "No way."

"I said I'd make it, and when Alejandra said no, I thought I might as well."

On the counter are spaghetti noodles, mozzarella, and raw squid. A packet of curry laksa sits to the side with a can of coconut milk. "Cheese curry squid."

"Curry squid cheese," he corrects. "Do you want to be sous-chef or relax here with some wine?"

"I can sous-chef if it's easy and I also have the wine. How did the call with your dad go?"

He pours me a glass of red and hands me some cheese to shred before starting to chop the squid.

"Not great. He wanted to know the details about our relationship."

I'd do anything to avoid that particular conversation with Edward. "What did you say?"

"I told him it was none of his business." His lips press together. "Then I told him I had to deal with work and hung up. I assume we'll talk again. Dad's tenacious."

"Won't he think it's his business?"

"I'm tired of worrying about what he thinks," says Teddy, chopping harder. "I can take care of it after we finish dealing with the fallout from the show."

"How's Michael handling it?"

"In a way that's almost unhinged from reality," Teddy answers in astonishment. "I think he's convinced himself it was a success and there's a conspiracy against him. He's tried to shift the blame for every decision."

"Like what?"

"You name it. Alejandra had done a bad job with the design and left him with a mess. The seamstresses were lazy. The producer was useless. People misinterpreted his vision. He even accused Environment Canada of messing with the weather predictions."

Since my hands are filled with cheese, I edge my foot over as the most sympathetic touch I can give at the moment. "Was it hard for you to watch?"

"Yes and no." Teddy wrinkles his nose and rubs his face on his forearm since his hands are covered with squid.

"How so?"

He washes his hands, speaking over the sound of the water. "A few years ago, I found a box with my mother's sketchbooks in a closet. One of them was filled with different versions of the Celeste logo that she'd drawn. When I saw what Michael had done to the name she worked so hard on, it was like getting punched in the gut." Teddy stands in the kitchen with a thousand-mile stare.

"Is there more?" I ask as gently as I can.

He takes a step to the refrigerator, opens the door, and then closes it. "My dad is a good guy. He's my *father*."

I shred so aggressively my grip slips on the cheese, and I yelp. Teddy comes over but I wave him off. "It's fine, didn't hurt."

"That's all the cheese we need. Want to mince some onions?" He hands them over when I nod.

"Your father?" I peel the papery skin off as he fills an orange Le Creuset pot with water to boil.

"Part of me recognizes that he saw it as a threat when I came in with new ideas, and a commentary on how he was running Celeste." Teddy oils a pan, his voice becoming contemplative. "I suppose it was, and I probably came in like a bulldozer trying to prove myself after what happened to Mars."

"It's also his job as the CEO to improve the business."

"CEOs are people, and people are not perfect, no matter how much they want you to think they are." He takes my onions to brown them and then adds garlic, the squid, and some green stuff that might be spinach and starts to stir. "I knew he wasn't a good leader for Celeste anymore, but it's hard to admit that about your parent. Especially one who only wants the best for you. I mean, he's giving me the company. What kind of ungrateful asshole am I? I was working behind his back, but after that show, I can't do it in private anymore."

I put down the noodles I was measuring out. "What do you mean?"

"The principles don't matter to him, just the perception. He's upset we're dating but he's more angry I made him look bad because he didn't know. Michael put on that reprehensible show, but he's only concerned about how it might turn into a scandal that affects the Opaline sale."

I raise my voice to be heard over the clatter of dry noodles going into the pot. "That's good news if they're concerned. It's what we hoped would happen."

Teddy busies himself at the stove. Soon, bowls of cooked squid and reheated risotto sit on the table. He pulls out a baking tray, then looks over to where I'm sitting with my wine and waiting, somewhat impatiently, for a reply.

"I talked to him about firing Michael. No sugarcoating. I said Michael was a liability and we should get rid of him and bring back Alejandra. He refused because he'd already told the Opaline board that Michael was a victim of a rogue employee who has been terminated."

I clutch my glass. "What a thing to do to Alejandra. Did you tell him about the design theft?"

He shakes his head. "No proof, so he would take that as an excuse to not believe me."

"Why?" I exclaim. "Why does your own father refuse to believe you? Why does he treat you like this?"

Teddy's eyes go wide, and he takes a step back, causing me to immediately apologize.

"I'm sorry. I shouldn't have said that."

He turns away and points to the bowls. "Do you want to form these into balls while I do the curry? Squid in the middle."

"Sure." I take the spoon he hands me and get to work, worried about the impact of what I said to Teddy. After I do about five balls, I say again, "Sorry."

"I don't know why he's like that," he says. "All I know is that Celeste has been the most important thing in his life since Mom died."

Teddy taps his wooden spoon against the pot for so long that I stand up to wrap my arms around him, rice and squid hands and all. Celeste was the most important. Not his son.

He leans back into me. "How did it come to this?" he asks quietly. "How did it come to me sneaking around on my own father to try to force him into not acting like a villain?"

I hug him tighter, burying my face in his neck. "I don't know."

"It's hard." He puts the spoon down and gently pries my arms open so he can turn around to hold me. "Sometimes it's like he's a stranger but he's so familiar."

He rests his cheek on my hair, and we stand there for a moment, me giving him the space to grieve. And it is grief when your faith in someone dies. I know, because it's how I feel with Mom and how I'd always taken her relentless positivity for a good thing. Now I see how damaging it can be, and although Jade warned me for years, it still hurts.

Teddy breathes a long sigh and kisses my ear, then steps away and takes up his spoon again. "It's not enough. He needs to make a public commitment to change, even if it puts him at odds with Opaline," he says. "You're on the right track. We need to push a bit more."

We contemplate this, me with my squid balls and Teddy squishing the laksa pack empty and dumping in the coconut milk before stirring.

"There's the meeting tomorrow," he says. "I can give him a final chance to make change there."

"That's a big step," I warn. "He's not going to take it well if you embarrass him in front of everyone."

"Someone needs to say it, and if it's not going to be me, then who?"

That's true enough. "We need a way to add more pressure if he refuses to listen." I think back to what got us here in the first place and what Vivian said about public shaming. "We could tape it."

Teddy understands instantly. "The initial leak. We could release what happens in the meeting. But we won't need to. Once he has to answer for Michael's actions in front of the company, he'll act."

"Are you sure?"

"He'll do the right thing." Teddy sounds as if he's trying to convince himself as well as me. "It's gone too far."

I'm less confident thanks to the fact that Michael is still there. "How about if Michael hasn't been fired forty-eight hours after that meeting, the tape goes out? Two days is enough time."

Teddy considers this. "That's reasonable. Do we warn him?"

I shake my head. "He might be able to stop us. Then we lose our leverage and Michael keeps his job."

"Okay," he says. "I just wish someone else could do it."

This makes me laugh. "Life would be easier like that."

He draws back to kiss me lightly, and I pull him in deeper. He runs his hands down my back and kisses me with a desperation that I return, drawing strength from each other's touch.

A pot hisses on the stove and he moves away.

"Back to work." He drains the noodles, then stirs in a bit of oil and puts them aside. I finish filling the tray with misshapen lumps that Teddy assures me will be fine as he puts it in the oven because he forgot to buy enough oil to deep-fry them.

"Nothing to do but wait until it cooks," he says. We wash our hands and move to the living room, where we collapse on the daybed and stare out the window into the dim twilight. Teddy drinks his wine and nibbles some of the almonds he brought out.

"What does this mean for us, then?" he asks.

"What do you mean?"

"This is getting complicated, and I want to know how you feel about it." Teddy looks steadily out the window. "Do you want to stop seeing each other?"

"No," I say immediately. I refuse to give Michael, Edward, or Gear Robins this much power over my life, and I'm confident enough in Teddy that I don't worry about hiding my feelings from him.

"Good." Teddy's downturned eyes close in relief, and he leans over to curl around me. I hadn't noticed how he was keeping his distance. "I've already decided to tell him that if he didn't want people dating, it should have been an actual policy rather than an unspoken expectation."

I poke at him. "That's one of my recommendations to avoid conflicts of interest."

"Good thing we snuck in under the wire." He tucks his face into my neck and wraps his arms around my waist. It's not the most comfortable position I've ever been in, but it's the most comforting. We sit for a moment, and Teddy is warm against me as he speaks. "I hate this. I want to bring you to company parties and events. I want to hold your hand on the street and go for lunch and check Questie clues without feeling like you're a Montague and I'm a Capulet."

"Juliet was the Capulet."

"She also had better clothes, so I'm claiming her." Teddy presses me back on the couch. He kisses my ear. "O, Dee, Dee, wherefore art thou a consultant to Celeste?" The kisses continue down my shoulder until he stops. "Shit, I forgot the next line."

"Deny thy," I prompt.

"Right, right. Deny thy, uh, laptop and refuse thy methodology."

I'm laughing so hard I nearly buck him off, so Teddy flips us so I'm on top. "Shakespeare would be proud," I finally say.

"It has promise," he says modestly.

"Apparently the original balcony scene was at a window," I say. "Elizabethans didn't know what a balcony was yet."

"Too bad for them." Teddy lies back and tucks his arms behind his head in a wordless invitation to do as I please. My skin heats up as I debate my first step.

I've barely started, sliding a hand under his shirt to watch his expression change to something more anticipatory, when the oven timer goes off. Loud beeping noises are devils that overcome even my desire to have my way with Teddy, so I jump off him, calling, "Dinner!"

Teddy grabs at me as I head to the kitchen, then follows a moment later, adjusting his clothes.

"It *smells* good," I say doubtfully, looking at the brownish lumps he pulls out of the oven.

"It's perfect." He sprinkles on cheese so it melts.

It only takes Teddy a minute to plate the food, and I can see why his nonna originally side-eyed it. He combines the spaghetti noodles with the laksa and fills a platter before adding the arancini and cheese and spooning on more laksa and more cheese. As a garnish, he sprinkles some chopped parsley on as if that will improve the overall brownness of the plate.

"If you don't like it, we'll order a pizza," he promises.

I prod at my lump with my fork. It has everything I like, so it can't be that bad. I slice it open.

"Your mother was a cooking goddess," I say after I polish it off in two bites and serve myself three more arancini. Somehow all the flavors have come together in a perfect medley.

Teddy looks happy I like it. "I'm glad I get to share this with you."

"Have you made it for others?"

He shakes his head. "I thought you'd appreciate it."

I touch his hand over the table. "Thanks."

He raises his glass. "To my mother, creator of curry squid cheese."

"To your mother, creator of Celeste."

We clink glasses and, as promised, spend the rest of the night not talking about work or Michael or any of it. It's a small reprieve from whatever's going to happen tomorrow, but looking at Teddy, his eyes closing as I bend to kiss him, I'm grateful we're facing it together.

THIRTY-SEVEN

I wake early to check the responses to Celeste's official statement and come across a story posted after I went to bed. It looks like Liz, bless her, had prevailed and forced Kylie to set up the interview with Fashion Eye.

It's also blisteringly apparent that Liz had vastly overestimated her bestie Priya's unconditional love. The interview has been presented in a Q and A format, and I scroll through rapidly, barely breathing.

Q: Some of the criticism of the show links its issues to Celeste's earlier leak showing lower-than-industry numbers for racialized staff at the company.

Liz Anton: Well, numbers don't ever tell the whole story, do they? [Laughs] I can assure you the two are absolutely unrelated. We value the experiences all people bring to the table, and many talented people worked on the Celeste resort wear show.

Q: Then you believe not having a single Asian person on the design team is acceptable even when showing a collection

supposedly based in part, however poorly executed, on Asian culture?

L.A.: Many would say Michael did a superb job. Culture is dynamic, and as an artist, Michael is in a position to absorb what's different and feed that back in a familiar way. He appreciates what other cultures have to offer us. As well, the majority of Michael's team is women. He thinks representation is very important in the industry, and he took their input seriously.

Q: Were there Asian women?

L.A.: Women with many perspectives, of course, including on different cultures.

Q: Liz, you haven't actually answered the question, so let me try again. Why does Celeste not hire more diverse staff? Why did you fire your only nonwhite designer under what are said to be mysterious circumstances?

L.A.: The tone of these questions is offensive and disrespectful, Priya. I offered to speak to you to set the record straight, and I'm very uncomfortable with the way I'm being attacked. As I said, Celeste is filled with people who are doing their best to be open-minded and inclusive, like me. I have no further comment.

Good God. I'm reading it again when Teddy texts me.

Teddy: Did you see Liz's interview?
Me: Did I ever.
Teddy: Dad's insisting Fashion Eye pull it down. Liz says her words were taken out of context. Not sure what context would improve it.

He switches to video, and I accept it. Teddy's seen me first thing in the morning, and luckily video calls disguise morning breath. "You look cozy," he says. He peers around me curiously, as if he can see past the edges of the screen to the rest of my room.

I pan the phone around. "This was my office before my family moved back."

"Are you sleeping on a cot?"

"Only the finest camping equipment for me. Did you talk to Liz?"

"Says the journalist deliberately tried to embarrass her." Teddy and I spend another couple of minutes reading through the comments and grimacing before he checks the time. "I need to get going, but I love seeing you in the morning. I wish it was more often."

"Me too. How's the plan for the meeting?" I had offered to help, but Kylie declined with a fairly brisk, "We have it covered."

"God only knows." He stands and props the phone up on the table. He's dressed for work in dark jeans with a thin sweater and tweed blazer, and he's added a gold Cuban link bracelet to his silver ones. It's a far cry from the boring gray suits of before and gives a worldly sexy professor vibe that I'm not complaining about. The only part of his appearance that speaks to any inner turmoil is his hair, which is a bit fluffy from running his hand through it.

"I like the blazer."

"Thank you." He adjusts a cuff and I nearly pass out. "It's from one of my old collections."

I sit up straighter in bed, the duvet falling off to reveal my men's style flannel pajamas. "Cute," says Teddy.

"Thanks. They're not designer."

"I'll make you some."

My alarm goes off—the sixth in my snoozing series, named *you are officially late*—and Teddy smiles.

"I'll see you later," he says.

As if to mock Michael's show further, the weather today is bright and sunny, mild enough that I take my coat off to tuck over my arm as I walk to work with a peppermint tea latte. I haven't warmed to Grandma's jasmine with milk, but I'd been intrigued enough to give the tea latte a try when I saw it at the café. It's surprisingly good, fresh but creamy. I have a coffee for Vivian, plain black with three sugars.

Before going to Teddy's for dinner, I gave her a complete rundown of the meeting yesterday, including what Michael had said. She asked how I was and told me I'd handled it as well as I could. I can only assume she held herself back with epic self-control from saying *I told you so* about Teddy and instead said I should be prepared for Celeste to call Will, which I knew but didn't feel better for her saying out loud. Then she told me to come in for a debrief and that we'd go to the Celeste town hall together.

Although I am a professional adult, knowing Vivian will be with me to observe what I sense will be a shit show of a staff meeting is welcome.

Vivian is working when I arrive, a deep line dividing her eyebrows. "Everything okay?" I ask, putting the coffee down in front of her. "Is Maya doing better?"

"Is this for me?" she asks, taking the cup.

"Yup. Figured you'd need the caffeine."

Vivian gives me a strange look, her long fingers with their perfect manicure tapping the lid. "Thank you." She sips it and her eyebrow raises. "Black with sugar."

"It's how you usually take it, but I brought a couple creamers."

"It's perfect. No one's brought me a coffee here before." Then she adds, "Yes, it was a bad day for Maya. My mom too."

She's slowly opening up to me, and I tick through what I'm used to saying. *It could be worse. Things will look up. At least they have you.* No, no, and no. "That sounds hard. I'm here if you want to talk."

"Thank you." She puts the coffee down. "I'm sorry you had to deal with Celeste on your own. That comment by Michael was unacceptable.

I told Will, but didn't think it necessary to mention his comments on your personal relationships."

"Thank you."

"You're welcome." She picks up her laptop. "I have a meeting I couldn't postpone, but it's quick."

"Got it. You saw the interview with Liz I sent?"

"I did." She pauses and then clearly refrains from saying something unprofessional. "We can talk more about Celeste on our way."

Will comes out of his office to loom over me as I try to pass by on my way to the washroom. He doesn't smile, and like a spider sensing a fly in the web, I know I'm in trouble.

"Daiyu," he says. He doesn't ask me to come into his office, merely points at the door. I follow, doing my best to keep a serene expression à la Vivian. "Celeste called me this morning. There was quite a list of complaints." He sits down and picks up a piece of paper. It's blank.

"Yes?" I say instead of immediately apologizing. "What were they?"

He puts down the paper and starts counting off on his fingers like I'm a child. "One, you involved yourself in a private internal meeting yesterday."

It's on the tip of my tongue to say Vivian thought it was a good idea, but I hold back. No need to involve her. "They needed the help."

Will frowns. "Two, you are having a relationship with the client."

"I have no personal relationships that contravene corporate policy," I say. That's true, and I'm getting angry instead of upset that I'm getting in trouble.

Will looks taken aback but holds up a third finger, which I want to snap in half. "Three, you openly challenged a senior executive at Celeste, Michael Madison."

"As Vivian told you, Michael made a racist remark to me," I say with as much calm as I can muster. "No one said a word to him."

"I'm sure you misheard."

"I didn't mishear."

"Now, calm down, Daiyu. No need to get emotional." Will waves his finger at me. "Michael's a well-respected man under a lot of pressure. I'm sure he didn't know what he was saying."

My face burns. "He knew what he was saying."

"We'll agree to disagree. It's not important, and I'm sure you were overreacting." He leans forward. "Four, and most important, you encouraged a Celeste executive to go unprepared into a hostile interview."

"What?" I half rise from my seat.

"You didn't set Liz Anton up for success. She's understandably angry with Gear Robins and has told us they're thinking of breaking the contract."

"I explicitly told her not to do the interview."

He shakes his head. "That's not what she says."

"Are you believing her over me? Liz insisted she was the best spokesperson, and I told them they were better off simply doing a statement."

"Calm *down*," repeats Will. "You're new, Daiyu, and most of these missteps can be attributed to Vivian's poor management."

"Vivian didn't do anything wrong." I sit up straight. "She has excellent judgment."

"Obviously not, because here I am talking to you."

"If there are any problems, they're my fault." My voice is getting louder.

"Vivian's job is to guide you so incidents like sleeping with your client don't occur."

I clench my fists. "How about dealing with a racist?"

"You're being a fool." In a British accent, this sounds even more cutting, and I glare at him.

"Vivian is an excellent and supportive manager."

"I'm not here to discuss Vivian but you and your future at Gear Robins. As of today, you will be moved to another role where you won't have client contact until you can prove yourself." He leans back in his chair. "You're lucky I'm giving you another chance. Of course this is contingent on an apology to Celeste and Liz Anton, and ending that personal relationship."

"The hell I will. Plus, Vivian has done nothing wrong, and neither have I." I get to my feet and have a brief moment of joy to be the one standing over Will. "Vivian provided the guidance I needed to cope with a difficult client, which means not giving in when they're wrong. She's shown me how to be a good consultant from being a great one herself, and she deserves much more respect than she gets here."

"Vivian's role at Gear Robin is not your concern," Will says.

The door opens behind me.

"However, it's mine." It's Vivian, with her predator smile and voice like the sweetest poison.

"Vivian, I'll speak to you later," Will says dismissively. "I don't appreciate you walking uninvited into my meeting."

"An invitation was extended when I heard you talking about me," says Vivian. "Down the hall, I might add, so half the office could hear as well."

"Later, Vivian."

"No, Will. *Now.*"

Will stands and plants his hands on his desk, causing him to lean right into me as he looks past to Vivian. I step aside, heart hammering because this is a capital-C confrontation. Outside Will's window, people are craning their heads to watch. One woman is nodding, mouth a thin line.

"I don't appreciate this, but if it's important to you, of course I can listen," says Will. "When I'm finished managing Daiyu, which I had assumed you could do."

"This is not about Daiyu," Vivian snaps.

"If your workload was too much for you to take her on, you only had to tell me you couldn't handle it."

"I did. Multiple times. You never listened."

He gives an almost avuncular sigh. "I hope this isn't about that request for leave. Your family is your responsibility and shouldn't interfere with work. I've already been more than understanding about your hours but I expect a certain degree of professionalism."

"Denying my leave and telling me I could work weekends and at night to make up for hours I take off during the day around client meetings is not flexibility, especially when you granted Paul the same leave I requested without any concerns. You've given me more clients than anyone else and refused to move any of them to other consultants."

"The work needs to get done and the others are busy." He sits down and temples his hands. "The people who work hard are the ones who get ahead. This is an opportunity."

She looks disgusted. "I don't need opportunity. I can do my job and yours. In fact, most days I do, but unlike you, I don't get paid for it."

"I beg your pardon?" He looks as if his desk had started speaking.

"I know the real reason you said no to my request," she says. "It's because you're a lazy and incompetent man who was promoted above his abilities. I pick up the slack, and you get to sit there like a little king and cash those checks. You'd be screwed if I left."

My entire body is frozen as I witness this. Neither combatant looks at me.

"You've got some nerve," says Will in a high voice. "You'd better watch yourself."

"Let's see. The Palladium project. I brought them in through one of my contacts. You took the credit. Traveler Equity. I made the connection, but you gave that contact bonus to your friend in sales. Who's run almost every staff meeting because you're too busy schmoozing so no one sees how out of touch you are? Me. Who does your budgets? Me."

The office is quiet enough to hear a pin drop. Will opens and closes his mouth like a fish as a red flush rises in a straight line up his neck. "I'm not pleased with you, Vivian."

"Excellent. Then we're even." The smile hasn't left her face. "By the way, I quit."

She nods at me, and I scramble out after her as Will shouts, "You can't quit! You're fired! Do you hear me?"

The door to his office slams shut against the renewed hum of office chatter. Vivian makes it to her desk with her head high, but her hands tremble slightly as she pulls her laptop from her bag to leave it on the desk. "Hell of a morning," she says.

"I'm sorry."

Vivian laughs. "I'm not. I feel good, Daiyu."

The blond woman who was nodding from the hall comes up to Vivian and speaks in a low voice. "I'm sorry, Viv. What an asshole. You deserve so much better."

Vivian reaches out, and they give a quick shake. "It was great working with you, Emma."

"You'll keep in touch?" Emma glares at Will's office. "When you're ready. I assume you'll want to decompress, but whenever you do, I'm up to restart our monthly lunches."

"Of course."

Emma jots down some information. "Personal email and phone number," she says. "Tell me if there's anything I can do."

I follow Vivian out of the office to the sidewalk, unwilling to stay in the office to witness further fallout. We don't say a word until we're on the street. Suddenly I realize I don't know if I got fired or what to say to Vivian. She's looking at the sky with an expression that's turning sour.

"Guess I've got plenty of time with Maya now," she says as she keeps her face up. Her voice shakes.

I put a tentative hand on her arm. I won't tell her things will be fine. I won't diminish what she's feeling. I don't say anything but try to provide silent comfort.

It takes Vivian a few moments of breathing deep and blinking hard to finally sniff. "That was a long time coming," she says in a contemplative voice. She drags her bag to her shoulder and starts walking down the sidewalk. I follow. "Thanks for what you said to Will," she says. "I appreciate it."

"It's true and you're welcome."

Vivian pulls her braids out of her ponytail to shake them out with a sigh of relief. "I've been thinking about leaving for a while but never expected to quit in a blaze of glory like that."

"I read about a woman who worked at a fish counter and spelled *I Quit* in haddock before walking out."

This makes her laugh. "I could have spelled it in methodology reports."

She glances up, and I want to tell her that I'm going to quit too. I don't even care if Will fires me. But that would be making this moment about me. If I do, I'll do it on my own and for once not add to Vivian's load.

"I see my streetcar," she says.

"You're going to be okay?" I ask.

"I will," she says, her face relaxing. "A friend of mine is a recruiter and she's always sending me jobs. But I think I might take some time for myself first. Myself and Maya."

"Will you stay in touch?"

She looks surprised. "You want to?"

"Of course!"

"I'd like that. Good luck, Daiyu." Vivian smiles. "You did well with Celeste. I want you to know that. You've got good skills and a better heart. You'll do fine as a consultant. Don't let this get to you."

"I'll try."

She gets on the first step and looks back. "And, Daiyu?"

"Yes?"

"Don't do anything silly like quit in solidarity," she says. "I can read you like a book."

The doors close behind her on my startled laugh, and she's gone, leaving me watching the streetcar move away. I wish she'd given me some more advice or instructions, but that's not her job anymore. I'm on my own, and my adrenaline is pumping through me like I'm in a sprint. I want more. I'm itching for more. I need the satisfaction of someone finally, for once, getting their just deserts. Vivian didn't deserve to lose her job, and Will doesn't deserve to keep his. Nor does Michael.

I was smart enough to grab my coat and bag when I left the office, and I glance at my watch. There's enough time to get to the Celeste staff meeting. No matter what, I'm going to see that through. I can deal with Will and whatever comes later.

I take out my phone and tell Teddy I'm on my way. I'll tell him about Vivian and Will after the meeting. Then I check that my voice recorder app is working. Forget Will. I have work to do, and I'm ready to make someone pay.

THIRTY-EIGHT

I sneak my way to the Celeste conference room where staff stand in groups or perch on the tables that have been pushed to the side. There's a podium at the front where Kylie tests the mic, and I melt into a group of women who work in the design studio and give me pleasant nods.

I try to relax but it's hard to focus when all I can think about is Vivian and Alejandra and who gets screwed over in this world and who gets to fail up instead of getting kicked down. The trip to Celeste hadn't calmed me despite a quick listen to my meditation app's session on *Chill is for penguins*. One section stood out for me, and I replay it in my mind. "To be chill about a situation is to not care. Do you care? Do you give the tiniest of shits? No? Then you are chill. Congratulations. You are also stagnant. To have no chill is to be a person who yearns for better."

I look at the portraits of the half-naked women that adorn the walls, the ones I've stopped noticing over the time I've worked here. They've receded into background noise, women as decoration no longer even pinging my radar as unusual, let alone something to be rectified or addressed. I don't like that. Right now, I have zero chill.

I take out my phone and text Teddy.

Me: I'm here. You okay?
Teddy: Yes. Calm. This is the right decision.
Me: You can do it.

No other messages wait for me. I wish Jean-Pierre had gotten back to us, but I have to respect his decision. There's a stir in the room, and I glance around to make sure no one is looking before I hit Record on my phone and leave it facedown on the notebook I'm carrying in my hands. It's showtime, and despite going to Paris and all the sneaking around, taping this meeting feels like the most transgressive action I've taken.

Edward comes in with his blazer off and sleeves rolled up. The deep lines in his face are visible from my spot at the back of the room, and his eyebrows have lowered until they almost cover his eyes. Beside me, a man whispers, "Uh-oh. He's busted out the shirtsleeves."

"We're fucked," says Travis. He glances over. "Eddy Boy's pissed. What'd you do?"

I ignore Travis. Behind Edward are Michael, acting like a righteous martyr being led to the stake, and Liz, wearing a wounded expression over her signature bolo tie. Teddy follows a moment later but stands to the side, off the riser. His face is serious as he scans the room but relaxes when he sees me at the back.

Edward glances down and shoves the mic aside. "Thank you for coming," he says in a flat voice that evinces no appreciation whatsoever. "I have a few things to discuss."

He surveys the room, hands gripping the podium like a preacher about to harangue us about our upcoming descent to hell. The crowd waits.

"Yesterday, something offensive happened. The much-anticipated resort wear collection was overshadowed by ludicrous complaints. I won't go into the impact this had on our sales team and reputation, but let me say it caused a lot of damage."

Travis laughs softly. "They acted like I was diseased," he says to the guy next to him. "One client sent me some bullshit email with their diversity policy, like anyone cares."

Edward glares around the room. "I'm told there have been minor concerns in the design studio, but Michael has assured me he's committed to working with the team and across the company to listen to your issues."

Teddy stares straight ahead with his hands in his pockets, chest rising as if he's taking deep breaths. When is he going to speak up?

Edward gives the podium to Michael, who surveys the crowd. "I'd like to address something," he says. "I've become aware of rumors that Celeste's designs have been derivative of other designers. It seems a member of my team has been taking inspiration, perhaps too closely, from younger designers and submitting them as her own."

I go up on tiptoes to try to see better. He must suspect that we're onto him and he's moved a step ahead to set Alejandra up. Why is Teddy not stopping him?

The noise in the room rises, and Michael holds his hands out to quiet the crowd. "I was as shocked as you, especially when I found them spying in my office," he says, speaking through that ever-present smile. "I suspect she...oh, sorry, *the person*, was trying to plant evidence against me."

No way. No *way* he's lying like this.

"Moreover, I take full responsibility as creative director for not having caught this sooner, although I acted the moment I knew the extent of the problem. I trusted that person and in doing so failed you, Celeste, and the fashion community."

My eyes hurt from how wide they are. A few of the women from Alejandra's team shake their heads, while others like Travis nod. Teddy looks at the floor. He knows the truth. Isn't he going to stick up for her? It's obvious from the whispers that everyone knows Michael's talking about Alejandra. Her reputation will be ruined. This is wrong, but what can I do if Teddy, who actually works here, won't act? The way he said he would.

"Good riddance," mutters Travis to his friend. "I never liked that chica anyway."

Oh, go *screw*. "That's a lie," I call. The words come out before I can stop them.

I might as well have pulled out a gun and started waving it around given the speed with which people stop talking and look at me.

"I'm sorry?" Michael says. He looks nonplussed that anyone would speak up.

I'm about to blow my career out of the water without any proof to back me up. It's Michael's word against mine. Vivian's gone, and so is Alejandra. I can't help them. Yet a single sentence crowds out everything else in my head, the last word latching to the first like an ouroboros. *I won't let you get away with this.*

My frantic eyes scan the room at the faces that are starting to settle into confusion or embarrassment or shock. Michael, bafflement swiftly transforming to anger, glares at me from the podium, his hair haloed out like a lion's mane. Teddy is agape, mouth slightly parted. A few people glance at each other as I stand there with my red face and shaking hands. The people around me move back a step.

"Looks like a female can be quiet when she needs to after all," says Travis. A few men smirk and one laughs out loud.

"Shut up," I tell Travis, jolted into talking.

His eyes bulge. "What did you say to me?"

I want to tell Jean-Pierre's story, but he hasn't given me permission. My hands are tied. I should have kept quiet. What was I thinking? Then I catch Jenna's eye. She's standing near the front, and she raises her fist to give it a little shake of solidarity.

One person is on my side, and that's all it takes to give me the courage to keep going. "Michael is lying. He's the one who's stealing from the designers."

Michael slams his hands on the podium as the crowd gasps. "You've got some nerve."

I remember the defeat in Jean-Pierre's expression as we sat on that pretty Parisian patio. "It's true."

"Enough of this." Edward comes forward and takes the podium.

"No, it's not enough." I look around. "I've been working here as the diversity consultant for three months. You say something offensive happened yesterday, but you know what that was? It was the show itself."

At that, a loud *hey* sounds around the room. Jenna stares at me with one hand on her mouth and her other hand in her pocket, but she's nodding.

"It's true," yells a woman from the corner. "I told you we needed to change it, and Michael told the stylist to ignore me."

"It was an embarrassment to the company," says another woman. "She's right. Alejandra is the one who always did the work. Michael got the credit, and he's the one who messed it up yesterday by changing her plans last minute and blaming us. It wasn't our fault, and I don't believe for a minute she stole a thing."

"Not another word," shouts Edward. "This is defamatory, and unless you have proof, Daiyu, I expect a full apology from you and from Gear Robins."

"Who's this magical designer?" calls Travis loudly although he's beside me. "Give us a name if you're going to accuse us of being thieves."

I hesitate because Jean-Pierre has not replied to my text. "I can't give their name. I promised I wouldn't because they're concerned about what will happen to them."

"No name? Nothing we can check. Convenient." Michael is almost crowing. "I hope you have good lawyers, because mine are the best in the country. You're going to regret this."

"They were under the impression that Michael was going to offer them an internship and wanted to look at their portfolio. They saw their designs in your work."

"Absolute bullshit," declares Michael.

Why the hell isn't Teddy talking? I look across the room to where Teddy is whispering urgently to his father. Michael can't be allowed to keep going like this. Not anymore. We agreed on it.

"Teddy can back me up," I say.

"What is the matter with you?" says Edward. "Ted has nothing to do with this. He might have made a few errors of judgment, but he's my son."

The look Edward gives me, like I don't know anything and I'm the error, goads me beyond endurance. "You don't know him as much as you think you do. He knows. We've been talking to a designer to convince them to come forward. We've been looking for proof. Teddy, tell them it's true."

There's nothing from Teddy, because he's staring at me with huge eyes. It slowly dawns on me that he's not going to back me up. In fact, he's looking at his father because I've told the entire company Teddy, the heir, was working behind his dad's back.

Edward turns to the room. "This meeting is over. If I hear a single word of this said anywhere, even in the goddamn *bathroom*, it's instant dismissal. Am I understood?"

I get out the door amid the shocked rumble of acknowledgment. I glance back once to see Teddy, who is staring after me. He looks stunned.

I've fucked up. Oh man, why did the universe not stop me? I need to get out of here, and I don't stop until I run through reception and get outside.

Then my phone falls, the seconds ticking by on the recorder. I'd forgotten it was running, and I slowly pick it up, wondering if I should delete it.

Instead I turn it off and put it in my pocket. I might have screwed up in there, but this isn't done, although I wish it was. I keep replaying Teddy's look of betrayal over and over again.

If ever there was a time for affirmations, it's now, and I whisper one to the sky. *Please, please let this all turn out.*

But I don't think it's going to work.

THIRTY-NINE

*H*ana plays with the stem of her wineglass. "Okay," she says. "That is a lot."

I didn't cancel on drinks because I don't want to go home. I can't go to Jade's because she and Opal have date night, which is sacrosanct. Alejandra isn't answering her phone, and Teddy is obviously not an option. I also can't be alone because I simply can't. So I sit with Hana and pour out my tale of woe on a poor unsuspecting woman who thought she was going to have a light, friendly, getting-to-know-you drink with a person she's met twice.

"Sorry," I say, gulping my wine. "Yeah, it is."

"What did Teddy say? Or Gear Robins?"

I look up, shamefaced. "I turned my phone off."

She freezes, glass in midair. "You publicly accused one of the top designers in the country of artistic theft and announced your secret forbidden executive boyfriend was plotting behind his CEO's back. Who is also his dad."

"I did those things although we hadn't confirmed, like, a label for our relationship or anything, so I would argue he's not my boyfriend per se."

"Correction accepted. Then you thought it was reasonable to say, 'I'm done for the day. Time for a well-deserved break'?"

"Yes."

"I don't blame you," she says. "Do you want to look at your phone?"

"No."

She eats a few of the brilliant green wasabi peas the server left with the wine and waits until it's obvious I have nothing more to add. Then she says, "How's this? We'll talk for a bit; then we'll check your messages. You need to read them eventually, so it might as well be after a glass of wine."

It's tempting to live in a hole of ignorance forever, but the tension between desperately wanting to know and not knowing will eventually snap me like a twig. "One glass."

"I'll hold your hand while you look." She pushes the peas over. "Knowing is always better when there's a problem you have to deal with," she says gently.

"What if you don't need to deal with it?"

"Then choose ignorance, absolutely. Unfortunately for you, this doesn't fall in that category."

I sigh and eat the peas, sniffing when the wasabi hits. "Thanks."

"I like to help." Her tone is joking but her expression is understanding.

Hana deftly guides the conversation during my single-glass reprieve from reality. She tells me about her recent trip to Seoul, where her friend is moving to live with her fiancé, who is also Hana's cousin, as they plan their wedding. When she casually mentions she'd met up with an old friend there, her face softens, and I grin at her. "A *friend* friend?" I tease.

She wrinkles her nose. "He's too huge a flirt to take seriously."

"Is he?"

Hana goes a bit red. "He texted me the other day out of the blue and asked me to stay single for the wedding so he could dance every song with me."

"He sounds sweet. Is he a good dancer?"

"Oh yeah." Hana nods. "Very good."

We sip our wine, and she tells me about her new job with an environmental nonprofit, almost bouncing with excitement at the new opportunity.

"Why did you leave your old job?" I ask. I have my phone in my pocket, and the edge digs into my leg. A quarter glass left.

"I kept saying the same things to every company," she says. "Nothing seemed to change, and it drove me wild with frustration. Then one day, I stopped caring at all, and I didn't like the person I'd become."

"I can see that." I drink down the rest of my wine, unable to take the stress anymore.

"If only my mother could." Hana looks at my empty glass. "Are you ready?"

I nod, but then my nerves get the better of me. "Will you look?"

"Are you sure?"

"I can't deal with it," I confess.

She takes my phone. "I reserve the right to clown you about any sexy messages I might see."

"Not a worry."

"Then here goes." She taps in my passcode as I tell her what it is. "First message. Your mom wants to know if you can pick up your grandmother's medication at the drugstore."

Of course. "Next."

"Alejandra, asking if you're okay. She heard about the meeting."

I look down at the table. "Anything from Teddy?"

She gazes at me with sympathy and hands the phone over. "You should read it yourself."

Teddy: We need to talk. Why did you do that? What were you thinking?

The acid burn of the wine rises in my throat. We do need to talk, and although Teddy rightfully expects a full apology, there's a nagging thought I can't get rid of. It doesn't excuse my behavior, but he should have said something, the way he promised. He let me down, but I feel my sin so outweighs his, he's the only one allowed to be upset.

I look back at the phone.

Me: We do. Tomorrow when we've had a chance to sleep on it.

This might be avoidant, but when I tell Hana, she nods in approval. "Giving feelings a chance to settle never hurts a conversation," she says.

I check my phone again. "Nothing from Will, so that's something."

"Good," she says with a clap of encouragement that makes me jump.

"Except I have to stress about it until Monday." I rub my wrists. "What a mess. Alejandra got fired. Vivian's gone. I destroyed Teddy's career and his relationship with his father. I definitely destroyed his relationship with me."

"You don't know those relationships are gone," she says. "They might be strengthened."

"I doubt it. All this for what?"

"For standing up for what's right." Her face is firm. "I saw this a lot, in all my jobs. People don't come forward because they're scared. If more people were brave, then less of this would happen in the first place." She blinks. "Wow. That felt good to say."

I give her a tiny smile. "It felt good to hear."

"Then my work here is done."

We split some nachos—I tear up when they make me think of Teddy; how tragic is that—and head out after another drink. Hana has gone above and beyond expectations for a first friend date, and I tell her so.

"Is this what life is usually like with you?" she asks. "It's exciting."

"You caught me at a transitional period." I frown. "One that is hopefully over soon."

She gives me an almost crushing hug. "Do your best."

I roll this over in my mind as I walk home. Not *don't worry*. Not *it'll work out*. Do your best. Hana acknowledged it was hard, it *was* a big deal, and that somehow made me feel better than being told it was all going to be fine.

The phone rings when I'm almost home, and I steel myself when Teddy's name appears. But I've been drinking, and I want to be calm and sober instead of saying something I'll regret. With the phone in front of me, I let it ring and ring and ring until his name fades from the screen.

Then I stand there for a long time before I go into the house.

———

I get upstairs without detection, no mean feat since wine, exhaustion, and general misery have made me clumsy. Once ensconced in my room, I lie on the cot and wonder how everything went so bad for me. I'd always had faith things would turn out, and until recently, they had.

I wiggle down to avoid the steel bar. The buzz from the wine has faded away, but I'm too keyed up to sleep. Hana was right. I did the right thing today. The result was less than ideal, but I'm proud of myself for speaking up. Too bad that's lessened because I feel terrible about Teddy. I curl up on my side, wishing things could stop being so nuanced.

I did what was right.

Then again, tipping the scale—Teddy.

Some tea might help. I pull on a quilted housecoat and make my way downstairs. Grandma is asleep so I creep around to put on the kettle in the dark kitchen and jump when Dad pops his head up from the basement like a groundhog. "Tea?" he whispers.

"Sure." I pull out another cup. "I'll bring it to you."

I brew the tea on autopilot and take it down, glancing around when I reach the bottom of the stairs. Even the nicest basement feels a bit unsafe, like someone can lock the door on you and leave. Mine is made worse by windows covered with tinfoil and LED lights glowing over Mom's weed plants.

Dad takes his cup and sips with satisfaction. "Good tea, Dee-bear."

We settle in the club chairs that used to be in my living room. The silence is soothing, and I think back to all the times in my life that he's simply been there, allowing me to be. I'd seen it as a fault, a way of letting my mother take center stage, but I had it wrong. There's strength in his active but quiet acceptance, how he doesn't try to mold me to the Dee he thinks I should be.

After a while, I get comfortable enough to say, "Dad."

He nods and waits.

"When you said that you move around obstacles like water."

Dad chuckles. "Are you still thinking about that?"

I press on. "I don't get how. I try to make changes, and I screw up. I don't try, and things go badly. I can't win."

Dad glances up at my first sniff, eyes widening as he sees my face. "Dee? Can you tell me what's wrong?"

The gentle tone of his voice is enough to send me over the edge, and I cry into my hands, body heaving. It doesn't feel good to cry. It hurts my throat and I feel nauseous. This is why bad emotions aren't supposed to surface. Forget wrecking your chances of attracting good things to your life by repelling them with negativity. They simply make you miserable.

Dad puts his hand on my back, a small touch that doesn't add to my sense of being overwhelmed. Slowly, I get control of myself, and Dad passes me a cup of water.

I snuffle into the glass and drain it, the residual sniffles and hiccups making the glass jerk in my hands. Then I put it on the floor and rub my neck, the muscles taut with tension, feeling a bit embarrassed at my outburst.

It takes a while until the words come, but Dad doesn't push me. "I don't think I'm like you," I finally say.

"How so?"

"I tried to not let things bother me. I tried to be happy like Mom. Neither works. I can't be those things."

He looks at the secateurs on the table. "I'm sorry, Dee."

My head shoots up. "Sorry for what?"

"For making you think you need to be like me," he says.

"It made sense when you explained it," I mutter.

"Maybe it's not for you, lah." He squeezes my shoulder. "You need to see what works for you, not live like me or Jade or your mother do."

"I'm trying," I say. "It's hard."

"All the worthwhile things are." Dad sits back in his chair.

"Mom doesn't see it the same way."

"Your mother..." Dad pauses. "She tries. She only wants you to be happy."

"That's the problem, though, isn't it? She wants that more than she wants anything else." I look at the scratches on the table. "We don't usually talk like this."

He looks astonished. "We talk all the time."

"Not like this. Not about things that matter."

"Ah. No. I never spoke to my parents about anything like this either." He shudders. "They would have been horrified."

"Are we breaking a family tradition?"

"Or starting a new one."

I lean toward him. "Thanks, Dad."

"You only need to be yourself, but sometimes that takes bravery." He smiles, eyes narrowing the same way mine do. "Should I tell you about how I came to Canada with only twenty dollars?"

"Dad." I shake my head. "We've heard that a hundred times, and the dollar amount keeps dropping."

He laughs and enfolds me in a huge hug that feels as safe as curling up in his parka did when I was a kid. "I'm proud of you," he says. "I should tell you more often."

"For what?"

"Fighting back against whatever it is that you're struggling with." He holds me close. "I never taught you to do that, because part of me hoped your mother was right and it was enough to try to be happy. I'm sorry you had to learn for yourself that it's not. I wish the world was kind enough that you didn't have to. So I'm proud of you."

Then he tightens the hug as I dash the tears out of my eyes.

———

Back in my room, I close my door and look in the mirror at my swollen face. Then I describe what I'm feeling, out loud and with no censoring.

"I regret what happened with Teddy."

Be honest, urges that voice. *Don't downplay it to make yourself feel better. You are not a bad person for having feelings.*

It's right. "I feel guilty I didn't keep his secret safe when he trusted me. He didn't keep up his part of the bargain, but that's no excuse."

I take a careful breath in and out and keep going.

"I don't want Grandma living in my house."

Instinctively, I glance around the room as if someone will hear and judge me for the awful person I am.

"I'm sick of having to be cheerful in front of Mom all the time," I say slowly. "I'm angry I haven't been able to be real to myself."

Stick with it. They're only words, and it's only me. Too bad I'm the hardest audience of all.

My mouth moves in the mirror as I dredge up all the words I'd anchored to the seabed of my life. "I envy Jade's attitude."

"I'm worried I'm not cut out to be a diversity consultant and I've failed."

"I'm upset my friends let me down. I'm embarrassed to find out I cared more about them than they did about me."

"I'm scared about saying all this."

It goes on and on, a recital of all the things I've kept closed in my heart for years, until I'm leaning against the desk, voice rough and mind exhausted. My face looks slack and dull, as if I had forgotten to tighten my muscles into their standard mask.

I didn't die saying those things out loud. In fact, I feel…fine? Not terrible, although I'm nervous about what happens because I sense the next step, in accordance with the Gospel of Jade, is taking action instead of hoping for the best.

I'll think about that in the morning.

No, not in the morning. All my manifesting and affirmations were about putting things off and hoping it would work out when I didn't want to face something hard. I can do what needs to be done, because I have in the past, even if I gave the credit to the universe. I was the one to do the night classes and renovate my house. I did that without waiting. I'm going to make changes now because my faith needs to be in me.

I pull out my old resolutions list from the drawer where I'd shoved it when my family moved in and slowly read through it. These are solid goals. It's my execution that needs a revamp. My eyes light on my vision board. It's good to have ambitions, but I want to open my mind beyond what I can cut out from magazines.

Down it comes, Paris café, happy salad woman, and all.

I look in the mirror one last time. "I will stop asking the universe to be my personal concierge."

I tried on the plane ride back from Paris, but I never truly stopped believing that a hand would dip down to help me out. Maybe one day I'll go back to affirmations, but I've been using them to avoid responsibility. I can make my life what I want by putting in the work. The universe can do its own thing. It's probably busy.

That's enough for now.

FORTY

The downside to extravagant inner transformation is there's an expectation the world itself has changed. How can a shift so titanic in oneself not be reflected in everything else? Yet all around me, people go about their usual business, and birds chirp, and Chilly takes dust baths as if everything is status quo.

This gap between my newly determined interior life and the steady constancy of the exterior world should make me unsettled and blue, but I find it invigorating. I made the right decision. I think I made the right decision. Did I make the right decision?

"It's the right decision," Alejandra assures me in a voice groggy with sleep when I call her in a fit of weakness in the morning. "You can do it. I always thought that woo-woo manifestation stuff was useless."

"I don't know..."

"Stop right there." Alejandra's voice firms. "You do know but you're scared. That's because it's scary to take risks."

"I never had to before," I whine. Mom's—and until very recently my own—belief system is to mitigate risks by pretending they're not there. "Everything was going as I wanted. This hurts."

"Life is pain, Highness."

I ignore her undeniably awesome reference. "I prefer being able to blame the universe for my screwups," I mutter.

"Those happen because we're not perfect. We also don't sit here beating ourselves up about it. We accept that we make mistakes, and we do our best to fix them. That's how you grow."

"Did you get this from a hot yoga class?" I ask.

"Rude, I only do restorative, and no. Look at me with Celeste. Am I moping?"

"A little bit."

"Well, I'm allowed. I'm not the one having an existential crisis."

"What if...?"

"Look, what if you stop what-if-ing?"

"You're right."

"I'm right?" She sounds skeptical. "Just like that, you agree with me?"

"You know what? I do. Yes." I didn't at first—I only wanted to get Alejandra off my case, even though I'd called her—but somehow saying it clicks my determination in like the final piece of a jigsaw. I am sure.

"Good, because with your personal emergency over, we need to talk about that recording. Are you sending it?"

Alejandra had been impressed that I'd gone through with the recording and had listened through the file I'd sent her yesterday after checking to make sure it was legal. I'd also given her a brief overview of what happened with Teddy, which I'd edited out. She hadn't said more than a long "Ohh," which spoke volumes.

"Tomorrow."

"Teddy knows?"

"I texted him a copy this morning, but he didn't reply."

I can almost feel her frown. "You know my perspective on Celeste."

"Burn it down."

"Exactly. His might differ."

"It might, but if Michael remains, nothing has changed." I bite my cheek. "I'm going to make it happen."

"As long as you're prepared for the fallout."

We hang up, and I open Questie as a distraction. The new puzzle is out but I don't have the heart to do it without Teddy, so I turn to my meditation app and find one called *News flash: hard shit is hard.* I lie on my cot, wince at the steel bar, and move to the floor. Then I listen.

"Here you are," says the man, who by this point I have decided looks like an Oxford don, complete with tweed suit and pipe. "Staring at the hard thing. You have a choice. Do the hard thing, or don't. I don't care. It's not my life. It's yours. What's it going to be, punk?"

I turn off Professor Inspiration as the music swells into a *Gnossiennes/ Music for Airports*/sea waves mash-up and get to my feet, needing to move. The house is strangely quiet—not even Chilly's wheel breaks the silence—and when I go to the kitchen, I'm surprised to find Grandma in her usual seat, turning a puzzle piece around in her fingers and staring at it with unseeing eyes. She doesn't look up when I come in, and with a shock, I realize this is unusual. For all this time, I thought ignoring me was standard, but the fact that I'm noticing her inattention means... maybe it hasn't been.

She starts when I open a cupboard and I realize she wasn't ignoring me. She'd been lost in thought.

"Dee," she says. It's pleasant to not have to hear my mother's determined good morning.

"Hi, Grandma." I grab some fruit out of the bowl. "Where's everybody?"

"Groceries."

"Want some mango?" It seems rude to eat in front of her without offering.

"I've never had it."

I pause. "Not had mango?" That's like never tasting bliss. I grab a plate and a knife and sit down at the table. The first slice through the green skin reveals the bright orange inside, and the sweet smell wafts over us. I put a few bits with a fork in a bowl and pass it over. She takes the smallest nibble, like Poppy trying any new food.

"It's good." Grandma sounds surprised. "Like candy."

"It's my favorite fruit after mangosteens."

"I never had this kind of thing growing up," she says. "We had apples and berries in the summer. It's what I'm used to."

I get up to wash my hands. *Do the hard thing.* I clear my throat and stare at the gummy spot on the window where the Niagara Falls thermometer used to be. It must have fallen during the winter. I flex my feet on the industrial gray anti-fatigue mat that sits like a dead pelt under the sink and feel that faint tension that I haven't been able to rid myself of since my grandmother moved in.

"Why did you dislike Jade and me so much?" I ask the window. Then I face her. "We were kids. Dad's a good guy. What gave you the right to treat us like that? Like you were better than us? Worth more than us? More important than us?"

Grandma stiffens and she hisses in pain as her hands tighten. "Dee. Do we need to talk about this?"

"No," I say. "We don't need to talk about it if you want things to stay the same. Do you?"

She looks at the puzzle of the Great Wall, and the silence fills the kitchen. Finally, she says, "No, I don't."

"Then we need to talk."

"Does it make it better if I tell you I was stubborn? That I got something in my foolish head and I couldn't let it go?"

"No, because the impact on us was the same, and the thing you got in your head was horrible. It was racist." She flinches at the word, but since it's much harder to be on the receiving end of that attitude than be accused of it, I continue. "It might be worse that you knew you were being unfair. Dad didn't deserve it. Nor did we. We were children."

"I know that now." She takes a puzzle piece and turns it in her fingers. "When your mother brought David home, it was a shock. You look down on me for it, but I was raised in a small town. David was the first Chinese man I saw in person."

"You never gave him a chance."

"No. I had ideas in my head—wrong, awful ideas. By the time I realized how bad a mistake I'd made, it was too late. I felt..." She casts her eyes down. "I'm ashamed of how I acted. That I was...that way."

She can't even say the word.

"You never apologized to him or us."

She gives a stiff shrug. "Too proud." Her wrinkled mouth turns down. "I regret it. I wish I could do it over, Dee, but I can't. I made judgments about your father and your sister that I wish I hadn't, but I was ignorant and depended on what I'd been told rather than learning for myself. I thought I'd be able to change it by living here, to start fresh."

"To change decades of the past like that? Without acknowledging the problems you caused, like we're supposed to forgive and forget because it's easier for you?"

"Not like that."

"No? Then how?"

"I'm trying." She looks at me. "That's no excuse either, but it's what I can offer."

I wish I could ask the universe to take the wheel, but steering my own life is my job now. "What I'm about to say isn't to punish you because of how you acted," I say.

She nods, and it takes me a second to gather my courage.

"This isn't working," I say. "This living arrangement, for any of us." Despite my best intentions, the words come out so fast they're almost unintelligible. "It's best if you leave." I force myself to slow down. "Not because of our relationship. I want to keep building that when you can bring yourself to apologize. None of us are happy or comfortable, and I'm tired of pretending it's all cozy when it's not."

I hear the familiar squeak of the door as it opens. Mom's voice calls down the hallway. "Hello, the house!"

"Here," I call, a bit pissed that I can't finish the conversation with Grandma, who is looking down at the table and tracing circles with her crooked finger. Mom and Dad chat as they take off their shoes, their voices drifting down the hall. I'm in no mood to deal with a family conference, but I've started this. I need to finish it.

"Why so serious?" asks Mom, looking from me to Grandma as she comes in the kitchen to drop a grocery bag on the floor.

This time, I feel Grandma's hand on mine despite what I just told her, and I speak up instead of telling Mom it's all fine.

"I've been talking to Grandma," I say as strongly as I can. "I'd like her to move out."

"What?" Mom takes a step back. "Don't be absurd. Where would she go?"

"To a retirement home," I say.

"Or my own apartment," says Grandma. "Dee is right. It's time."

"No," says Mom, the lines on her forehead deepening. "I don't understand. This is working fine. We're all getting along!"

"We're not." I look at her.

"It's a challenge," she says. "We're not giving up."

"I am looking at this realistically," I say. "I don't want this. None of us do except for you."

"Dee?" asks Dad.

I turn to him. "I don't want to be so scared of conflict that I hold back anytime there's a risk of someone getting upset."

It's fine to be water, but sometimes it's better to be the rock.

"Dee, that's enough." I've rarely heard Mom get mad, but she might be getting there.

"There were alternatives that didn't involve you moving in with me," I say. "I should have said that in the first place."

Mom squares her shoulders. "This was the best."

"Because you organize life in the way that works for you," I say, trying to control my voice so she pays attention to the words instead of the delivery. "You want a family the way you picture it, all happy and together. That's not who we are."

"Is that what you think of me?" Mom's voice breaks.

"I tried to tell you before."

"No, you didn't." The way Mom says it, the immediate denial, makes Grandma's hand tighten on mine. "You don't feel that way."

"What if for once, you tell me that you understand instead of telling me I'm wrong?" I burst out. "What if you say it's okay and let me be me?"

There's silence in the room until Grandma speaks up. "I agree with Dee." No one speaks, and she continues. "David, I was wrong about you, and I was judgmental because of who you are." She tugs the leg of her pants, clutching it and releasing. "I've had time to think as I've gotten older. Time to regret. Time to know I need to change."

She looks at me, and her mouth works as if she's struggling to say something, but nothing comes out.

Then she manages it, the words I thought I would never hear. "Dee, David, I'm sorry. I'll tell your sister, too. I apologize for the way I treated you. This situation might have been different had I been a better woman, but I want to move past it. In our own time, and if you'll let me."

I don't have an answer, and when I look at the rest of my family, it's clear they're as shaken as me. She gets up, and we say nothing as she limps out of the kitchen. I feel battered but Mom looks stunned, as if Chilly had started to talk. Dad comes and puts a hand on her arm.

She looks at it for a moment, then shakes it off. "Too much fuss. I'm going upstairs," she says to no one in particular.

Dad and I look at each other as Grandma speaks to Chilly in a soft voice from the other room. Then he comes over and pats my shoulder.

"Good job, Dee-bear."

"Thanks, Dad."

"Tea?"

I nod.

"Heather?" He raises his voice. "Tea?"

There's a pause and then, "Yes, thank you."

This isn't over yet, but it's enough for now. I settle down at the table to watch him take down the tea bags and the jasmine pearls, and I wonder how to tackle the next hard thing.

Teddy.

FORTY-ONE

DAILY AFFIRMATION: STILL NOPE.

On Sunday, I wake to the soulful sound of Patsy Cline, and a primal part of me immediately reverts to back to childhood, as this was the soundtrack to the household weekend chores for decades. Mom is firm that a spotless house is necessary for a bright mentality.

I text Jade, the only person who will understand.

> **Me:** Am I crazy for feeling so lonely?
> **Jade:** LOL Sunday morning memories. Opal refuses to play that song because it triggers my trauma response and I start fear cleaning.
> **Me:** Sounds like that's something she'd want to encourage.
> **Jade:** Me dusting the baseboards, yes. The insistence that everyone join in because if you've got time to lean, you've got time to clean, not so much. What's up?

I tell her about last night's conversation, and Jade calls.

"Holy shit," she says, sounding awed as Patsy's voice filters through the door. "You did it. You cut the cord. You're Cameron staring at that trashed Ferrari."

"In the movie, it wasn't a real Ferrari. They couldn't afford to wreck one, so they put a fake body on a Mustang."

"That may be, but what you did was real enough. Good for you. How do you feel?"

"A little worried about what's going to happen next."

"Nothing. Mom can't change," Jade warns.

"Grandma changed," I point out. "Or she's trying."

"Trust me on this, Dee. I've been trying for years. Don't get your hopes up." She sounds defeated.

Jade has to get the kids ready for swimming, so we hang up. I lie in bed remembering all those unappreciated Sundays when I could do what I wanted in my own house and knowing that soon, I'll have them back. That cheers me up, a tiny bit. I get dressed and sneak out to a café because I'm gutless and want to avoid Mom. Emotional hangovers are worse than tequila ones, and I'm worried about what to say to her. The only thing worse than Mom confronting me is her proving Jade right by pretending it's all fine, like she does after every fight.

The day is bright and sunny, and the café is quiet as people file through to pick up drinks. It's a perfect day for Questie, and I pull out my phone, wondering if I should text Teddy. We need to talk. I want to talk, but he didn't text me back yesterday and I was too scared to try again.

However, when I was at his place we'd decided to give it forty-eight-hours before we leaked the recording. That expiry date is coming up fast.

Text him. Text him now. I shake out my hands to get the feeling back in—stress has made them numb—and the screen lights up.

Teddy: Can you meet me today? In an hour?

I'm about to tell him I was just going to message him when I decide that sounds fake. Instead I nod at the screen before realizing it won't translate to text.

Me: Of course, where?

He sends me the name of a place that's between our houses, and I barely check the address before I head out, walking to calm myself down and counting sidewalk squares as a coping mechanism. I keep losing count around fifty and give up. When I get to the café, I'm twenty minutes early, so I duck into a food emporium—it's too fancy for a grocery store—to waste time picking up and putting down fifteen-dollar jars of olives. As I gaze at a display of salt in the colors of a muted rainbow, I practice what I'm going to say. I'll apologize, that's certain. I'll ask what happened and do my best not to sound judgmental, since he did kind of screw me over. Then, I'll tell him I'm sticking to our plan about the tape. Finally, after the business part of the meeting has concluded, I'll ask him what's going on with us, with the same calmness as I will conduct the rest of the conversation. I glance at the time. Ten more minutes to keep my nerve up.

"Dee?"

Teddy peers through a gap between the shelves as I poke a box of pasta shaped like narrow lasagna. I nearly drop it and end up somehow batting it back in place on the shelf.

"What are you doing here?" I ask, staring back. His face is paler than usual, with pronounced stubble and hair falling over his glasses.

"I was early."

"Me too," I admit.

We walk to the end of the aisle and wordlessly head to the café next door. I order first and ask Teddy what he wants. "I can pay," he says.

"Teddy. Please."

He orders and we take our drinks to a table in the corner, where he sits down without removing his coat.

"Do you want to start?" He sounds calm, his voice the same in a way that gets my hopes soaring that we can fix this and stroll away hand in hand.

I practiced this. I can do it. First, the apology.

"I'm sorry for what I did in the meeting," I say. "It was wrong of me to say that to your father."

"Thank you."

There's a silence, and my heart starts doing dips in my chest. "Umm, I hope you sorted out things with him?"

"Not quite. I told him what I thought about how he's running Celeste. He told me he knew what was best. I told him he was wrong and that if Celeste was going to be mine, we needed to make changes and that included postponing Opaline until we fixed our own house. He said not a chance in hell was he giving up on Opaline and he definitely wasn't going to sacrifice Michael to the woke mob. Then he gave me a speech about loyalty and said me being unable to keep it in my pants was proof that my judgment wasn't to be trusted. We haven't talked since."

I feel sick. "That's awful."

He makes a sound that might pass for a laugh. "It's not an ideal situation."

"What happened?" I ask. "You said you would confront your father about Michael in the meeting. Why didn't you back me up?"

His eyes focus on his coffee. "I *was* backing you up. I was warning him that he had one last chance before I called him out publicly." He looks up. "Four seconds more was about all I needed."

"You had plenty of time before that," I say, getting a little angry that he seems to think this was my fault. "You could have spoken up when Michael was trashing Alejandra or when Travis was on my case. I was alone, and I don't even work there!"

"I'm sorry, Dee." He blows out his breath. "You're right. I could have."

"Then what happened?"

"I was scared, you know? Dad had let the executives see his notes for what he was going to say, and I wrote this little script so I knew where to step in. I was waiting for it like a fucking actor waiting for my line. Then the meeting went off the rails, and I froze long enough for the whole thing to go to shit."

"You were scared?" I stare at him. "You did Paris Fashion week, and this scared you?"

"Family is different," he says, and I don't have an answer because he's right.

"Is Michael there still?"

"He is, yeah."

I take a deep breath. "I'm going to send the tape. I took out the part at the end. About you. Us. Are you okay with that?"

He shrugs, and it's like being with that old Teddy, the one who didn't care. "Go ahead. I doubt it will make a difference."

"Don't say that."

"Why not when it's true?" He gets up to go.

"Teddy, are we good?" My voice chokes off at the end as I try to swallow my fear that he'll say no.

"Dee." He steps away. "It's all a bit raw. You didn't mean to say what you did, but I need some time to figure everything out. Work is a mess, and it's going to take a while to fix things. Or decide if I want to."

"Teddy, I..."

"I'll talk to you later."

Then he leaves and I'm alone in a bright chic café, staring at my still-warm cup of untouched tea. For the first time, it occurs to me that Teddy might have found what I did unforgivable. There might not be a way back from it.

No, that won't happen. Then I stop myself from forcing the thought away. It might happen. Ignoring it won't stop the problem. It's up to Teddy, but no manifestation, no hope will stop him from coming to his own conclusion about how he feels.

I hate this.

Well, I might not be able to make a difference with Teddy, but I can in other places. With shaking hands, I take out my phone and check the email I'd saved to the drafts folder of the fake account I'd set up, and addressed to priyakumar@fashioneye.com.

Then I don't even second-guess myself. I click Send.

FORTY-TWO

*P*riya gets back to me by the time I return home, wanting to verify the audio and know more about its context. I send her to Alejandra, who has offered to provide more details as long as she can stay anonymous, since her lawyer would lose his mind. Apparently their talk went well, but when I check first thing Monday morning, there's nothing up.

Nor is there a good-morning trivia text from Teddy.

I don't have time to worry about it, since I'm probably getting fired in about two hours even though I haven't had a call from Will or anyone else at Gear Robins. The weekend has leached most of the defiance out of me, and my thoughts ping-pong remorsefully between work and Teddy and Mom and Grandma until I want to crawl into my cot and cry.

Really wish I hadn't given up manifesting.

The commute goes too fast, and I trudge up the stairs at Gear Robins, pass the motivational quotes, and put my bag down on the desk, wondering if it's my last time. The woman who had talked to Vivian the other day comes over with a smile. Emma, that's her name.

"Daiyu, can we talk?"

"Sure." Lowering my head to avoid eye contact with anyone, I follow her to Will's office. She sits down in his chair and motions for me to take a seat. I perch gingerly on the edge and look around for clues as to what's going on.

"Vivian speaks highly of you," Emma says.

Normally I wouldn't be averse to hearing some accolades about myself, but I'm a little rattled about why I'm sitting in Will's office with a woman who is not Will. Have I somehow walked into the life of one of those other multiverse Dee Kwans? I wonder if this Dee Kwan kept Teddy's secret.

Emma puts me out of my misery.

"Will has left Gear Robins," she says. "Between us, after the incident last week that resulted in the company losing Vivian, it was decided he would do better elsewhere."

"He got *fired*?" I stare at her. This is not what I expected. Wills don't get fired. They get promoted or moved to another department or sometimes warned.

Emma smiles. "I'll be taking over as director."

What does this mean for me? "Is Vivian coming back?" I ask.

Emma picks up a pen and twirls it around her fingers, frowning. "I'd like to be transparent with you. Vivian was asked to take this role on and refused. I spoke with her before I accepted. She has a lot of history here, and more than that, she was the best consultant we had. She should have been offered Will's position when it came up two years ago."

I nod.

"She also told me about your experience with Celeste. Suffice it to say that we don't put up with verbal abuse from our clients, and I plan on severing that relationship today." She makes a face. "Although they might beat me to it."

"You believe me?" I ask.

"Of course." She says it so simply that it floors me. "I'd like to think your experience here, short as it's been, is unusual, but it isn't. I'm making some changes, and I believe you can have a big part to play in the department. Vivian also mentioned some of your concerns with the limitations of the People First model, which I share."

"I'm not getting fired?" I ask cautiously.

Emma doesn't laugh, as if she understands how bad the past couple days have been. "No. In fact, Vivian told me about how you guided Celeste in their communications. We can use that expertise. Would you be willing to take that on as part of your role?"

I'd forgotten how much I liked the rush of dealing with an issue in the moment and deciding the exact thing to say. "I would," I say. "I missed doing that."

"Good." Emma holds out her hand for me to shake. "I'm glad we get to keep you."

She waves me out and I almost float to my desk. I didn't get fired. I have a job, a job that I'm excited about again.

If I consider my day from a work perspective, it goes fairly well. By the end, I've been called into a few meetings to serve as a communications consultant to the consultants, which kept my mind off Teddy. I even meet some people who have been working off-site. One of them, Omar, is especially hilarious and shows me photos of his cats that his wife dressed in squirrel costumes before inviting me to his weekly lunch with people from other departments.

Vivian texts me before I leave.

Vivian: Congratulations on the new role. You'll do great.
Me: Did Emma tell you?
Vivian: She's good. You'll like working with her.
Me: I liked working with you.
Vivian: Apart from some obvious issues, I liked working with you as well. You gave me some perspective on what matters. After my husband died, I was so busy trying to build a good life for Maya I forgot why I was doing it.

It's much easier to be honest on text sometimes. I don't think Vivian would have said that to me in real life.

> **Me**: I'm glad.
> **Vivian**: Me too. We'll have coffee soon.

———

Despite the turnaround at work, I'm almost physically sore with misery about Teddy by the time I get home. Knowing it's only Monday isn't helping. Plus, Fashion Eye still hasn't posted anything.

Mom is outside in the garden wearing Dad's parka to ward off the spring evening chill. I hesitate at the drive, wondering what to do when she stands up, hands on her back, and looks at me. "Do you want to help me turn the soil?"

"Okay." I put down my bag and take the shovel. I like digging, and Mom points me to the raised bed she always used for tomatoes—a tradition I continued last year so I could present her with Early Girls from her old garden. At least I wore basic boots and not dress shoes for work.

We dig in tight silence for a few minutes. I'm too busy thinking about Teddy and what's going to happen when the audio from the meeting is released to pay attention to much more than the rhythmic feel of the shovel hitting the dirt.

Mom chops up a chunk of sod. "I want you to reconsider about your grandmother."

I should have seen this coming. "No, Mom. It was a conversation between us, and we decided."

Her lips tighten. "I thought I raised you to be more compassionate."

That stings enough that I look her right in the eyes. "I'm being compassionate to me first this time."

We continue to dig.

"I don't want you to not be yourself," Mom says abruptly. "Like you said. It's not a crime to want your child to be happy."

I keep digging to give myself time to map out a reply before I say, "I know you want that for me."

"Then why are you so upset?" She jams the shovel into the ground with her foot. "Why is it bad to be positive?"

I scrape at a little weed that's barely poked above the surface. "It's not."

"I don't understand you. You or your sister." She sounds discouraged. "Why you want to choose the most difficult lives for yourselves."

"It's not difficult. It's real." I dig out the weed and turn it over so it disappears under the soil. "Sometimes I need you to accept that I'm upset and that it's not a judgment on you or going to ruin my life."

My voice has raised enough that a woman walking her dog on the sidewalk pauses. Mom and I work until she passes. "I hate to think of you being miserable," she says. "You deserve better."

"I deserve to have you respect my feelings instead of making me feel bad for having them."

To my shock, her eyes fill with tears, and a small smile wavers on her lips.

"Mom?" I ask uncertainly.

"Your father told me we should think of a better plan for your grandmother, but I insisted it would work out. I said it would bring us closer as a family. I guess I was wrong."

I reach out and touch her arm. "Not totally wrong. There were some good things that came out of this. It's been enough, though, for all of us. Don't you miss being up north?"

She nods. "Your dad always says I should listen to him," she says wryly as she dries her tears.

"You should listen to all of us."

"We'll see, sweetie. I'll try." She sighs. "I'm going to go for a walk to clear my head."

She gives me a quick hug and leaves her shovel stuck in the ground. I watch her go, her pace slow in the twilight. Should I go with her? No, I'll give us space to think.

There's only a bit left of the ground to prepare for planting, so I dig quickly, my mind occupied with Mom and Teddy and what's going to happen next. When I finish, I grab the shovels to bring back to the shed. The small weed I thought I dug up peeks out from the dirt. As I'm about to grind it down with my foot, I change my mind and clear it a bit of space.

It should have a chance too.

FORTY-THREE

The text from Alejandra comes as I'm leaving work the next day.

Alejandra: We need to meet asap.

There are two links underneath, both from Fashion Eye. The first is the audio file from the Celeste staff meeting, and I quickly check the story, heart thumping so much my fingers shake.

"A shocking staff meeting at Celeste shows the depth of its toxic corporate culture," it begins. That's true enough, and Priya has used quotes from an anonymous source—Alejandra—to provide damning context. It also links back to the leak that caused Gear Robins to work with them in the first place. I can listen to the audio later, because I want to know what the second link is.

Exclusive interview, it reads in red font. **Ted Marsh, formerly of Mars and VP at Celeste.**

Teddy gave an interview? I start reading and forget to blink. It's another Q and A, but instead of Liz humiliating herself, it's Teddy talking about the need for sustainability and fair treatment in the industry. That would be startling by itself given the timing of our meeting leak, but what makes it stunning is that Teddy outlines specific practices at Celeste and how he plans to change them when he's CEO after his father.

Q: There are rumors that fashion conglomerate Opaline is buying Celeste.
Ted Marsh: Certainly that was under consideration and is my father's dream, but my goal is to make Celeste better, not bigger. We have fundamentally different business philosophies that make Opaline unsuitable for Celeste.

Then it gets to the juicier part.

Q: You know there's audio accusing creative director Michael Madison of threatening and stealing from younger and—we were told anonymously—marginalized designers.
T.M.: It's true.

Q: In the recording, no designers are named. How can we believe it?
T.M.: Michael targeted people who have limited power in the industry and are rightfully concerned about the impact on their careers. However, there's enough circumstantial evidence to warrant a very strong look at Michael's processes. I personally have been pushing for his termination given his treatment of people on his direct team alone.

Q: This is an unexpected take, given your father is head of Celeste and one of Michael Madison's staunchest allies.
T.M.: It's the right thing to do, and as well as being what's right, it's smart business. Look at the data. More diversity leads to

better decisions, better performance. Paying a good wage and working with our long-term suppliers reduces the time and labor involved in turnover and sourcing. These are facts. We maintain our advantage by working with talented people, not keeping exploiters on staff. CEOs say business isn't personal, but they stick by their friends and hire who they know instead of the best for the job. I should know.

I can't believe it. His father is going to be apoplectic. Do I call him? I waver, then decide to meet Alejandra first. She might have more information. But when I do, she's as lost as I am.

"I have no idea why he did it." She points at the beer in front of her. "No table service."

I go up to the high oak counter and come back with a pint, two shots of rum, and a bag of all-dressed chips that I open so it forms a flat surface with the chips in a little pile in the center. "Cheers," I say distractedly.

"I can't believe Michael hasn't been fired yet after all this," she says, peering into her rum as if it has answers for her. "Also why are you asking me about Teddy? Still not talking?"

I drink the rum too fast and cough. "He wanted some distance to think."

"Oh dang. Makes sense, though. You fucked him over royal." She sees my face. "Sorry."

"No, it's true." I fold up the empty chip bag.

"Do you want another drink?"

"The last thing I need is more depressants."

We're debating if Michael can survive this latest hit when Alejandra checks her phone. Her thick eyebrows shoot up her forehead.

"What?" I ask, voice getting shrill. I can't take much more. Then my phone dings and I find a message from Jean-Pierre.

"Fashion Eye," Alejandra says.

I'm too busy reading the message, which has a link.

Jean-Pierre: I've been thinking about what I want to do.
Although I appreciate your offer and support, it's my story,
not yours. I will be the one to tell it.

I click the link. **Young designer accuses Madison of theft; harassment.**
I twist my neck until Alejandra tilts her screen; we're looking at the
same story. We stare at each other; then I detach her hand from my
arm. I hadn't noticed she'd grabbed onto me.

She reads aloud. "'Michael Madison stole my work and threatened
my career if I tried to get what I was owed. I let him silence me once,
but it's my turn to speak.'"

The story is as he told me, complete with screenshots of texts and
time-stamped examples of his work, demonstrating without a doubt
he had been creating these designs well before Michael claimed them.

"What is going on?" she says. "I mean, I'm glad he changed his mind,
although I would have welcomed it last week even more, but Jesus."

I stare at the dusty black of the painted ceiling. "You know, I might
have another drink after all."

I go and get us fresh pints as we settle down to our phones, each of
us calling out what we find.

"Social media is melting down," she reports.

"There are pro-Teddy and pro-Jean-Pierre hashtags."

Within an hour, it's clear that, at least in a specific subset of the
internet, Teddy and Jean-Pierre are heroes. Teddy, despite being a rich
man's son (this part was emphasized by most users), is being lauded
for trying to do what's right. Clips from Teddy's interviews discussing
sustainable fashion from when he ran Mars start to circulate. There
are also a disconcerting number of posts commenting on his hotness,
which seems irrelevant even if true. Memes of Jean-Pierre as David
appear as well as commentary on *his* hotness. We watch as his follower

count skyrockets, along with comments asking him for collaborations, far outweighing the inevitable trolls.

I sit there and have a freak-out. "Do I call Teddy?" I ask Alejandra.

"You've had three drinks. I don't think you should talk to anyone right now. Definitely no social media. Am I understood?"

That makes sense, but... "I want to. I want to support him."

"Yes, because you're drunk and think everything is a good idea. He asked for space, didn't he?"

"Yes."

"You should respect that, especially during what I assume is an extraordinarily stressful time. If he wants to talk to you, he knows your number."

If Alejandra had reached across the table to slap me, it would have hurt less. I'd conveniently let myself forget communication works both ways. "Right," I say heavily.

"Good. I didn't want to take your phone away, but I would have without hesitation." She glances down. "Holy shit. Look."

We read together. "'Celeste has announced the departure of creative director, Michael Madison. Recent scandal has rocked the luxury firm...'"

"I've said it before and I'll say it again. Fuck that guy." Alejandra's smile almost reaches her ears. "What a great day."

I text Jean-Pierre, sending him the link about Michael.

Me: Thank you.

His response comes in a moment.

Jean-Pierre: I did it for me. But you're welcome.

We pay up and go outside, feeling numb at the number of shocks we've experienced. "What happens now?" she asks, glancing up the street.

"I guess we find out."

"I guess we do."

We grimace as, to date, that hasn't worked out the best for us. But today gives me hope things might be changing.

———

I arrive home to a crash followed by Dad's shout, causing me to fly into the hall, then pause because the way is blocked by a huge wooden structure with Dad struggling beneath it. "What's going on?" I ask, dropping my bag and wondering how much I drank.

"Dee, give me a hand with this," he pants.

We maneuver it into the front room, and I take a step back. It's a cage made of strong mesh and with platforms for Chilly to run around and do his chinchilla thing.

"Did you make this?" I say, admiring it.

He nods and turns to Grandma, who is running her hand along the wooden frame with a cautious hand. "I thought Chilly could use a bigger cage," he says. "With a new wheel."

I reach in the old cage and hand Chilly to Grandma, who holds him close while we position the new one. She puts him in, and Chilly's whiskers wriggle as he hops from a platform to poke his head in a burrow hole. Then he stands and looks happy. It's hard to tell.

"I hated that old wheel," says Grandma thoughtfully.

"Me too," Dad says.

"This will be perfect for my new place," she says. "I'll have more space there."

"Chilly can get used to it while we're all here. In case I need to make repairs before we go up north." He winks at me. "Back in time for the blackflies and fishing."

This is the first time I've had Dad confirm they're leaving, and a wave of relief overtakes me. I'll have my house back, and more than that, I did the hard thing.

He looks at the old cage. "I'll take this out."

Before he can leave, Grandma reaches out and almost touches his arm. "Thank you, David. I appreciate this."

Then she glances down like she's embarrassed. Dad is also staring down, and it's clear neither of them have any idea where to go from here. It's a start, but there's years of hurt to work through, a task and a half for two people who would prefer not to talk about feelings or the past. Maybe they don't need to. The cage in the living room is a message as strong as a letter.

I break the silence with the old standby. "Tea, anyone?" I should have bought shares in Twinings for the amount we drink as we work our way through this.

They look at me in relief. "Yes," says Grandma.

"I'll be there as soon as I finish tidying," says Dad.

Grandma follows me to the kitchen and sits so she can admire Chilly in his new habitat.

"How's your hip?" I ask, picking up a piece of the latest puzzle and putting it back on the table. It's a night view of the Petronas Towers.

"Better. The exercises help. I might go for a walk."

"A walk?" I look at her. This is the first time she's left the house of her own volition.

"I might. Oh, look, Chilly is trying his wheel."

There's not a single squeak. I sigh with relief, thinking about the hours of uninterrupted deep sleep coming my way. I make the tea, doing my best not to rush so I don't burn myself, and then go upstairs to think about the day.

———

An hour later, I'm too restless to relax and go out on a desultory stroll, debating whether I should call Teddy despite Alejandra's excellent advice. There's an old Questie clue location in the park nearby, and I wander over to check to see if it's there. It is, a small *L* on the back of a bench. I haven't played Questie lately, given the current status of my life, and when I check the leaderboard, SunnyDay and Teddy9 have dropped to fourth and fifth place.

I'd like to care, but I feel a bit numb. I sit on the bench, kicking my legs, then look over to the lamppost with that same neon sheet asking people to take what they need. No, not the same one. It's new, with all the tabs intact. No one has needed anything yet, but this time, I do.

My hand hovers over the tabs before finally settling on the one I want most, which was missing from the first sheet back in the winter. I might be trying to get off my addiction to manifesting, but part of me will probably never stop believing in signs from the universe. This one is flashing red lights and sirens.

Love, says the tab in my hand.

I want love, and suddenly I know how to get it. Or at least ask for it. Because all I can do is ask.

FORTY-FOUR

I text Teddy the next day when I'm sober.

Me: I saw the interview on Fashion Eye. It was incredible.
Teddy: Thank you.

I sit down at my desk and parse out those two words for what seems like forever because he doesn't offer any more information about how it came about and what happened after. Do I text back? Do I assume his answer means all is forgiven? I could ask but I don't want to push him. As Alejandra says, he's going through a lot right now. Paralyzed by indecision, I don't do anything.

Also, I have a plan. It takes a full two days to get everything in order because I want it flawless. When I'm done, I spend twenty minutes on Saturday morning hyping myself up to text him.

Me: Please don't leave this reference on read 9144361.

It's a clue. A Questie clue for a secret puzzle. My heart leaps into my throat as I press Send. Creating the puzzle had been both more difficult and more exhilarating than I'd expected. To rule out any issues with misinterpretation, I'd spent hours thinking through all the possible answers he could get for each clue. For instance, if he tries 9144361 as a phone number with a Toronto area code, he'll reach an angry old man (416), a fax machine (647), or an automated message for a defunct restaurant (437). It's not a GPS location, and a substitution code results in the nonsensical word IADDCFA. He needs to make the connection between the word *reference* and reference books and realize the number is a Dewey decimal call number that leads to Paris guidebooks at the Toronto Reference Library, which is also hinted at with the word *read*.

I grab my bag and head to the library to wait, my feet so heavy every step is a struggle. It's overcast but with a thick humidity that gives my straight hair a slight wave under a thin veil of frizzies. I'm sweating under my jacket, but my fingers are cold. Everything about the day screams, *Get back home and lie in bed feeling sorry for yourself,* but I no longer take orders from the universe.

The ride to the Toronto Reference Library is thankfully short but I can't sit still and pace up and down the train as the other passengers ignore me. I pass through the turnstile into the huge atrium before heading straight to the stairs. The 900s are on the second floor, and I do a quick check but I don't see Teddy. That's fine. This is fine.

An old woman with dyed copper hair peruses the books in the section I need, and she shoots me a dirty look when I hover behind her chanting, "Four three six one," as I try to locate my book. There it is, a pedestrian guide to Paris with a photo of Sacré-Coeur on the front. There's a small paper tucked inside, where I put the clue last night for Teddy to find.

I pull on a hat and sit at one of the desks to wait with a clear view of the aisle. Ten minutes pass and I get up to walk around, my head hammering with my heart. Twenty minutes pass, then an hour. I fidget so much in the chair that it starts to squeak. Doubt assails me. He hasn't texted. Maybe he didn't get the clue. Maybe he's not in town. This was an awful idea.

He might not want to do it. He might have deleted the text. He might not care at all. I'd been so intent on doing the puzzle that this has not occurred to me as an option, and it prompts an immediate sense of heightened panic. He has to do it. It's my big apology and thank-you for him stepping forward with that interview. I want to throw my desire out to the universe, but then it fades. I put myself out there, but the only person who can make Teddy decide to do this puzzle is Teddy.

One hour, I decide in a strange calm as if I'm observing myself. One more hour, then I'll go home. If he does it later, then he can contact me. If he doesn't do it at all...well, I tried.

I stare at the wooden desk with my hands gripped tight underneath it, each minute eroding my confidence. Someone has carved a heart with LC + EA in the wood so long ago the ink has faded away, leaving only the indent of the letters that I trace with my fingertip. Over and over, until my skin turns pink, then red.

He's not going to do it.

Five minutes left.

Leaving the lovers' initials, I pull out my meditation app because although I might be trying to give up a lot of my former ways of thinking, this has stayed. *Waiting is a total bitch* looks like it might suit my needs, so I glance at the woman with copper hair and plug in a single earbud. I have no idea why I feel having in two will affect my ability to see Teddy, but I don't fight it.

This one starts with birds chirping, as if we're in a glen. "Sitting there like a total asshole, huh?" comes the man's voice.

Three minutes left.

"Thinking about time and how it flows?"

I keep listening as he talks about time's continuum. One minute.

Then the hour passes, but I can't make myself move.

"Every second feeling like a year? I bet it does, which is good if you remember each moment brings you closer to death. Don't waste them."

That's it. Teddy's not coming. I press Stop and start to stand, then drop back in my seat because a man appears at the top of the stairs, Celeste bag slung over his shoulder. He looks around, and I angle my head down slowly to avoid drawing his attention. I am mentally defenestrated, mind blank of anything but him.

Teddy looks unusually disheveled. His shirt is untucked and wrinkled as if he'd plucked it off the floor. His hair is a bedheaded mess, and one shoe is untied. He checks his phone and the numbers at the end of the aisles and his phone again before disappearing down the row.

Utter bone-deep relief fills me, so fierce I get shaky. He's giving me a chance. I train my gaze on that aisle like a sniper, not moving and barely blinking until Teddy comes back out with the paper in his hand and a frown on his face. This clue is *I pray you find the pot of gold on this street.*

Teddy starts down the stairs and I sneak to the balcony to watch discreetly. When he pauses at the pride flag near the doors, I can almost see the switchboard in his brain making connections. Rainbows. Pots of gold are associated with rainbows, and there are rainbows all over nearby Church Street, which is the *praying* part of the clue. The pot of gold is at the end of the rainbow, so he should check for a clue at the end of the street. At least I hope that's close to his thought process, because I've drawn a heart with the letters *TM* and an arrow pointing to the clue tucked under a rock on the building right at the intersection.

He leaves the library, and I don't follow because I don't want to get caught, and it's a little creepy to slink around after him. The clues should take him about an hour and go as far south as Grange Park past the art gallery and back up to the library. They're easy enough so he doesn't get frustrated and so that I could be sure the clues worked, since I've never made a puzzle before. While I wait, I hide a new clue in the book, a slip of paper that says, *Map it.*

By the time Teddy gets back, I'm cursing myself for making the puzzle both too long and not long enough. My nerves have stretched to the breaking point because the fun's over and the hard part is here. He finds the last clue, goes to the other side of the library where chairs are set up by the window, and sits down with his phone.

I wait a minute and then walk up behind him. Teddy is so engrossed in what he's doing that he doesn't notice me check his screen to see if he has the correct answer.

He does. When they're plotted in a map app, all the clues come together to form a heart.

"I knew you'd solve it," I say, sitting beside him. I try for casual but sound strangled. "You were always amazing for the second-best player."

"Have you been here the whole time?" he asks, looking between me and the screen.

"Shh." The old woman from earlier glares at us from under her heavy bangs. "This is a library. For quiet!" She's yelling by the end, and Teddy and I mumble apologies before he motions with his head toward the exit and we scramble out of our seats.

Conscious of the quiet police, we don't talk until we're outside.

"You didn't text to tell me you got the puzzle," I say.

"I wasn't sure what it was. I wanted to wait and see." That sounds cold, but when I risk a look at his face, he's smiling. It's only the slightest curl to his lips, but it's enough to give me hope.

We walk west toward Yorkville, automatically finding ease in movement. We cross through the little park that mimics forests, waterfalls, and a marsh to climb on top of the shattered rock sculpture and sit down to watch the rich people and tourists shopping and drinking expensive coffees. We look at a flock of pigeons that surround a seagull bullying a sparrow. Anything to avoid looking at each other.

He sighs. "Dee, let's get it all out instead of dancing around. Total emotional honesty."

"Okay." There's a glass ball layered around my heart, so thin that every breath makes it shake. I ready myself to feel it shatter.

"I was upset after that meeting. No, don't interrupt," he adds as I open my mouth. "This is hard enough, so I want to finish."

I nod and he continues.

"I was angry with myself. We had a plan, but when the time came, I failed. I felt like I was the same man I'd been before I met you, and I was embarrassed that I let you down."

My gaze stays on the black-speckled granite we're seated on, and the first cracks appear in the glass ball.

"There you were, risking it all to confront Michael, and I froze. I was so proud of you and ashamed of myself. That's why I needed some time. I wanted to think about what had happened to me." He looks over. "That's why I was upset. It was at me."

"I shouldn't have spilled your secret like that."

"No, but you wouldn't have had to if I'd stood up for you and Alejandra. I'm sorry I didn't. That was wrong of me, and I feel sick every time I think of it." He grimaces. "Which is a lot."

"Why did you do the interview with Fashion Eye?"

"Because it was time for me to stop hiding. I'd told Dad what needed to change, but he thought I'd quiet down the way I had in the past. He thought he could control me through Celeste the way he used to."

"Used to?"

He laughs. "My interview was like dropping a bomb, and Jean-Pierre coming forward was like bringing out the flamethrowers. Opaline was furious. They told my father to fix the problem if he wanted the sale."

"That's why Michael finally got fired." I smile at him. "At least there's one victory."

"Two. I don't have to answer to my father anymore. I can be my own man again."

"He's leaving Celeste?"

"No. I quit."

The screeching of the seagulls fills in the silence. "You what?"

"I quit because Dad refused to change at all, and after I did that interview, he doubled down. He only fired Michael under duress and was already planning to bring him back when this settled. He knew Michael was taking credit from Alejandra and didn't care."

"Teddy, that's huge. You gave up Celeste."

He sighs. "I love my dad, but I can't respect him after this, and I couldn't keep on in that half a life I'd been forced into. Not now that I've been living in color again." He looks over. "He told me to stop seeing you."

"What?"

"That was the final straw."

We're quiet for a minute. "Now what?" I ask carefully, trying not to take too much hope from what he said.

Teddy runs his hand over the rock. "You did me a puzzle."

"I did."

"As an apology, or have you changed your mind about trying out for a Questie position?"

"I wanted you to feel like I cared." A kid's balloon floats by us with the orange ribbon trailing. "I do care, I mean. I wanted to show you how much."

"By having me run all over the city?"

"I didn't think of that," I say, abashed.

"I liked it." He grins. "Was I faster than you expected?"

"No," I say. He glances over and I laugh. "A bit."

"Best player," he says complacently.

"Fifth as of this morning according to the leaderboard."

Teddy frowns. "I don't like that."

"We could play again? Get our spots back?" I ask tentatively.

"I do have a lot of free time," he says. "Since I'm unemployed."

"I'm sorry."

"I'm not, surprisingly." He smiles. "Time for a new dream."

Don't worry, universe. I've got this. I pull the glass from my heart and hold it up to the sun like a crystal, letting it reflect everything I feel.

"Me too," I say. "You said you were living in half a life, but so was I. You listen to me and make me feel like I matter. Like my feelings matter. You made me realize I can be myself, and that's good enough."

"You're more than enough, Dee." He's watching me intently.

"I want you," I say. "I want to sit in the studio and work on Questie clues while you sew or draw or do whatever you want. I want to go on inspiration walks. I want to be with you exactly as I am, even if that me is sometimes sad or miserable or in a bad mood."

Then I wait. I've laid it all out there, and I'm not playing any games.

"That's good, because I want the same thing."

"You do?"

"I want to play games and send you trivia and have you dazzle me every day with how incredible you are. I want to be the trash can to your Oscar."

I give him a look. "That's...bizarrely romantic? Kind of?"

"It should be because I'm in love with you. God, that feels fantastic to say." He looks me in the eyes. "I was teetering on the edge of it even before we met in person the first time. Then I saw you and it was over for me. I was a goner."

He's smiling that upside-down smile that gets me every time, the one I thought I'd never see directed at me again. "Is this a yes?" I ask. "Best Questies?"

"We'll need a new name." He wraps an arm around me and pulls me in. "I'll think of one."

I relax for the first time in days and burrow into his shoulder. "The puzzle was that good?"

"Your puzzle was much more impressive than me googling weird facts."

"Like that the inventor of Pringles is buried in a Pringles can?" I kiss him when he laughs, on top of that rock in the middle of the little square.

"That's...bizarrely romantic? Kind of?" he teases.

"How about that I love you?"

"Better." He lets me tug him over for another kiss before burying his face in my neck. "Much better." His voice is muffled. Then he pulls back, eyebrows knit together.

"What?" I ask.

"Something I've been wondering," he says slowly. "After all this, we still don't know who was behind the first Celeste leak."

I yank him back. "A puzzle for another time."

Teddy grins. "One I have no doubt you'll solve." He leans in and kisses me again as the pigeons rise up in a single iridescent gray cloud to cover us from view.

EPILOGUE

*T*ea?" Teddy's hand hovers over the kettle as I come into the kitchen.

"Mmm?" I'm distracted by the sight of his chest since he's only wearing pajama bottoms. I'm cuddled in the matching top, which barely reaches midthigh. "Right, tea. Yes."

He puts the kettle on and starts slicing an apple. "We need to leave for the airport soon."

"I'll be ready. Did all your freight arrive?"

Teddy nods, focused on forming the apple slices into a circle before adding some berries to make a pretty little fruit sun. Then he turns his attention to the toast. "Jean-Pierre called last night after you went to bed. It's all there. Fashion Week is always chaotic, so that's one less thing to worry about."

I eat the apples he slides on the table. "Alejandra said it was looking good."

He nods. "She's got it under control."

Teddy's back is to me, and I admire the tapered V of his body before he turns around. It's nice to have him here in my house. Since he took over as CEO of Celeste, it's been busy, and we take advantage of every opportunity to be together.

It's been a strange year and a half. Thanks to the mess with Michael, Opaline stepped away from the Celeste sale, providing Teddy with a somewhat pyrrhic victory. After getting eviscerated by Fashion Eye and ZZTV among others, Edward had been put in the tough position of having to look for a way to save his company due to plummeting sales just as another group, Worldspan, came knocking. Intrigued by Teddy's plans to transform the business, they offered to buy a majority stake if Teddy took over. Edward had reluctantly decided that having Teddy run Celeste was better than a stranger and stepped down as CEO, although he remains on the board. It's taken a long time for them to repair their personal relationship, but last month, Edward told Teddy he was doing better than expected. Teddy considered that high praise but was more excited by Worldspan's decision to use his sustainability work at Celeste as a template for other companies under their umbrella.

After getting fired and with more young designers coming forward, Michael was quickly removed from his positions on various fashion councils and boards. I hear he's trying to get work as a consultant. It's not going well, and the gossip says his loss of influence hit hard. I find it difficult to feel bad for him.

Alejandra works with Teddy as Celeste's creative director, and watching the two of them wrangle over the correct length for a brace-let sleeve is like watching two siblings fight over what show to watch. It was Alejandra who convinced Jean-Pierre to join Celeste as a designer. He continues to live in Paris with his boyfriend, but he comes back to visit often. Teddy is thriving in his role as mentor for the two as well as other up-and-coming designers, including the mysterious J, who turned out to be a talented young woman named Jazna. She had in fact given Michael her sketchbook after he said he had an internship opportunity. Although Teddy continues to create his own designs, it's limited to private collections only for me. I've gotten used to people taking photos of my outfits and posting them on street fashion sites. I've even been featured on best dressed lists.

With Alejandra and Jean-Pierre on board, the new Celeste hit the fashion world like a bomb. Teddy had done some test drops featuring the new fabrics and the duo's designs, which were universally lauded. As well as leading the company, Teddy's become a global spokesperson and activist for fashion sustainability, which he loves. I'm happy for him, but it was a shock for me to come into a room and find Teddy on a call cracking jokes with people whose faces I more commonly see on billboards and movie screens.

"Did you put your out of office on?" asks Teddy as he spreads the toast with butter.

"Last night." I'm the lead for all Gear Robins's diversity communications, and I love it. Emma is a fantastic manager, and she's opened up doors I didn't know existed. Hana keeps asking me to come work for her nonprofit, but I like where I am. She tried to lure in Vivian, too, but Teddy asked her to be the chief diversity officer for Celeste. Worldspan often comes to her for advice, and Vivian can work a flexible schedule to help care for Maya, who has good days and bad. Luckily, Vivian's mother's health has improved enough for her to help out occasionally. I do as well, spending time with Maya watching movies or simply keeping her company so Vivian can take some time to herself. Sometimes, when she's strong enough, we play Questie, which is a blast.

Vivian joined me for dinner last week to say goodbye to Hana, who was off to Seoul to visit family. Or so she said, but I have my suspicions about who she's there to see. She'd been a little too giddy about a visit to an auntie.

Teddy pours out the hot water for tea and checks his phone. "Jenna has a new candidate for me to meet," he says. "From the latest posting."

"That's good."

Jenna is already in Paris looking for talent. She'd been the greatest surprise of all. After Teddy took over at Celeste and Gary was quickly shuffled out—Liz had been let go as well—she'd come to Teddy and laid out why he needed a better HR strategy. It turned out that she had been an HR manager before deciding she wanted to work in fashion and taking the job as Gary's assistant. Impressed, he'd offered her Gary's role, and she'd said, "There's something you should probably know. I was the one to leak the diversity numbers to Fashion Eye."

Teddy had been stunned. Me too.

She'd told him she understood if that was an issue for him but she'd tried every channel before deciding to take it external. "Things needed to change."

Teddy had nodded. "You're hired."

We'd popped champagne when that mystery was solved. It had driven me wild to not know.

Teddy brings over the tea and sits down. "Aren't you cold?" I ask, staring unashamedly at his chest.

"Aren't you?" he asks my legs.

"You like me like this."

"Well, you like me like this, so it's worth a bit of suffering." He laughs when I nudge him with my sock-clad foot, a slightly less sexy but cozy addition to my outfit.

My phone rings. "Good morning. I'm jealous about Paris, I want you to know," Jade informs me when I put it on speaker.

"When you went to Paris, you got food poisoning from steak tartare and projectile vomited off the top of the Eiffel Tower. You swore you'd never go back."

"I promised Opal a honeymoon she'd never forget," says my sister proudly. "I didn't lie."

"I'm sure that's not what she had in mind."

"Probably not, but as Mom delighted in telling us, you get what you get, and you don't get upset."

"You hated hearing that."

"It's different when it comes from me. Anyway, we're off to Heather's.

I called to tell Teddy bonne chance with Fashion Week and to remind him I'm waiting for the personalized sukajan jacket he promised."

"It's coming as soon as Dee's is done," he calls at the phone before I hang up. "The kids going swimming?" he asks me.

"They are." Grandma's new active retirement home has an indoor pool that is a magnet for Nick and Poppy. They go over every couple of weeks to play with Chilly and splash around before having a lunch of dino nuggets and ice cream with my grandmother, who usually has a new puzzle to swap with Opal. It's been difficult for Jade to get used to, but she's slowly warming up to Grandma and the idea that it's possible for them to not rebuild but build something new.

Their next trip is to my parents at their cottage up north to see the autumn leaves. Mom's into knife throwing at some hipster place the next town over, and she sent Jade and I photos of her looking like an L.L.Bean version of Lara Croft captioned, The new axe throwing! with five happy face emojis. Whatever twists her crank. Mom remains Mom, although she's trying. The other day, I told her I was having a rough time, and she said, "Things will—"

"Mom."

"Right, sunshine." I heard her take several breaths before she spoke as if reading from a script. "That's too bad. Would you like to talk about it?"

Like all of us, she's a work in progress. I've talked with Dad a few times about how he approaches conflict. It's not my way, but it's interesting.

"Toast?" Teddy passes over the plate. "By the way, when are you seeing Marianne?"

"In two days," I say, perking up. While Teddy will be meeting with people for Celeste, I'm going to work with my new friend Marianne to set up my first international Questie game. It took me a long time to get the courage to send in one of my puzzles, but it was accepted immediately. The SunnyDay puzzles are some of the most popular on the platform, which thrills me, and I've become online friends with Marianne, known as TigerCloud, who is great to bounce ideas around with. I found out that although the Mensa part is true, she doesn't have any crossword puzzles in the *New York Times*. She's more of a sudoku fan. Teddy insists on trying all my puzzles first, and the time we spend testing them are some of the best hours in my week.

I sniff around. "What's that smell? It's amazing." It's an earthy scent that I detect over the toast.

"New candle." Teddy looks sly. "It's called Cannabis."

"You're kidding." I breathe in. "Mom's plants never smelled like that."

"Thank God we finally got that smell out of the walls." Teddy takes my cup. "More tea?"

I glance at the time. "How long until we need to leave?"

"An hour from now."

I grin up at him. "You know, this outfit *is* a bit cold."

He slowly puts the cup down, a little smile playing on his face. "An hour seems like plenty of time to warm up before we go."

"It does."

He pulls me up against his chest. "We can't miss the flight," he whispers in my ear. "Not another one."

I slide my hands around his back. "Set a timer."

"Romantic." Then he does, but when he kisses me, it's like he has all the time in the world.

Acknowledgments

A book would be an impossible endeavor without the kindness, generosity, and expertise of many people.

This was a tricky book to write. I think it fair to say the last few years haven't brought the advances in diversity and inclusion many had hoped for.[1] At the time of writing, only a small proportion of the billions of dollars recently promised to support DEI programs have been disbursed, and a 2021 report by the *The Washington Post* found that much of the money had been promised not as direct support but was "allocated as loans or investments [companies] could stand to profit from, more than half in the form of mortgages."[2] There remains much work to be done.

I spent a lot of time researching the diversity and fashion industries, and I've added a select list of resources on my website. However, I take full responsibility if I've misunderstood the information presented to me. I repeat: It's totally my fault if I got anything wrong.

I also want to say that I personally am a big fan of affirmations and hyping yourself up (someone's gotta do it). I regularly beg the universe for favors, and one of the affirmations used in *The Takedown* is one I say almost every day. However, Dee's experience is specifically with how

1   "Annual Report Card on Gender Diversity and Leadership," Prosperity Project, accessed February 1, 2023, https://canadianprosperityproject.ca/data-tracking.

2   Tracy Jan, Jena McGregor, and Meghan Hoyer, "Corporate America's $50 Billion Promise," *The Washington Post*, August 23, 2021, https://www.washingtonpost.com/business/interactive/2021/george-floyd-corporate-america-racial-justice/.

invalidating some elements of positivity can be when it forces people to deny how they feel or shifts responsibility to individuals while ignoring the impact of systems and groups on mental health and well-being.

Now for the thanks!

To you—thank you so much for giving me (and Dee and Teddy) your time. I'm incredibly grateful to be able to write stories that matter to me and to be able to get them in your hands and ears.

To Allison Carroll at Audible and Mary Altman at Sourcebooks, who continue to believe in my stories and work tremendously hard to help me find the book buried under the manuscript I send in. Every time I see a little happy face in the comments, it fills me with joy.

To the teams at Audible and Sourcebooks who work on everything from marketing to edits to design to production to publicity and help at every stage to make the book as good and as widely read as it can be.

To my agent, Carrie Pestritto, who I'm eternally grateful to have in my corner.

To my incredible beta readers, who provided excellent feedback and answered many questions: Allison Temple, Candice Rogers Louazel, Farah Heron, Jackie Lau, and Shari Keen. Allison also has the dubious pleasure of having to hear me agonize over scenes I had to cut (and there were many) during our weekly writing dates.

To Ariana Gonzalez Stokas (who also beta read *The Takedown*), Nisha Sharma, and Renée Charles for answering my questions about the diversity industry and diversity work. Although their thoughtful insights helped to inform the book, none of the specific situations Dee and Vivian encounter are based on what they shared with me. I have the deepest respect for everyone who does diversity and inclusion work and who dedicates their time and expertise to helping the world be a more fair and just place.

To Adrienne Shoom, who gave me excellent suggestions on where to direct my fashion research.

Finally, as always, Elliott and Nyla. Thank you for putting up with me.